SERPENTS RISING

SERPENTS
A CULLEN AND COBB MYSTERY
RISING

DAVID A. POULSEN

DUNDURN
TORONTO

Editor: Jennifer McKnight
Design: Laura Boyle
Printer: Webcom
Cover Design: Jesse Hooper

Image credits: Snakeskin ©1joe/iStockphoto. Cityscape ©ImagineGolf/iStockphoto.

Library and Archives Canada Cataloguing in Publication

Poulsen, David A., 1946-, author
        Serpents rising : a Cullen and Cobb mystery / David A. Poulsen.

Issued in print and electronic formats.

ISBN 978-1-4597-2172-2 (pbk.).--ISBN 978-1-4597-2173-9 (pdf).--
ISBN 978-1-4597-2174-6 (epub)

        I. Title.
PS8581.O848S47 2014   C813'.54   C2014-901031-1
                                                C2014-901032-X
1   2   3   4   5 ,   18   17   16   15   14

We acknowledge the support of the **Canada Council for the Arts** and the **Ontario Arts Council** for our publishing program. We also acknowledge the financial support of the **Government of Canada** through the **Canada Book Fund** and **Livres Canada Books**, and the **Government of Ontario** through the **Ontario Book Publishing Tax Credit** and the **Ontario Media Development Corporation**.

Care has been taken to trace the ownership of copyright material used in this book. The author and the publisher welcome any information enabling them to rectify any references or credits in subsequent editions.

J. Kirk Howard, President

Visit us at
Dundurn.com | *@dundurnpress* | *Facebook.com/dundurnpress* | *Pinterest.com/dundurnpress*

Dundurn
3 Church Street, Suite 500
Toronto, Ontario, Canada
M5E 1M2

To my family: my dad, Lawrence; my mom, Leona; my wife, Barb; and to Murray, Amy, and Brad and their families. This is for you with endless thanks and love.

"Whom I will trust as I will adders fanged."

— *Hamlet*

PROLOGUE

May 2005

D^{ate} night.

We'd gone to a movie — *Million Dollar Baby* — long after everyone we knew had seen it. It was one of those theatres that plays really good films but months after they're first released. The movie was Donna's choice. She cried through the last half hour. I hung in until the final ten minutes. We sat through the credits to let our eyes dry before we left the theatre, holding hands and smiling at each other as we made our way up the aisle toward the lobby.

We stopped for a drink on the way home. The Kensington Pub, one of our favourite places. Donna liked it because it made her think of England, where we'd never been but kept promising each other we'd go one day. I liked it mostly because it was a place that made Donna happy. And I like beer. Donna had a white wine, I drank a Mill Street Coffee Porter. We didn't talk much about the movie. In a day or two, over breakfast or maybe dinner, we'd discuss it then.

When we got home, I went inside just long enough to change my clothes. Donna came to the door to say goodbye, already in a nightie that reminded me how small she was.

Her slim jogger figure was not without contours; her curves were evident through the nightie and I inwardly cursed having to leave. She slid her arms up around my neck. "Maybe you should phone in sick." She nuzzled my neck.

"Clint Eastwood always brings out the tramp in you," I told her. "Which made sense when he was Rowdy Yates. Or even Harry Callahan. But now ... whoa."

She laughed. "I'll settle for you going in late. At least an hour."

I kissed her and she kissed back, which did nothing to diminish the very non-work-related feelings I was trying to suppress. I gently separated us, turned to the door, and stepped onto the front step, her "Your loss" and throaty laugh ushering me outside. I stopped on the step and glanced back at the door and the tacky little sign Donna had insisted we place just above the doorbell; she'd had it made at a booth at a farmer's market a few years before: THE CULLENS LIVE AND LOVE HERE.

I jumped down and did a not bad imitation of the guy dancing in the Viagra ad on my way to the car, knowing she'd be watching from the living room window. Watching and laughing as I drove off to work.

Work — a meeting with Martin Caveson, a lawyer who made a living representing the seamier element of Calgary's criminal population. His office was near the Victoria Park police station. The area had once been a badass part of town — a home turf for the city's drunks, crackheads, low-end prostitutes, and a couple of the nastier gangs. Now that the Calgary Stampede had bulldozed most of the old neighbourhood for the expansion of its grounds, Vic Park was gentler, though not nearly as interesting as it had once been.

But Caveson had kept his office right where it had always been. His clientele had farther to travel, but it didn't seem to diminish business any. In fact, in the three-quarters of an hour I was there the phone rang three times. Caveson did me the courtesy of not answering any of the calls.

The shaved head was the first thing you noticed; Caveson was sixty-ish, well dressed, even for an evening meeting, light blue sport jacket over a pale yellow pullover sweater, the collar of an expensive dress shirt and perfectly knotted tie, also yellow, poking out over the crew-neck of the sweater.

He didn't get up as I entered the office. He'd made no secret in our previous meetings or my phone call of a couple of days earlier that he harboured a long-standing and unshakeable dislike for members of the media.

He looked up from some papers as I came in, gave me a mouth-only smile, and nodded at the well-worn chair opposite the desk. I sat. His desk looked teak or something equally exotic; a high-end Apple computer perched on a wing of the desk at an angle that made it impossible for the person sitting opposite Caveson to see the monster screen.

The chair he was sitting in looked both comfortable and expensive. Original pieces of modern art dotted the walls and even the plant in the corner to the left of the desk looked like it had been imported from a country with a hot climate and a long name.

I pulled out a notebook and pen and got ready to take notes. Caveson had warned me up front that a tape recorder wouldn't be permitted.

The night had cooled and Caveson had his window open, reminding me of just how much it had cooled. About ten minutes into our chat, I stood, zipped up my warm-up jacket, and sat back down. Caveson didn't make a move to close the window or even acknowledge that the person sitting in his office — arguably his guest — was uncomfortable. Sweetheart of a guy, Caveson.

I was interviewing him for a series the *Calgary Herald* was doing on crime in the new millennium. Now that we were five years in, where were we at — more crime? Less? The different kinds of crime. Where did kids fit in? The impact technology was having on crime. The impact crime was having on technology. That kind of thing.

I was co-writing the series with two long-time friends and colleagues, Janice Mayotte and Lorne Cooney, good journalists, both of them, Janice the better writer, Lorne the better digger. The research was going well and I was excited about what we might end up with. Still, some parts of the project were less fun than others. Caveson fell into that category. I had drawn the short straw, which meant a late-night meeting (the only time he'd see me) at his office (the only place he'd see me).

For a while I thought I might actually get something. A name or two that we didn't already have, maybe even a peek at what the city could expect from its less desirables in the next few years. But Caveson, after spending the first twenty minutes of our meeting telling me that he was unquestionably the best person to talk to for the information I was seeking, spent the next twenty letting me know that he wouldn't be sharing any of it.

I managed to leave his office without telling him that I thought he was the slime in slime ball, and congratulated myself for exercising remarkable self-restraint. I dutifully drove back to the *Herald* building, parked my aged Volvo in the parking lot on the east side, and walked up two flights of stairs on my way to the cubbyhole I laughingly referred to as my office. I was determined to get into my computer what little real information I had wheedled out of Caveson.

I never made it. Lorne Cooney was pacing, head down, back and forth in the hallway outside my office door. I saw him before he saw me. The sheen on his brown-black face was evidence that the building furnace had not yet been fixed and I would be transcribing my notes in sweltering discomfort.

The joke around the *Herald* for the last few days had been, "writing is hell." Journalist humour.

I grinned. "You must have something real good to drag your sorry ass down here at this hour."

He looked up, saw me. "Jesus Christ, man. Why do you even bother to own a cell phone? I've been calling you for a half hour at least. Even tried to get you at Caveson's office. No answer there." The hint of the Caribbean that was barely evident in Lorne's voice became more pronounced when he was agitated. He was agitated now.

"Yeah, his phone rang but —"

Lorne stepped close to me. The look on his face was all wrong, way too tight, too tense, something …

"You need to go home right now."

There was no little turn at the corners of the mouth, no prankster trying not to laugh, not this time. No smile, not even in the eyes, which is what usually gave him away.

"Why … what…?

"Adam, you've got to go *now*. Webster called me from downtown. Said he'd dispatched two cruisers to your house and —"

Everett Webster, police sergeant.

I wasn't there for the end of the sentence. I had already run out the door, back down the two flights, sprinting for the parking lot. I didn't know what Lorne was talking about but I knew it was bad. And it was at my house.

Donna.

I made the thirty-five minute drive in twenty, maybe less. From a block away I could see flashing lights, lots of them; could hear sirens as two emergency vehicles screamed through an intersection that was normally, even in the middle of the day, quiet — an in-home hair stylist on one corner, residential homes on the other three. Tonight there were people on all four corners, standing in little groups like they were waiting for the Stampede parade to pass their location. Except they were all facing one direction ... watching and pointing.

I turned the corner and saw the flames leaping into the night sky.

Please God. Please. Please.

By then three fire trucks were in place. Firefighters were running, their work a frenzied race, with a maze of hoses, all aimed at the house ... my house ... *our* house. I couldn't get closer than three houses away. I jumped out of the Volvo, not bothering to shut it off or close the door.

I ran, not knowing what I'd do when I got there but knowing I had to get into the house, find Donna, get her out.

This battle was already lost, the firefighters' work next to useless. It was too late to do much more than keep the fire from spreading to neighbouring houses. My home was unrecognizable, a lot of the front of the house having collapsed — the flames everywhere.

Even with all the flashing lights and the glow of the flames, or maybe *because* of those things, it was hard to see. I ran into what felt like a wall. This wall moved. And spoke. Wally Neis had seen me running, put his big body in front of me, and got me stopped halfway up the sidewalk. Wally Neis: former classmate, former high school football teammate, deputy fire chief, and maybe the strongest man I knew.

"Nothing you can do, Adam." He bear-hugged his massive arms around me and another firefighter and two cops had hold of me as well.

I fought to get loose. "I'll fucking kill you right here. Donna's in there. I've got to —"

"Nothing you can do," Wally said again.

Still I tried to get free. And I *would* have killed him if I'd been able to get my arms loose. I'd have killed them all. I'd have done anything.

"Adam, listen to me, she's not in there."

The words registered and I relaxed my body slightly. "Where is she?"

The answer didn't come right away. "We ... we found a body. I'm sorry, Adam. It's burned ... real bad. But we think it's Donna."

I struggled to turn my head ... felt Wally release me as I saw the tarp on the lawn, covering something.

Someone.

A police photographer stood nearby studying his camera, maybe looking at the pictures he'd already taken. A cop and someone who looked medical were standing next to the tarp talking, the policeman writing something in a notebook.

I moved toward the tarp and whoever was under it.

But I knew.

I knew.

May 4, 2005. The night the first half of my life ended.

The second half of my life started badly and stayed that way for a long time.

Knowing Donna had died horribly, then learning that the fire had been deliberately set, that someone had murdered my wife, realizing that I had to have been the one the killer wanted to die, or that the arsonists had simply made a mistake, burned down the wrong house, killed the wrong person … it was all incomprehensible. And impossible.

I spent the first weeks of long nights sitting in an armchair in the living room of the apartment I had rented on Drury Avenue, staring at the wall opposite and thinking the same thoughts over and over. *Why had that night happened? Was I to blame?*

Then came the investigation — and the suspicion that I had set the fire. It was beyond painful. Webster and most of the cops — I knew some of them from my work on the crime beat — were pretty good. They made sure I knew that none of them believed any of this shit. However, a few of the people I worked with, even a couple of my bosses at the paper and the investigators the insurance company sent, were a different matter. The latter were very good at what they did, but I hated the bastards.

One of them, a round mound of self-importance named Macrae, made it clear he was convinced that if I hadn't actually set the fire, I'd had someone do it for me. He even managed to get charges laid against me.

Conspiracy to commit arson with intent to cause bodily harm. The charge was based on one piece of evidence that Macrae found compelling — one of the neighbours, a guy I'd only spoken to a couple of times in the three years he'd lived in the neighbourhood, had seen someone who looked like me out in the backyard the day of the fire doing something near my fireplace woodpile. The *something* the neighbor saw involved the *someone* spreading what might have been some kind of chemical in and around the logs, presumably for the arsonist to set ablaze later when I was conveniently out of the house.

As for motive, Macrae had it all worked out. He convinced himself I was having an affair and murdered my wife in order to be free to pursue my real love. Checked phone bills, my Day-Timer, phoned people I had meetings scheduled with to make sure we'd actually met. Found nothing but remained unfazed.

With all those mights and maybes, the neighbour's musings about *possibly* seeing me near the woodpile wouldn't have earned a second look in a first year college criminology class. But in a case where there was damn little else that qualified as credible evidence and because the fire department investigators determined that the origin of the fire was at or near the woodpile, and, most of all because Macrae was looking for anything that made his theory more solid, it all took a long time to go away.

Macrae and his people couldn't find anything more and I was finally dropped as a suspect. The day after the charges were set aside, I quit the *Herald*. That had been coming anyway. The newspaper business was changing. A nine-month-long strike that ushered in the new millennium had resulted in many of the best and brightest writers leaving the paper. They probably did the new publishers a favour.

Fewer full-time writers meant less overhead, no benefits to pay. It was cheaper to hire freelancers and stringers on an ad hoc basis.

I was now one of those freelancers. And I'd done okay with it. Even won an award for a piece on the bad shit people could learn on the Internet: how to build your own roadside bomb, how to poison your spouse and get away with it, how to manufacture crack in your basement…. Most people already knew a lot of what I was telling them, but nevertheless I won some minor award that I didn't bother putting on my wall. Nobody would see it anyway.

I wrote a book too, a kids' book. That was something I was proud of. Unfortunately it was published by a company that was very good at creating nice looking, well-edited books but couldn't sell iced tea in the desert. My book, *The Spoofaloof Rally*, disappeared from the shelves of Chapters and every other Canadian bookstore faster than beer at a rodeo dance.

So I kept flogging stuff to the papers and a few magazines. And it had gone well enough. I was making my rent payments — I never bought another house even after the insurance company finally settled with me. I was making a pretty good living at a time when a lot of people were struggling to get by. I didn't really mind that part of my life.

It was the rest of it, the part that included knowing that whoever had killed my wife had never been found … that part of my life was always there, never went away, and I hated every minute of it.

And there was one other thing — the note that I was sure had come from whoever had set fire to my house.

It came a year to the day after Donna died. It read:

> The Cullens live and love here. I guess
> not anymore. Ha ha.

One sheet of white paper, folded in half, the typewritten message on the inside.

I'd gone to the cops. Nothing. I'd even hired a private investigator I'd known when he was on the police force, a guy named Mike Cobb. Smart guy and he tried hard. We went back through every story I'd ever written that could have even remotely pissed somebody off. Examined in detail my personal life back to grade school. Friends, enemies, relatives, school mates, teammates — he looked at all of it. And wasn't able to turn up a thing.

The cops raised the possibility, a legitimate one, that the note writer might be a crank — some heartless bastard who had read about the fire and decided to play the cruelest of jokes as a follow-up. Cobb couldn't see it and neither could I. The message coming a year to the day after the fire, the reference to Donna's corny little plaque that had sat next to the front door….

Eventually the cops came to agree with what Cobb and I had already concluded.

There was someone in this world who hated me.

ONE

It was annoying. A noise I couldn't quite get my head around. A loud noise. A loud *banging* noise.

It was playing hell with my sleep. Sleep that I needed to combat the hangover that was sure to be an unpleasant reality once my sleeping was done. Which I was hoping wouldn't be for some time.

The banging noise seemed to have other ideas. I sat up in bed, looked over at the digital clock. 8:35. The banging had been joined by another noise. Yelling. It occurred to me that the person doing the yelling might be the same person who was doing the banging. I was about to shout something disagreeable at the noisemaker when I realized that what he was yelling was my name. And what he was banging on was my door.

I threw the covers back and stood up. It didn't feel pleasant to do that but I didn't think I'd die from it either. I stepped over the clothes I'd worn the day before, walked to the door, leaned on it and said, "I'll make you a deal. You quit making that Goddamn racket and I'll open the door in sixty seconds."

The yelling and pounding stopped. The person on the other side of the door said, "Deal."

I found the light switch and flipped it on, a decision I instantly regretted. I walked to the sink, shook three Extra-Strength Tylenol out of a bottle that was sitting on the counter, and gulped down the pills and two glasses of water. I turned away from the sink, reached down, extricated a pair of well-worn jeans and an ancient Bryan Adams *Waking Up the Neighbours* T-shirt from the pile on the floor, and threw them on the bed. I sat, pulled off my sweat pants, and in relatively few attempts was able to exchange the sweats for the jeans and T-shirt.

The voice outside the door said, "You're at forty-five seconds."

"Shut up."

"I've got coffee out here."

"What kind?"

"Starbucks. Pike Place. Grande."

I stood up, crossed the floor a second time, and opened the door. Mike Cobb looked down at me. I'm not a little guy, but I was small standing next to Cobb. He smiled. "Milk and sugar or black. I don't remember."

"Milk and sugar."

He extended one hand.

I accepted the coffee and stepped back to let him in. My apartment is a large bachelor, which means the bed is in the living room, the far end of the room. I led Cobb to the kitchen/living area, gathered a couple of days' newspapers off the table, and threw them on a pile next to the fridge. I pulled out a chair and sat down.

I more or less pointed at one of the other chairs at the table and Cobb also sat. He was wearing a brown leather jacket over a bulky knit tan sweater. Wrangler jeans with no belt. New Balance trainers that looked fresh out of the box. A Jersey Boys ball cap sat just slightly off centre, revealing light brown hair parted on the left with no hint of grey at the temples, though he had to be getting close to that time. Cobb had never told me his age but I figured he was maybe five years older than me, which put him in his early forties.

I thought about apologizing for the mess but decided against it, first of all because mess is a relative term and I'd seen my apartment look much worse, and secondly because people who drop in unexpectedly this early in the morning can damn well take the place the way it comes.

"See you got rid of the moustache," I said.

"See you grew one," Cobb replied. "Kind of evens it out."

We sipped coffee. He removed the ball cap and set it beside him.

"You busy?" He was still smiling.

"Do I look busy?"

"No. You look like crap but you don't look busy."

"Banging, yelling, *and* insults. To what do I owe the pleasure?"

I'd talked to Cobb a couple of times since he'd tried to help me with my arsonist/anonymous note writer problem. I'd used him as a resource for a couple of stories I'd done that had a crime focus.

I looked at him. Though hadn't been able to track the person who sent the note — and also very likely burned down my house and killed my wife — Cobb had worked hard at it, then returned half his fee when he wasn't successful.

He didn't answer. Instead he stood and walked around, surveying the apartment. He'd never been in here before. He stopped at the stereo and CD collection, a series of boxes and stands that takes up a third of the space.

"There are record stores that don't have this kind of selection. You actually listen to these?"

"Yeah."

"All of them?"

"Yeah. Listen, Cobb, I'm betting you didn't come over here at the crack of damn dawn to discuss my music preferences."

"It's 8:44."

"The crack of damn dawn."

He turned away from the music to look at me, then came back to the chair at the table and sat down again.

"I could use your help with something."

"Sure, just make an appointment with my secretary. I may have an opening next Tuesday."

"I was thinking more like right now. There's a bit of urgency to my request."

"I'm listening."

"Good because this will take a little time." As if to reinforce what he'd just said, he pulled off the jacket and draped it over the back of his chair.

I drank coffee. Waited.

"A guy came by my office yesterday morning, a guy named Larry Blevins."

I looked up from the coffee. "Don't know the name."

"You will. Blevins has a seventeen-year-old son, Jay. High school dropout, got into alcohol in more than a recreational way in tenth grade, moved on to drugs a year or so later, was out of school a few months after that."

"Cocaine?"

A small nod. "Kid has eclectic tastes. Crack's his main thing though. The family's tried every way they could think of to get the kid off the juice and off the street — treatment, counselling, spent a lot of money, threw him out, took him back home, tough love, real love, all of it. Last week the kid ended up in hospital; they almost lost him. Overdose. The family figured maybe this would be the thing that might get Jay motivated to get off the stuff."

"I think I know where this is going," I said.

Cobb nodded again. "When they got him home they talked about it, cried, begged, bargained, all the stuff they tell you you're not supposed to do. Four nights ago Jay got some money and the car keys out of his mom's purse and took off.

"Night before last Blevins is out driving around some of the seamier areas, looking for the kid. Said he's done that before, never found anything. This time he spots his wife's car in a parking lot a few blocks from the Saddledome, figures he's maybe close. Keeps cruising, gets lucky this time, sees a friend of Jay's, also a user, coming out of a house carrying something. There's another guy on the porch of this place, badass-looking guy … Blevins figures he's found a crack house."

"Good guess," I said.

Cobb nodded. "This other kid, his name is Max, leaves and badass goes back inside. Blevins decides he's going in there."

"Shit," I said.

"It gets worse," Cobb looked at me. "Blevins hunts and he's a gun collector, has a handgun with him. Decides to take it along thinking he might wave it around a little, scare the crap out of these creeps and warn them off selling product to his kid. Figures he'll tell them that if they do, he'll come back. Like Sylvester Stallone. His words, not mine."

"The gun loaded?"

"Uh-huh."

"I've got a hall-of-fame hangover and I can see a hundred holes in his line of thinking."

Cobb shrugged, noncommittal. "Maybe. But you don't have kids. Never had to go through what Larry Blevins has. Desperate people do desperate things. Stupid things, because they're not thinking clearly. Blevins knows that now."

Cobb paused and we both drank some of our coffee. He set his down, resumed the story.

"The door's open so he walks in. One guy's on a cell phone, the other one, the same guy who'd been on the front steps with Max, is sitting behind a table. There's a bunch of stuff Blevins has seen in pictures on the Internet spread out all over the table."

"I've seen those pictures," I said.

"He tells them why he's there."

I whistled. "This guy's got balls."

"Big time. The first guy, the one behind the table, says he's never heard of anyone named Jay. He sticks with that for a while, laughing like it's all a big joke. Blevins wasn't sure what he said that changed the guy's attitude, but suddenly the guy goes from all smiles to mean as a snake — tells Blevins to get his ass out of there, or he'll put him out."

"And all this time Blevins is holding a gun."

Cobb nodded.

"The dealer *also* has balls."

"Now he tells Blevins that Jay's one of their most valued customers, says they could work up a family package if he really wants to bond with his son. Blevins actually points the gun at him, but that just gets the guy laughing again, like it's the funniest thing he's seen in a long time. Just then the front door opens and a girl, younger than Jay, walks into the place. Blevins said she looked maybe fifteen, sixteen.

"Laughing Boy says something about how now the fun would really begin, because Carly doesn't have any money and she needs a load. Blevins tries to take the girl by the arm and push her back out of there but she twists away, tells him to fuck off. The guy behind the table stands up, starts coming around the table. Blevins tells him to back off but the guy keeps coming. Blevins said he was tall, real tall, maybe six-six, but he isn't laughing anymore and he's got something in his hand. Maybe a knife, Blevins wasn't sure.

"Blevins shoots him. Twice."

"Jesus."

"Then everything gets loud. The young girl, Carly, she's screaming, the other guy is yelling and knocking over chairs and stuff wanting to get out of there. Blevins told me he thought the guy was trying to get to the back door. Anyway, wherever he's going he isn't fast enough and Blevins shoots him too."

Cobb stopped talking. Neither of us spoke for quite a while. I've covered crime in Calgary for a dozen years and I've heard lots of stories, some bad, some *real* bad. This was one of the real bad ones.

Desperation.

"What about the girl … Carly?" I was almost afraid to ask. If Blevins had completely lost it, who knew what else he'd done?

"Blevins didn't know. He thought she ran out the door … the front door. When he went back outside he didn't see her. He got in his car and drove away."

I took a breath.

"What did Blevins think you could do for him?"

"Nothing. That wasn't why he'd come to see me."

"What then?"

"He's worried about Jay. That he might be in danger."

"Why? Was the kid there?"

"No, but the guy on the cell phone, Blevins said it was like he was doing play-by-play, telling whoever he was talking to that Jay-boy's old man is here and oooh he has a gun and he's such a scary man … same deal, like it was all a big joke.

"Blevins figures, and he's probably right, that whoever was on the other end of the line will know who shot those guys. Might even think Jay *was* there, with his old man. And he's worried that maybe they'll try to get to Jay … a payback thing."

"Were the two guys dead? Did he check?"

"He says he didn't but he put two in the middle of the first guy's chest. The second guy, the one on the cell phone, he got him with a head shot. He figured they were both dead."

Two in the middle of the chest. Head shot. "The guy was good under pressure."

"Real good."

"And Blevins wants you to…?"

"Find Jay. If these guys' bosses, associates, partners, whatever, go looking for him …" Cobb didn't finish the sentence.

"The kid could be hard to keep safe. If he's using and

needs to make a buy …" It was my turn to leave a sentence unfinished.

Cobb nodded. "I know that. So does Blevins. But he's hired me to try."

Another long silence.

I rubbed my hand over the stubble that was the result of not having shaved for a couple of days. Cobb may have been right. I likely did look like crap.

"You think Blevins's story was for real?"

"I already checked. Made a couple of calls. Two shooting victims, no information on the condition of the victims, found at a house on Raleigh Avenue."

"Okay, so it sounds like it's the real deal."

"When Blevins finished talking to me, he walked over and dropped a handgun into one of my filing cabinet drawers. Guess he didn't think he'd need it anymore."

"Let me guess — the two guys were shot with a handgun that matches the make and model of the one Blevins deposited in your filing cabinet."

"Check."

"What about Blevins?"

"He said he'd be turning himself in but needed twenty-four hours to take care of a few things."

"I hope shooting some more people wasn't one of the things he had to take care of."

"I asked him that. He said it wasn't."

"And you believed him."

"He's not a nut, Adam. He's a guy who lost it and shot two people who were hurting his son. Something that in his position I could have done. He's aware of what he did and all he cares about is keeping the kid safe."

I stared at the ceiling for a while trying to make sense of it. With limited success.

"I guess that brings us to me. When you came in here you mentioned wanting my help."

He nodded. "My time on the force, and even the work I've done since, I haven't spent much time on the drug side. I've had my share of dealing with crimes that were *fuelled* by drugs and even motivated by the need to obtain the resources to make a purchase, but that's not the same as being up to my ass in the drug culture. So my expertise is limited."

"You want me to provide information that might help you find Jay or assist you in the actual search?"

"Both would be good. I know you've written stories on the drug scene here. If I remember correctly, a couple of them focused on crack. I thought you might know some people who might know some people. Or at least where I might start looking."

"As in who might be the bigs behind the house on Raleigh Avenue?"

Cobb shook his head, then waved a hand. "Don't get me wrong, that's information I wouldn't mind having. But I don't imagine you know that." His eyes narrowed. "No, my only real shot is to find the kid before they do. Which is why I mentioned urgency earlier."

I looked around the room. "Okay, you finish your coffee, while I find my socks."

"A clean pair not an option?"

"It would be if I'd washed clothes in the last couple of weeks."

Cobb stood up. "You haven't told me if you're going to help me. If you're not —"

"I can't make important decisions in bare feet." Trying to lighten the mood. I resumed my search and discovered the socks under an Oklahoma State Cowboys sweatshirt.

"Anyway, you're right. If you read the stuff I've done on the crack industry in our city you know I never really got past the street sellers. Most of the sellers are also users and they protect the guys at the top, first of all because they're the employers, sort of a job loyalty thing, and secondly, they don't want anything bad to happen to their own supply."

"So, like I said, the only way I can approach this is to find the kid before they do."

I nodded. "And I'm guessing you may not have a lot of time."

"Which, as you pointed out, brings me back to you. Any ideas as to where I might start with a kid like Jay? Or Max?"

"Well, there I might be able to help a little. I mean we might start with some of the areas that are hangouts for users. The bigger the user, the crappier the places they tend to hang out. Unless of course the kid comes from money. Those people tend not to be sleeping on the streets and under bridges."

"I didn't get a sense from Blevins that they're wealthy people."

"Right. Streets and bridges it is."

"Sounds like bad movie stuff."

"What I saw when I was researching my stories was a *real* bad movie."

Cobb pulled my down-filled jacket off a door handle and handed it to me. "So you're willing to help?"

I took the coat, pulled it on, checked pockets to make sure my gloves were there.

"Yeah, but don't get the idea that I'm all about doing my civic duty or helping the less unfortunate. There might be a story here, maybe a compelling one. I'm not talking about the concerned-dad-shoots-drug-dealers story. Everybody will have that. I'm talking about the what-happens-after-that angle. If it turns out to be good, I want to be the one writing that story."

Cobb looked at his watch. "Let's go."

TWO

We took Cobb's SUV, an older Jeep Cherokee with four wheel drive and the biggest engine Jeep makes. While we drove, Cobb filled in a few more missing pieces.

Blevins had given him an envelope filled mostly with cash — I didn't ask how much — the address of the house on Raleigh, and a picture of his son. Blevins had said the picture was a year old but that Jay hadn't changed much. A little skinnier and a couple of tattoos, rattlesnakes, but they were on his shoulders and upper arm, not visible if he had a shirt on. The envelope also contained the name of Blevins's lawyer (in case the money was insufficient) and Blevins's own business card with his home address on the back.

"What do you think Blevins was wanting to do before he turned himself in?"

"I really don't know. Maybe try one more time to find the kid. Or look after personal stuff, financial stuff. He didn't say. I offered to help him with the surrender to the cops but he said he'd handle it on his own. Besides, he wanted me to get started ASAP with looking for the kid."

We got where we were going in a hurry, partly because the area wasn't far from where I lived and partly because Cobb seemed determined to test the Jeep's speed capabilities.

We started in a part of Calgary that shoppers and diners don't usually frequent. I reasoned that Jay Blevins would have tried to stay fairly close to where he was buying drugs. Convenience.

Inglewood is Calgary's oldest neighbourhood and has made a comeback from a couple of decades ago when it wasn't a place you wanted to be. Now, as the transformation moves forward, it's a funky mix of mostly good and some not so good — both in its architecture and its populace.

Cobb found a parking spot between a couple of sub-compacts and we stepped out into a maze of buildings three quarters of a century old or older. The not-so-good part of Inglewood: a military surplus store, a couple of warehouses, what was once a hotel, a few shelters, the Salvation Army, street counsellors, a couple of community churches run out of very non-church-like buildings. I'd been here before when researching stories and I guessed that Cobb, even if drugs hadn't been his focus as a cop, was not unfamiliar with the area.

I suggested we start with the shelters. Blevins had said Jay had taken off before, sometimes for fairly long periods of time. He'd need a place to sleep, would know what was out there.

A couple of people hanging around outside the Sally Ann knew Jay Blevins; he had stayed there a few times. But if they knew where he was now they weren't willing to share that information.

Cobb and I headed inside. I knew one of the people who worked there — a pastor who ran twelve step programs out of the Sally Ann and a couple of other re-hab centres in other parts of town. I'd interviewed Scott Friend a few times, and found him to be optimistic with-out the over-the-top cheery you see on the religion chan-nels. I knew he spent a lot of time on the street and hoped he'd be in.

He was. He was sitting at a wooden desk working on a sandwich and tapping at a keyboard. He looked up, recognized me, and stood up, smiling.

"Adam, how've you been?" He extended a hand.

I shook it. "Good, thanks, Scott. This is Mike Cobb. Mike, Scott Friend." They shook hands. "We're looking for someone," I told him. "I wish we could take time to visit but it's kind of urgent."

He looked at me. "No need to apologize. I hope I can help."

Cobb showed him his P.I. card, then held out the picture of Jay Blevins. "Know him?"

Friend took the picture looked at it for several sec-onds, handed it back, and nodded. "Sure, I know Jay."

Cobb tucked the picture back in a jacket pocket. "Seen him lately?"

Friend shook his head. "Not in … I'd say a month, anyway. Is he in trouble?"

"We're not sure. Just need to talk to him. A family matter."

Friend looked at me. "But urgent."

"Yeah," I said

"I heard he had an OD episode. I'm guessing he must be okay or you wouldn't be looking for him."

"Yeah, he recovered from that," Cobb said.

Friend nodded. "And he's back on the street."

"Uh-huh."

"Using?"

"Looks like it."

"We get a lot of people looking for family members. Some hire guys like you." Friend said it casually. "Most don't find the people they're looking for. Mostly because the people they're looking for don't want to be found."

"He attend your meetings regularly?" Cobb asked.

Friend shook his head. "He'd start with the best of intentions, come to a couple of meetings, then drop out of sight and go back to using. That happened three, maybe four times."

"Any idea where Jay lives when he's on the street? Where he stays?"

Another head shake. "Sorry, I'd like to help but I really don't know where you might look ... other than maybe the other shelters."

"How about a guy about the same age as Jay? Name's Max Levine. They were friends. Or a girl named Carly? Don't have a last name. Probably younger than Jay or Max."

Scott Friend thought, then shook his head slowly. "Sorry, can't help with either of them. Maybe try some of the folks outside." He pointed at the people we could see through the windows that faced the street.

"Thanks, Scott," I said. "Good to see you again."

Cobb handed him a business card. "If you happen to run into him or hear anything about where we might look, I'd appreciate a call. And thanks."

Friend took the card, nodded. "Any time."

We had no luck on the street with Max Levine or the girl named Carly. It seemed to me there was a less cordial feel to our second pass through the people outside the Salvation Army building.

Cobb and I split up to cover more ground faster. We mapped out two routes that would take us to several places where a runaway kid might hang out. We'd meet up two hours later outside a take-out pizza joint on 9th Avenue.

I got two hours of nothing. A couple of times I thought the person I was talking to knew something but wasn't about to tell me. Code of the street people.

When I got to the rendezvous point, Cobb was already there but he wasn't alone. He was engaged in a conversation with a short, bearded man wearing a bundle of winter clothes, none of which were what could be called colour coordinated, including his mitts, one of which was tan and huge, the other not a mitt at all but a glove, orange with blue trim.

The conversation was one-sided. Cobb was doing the talking, his voice low and controlled but forceful. He saw me, paused, and indicated I should come over.

"Adam Cullen, meet Ike Groves, the Grover."

I nodded. Ike Groves did not respond.

"Now Grover, we've talked about the importance of manners. Say hello to the gentleman."

Groves growled something that approximated hello. Cobb turned toward me without removing a hand from the shoulder of a coat that may have been tan once but was now the grey-brown of undercooked hamburger.

"Grover here was just about to tell me what he knows about a particular house not far from where we're standing where some enterprising people are selling illicit products, isn't that right, Grover?"

Groves looked around ... worried.

"My friend Grover lives in the neighbourhood and knows everything, but sometimes he's reluctant to share information with his friends. I was just reminding him about his involvement in an ill-advised scheme involving a number of automobiles that didn't belong to him but somehow turned up in a storage garage he was renting."

Groves squirmed but the hand remained firmly attached to his shoulder, and even with the coat as padding I guessed that the shoulder was in some discomfort.

"Happily for Grover the police never learned about the vehicles in question," Cobb turned to Groves in mid-sentence, "but who *did* know all about the operation and chose not to inform the authorities about what was going on in that garage, Grover, who was that again? Speak up, I'm having trouble hearing you."

"You, Cobb, and I appreciate it but I can't say —"

"Oh, now see Grover, there's a word I hate — that word *but*. Now what would have happened on that stolen auto thing if I'd been thinking, 'I don't really want to turn my friend Grover in for doing something very illegal, *but* …' Thing is, Grover, there was no but then and there really shouldn't be a but now. You can see my point here, can't you?"

Groves winced and I was fairly sure the grip on the shoulder had just got tighter.

"Alls I know is that there's a guy owns a few houses around here. Maybe three or four. That's one of them. He buys places cheap, fixes 'em up a little bit, rents 'em to people who have … business interests."

"Crack houses," Cobb said.

"You didn't hear that from me."

"This particular house — you know the tenants?"

Vigorous head shake. "Uh-uh, and that's the truth, man. From what I hear I don't wanna know."

"Bad guys?"

"There's bad guys and there's *bad* guys. These are guys people like me stay away from."

Cobb said, "Jay Blevins."

"Who's that?"

"That's *my* line, Grover. You know him?" Cobb held out the picture.

Groves studied the picture, thought for a few seconds. "I've seen the kid. Didn't know his name. Pothead, crackhead, maybe other shit too."

"He ever buy from you?"

"Aw, come on, Cobb, you know I don't —"

Louder. "He ever buy from you?"

"Naw, I've seen him on the street a few times. Goin' in and out of shelters. I don't pay attention to them kind."

"Because he's not one of your customers?"

"Punks like that attract the wrong kind of people. Parents, cops, guys like you. Like I said, I steer clear."

"When's the last time you saw him?"

Another shrug. "No idea. Month ago maybe … or maybe two."

"Where?"

"Told you man, I don't pay attention to punks like him. Bottom feeders. Low life, you know?"

"I can see how having to associate with riff-raff like that would be upsetting."

"Yeah, so now you know what I know and you can let go of my shoulder."

"I need a name, Grover."

"What?"

"A name. I'll buy your story that you don't know the people in the house. But I need the name of the owner. The guy with several properties."

Groves shrugged. "Shit, how would I know that?"

"Guy owns three or four places around here that house the kind of businesses you described. You know who owns them."

"Jesus, man …"

"The name."

Groves winced again, looked over at me, and leaned closer to Cobb, whispered something. Cobb let go of the shoulder, took a step back. "Now, Grover, I'm hoping you aren't thinking that you can mess with me, because if that happens, it will come back to haunt you."

Groves feigned indignity. "I wouldn't do that. You know me better than that, Cobb."

"One last thing, Grover — you hear anything, I mean *anything* about that house or the people in it, I'm your first phone call. You got that?"

Grover didn't answer and started moving quickly away from us.

Cobb and I watched him walk away, flexing the shoulder, rubbing it with the other hand.

"Friend of yours?"

"Yeah," Cobb managed a half smile. "We're real tight. He was one of my informants back in the day. And I wasn't kidding — there isn't much that happens in this part of Calgary that Grover doesn't know about. Kind of fortuitous running into him."

"You think he knows about the shooting?"

"If he doesn't he will soon. The question is, will he call like I told him to."

I looked down the street. Groves had already disappeared. I looked back at Cobb. "How'd you make out?"

"Like the song says, 'I got plenty of nothin'.' You?"

"Zeros. I asked some guys that looked like regulars on the street person circuit. A couple of vague, 'Yeah, I think sos' as far as having heard the name, but that's it. Scouted the area under the train bridge. Three or four people sleeping. A couple of guys just sitting, not talking, not sleeping — just sitting. They didn't know Jay. At least that's what they said. They didn't change it up even after I told them the kid could be in danger, so maybe they really *don't* know him. Hard to say."

"I didn't expect it to be easy. And if Jay's old man has tried to find him before, the kid might be pretty practiced at leaving no trail."

I nodded. "Could be."

"Looks like I've got a stop to make before we carry on with looking for the kid. Follow up on what my friend Grover told me. Won't take long. Care to come along?"

"Wouldn't miss it."

Gifford Sharp was a realtor, his office located in a strip mall not far from the University of Calgary. We'd caught a break in traffic. In just under a half hour we were parked in front of Sharp's office, the Jeep nose in to a tired two-storey, red brick building, flanked by a hair stylist and a computer repair place that didn't look open.

Cobb sat, not moving, staring at the window that said "Gifford M. Sharp, Realtor, Million Dollar Club."

"Million dollar realtor, fifty dollar office," Cobb said as he climbed out of the Jeep. I followed him onto the sidewalk and through the door that took us into the office.

Apparently being a million dollar club member doesn't mean you can afford office help. One man sat at the only desk, staring at a computer screen. He was fifty-ish and bulky in a wrinkled grey shirt and loosened red tie with what looked like post-modern penguins on it hanging limply around a thick neck that sported a schematic of prominent red veins. Dirty fingernails. He looked over the top of the computer screen as Cobb stepped up to the desk.

"Why do I get the feeling you guys aren't looking for a nice four-bedroom with a spacious yard and several recent upgrades?"

"Gifford Sharp?"

The man eyed Cobb for a few seconds before answering. "I'm him," he said. "If you're in the market, it's Giff."

"I'm Mike Cobb. I'm a private investigator looking into the shooting at your house on Raleigh."

Sharp looked back at the computer screen, tapped a couple of keys, looked up again. "I already talked to the cops."

"We won't take much of your time. Just wondered if you could tell us who your renters are."

"I could, but like I said, I already spoke to the *real* investigators." He dragged out the word "real."

I reached in my pocket, pulled out a notepad and a pen, flipped open the notepad. Cobb saw me do it and said, "This is Adam Cullen, reporter for the *Herald*."

Sharp shifted his eyes to me. "I don't need no publicity here."

I steadied the notebook, pen poised to write.

"We don't *need* to give you any," Cobb dragged out "need," a couple of beats longer than Sharp had with "real."

Sharp said, "What do you want to know?"

Cobb said, "Your renters — who might they be?"

"Outfit called M and F Holdings."

I put my notepad away.

"How long have they been renting the house?"

"Just coming up on two years. I bought it in January, had it rented by February 1." Proud of that.

"How did the rental come about?"

"Two people walked in here, just like you did, except it was a man and woman."

"What were their names?"

"Smith."

Cobb raised his eyebrows.

Sharp shrugged. "I'm not the government. I don't ask for ID. People sign a contract, give me the first and last month's rent and the damage deposit, they move in."

"How much rent?"

Sharp cleared his throat.

"What was that?" Cobb leaned on the desk.

"Two thousand."

"A month?" I asked.

"Yeah, a month."

"So they gave you four thousand dollars and the damage deposit," Cobb said.

A beat.

"Not exactly."

"Then *what* exactly?"

"They … uh … paid for a year in advance."

"Twenty-four thousand."

"Well, actually, thirty-four."

"Sorry," Cobb said. "You lost me there."

"Twenty-four grand for rent, another ten damage deposit."

"You normally charge ten thousand dollars damage deposit on your rental properties?"

Hesitation. "Not normally, no. It was … uh … their idea."

"So they wrote you a cheque from M and F Holdings for thirty-four large in advance."

"Right."

"And no catches?"

"No…. Well, only one. They told me they didn't want me coming around the house — no owner drop-in checks or anything like that."

"And for thirty-four thousand clams, I'm betting you didn't see that as any kind of obstacle."

Sharp shook his head again. "Look, I got work to do here."

"What happened when the year went by? You see the Smiths again?"

"Just her. She came in a couple of weeks before the lease expired, paid up again."

"But just twenty-four thousand this time, right? Because the damage deposit had already been paid."

Sharp looked down, didn't answer.

"Let me guess, Mr. Sharp. It was thirty-four thousand again and maybe a reminder from Mrs. Smith that you didn't need to be coming by the house."

Sharp didn't look up.

"Mr. Sharp?"

"Yeah, something like that," he looked at me. "You ain't writing any of this in the *Herald*, right?"

I tapped my pocket and smiled at him.

Cobb said, "What did they look like?"

"The Smiths?"

"No, Giff, the Obamas. Who are we talking about here?"

"She was a looker. Classy broad, expensive clothes, tall, dark hair, nice smile, not movie star looks but not far from it."

"You see what they were driving?"

"Uh-uh."

"What about Mr. Smith? What did he look like?"

"Hard to tell. I was looking at *her*, you know what I mean?" He chuckled. Neither Cobb nor I smiled. "Big guy, not in terms of height but broad like a football type, maybe a linebacker, you know? Probably works out or maybe does steroids, what do I know. Hair sort of reddish, I think. I only saw him once, I don't remember exactly."

"Guy writes you a cheque for thirty-four grand, you don't recall what he looked like? Why am I having trouble with that?"

"Had one of those noses that looked like it had been broken a time or two. Maybe fights or something. And real big hands, I remember that. Good dresser too, like her that way."

"How old?"

"Mid to late thirties maybe. Both of 'em."

"And you never went by the place since that first time they came in."

"That was part of the deal."

"That isn't what I asked you."

"I might've drove by a time or two, just to make sure the place was still standing."

Cobb laid the picture of Jay Blevins on the desk facing Sharp. "You ever see this kid? Maybe during one of your drive bys?"

Sharp looked at the picture, picked it up and handed it back to Cobb. "Never seen him. Who is he?"

"Missing kid we're trying to find for his family. A kid who did some buying at the house you rented to the Smiths."

"Don't know anything about that."

"I'm sure you don't. Appreciate your time, Giff."

Sharp handed each of us one of his cards. "You ever lookin', give me a call. I've got some nice condos in the southeast … *nice* condos. Or if you know somebody and send them my way, I usually offer a five hundred dollar incentive, but you guys, seven fifty."

I took the card. "Is that Sharp with an 'e'?"

I smiled at him as Cobb turned and led the way back outside. I fought the urge to grind the business card under my heel on the way to the door. Cobb didn't say anything until we were back in the Jeep.

"Sharp," he said. "Middle name Notso."

"I'm not sure about that. Seems pretty savvy to me. I don't know of many landlords pulling down that kind of revenue."

"Good point. By the way, nice touch with the notepad."

I grinned and Cobb chuckled.

"You hungry?"

I looked around hoping there was another option besides the donair spot a few doors down. "I am, but I'd be a whole lot hungrier if we were anywhere but here."

He nodded. "Got any more ideas as to where we might look for Jay Blevins or Max Levine?"

"A couple."

"Good, let's grab a sandwich somewhere and get back at it."

"We can do better than that — head down to Chinatown. We do dim sum and talk to a couple of guys I know. Longshots maybe, but worth trying."

Cobb looked at his watch.

I said, "There's a place that'll get us in and out fast. One of the people I think we should talk to works right near there. The other guy won't be hard to find. Both of them are … uh … connected."

Cobb nodded. "Let's do it."

Twenty minutes later we had miraculously found a parking spot on 3rd Avenue just off Centre Street and were sitting at a corner table at the Peking King. The "King-King" as it's known to the locals is one of those *best kept secrets*, virtually unnoticed and unknown except to the Chinese residents of the area and a few non-Asian types like me who have stumbled across it by accident.

Cobb told me he didn't know dim sum from chop suey so I ordered a few things I thought were conservative enough for the fledgling diner: shrimp dumplings, steamed wheat buns with pork filling, a couple of bowls of duck egg and pork congee (a kind of porridge with non-porridge-like stuff mixed in), some lotus leaf rice and, to test Cobb's limits at least a little, a few Phoenix talons — deep fried chicken feet served in a black bean sauce.

Cobb did well, eating at least a little of everything — he seemed to like the dumplings a lot, the congee somewhat less and, to my surprise, he went back at the Phoenix talons a second time.

As he chewed on a wheat bun, he looked at me and nodded. "I wanted to thank you for this."

"I don't need much of an excuse to come to King-King."

"I meant helping me look for the kid."

"Haven't helped much so far. You think he's in real danger?"

Cobb's shoulders moved up a couple of centimetres, then back down. "If I was a betting man, I'd lay five to two on they go after the kid. Show the world nobody fucks with them, that kind of thinking."

"A lesson."

"Something like that. These two guys you mentioned, what's the deal with them?"

"One of them, Jackie Chow, works down the street, runs an adult video store. Sells more than videos there. The other guy is a part-time pimp, part-time dealer. Buys and sells guns as a sideline. I only know his first name, Yik. Bigger player than Jackie Chow but not the top banana. Not a nice man, but I did him a favour once and if he's in the mood he might tell us something interesting."

"Yik."

"Yeah, he doesn't like it if people make humorous remarks about his name."

"Maybe he should change it."

"That would be the kind of remark I'd avoid."

Cobb shrugged. "What kind of favour?"

"It was while I was doing the series on drugs in Calgary. I'd met with Yik and he'd filled me in on the coke scene — without any names, of course — in this part of the city. While we were having coffee at a place not far from here, a couple of cops came into the place wanting to be macho. They spotted Yik and thought this would be a good time to interrogate, aka hassle, him. I let them know I was a newspaper guy and then made a big deal of taking down badge numbers, descriptions, anything I could think of; I wrote down their questions as fast as they could ask them. They either got nervous or pissed off and finally stomped out of there. I didn't think it was any big deal but Yik liked that I backed him. We'll see if he remembers."

"That notebook of yours is a handy little implement."

"Sometimes." I grinned.

We finished the main course and though I recommended he try the Malay steamed sponge cake for dessert, Cobb settled for green tea. I ordered an egg tart and opted for oolong tea.

When my dessert arrived, Cobb pointed at it, not in a good way. "What is that?" It was an accusation disguised as a question.

"It's called an egg tart."

"I know that. I heard you order it. What's the stuff on top that looks like hay?"

"Bird's nest."

"Sure, that's what they call it. What *is* it?"

"Bird's nest." I tucked into it.

"Nice."

He watched me eat for a while. "I haven't asked you because I think I know the answer but did anything further come up in connection with your wife's death? Any leads? Suspicions?"

I shook my head, set my spoon down. "Nothing."

"I wish I could have helped you more than I did. That damn thing still doesn't make sense to me."

"You did all you could. I wasn't unhappy with your investigation."

Cobb nodded. "I know you weren't. But I was. I wanted to get the son of a bitch."

I nodded.

Cobb stared at his tea cup, not seeing it. "I think about it sometimes … even after all this time. That there must have been something we … I missed."

"The arsonist didn't give you or the police and fire investigators much in the way of clues."

"Maybe. But there's something or someone out there that if we could just find it, or him, we could finish this thing. I've thought about it a lot. Sometimes I even wonder if we shouldn't have looked a little closer at your wife."

I stared at Cobb. "What do you mean?"

"I know you said she didn't have any enemies but I sometimes wonder if there wasn't something, maybe, in her past."

I shook my head. "I know it's tempting to think about especially when we've got nothing else, but as I said then, there just isn't anybody who could possibly have any reason … Look, I know every guy thinks his wife is perfect, but —"

"Not every guy thinks that."

"You're right. And I know I sound like a parent with the smartest, best-looking kid in the world, but Donna was the person others came to when they were having some spat or other, they'd ask her for advice, like an unofficial counsellor. I just don't think —"

"I know. I get that. But what about before she knew you? Something in her more distant past. Not necessarily something *she* did or even knew about. Maybe some guy that had the hots for her in college and years later the guy's a whack job and decides to show her that nobody gets away with dumping him. I know it sounds farfetched, but believe me, Adam, weirder shit than that — a lot weirder — has happened. And *does* happen."

"Believe me, I've thought about it, gone through every moment of our lives together, every conversation ... I just don't buy it. Even her growing up. We talked about that, the way couples do. Donna was the braces and glasses kid in school, kind of geeky, she didn't become the beautiful woman ... okay, there I go again."

"It's okay. I saw pictures. She was beautiful."

"But she wasn't that way all her life is all I'm saying. She didn't really bloom until she was pretty well through university. Didn't even date much. And if there had been a guy like the kind you're talking about, she'd have told me."

Cobb took a last drink of tea. Nodded. Not looking convinced. "Anyway," he started to rise. "We've got other things we have to take care of. Let's go talk movies with Jackie Chow."

The video store was as unpleasant as I'd remembered it. A big window that faced the street didn't let much light in, mostly because it was covered in posters that announced "XXX Rated," and had the word ADULT plastered all over it in foot-high capital letters and repeated at every angle possible, sometimes the letters overlapping. Artistic.

When we went into the store, a bell jangled to announce our arrival. We were the only people there. No one at the counter. I figured the jangling would bring Jackie Chow or someone at a dead run to head off shoplifters on a street where shoplifting was like breathing. I was wrong.

The store was decorated in a minimalist motif. A couple of posters on the chipped plaster walls, all of which needed painting. The most recent coat had been a light blue once, now it was the colour of washed-out denim. The floor, however, looked relatively clean, maybe because it's easier, and cheaper, to sweep than it is to paint. There were a couple of aisles of empty DVD cases. Not a lot of stock. I was reminded that renting movies wasn't the primary business conducted in the store.

Cobb checked out some of the merchandise while I read the titles on a flyer that was stuck on the wall with a single piece of aging Scotch tape. "Top 10 Adult Films of the Month." No indication what month. Probably didn't matter. *The Virgin Surgeon*, *Depth Chart*, and *Insatiable Nurses* were the top three. The latter had a promo line that read, "In this hospital anything goes and everybody comes."

I quit reading. "This place always makes me want to have a long bath in disinfectant."

"Roger that," Cobb looked around, impatient. "Much as I'm enjoying all this exposure to culture, we need to keep moving. Is our boy here or not?"

On cue Jackie Chow came out of the back part of the store carrying a newspaper and a half-filled Styrofoam coffee cup. He stepped behind the counter and looked at us. "Gentlemen."

He hadn't changed much. Average height, still thin, too thin to be healthy. He was wearing a *Les Miserables* T-shirt. I guessed Value Village. Jackie Chow didn't strike me as a guy who got to a lot of Broadway musicals. The makings of a moustache sat above his mouth, dark eyes set close together, grey ball cap with the letter L sitting fashionably off-centre on his head.

I wasn't sure he recognized me at first. I stepped closer to the counter.

"Hey, Jackie. Adam Cullen. Writer … freelance. I interviewed you a couple of times. Drug stuff. Crack and a few things."

Chow raised a pair of glasses to his face, studied me, took the glasses off again and set them on the counter. "Sure, I remember. Newspaper dude. Didn't use my name. Kept your word. That was good."

"Yeah. Jackie, this is Mike Cobb. I'm helping him find a kid who's missing. Might be in some trouble."

Chow smirked. "Most of the kids around here are missing. A lot of them are in trouble." He kept looking at me. Hadn't glanced at Cobb. "Cop." Cobb pulled his wallet and showed Chow his PI card. Chow didn't bother to put his glasses on and barely glanced at the card. "I'm pretty busy here so if you don't mind —"

"I can see how busy you are and Mr. Cullen and I don't want to keep you from all that industry any longer than necessary." Cobb set an elbow on the counter, just grazing the eye glasses. "Just like you to take the time to look at a picture." He held out the photo of Jay Blevins.

Chow glanced at it. "Don't know 'im."

"Yeah, maybe try again. With your glasses on. Just in case."

Chow looked at Cobb. Not scared but wary. Cobb straightened, lifted the glasses, held them out.

Chow took the glasses, set them on his face, looked at the photo, then handed it back to Cobb. "Like I said, I don't know the kid."

Cobb said, "So he's never come in here to buy any 'movies'?"

Chow looked down at the counter then up at me. "I

ain't seen this kid. Here or anywhere else. And I got work to do."

I moved closer. "Jackie, you hear about what went down last night?"

A flicker of interest. "As in?"

"As in a couple of dealers getting wasted."

Slow nod. "Yeah, I might have heard about that. This kid have something to do with it?"

"He's what the police call a person of interest. We'd like to find him before they do."

"If the kid had anything to do with those two guys getting blown away, the cops are the least of his problems."

"Any idea who might be a bigger problem for him?"

"Nope," Chow shook his head. Too quickly. "But the word is that the people who are behind the residence where the two gentlemen were shot are not happy. And when they aren't happy, it's not a good thing." Chow looked at Cobb for the first time. "For anybody."

Cobb pulled a business card out of his shirt pocket, dropped it on the counter. "If he happens to drop in, or if you see him somewhere or hear about him, I'd appreciate a call."

Chow picked up the card, crumpled it in his fist. "Nice chatting with you gentlemen." Still avoiding eye contact with Cobb.

"Thanks, Jackie," I said.

I looked at Cobb to see if he had anything else he wanted to say or ask. He turned away, not doing a real good job of hiding his disgust. Back out on the street, both of us took deep breaths. Like we were trying to get the place out of our lungs. Bad air out, good air in.

Cobb grunted, "I didn't like that guy."

"No one would have guessed. At least now I know who's who when we do good cop, bad cop."

"I could use some of that disinfectant you mentioned."

"The next guy makes Jackie Chow look like Robin Hood."

THREE

"We can walk. It's not far." I pointed south on Centre Street, toward downtown.

We stopped at a kiosk where all the publications were in Chinese. I bought two coffees, handed one to Cobb, and we continued walking south, turning left after another block. I thought about how bad the odds were that we'd find a drugged-out kid who didn't want to be found. On the other hand, Jay Blevins wouldn't know that some real bad guys might be looking to use him as a lesson in street cred, and he also wasn't aware of Cobb and me.

So maybe.

"How'd you come to know about this Yik?" Cobb's eyes were busy, taking in windows on second and third floors, alleys, people passing us, cars on the street. I was reminded that he'd been a cop.

"When I was researching the drug stuff, his name came up a lot. Mid-range importance. Tough guy. Has a lot of people who work for him, more or less."

"More or less?"

"It's not like a corporation. Not at this level. No job descriptions, no benefits. You sell for the man, you get paid, you buy to feed your own habit, get wired, wake up, and start over. Yik keeps a set of books, very businesslike; he knows who owes him what and when it's due on a minute-to-minute basis."

"Plus he's got hookers and guns."

I nodded. "Different sets of books. Same business principles apply."

"And you have no idea who's above him?"

"No. I heard lots of names, most of the time from people who knew less than I did. Rumours. Wishful thinking. Pulling names out of thin air, a lot of that."

"Wishful thinking?" Cobb looked at me.

"Somebody hates somebody, they hope they're involved in something crooked so that someday they'll go down. So they suggest that person actually *is* involved. Sort of start the ball rolling."

Cobb didn't get to respond. Yik and two guys, both Caucasian, who looked big enough to play on a defensive line and mean enough to eat people's pets, came out of a doorway with a sign above it that read, Lam Fong Soon Tong Society. They started toward us and Yik saw me, didn't recognize me at first; then a glint of recognition came to his face. His mouth moved maybe a millimetre; it wasn't a smile. Yik wasn't a smiler.

I tapped Cobb's arm to let him know that the guy approaching us flanked by two gorillas in expensive suits and overcoats was Yik. He wasn't wearing a suit but his clothes were designer all the way, topped with a leather coat that went to his knees. It was open to show starched jeans and a western plaid shirt, all a perfect fit, all expensive.

Yik stopped in front of Cobb and me, held out a hand. I shook it.

"Cullen, long time. Last time I saw you, there you were helping me with a bit of cop unpleasantness and now the next time I see you you're packing a cop with you. Why is that, man?"

"*Ex*-cop. Private investigator now." I figured BS'ing Yik would be a bad way to start the conversation. "Mike Cobb, this is Yik."

"And friends," Yik indicated the two guys with him. He didn't offer a hand to Cobb. "I hope you're not investigating me, Mr. Cobb."

"No reason to do that that I know of," Cobb said.

"We're looking for somebody," I told Yik. "A kid. Kind of a favour to his dad. He's worried about the kid."

Cobb pulled out the picture of Jay Blevins, held it out. Yik took it, made a show of holding it in front of each of the goons, neither of whom took his eyes off Cobb. Yik looked at the photo, shook his head, handed it back to Cobb.

"Sorry," he said, though his face didn't look real regretful. "Kid a user?"

"Yeah."

"Can't help you. See you again Cullen." He started forward.

"It's kind of important. If you have any idea where we might look for him.…"

Yik stopped, looked at me, then shook his head and started forward again.

"Uh, one question, I'm also doing a little research. You know me, always working a story, trying to make a buck."

"Aren't we all?"

"So about that question.…"

He gave me a look I couldn't read. "One question. All right, I owe you. I'll give you one question, then we're even and after that I don't want to see you again, you hearing me Cullen?"

I nodded. "Fair enough. I was wondering, for the purposes of the story I'm writing, if you could direct me to someone who might know something about the shooting last night. Over in Ramsay. Crack house, a couple of dealers."

Yik's face didn't move but he didn't answer right away. Thinking. "I know about the incident, Cullen. My advice is you'd better leave it out of any story you're writing." He started moving again.

"Come on, Yik. You told me you'd answer one question. That's my question. Let's say I *was* going to mention it in my story, I'd sort of like to have my facts straight, you know."

Yik's mouth moved again, about the same amount as last time. "All right, that's your question. Here's my answer and I'm giving you this only because of before, you understand what I'm saying here?"

I nodded. "I understand."

"That house ain't Asian. Different group. And here's the bonus, Cullen. Badass guys. It would be a big mistake to walk up to them like you did with me just now."

"If it's not Asian, what should we —"

Yik took a half-step forward, stopped. "You've had your one question, Cullen. I won't say I'll see you around because that isn't going to happen. So let's just leave it at goodbye."

"What about M and F Holdings? Ever hear of a company by that name?"

"Same answer, Cullen. Don't try my patience."

As Yik moved ahead, the gorilla opposite Cobb

stepped forward too, expecting Cobb to move. Cobb didn't move. A game of sidewalk chicken.

"Now, gentlemen," Yik said, the tone of a dad to his kids. "Remember the golden rule."

He very deliberately stepped between Cobb and me and headed off down the street. The gorilla stepped around Cobb and followed, his shoulder just brushing Cobb on the way by. I realized that Cobb had not said a word in that entire exchange. Probably a good thing.

I'd never actually seen Cobb in action before today. When he'd investigated the fire and the note, he'd worked on his own, reported in a few times. I guess I hadn't expected somebody out of a Bruce Willis movie.

We turned and watched the trio walk toward Centre Street. I looked at Cobb. "Why is it I get the feeling that if I'm going to hang out with you I better make sure my health care premiums are up to date?"

He didn't answer.

When we were back in the car, I said, "You believe him?"

Cobb shrugged. "He was playing it up. Telling you he knows more than you do, that he's a big deal in this world." He waved a hand to show what part of the world he meant. "And he's not afraid of us so there was no reason to lie. But I did get a sense that he was maybe a little nervous when it comes to whoever his rivals are over there in Ramsay. In fact, he might be more than a little scared, even with his goons beside him."

We spent the rest of the afternoon on Calgary's darkest, meanest streets. More homeless shelters, a couple of church-run basement flophouses manned by tired looking, well-meaning people. We stopped everyone who looked younger than thirty — there were lots of them — to show the photo and ask about Jay Blevins. A few times glimmers of recognition tried to work their way through fog-shrouded minds. But never did. All we got from a couple of guys was that they knew Jay, had seen him around, maybe even talked to him, but had no idea where he'd be or even who we might ask for a little more in-depth information.

Some neighbourhoods take on a vibrant, pulsing new persona as the darkness of night falls. This one did not. The film noir feel to the place was palpable.

Cobb and I had split up again, agreed to meet at seven on the corner of 9th Avenue and 8th Street. There was a used bookstore there, a good one. The temperature was dropping fast and a north wind was starting to whip around me as I walked. Though we'd had a couple of snowfalls, this was the first real blast of winter cold and reminded me that this season was fourth on my list of favourites.

I tried to bury my face in the scarf I'd had the foresight to stuff in a pocket of the down-filled jacket I was wearing. Gloves too. Good.

I approached a Goodwill store that doubled as a shelter. Small place, wouldn't house many residents. The sign outside said LET THE SUNSHINE INN. A woman stood just outside, leaning against a red-faded-to-dirty-auburn brick wall.

She was holding a chipped, orange coffee cup, full of what looked like coffee, or maybe tea, steaming a little. Both hands around the cup. She had short blond-brown hair, gentle contours to her face, early thirties, not tall, not short, tired looking, like the building she was leaning against and like most of the people around here. Except she was better dressed than most. I stopped in front of her.

"Let the Sunshine Inn. That the name of the place or does somebody really like the song?"

She straightened only slightly. "Maybe both."

"Do you work in the Goodwill store?"

She regarded me with what I took to be mistrust. "Volunteer."

I nodded. "Been doing that long?"

"If that's a pickup line, it's one of the worst ever." A smile softened the words.

I returned the smile. "You should hear my others, they're even worse." I held out my hand. "I'm Adam Cullen. I'm looking for someone, a kid I was hoping you might know or at least may have seen around here. His name is Jay Blevins."

She sipped the drink, her eyes on me over the top of the cup. "Police?"

I shook my head. "Actually I'm a writer. A journalist." Again the mistrust in eyes that looked like they'd seen some of the downside of life. "But this doesn't have anything to do with a story. A friend of mine and I are doing a favour for the young man's father. He's worried about Jay."

"Aren't they all?"

I shrugged. "Maybe."

She didn't answer.

"This one's different," I said. "This is a dad who's not just worried about the kid doing drugs. Jay could be in some danger, real danger, and it's important that we find him as soon as possible."

"Good Samaritans, you and your friend." Her voice was slightly husky, like she'd just woken up. I always liked that kind of voice.

"Actually, no, we're not. I guess it's not really a favour in the strictest sense. My friend is a private detective. Jay's father hired him to try to protect the kid from a potentially serious threat." I sketched in general terms what had happened on Raleigh and the possible link to Jay.

"And you're helping because…?"

"Yeah, I don't really qualify as a good Samaritan either. I lied when I said it wasn't about a story. I mean, I'd like to find the kid and help him, we both would. But I'm a journalist. I'm always on the lookout for a story."

She sipped her drink, thought about it. I stared at the cup, tried not to shiver. When she spoke again, her voice had changed; it was still husky but softer now.

"Jay's a good kid. Messed up on crack, but a good kid. You wish … I mean you wish all of them could get off the shit but there's some, like Jay, you *really* —" She stopped, took a last sip of the coffee, tossed the last few drops in the direction of a street garbage container that looked like it was largely ignored by most people. The sidewalk around it made it evident that this wasn't a noted recycling area. "Come on inside. I have to get back. I'm working the food bank tonight." She turned and headed inside.

I followed her and immediately understood why someone would want to take their coffee break outside, even on a cold night. The air in the place was a cross between exhaust fumes and stale milk. There was another smell mixed in there too that I couldn't quite place — wet dog maybe. The total effect was a smell that I'd have thought would put food bank shoppers off their game.

As I closed the door behind us she turned to me. "Jill. Jill Sawley. You can hang your coat up over there if you want."

She pointed to a wall off to the right and a coat rack that was a rough cut two-by-four and several nails. None of the nails were at the same height or protruded from the two-by-four at the same distance. A couple of coats hung next to a pair of blue smocks, the same shade as hospital gowns. Jill hung her own coat on a vacant nail, took down one of the smocks, pulled it over her jeans and Gap hoodie. An interesting mix of fashion.

I wasn't sure why she'd suggested I remove my coat. She cleared that up for me right away. "I can tell you about Jay, but it'll cost you. We had a couple of big donations come in tonight. I could use help sorting."

I looked at my watch. Twenty to nine. It was maybe five minutes to the bookstore so that left me fifteen minutes to spend talking to Jill. And sorting. Since she was the most promising source of information to date — virtually the *only* source of information — I figured the fifteen minutes might be well spent. And I'd get a chance to do a little volunteering. Good for the soul.

I hung my coat on the nail that had formerly held the smock. "Okay, where do I start and what do I do?"

She pointed to a table stacked high with cardboard boxes. I actually rolled up my sleeves, ready for work, but with no idea what my role was to be.

"Boxed goods and paper-wrapped stuff over there, canned items on those shelves. Anything perishable has to go out of here right away so set it out on that table next to the back door."

"Right." I sorted and Jill talked while she filled cardboard boxes with a mix of items.

"First time I met Jay was at a pancake breakfast one of the service clubs puts on every year. It was December a year ago, so eleven months I guess. About a week before Christmas. I was a volunteer server. Some corporate big-wigs and a couple of politicians were there supposedly to help, but mostly for the photo ops.

"Jay … he looked lost, didn't even know if he was allowed to have the breakfast. I happened to see him, and told him he was welcome to join in. I noticed he didn't seem to know many people so I got some pancakes and juice and sat down across from him. Good-looking kid; he looked like he should have been the quarterback on the football team or learning his lines for the school play.

"Anyway, it was obvious he hadn't had a lot of good meals in a while so I just let him eat. I could tell he was really enjoying the breakfast, every few bites he'd nod as if to say 'now that's a great chunk of pancake right there.' When he was finished we both got another cup of coffee and sat back down. Small talk for a while, then he told me about himself. Or at least he told me some of it. Soup and canned spaghetti on that middle shelf."

She pointed and I nodded.

"Turns out he was pretty much as advertised. Even though he looked like he'd been on the street a while, he had something about him that told you he had come from something a lot different. Sure enough, he had played on the football team, he told me that, although I'm not sure he was the quarterback. Clean cut, went with one of the prettiest girls, got decent grades, drove a cool teenager car — one of those guys who didn't give anybody much trouble. Like I said, a good kid."

"I have a feeling the story is about to turn."

Jill nodded. "Depression. All that great stuff going on, looked like he had it all but inside he hated himself, hated his life, even talked suicide. Doesn't remember when it started, just remembers feeling like that as far back as junior high. His parents got him into counselling, some drug therapy. It was hit and miss. He'd go along for a while feeling okay, then it was like the world, all of it, was a real bad place to be. Then when he was in eleventh grade, his parents split and the universe seemed to crash down around him. They got back together after a couple of months, but it didn't get Jay back to what he'd been. He started skipping, hanging out with different kids at school, badass kids, he broke up with the pretty girl, started staying out later and later. At first it was alcohol, then pot, and the downhill slide was on. A few months later he was living on the streets, doing whatever it takes to get money for the next buy."

She'd stopped filling boxes while she talked about Jay but now she started again. With attitude, like she needed to be doing something. *You wish all of them could get off the shit but there's some, like Jay, you really ...*

"He told me he'd tried to kick it a few times but couldn't. I believed him ... about trying to get clean. I guess I *wanted* to believe him. And I know he went back home a couple of times. But it never lasted."

"Did you see him after that, after the Christmas breakfast?"

"A couple of times, but never like that. He'd say hi but he seemed to want to keep moving. It was like he didn't want to connect with anyone. Like he'd chosen that other life. Made the same choice so many of them make."

Her voice had grown quiter. This was someone who had seen the dark side of this world but was not a street tough woman. What was happening around her, all the misery of these streets, got to her. That's when I remembered she wasn't a professional — she'd said she was a volunteer.

"And you don't know where we might find him? Or who we could talk to who might know where he is?"

She shook her head. "Last I heard he was camped out in a park area over near the Stampede grounds. But that was in the fall. Too cold for that now. So I hope … I'm guessing he's in a building, a house or something somewhere."

I rolled my sleeves down, pulled on my coat. "If you should happen to run into him or hear anything, maybe you could let me know. It would really help and it *is* important." I wrote my cell number on a piece of paper and handed it to her. She took it, glanced at it, stuffed it in the pocket of her jeans. "And thanks for the insights. It's tough seeing what happens to these kids." It was weak, but it was the best I could come up with.

She nodded again, looked up at me. "I hope you find him. And I hope you can help him."

"So do I." I turned and headed back out onto the street.

The cold had deepened and the wind was stronger, the combination of the two making the night still more unpleasant. I looked at my watch. I'd be a couple of minutes late getting back to the bookstore.

When I got there, Cobb was inside talking to the proprietor, showing him the picture. The guy was older, with a long grey ponytail and both arms a roadmap of tattoos. He was wearing a T-shirt that read "I'm Kissable." I wondered if this guy and Jackie Chow shopped at the same Value Village. He was shaking his head. Judging from the look on Cobb's face, this was the latest in a line of similar responses.

When we were outside the store, Cobb said, "I hope you had better luck than I did."

"Nothing?"

"With a capital *N*."

I gave him the Coles Notes version of my conversation with Jill Sawley. He nodded a couple of times, then pointed a thumb back in the direction of the bookstore.

"This guy mentioned an old warehouse not far from here. Some company was supposed to turn it into lofts. When the economy softened, the company folded and the place has been sitting vacant. Mostly squatters there now."

"Worth a try," I said.

"My thinking exactly."

We headed for the car, walking fast. The cold was intensifying. I was hoping Jeep made good heaters.

I didn't have time to find out. The drive to the warehouse didn't take long enough for the heater to generate more than cold, then merely cool, air. We were on a street that whoever built it had forgotten to finish. South of 9th Avenue a couple of blocks, then left. A sign told us it was Garry Street. Looking east, we could see that it just kind of stopped. Dead-ended up against a hill that probably shouldn't have been there. I pictured a gaggle of 1930s engineers working on their drawings and noticing the hill after the street was started. Saying screw it and moving on to another project.

We parked under a sign that said, VEHICLES TOWED TWENTY-FOUR HOURS. I wondered why the sign was there. It wasn't like the curb in front of the warehouse was a prime parking spot. Cobb must have thought the same thing.

We walked to the front door of the building. A faded sign above the doorway told us that this had once been the home of Mainwaring Tool and Dye. Beneath it a smaller sign, even more faded, announced "De iver es At Re r."

We tried both sides of a set of double doors — they were either locked or had simply sealed themselves shut with years of disuse. Cobb stepped back, looked up at the front of the building. Some of the windows were gone completely, others were broken, a few were intact. I followed Cobb's eyes to one particularly dirty but intact window. Third floor.

A man in an undershirt sat smoking and staring down at us. Cobb motioned to him that the door was locked and tried to indicate to the man that we could use his help getting in. The man behind the filthy pane of glass took a drag on the cigarette and continued looking at us. Didn't move.

"Let's try the back. Unless that's a robot up there, there has to be a way into this place."

I found myself hoping that maybe the smoker *was* a robot and we wouldn't get in. To no avail. The back door was not only open, it was gone.

We stepped over broken chunks of cinder block, two-by-fours and bricks, remnants of the unfinished construction, into the building. Cobb pulled out the kind of flashlight you see in cop shows and aimed it at the hole that had once been a door.

Straight ahead was a large open area where I guessed that back in the day people did whatever you do in a tool and dye plant. To the left was a set of stairs leading up to where the lofts would have been located, had they been completed. Beyond the stairs was an elevator, the door carved, scratched, and painted with graffiti. There was a hole in the wall where the buttons for the elevator should have been.

"Think I'll take the stairs," Cobb said.

I followed him. We moved slowly, not because we were trying to sneak around but because the stairs appeared to have been there from the building's first life and hadn't received much if any attention during the short-lived renovation.

We came out on a second floor that looked and smelled like it was the building's garbage dump and communal toilet. As Cobb directed the beam of light first left, then right, I stared down at the mounds of garbage and human filth.

"How is something like this not condemned?"

Cobb didn't answer. I was hoping he wouldn't suggest we try to navigate our way through the refuse and he didn't, opting instead to follow the stairs up to the next floor.

When we reached the top of the stairs we entered a narrow, dark hall that led off in both directions, like the hallway in a hotel. And like a hotel, doors stood on both sides at regular intervals leading into who knew what. My guess was that this part of the renovation had begun and what were to be lofts had at least been framed in.

A small generator hummed away about halfway down the hall to the right and a lone light bulb hanging from a protruding board offered what light there was. Cobb stowed his flashlight and we started off in the direction of the light. As we walked, it became clear that some of the doors were hanging by their hinges; others were missing altogether.

The first door we came to had no handle but was closed. Cobb studied the door for a while as if trying to figure something out. He didn't say what and finally knocked.

No answer. He knocked again, waited maybe thirty seconds, then pushed on the door. It offered no resistance.

Flashlight out again. We were looking at a room about the size of my own, framed and drywalled but not painted. Holes in several places in the drywall. A couple of rooms led off of the big room; they were intended to be a kitchen and bathroom maybe. The main room was empty but for a sleeping bag piled in a heap on the floor, a few cases of empty beer bottles, and a discarded cereal box — Honey Nut Cheerios — in one corner. A large grey and white cat, surprisingly healthy looking, watched us, unconcerned.

"Anybody home?" Still no answer.

We stepped into the room. Several candles and a box of wooden matches lay next to the beer bottles. I lit the longest of the candles and moved to one of the rooms leading off of the main room. I peered into what I guessed was to be the bathroom, though nothing was plumbed. Part of a newspaper lay on the floor and I bent down to note the date. November 17. Less than a week old.

I stepped back into the main room at the same time that Cobb returned from the other room. "Kitchen," he said, "but all that's in there is a wooden crate, two empty wine bottles, a used syringe, and half a Coke can."

"Stove," I said. Heroin users had taken to using half a soft drink can to heat their smack. Better availability. Easy to use.

"Uh-huh."

"Someone's been here not that long ago." I told him about the newspaper.

We stopped at the door and looked back into the place.

"The cat looks like he's doing okay," I said.

"Maybe he likes Cheerios."

Cobb stepped out into the hall. I followed him and we moved on to the next place. This one had no door but a stained and tattered makeshift curtain hung limply from a couple of nails. Again Cobb called and again received no response. He pushed the curtain aside and we stepped in, did the tour — same layout as the last one. This one looked a little more lived in. Rumpled clothes on the floor, another sleeping bag, this one rolled up, lay next to a makeshift ashtray that was overflowing, mostly cigarette butts, a few roaches.

Several bricks supported a length of board that served as a counter or cupboard or maybe both. Two tins of cat food, a large jar of peanut butter, a plastic-wrapped half loaf of bread, a deck of cards, and one bottled water container, half full, occupied space on the board.

"Must eat out a lot," I said.

Back in the hallway we continued down the hall, past the generator, still humming, a couple of black extension cords leading away from it. The third door in the hallway was closed and had a handle. Upscale. Cobb knocked once, then again, louder.

A male voice from inside said, "Yeah."

"All right if we come in?"

"What d'ya want?"

"We're looking for someone, wondered if he might live in the building."

"Shit."

Cobb looked at me. I shrugged.

"All right if we come in?" Cobb repeated.

A pause, then, "Yeah."

Cobb gestured for me to step back, turned the handle and pushed the door open, stepping to one side as he did.

He slowly leaned forward, looked in, nodded to me, and stepped across the threshold. I followed him inside.

The man was the one we'd seen from outside. He hadn't moved and didn't now. He was turned away from us, sitting on a stool, still staring out the window. I didn't get a sense that he was actually looking at anything.

He was wearing a dark blue sweatshirt, faded blue jeans with no belt, and some kind of slippers that looked like deck shoes. No hat, and what hair he still had was mostly grey. It hadn't been combed in a long time. He was either the toughest person I'd ever met or he had two or three shirts under the sweatshirt. The room was the temperature of a meat locker.

It was also the cleanest we'd seen to that point, which isn't saying a lot. And there was actual furniture — a worn armchair in one corner, a TV with rabbit ears adorned with scrunched up tinfoil at the tips in another corner, and a refrigerator with a cord that ran into the other room. I guessed if I followed the cord I'd find the other end hooked to the generator in the hall. A space heater was also plugged into the extension cord. Its effect was negligible. A second heater sat unplugged a couple of feet away. I wondered if it would be bad manners to go over there and plug it in, decided it probably was.

There was a kitchen table with two chairs sitting to our left, a dishpan with an inch or so of water in it perched on the heater that wasn't heating. But what jumped out at me was a potted geranium, healthy and well-tended, sitting in the middle of the kitchen table. I wasn't sure how the plant survived in the polar-like conditions, but maybe where it was — closer to the functioning space heater — the climate was somehow more tropical.

"Excuse me, sir," Cobb said in a low voice, "my name is Mike Cobb and this is Adam Cullen. We don't mean to disturb you but as I was saying —"

"Yeah, you're looking for somebody." The voice was sandpaper on mortar, rough but not very loud. And somehow not mean. Mostly he sounded tired, or maybe unwell.

"A young man, late teens," Cobb continued. "We thought it possible he might stay here sometimes. We're wondering if you might know of him."

The man didn't answer.

"If you don't mind, I'd like to come over there and show you a picture of him, see if it rings any bells."

"Rings any bells," the man said.

Cobb crossed the room, held the picture in front of the man on the stool. No reaction at first, but eventually the man moved in slow motion, his head pivoting just slightly to the right as he seemed to study the photo. Then nodded slowly.

"Forget his name, crackhead kid. He's okay though. Borrowed some winter gloves from me … hasn't brought 'em back yet. Ray or Clay or something."

"Jay Blevins."

The man nodded. "Borrowed some mitts from me."

"When was the last time you saw him, Mr. … uh …"

"Morris. Not Norris. Last name, not first."

"Right, Mr. Morris. When was the last time you saw Jay, do you remember?"

"Couple of days ago. Not here. On the street, out there." He lifted his chin to indicate outside.

"Which street?"

A long pause. "I don't remember."

"Did you talk to him?"

"Sure, said hey, asked him how he was doin', stuff like that."

"Does he stay here?"

For the first time Morris turned away from the window, swivelled slowly on the chair, and faced us. "Not enough room in here."

The face was lined and creased and the nose was off-centre a little and bent. Thin lips, set back in a face that had gone unshaven for a few days. Looked like he still had most of his teeth. Morris was a man who might have been handsome once.

"Yeah, I meant in the building," Cobb said.

"Down the hall … at the far end. But he hasn't been here for a while."

"How long since he was last here?"

"Don't know … month maybe."

"Think he'll be coming back?"

Morris shrugged, turned his head a little more, and saw me for the first time. I could see him more clearly now and realized that we were talking to a man who looked, sounded, and moved like an old man, but who, I guessed, was maybe forty, not more than forty-five.

Cobb said, "When you saw Jay a couple of days ago, did he happen to say where he was staying?'

"Don't think so."

"Are you sure?"

"Pretty sure."

"And you don't have any idea where we might find him? Where he sleeps at night when he's not here, who he hangs out with?"

"Not enough room in here."

"Yes, sir, I understand. Do you know where he sleeps when he's not here?"

Pause.

"Nope."

"Mr. Morris, it's important that we find him. Jay could be in some danger, some bad people are looking for him. You have any idea at all where we might find him?"

Morris shook his head. No pause this time. Definite.

"Anyone else you can suggest we might talk to? Someone who might know where we might find Jay?"

"There's always kids in and out of that place at the end of the hall. Maybe one of them." He turned back to the window. The interview was over.

"Thank you, sir," Cobb said. "We appreciate your time."

Morris didn't answer and we left him and stepped back into the hall. I closed the door gently behind us. Cobb didn't say anything but led the way back down the hall.

Cobb held the flashlight out in front of us, allowing the light to illuminate the last door at this end. It was covered in graffiti art. Someone had talent. There were a few lines of poetry gracing the door's surface — or maybe it was prose — that mostly seemed to be exploring creative ways to adapt the word *fuck* to different parts of speech.

Cobb knocked, got no answer. He didn't bother to wait this time, pushed the door open, and let the beam of the flashlight work its way around the room. "Anybody home?"

Again there was no response so he stepped inside just far enough to let me move up beside him. We surveyed the main room. Stuff, a lot of it, covered most of the floor and a couple of makeshift tables that occupied the centre of the room. Two mattresses, clothes strewn in heaps on both of them; four chairs, none of them matching; several garbage bags, all of them crammed with something, garbage or possessions — it was hard to tell which.

There was more graffiti on the walls, and paper, sheets of loose leaf and a couple of pads of lined paper, several battered paperbacks, and an even more battered Bible lying amongst the rest of the stuff. The room didn't look or smell bad, really. I'd seen friends' teenagers' bedrooms, and this wasn't all that different. Too much stuff, none of it actually put away — chaos but not filth.

We walked around the room, looking for ... I wasn't sure what. I picked up some of the pieces of paper, more of the kind of art we'd seen on the door and walls. Same artist maybe. One scrap of paper was a note that read,

> Zoe, please come home or at least call.
> Your Dad and I love you and we're going
> crazy not knowing where you are and if
> you're okay. Please, please call or send an
> email. We just want to hear from you.
> Love
> Mom and Dad

No way of knowing how the note had got to Zoe, assuming Zoe was one of the residents of the place, or whether she'd answered it.

Cobb and I worked our way through some of the stuff, but while there was lots of it, most of it clothing, there wasn't much to identify the occupants of the place or offer much help with our search. Again another room, this one with a door. It was open and I glanced in — more stuff, possessions that defined the word meagre. Stacked and stashed in an attempt at order.

After maybe ten futile minutes, Cobb said, "Let's get out of here. I've had enough."

Neither of us spoke until we were outside. It was dark by then and I was instantly aware of a different look to the street. Different sounds too. It seemed even less friendly, more serious … dour. It wasn't a place I'd have wanted to be by myself. Cobb looked up and down the street, rubbed a gloved hand against his jaw, then turned to me.

"Any more ideas as to where we might look?"

I shook my head. "No, and I'm sorry I haven't been much help up to now."

Cobb looked at me. "No apology necessary. If finding missing people was easy, I'd be out of a career."

"I guess."

"I'm bagged. I say we call it a day and start again in the morning. Are you game for another day of this?"

"In for a penny, in for a pound," I said.

FOUR

We started in the direction of the car but had only gone a couple of steps when a girl crossed the street coming our way. She was carrying something bulky and paid no attention to us, probably deliberately. She passed us and looked like she might be heading for the back of the building.

I decided there was nothing to lose. "Zoe?"

She slowed, almost stopped, then picked up speed. Turned the corner of the building.

"Zoe." I called again and started after her, Cobb right behind me.

As we came around to the side of the building, I thought we'd lost her. Black night, no illumination here from the street's lone streetlight. A shadow moving just ahead.

"Zoe?"

She kept going, now around the back of the building.

Cobb said, "We just want to ask you about Jay Blevins. He's in trouble and we need to find him. To help him."

We came around the corner and she had stopped right at the hole in the wall entrance. The tiny amount of light from the interior of the building was enough to let us see her face.

I'd have put her at seventeen or eighteen. Pretty, or could have been with a little attention to her appearance. Her clothes were thrift store head to toe. Her light brown hair, what I could see of it, was a maze of tangles; a scarf haphazardly covered the rest. The bulky item she was carrying was a garbage bag. There was no way of knowing what it contained.

She was looking at us. More angry than scared. Or maybe pretending to be tough. "Stay right there or I scream and fifteen guys will be down here to kick the livin' shit out of both of you."

Fifteen guys. She might have been able to rustle up three or four, counting the cat, but I didn't think pointing that out would improve our chances of getting information from her.

"You don't have to do that. We're trying to find Jay. It's important. If you could help us —"

"What kind of trouble?"

"I … what?"

"You said he was in trouble. What kind of trouble?"

Cobb answered. "We think some people might be looking for him. If they find him, it could be very bad for Jay. He doesn't know, at least we don't think he knows, that he's in danger. We need to tell him and help him if he'll let us."

"How do I know you're not those guys, or cops, or guys his parents have sent out to bring him home?"

"I guess you don't. We can show you our ID if that'll help. I'm a private detective. Jay's father hired me to find him. But not to get him to go home, just to keep him from getting hurt by the people I mentioned. This gentleman is a journalist. He's helping me."

"Jay doesn't want to go home."

Cobb shook his head. "Like I said, this isn't about him going home, Zoe. This is a lot more serious than that, believe me."

"Zoe," I spoke softly, hoping my voice conveyed sincerity. "We don't want to hurt you or Jay. That's not why we're here."

"Okay, let me see your ID."

Cobb pulled out his wallet, stepped forward with it. I fished in my pocket, found mine, and extracted a driver's licence and Press Club membership. It wasn't great but I hoped it might convince her. I started forward.

"Hold it," the sharpness of her voice echoed off the building. "Only one of you." She pointed at me. "You, the little one, you bring the ID for both of you."

Cobb handed me his PI card. I guessed he was trying not to smile. *The little one.*

I stepped forward and extended my arm in order to keep some distance between us, handed her the IDs. She held them so that she could examine them in the light, then passed them back to me.

"Come on," she said and turned and went into the building.

We followed. No one spoke as we retraced our path back up the stairs to the last place we'd been in. When we got to her door I said, "You want me to go get the light bulb?"

"I've got light. Wait here." She went inside, closing the door behind her. She was gone long enough that I looked questioningly at Cobb. He stared straight ahead, waiting. More patient than I was.

The door opened. Zoe stepped back, made a motion with her hand that seemed to indicate we should come inside. Cobb went in first and I followed him.

She was right. She had light. Candles, eight or ten at least, in various shapes and lengths, were lit, giving the room a very different feel from when we'd been in it before. She'd even pushed a few things around. Tidied a little.

She closed the door behind us, directed us to a lawn chair that hadn't been set up before, and a board set across two piles of magazines. Cobb let me have the chair, he sat carefully on the board. She sat on the floor opposite us.

"So you are Zoe."

She nodded.

"What's your last name, Zoe?"

"Tario."

"Thanks for talking to us."

"I can get you some water."

Cobb declined and I started to but thought better of it. In some strange way, I felt that this street girl was doing her best to be hospitable and that water was probably all she had to offer us.

"Thanks," I said. "I'd appreciate a water."

She got up, reached behind her for a plastic jug of water, poured some into a glass that may or may not have been clean. She handed me the water with a flicker of a smile at the corners of her mouth.

"I hope you like *cold* water." She shook the glass and I could hear bits of ice hitting the sides.

"Cold's my favourite." I said.

Another flicker, then she sat back down and looked at Cobb. "Why should I help you guys?"

"Because you'd be helping Jay," Cobb said. "It's like we said before, there are some other people who might be looking for him. If they are, it's imperative that we find him before they do."

"Who are these people?"

"We're not sure."

"Pretty vague."

"I wish I could give you more definitive answers but I can't. You're going to have to trust us."

"Do you have any idea how many times I've heard that in my life? From my favourite uncle who was a pedophile to my first boyfriend who turned out to be violent to the two cops who arrested me for shoplifting and offered me some interesting ways to avoid being charged to … there's more, but I'm sure you get the picture. So, bottom line, I don't *have to* trust you."

Cobb glanced over at me. I could see he was thinking about how much he'd tell her. He nodded. "Two drug trade guys were killed last night. A house over in Ramsay. Crack dealers … they were shot."

Zoe looked thoughtful, nodded slowly. "I heard something about it on the news. There was a radio playing at a shelter I stopped at to get some blankets."

Blankets. That explained the garbage bag.

"It's going to be bloody cold tonight," I said. I shook my water glass to remind her just how cold. "Why didn't you just stay at the shelter?"

"I like it here."

When neither Cobb nor I responded she added, "I sort of wanted to be here in case … someone comes here."

"Jay?" I asked.

She didn't answer. Turned instead to Cobb. "What's the shooting have to do with Jay?"

"Maybe nothing," Cobb looked down at the floor for maybe a millisecond then back up at Zoe, his decision made. "The guy who shot those two men was Jay's father. He's worried that the guys who are higher up the food chain might want revenge for a couple of their guys getting snuffed."

"So why wouldn't they want to get their revenge on Jay's father?"

"They will want that. But if they're not successful, or even if they are, Mr. Blevins is concerned that they might want to go farther. If he's right, then Jay could become a target. Or maybe already is."

Zoe didn't say anything for a couple of minutes. She seemed to be digesting the information.

Cobb let her think about it for a while. "Do you happen to know that house? It's on Raleigh Avenue."

Zoe pulled a cigarette out of her jacket pocket, not a pack, one lone cigarette. She lit it from one of the candles, took a drag, blew smoke above our heads. "I know it."

"You a user, Zoe?"

She shook her head. "Was. I've been clean for almost four months. Went through a program and got off it … for now. I guess we'll see."

I appreciated her honesty. None of the "I've never used" or "I've beaten the thing for life" that you hear from a lot of users.

"What do you know about the house?" Cobb asked her.

"Not a lot. Jay bought there quite often. He took me with him twice. I hated the place. Real creepy guys. I remember one was called Stick. Real tall. The first time I went there with Jay, that asshole, Stick, offered to show me why he had that particular nickname. Total jerkoff."

Blevins had told Cobb one of the guys was very tall. Maybe Stick was one of the victims.

"Who else was there, do you remember?"

"The first time it was only Stick and two kids who

looked junior high school age making a buy. The second time, it was like Walmart on Saturday night — people everywhere. Stick was there and another guy was doing the selling and distributing. I didn't pay much attention to who was in there, mostly I wanted to get out and gone as fast as we could. After that time I told Jay I wouldn't go there anymore. He said he'd buy for me — that was when I was still using."

"Crack ... that what they sold there?"

"Crack, ecstasy, blow, lots of other stuff. One stop shopping."

Cobb nodded and leaned forward. "Jay ever say anything about the people who sold out of that house? Like who they worked for?"

"No. I even asked him once. He said he didn't know and didn't want to know. Just as long he could get what he needed he didn't care if Stephen Harper owned the place."

"Yeah, I'm pretty sure it's not him," Cobb said, smiling.

Zoe didn't return the smile.

"Listen, Zoe, we don't know who runs that place either and we don't know if it's the same people Stick and his pal report to ... or maybe *reported* to is more accurate. But we've talked to some guys who are in the know and they've told us that these aren't people you want to mess with."

"So why are you messing with them?"

"Because a scared dad hired me to protect his kid. And that's what I'm going to do, but I could use your help."

"Trouble is, I don't know where he is. Jay isn't what you'd call reliable. He'll tell you he's going to be somewhere at a certain time and show up a few hours later, or the next day, or not at all."

There was a knock at the door. Sitting there grouped around the candles, talking in low voices, we hadn't heard anyone approach. I have to admit I jumped. I think Zoe did too. Cobb stood up, turned to face the door.

"Yeah?" Zoe called

A gravel voice answered. "I got an extra heater and a cord. I'll leave 'em right here."

"Thanks, Jackie," Zoe called again, then looked at us. "Jackie Morris. My neighbor. Good guy. One person I *can* trust."

"We met him." Cobb sat back down.

We waited and no one spoke until we heard shuffling footsteps moving away from Zoe's door.

Cobb said, "You were saying that Jay isn't reliable."

Zoe looked at each of us in turn. It looked like she was deciding whether she ought to be critical of Jay in front of strangers.

"Sometimes he's great. When he's sort of in control of his life, everybody loves him — he's funny, smart, creative, considerate … just a good guy. I know that sounds, I don't know —"

"We've heard that same description of him from other people," I said.

She nodded. "Anyway, Jay is pretty heavily addicted. He's tried, really tried, but he can't seem to stay clean, at least not for any length of time."

I sipped my water. "Back to my earlier question: is Jay the reason you're here tonight instead of somewhere warm? You're expecting him?"

She hesitated then smiled a little. Shy. "Not expecting, exactly. More hoping."

"If he doesn't show up here, is there anywhere you could suggest we look?"

"If I knew, I'd look there myself."

Cobb said. "So you haven't seen him in a while."

"A week, maybe more. Like I said, he tends to disappear from the radar sometimes. Real hard to find then. I've given up looking. I just live my life and if he comes around, great, if not …" She shrugged.

Cobb stood up. "Thanks Zoe. We do appreciate the help. If you hear from him or *of* him, I'd appreciate a call." He handed her one of his cards.

"Likewise."

"Fair enough. You have a cell phone?"

"Uh-uh. The thing with having a cell phone is they expect you to pay the bill now and again."

Cobb nodded. "If we find out anything, I'll get word to you." He turned toward the door.

I finished my water, set the glass down, and stood up. "Zoe, just wondering, I know it's none of my business, but have you answered that note from your parents?"

She looked over at the note, then back at me.

"Sorry, we weren't really snooping, just trying to find out if Jay —"

She waved an arm. "It's okay, and no I haven't. My bad, huh?"

"I don't know anything about your relationship with your parents. It just sounded like they're worried, that's all."

"That's another story for another time. I'll think about letting them know I'm okay."

I nodded, turned, and followed Cobb to the door. As we stepped into the hall, the space heater and neatly coiled extension cord were sitting next to the doorway. The heater didn't look like it would generate a lot of warmth but maybe it would help if it was right next to you. Maybe.

Cobb didn't say anything until we were back on the street. The temperature had dropped a few more degrees but the wind had let up. A few flakes of snow drifted down. It wasn't a bad night, especially if you were going home to a house with a furnace and a warm bed.

"The offer still stand? We have another go at this tomorrow?"

I nodded. "The offer still stands."

It was a quiet ride back to my place. I thought we might stop for a drink, do a little recap of the day and what we'd learned. But I was relieved when Cobb seemed intent on taking a straight line back to Drury Avenue. I was too tired to make much sense and mostly wanted a hot shower to get the smell and feel of the places we'd been off me. And sleep, I wanted that most of all.

As we turned the corner that led to my apartment building, Cobb took a breath, exhaled, and said, "Interesting day."

"It was," I agreed.

"Listen … thanks."

"I hope we get a little closer to the kid tomorrow."

Cobb pulled to a stop in front of my building. Reached across, shook my hand. "See you in the morning. How about eight?"

"I'll try to be a little more ready for action then I was *this* morning."

Cobb smiled and I stepped out into the street. The Jeep had turned the corner and disappeared before I had the front door of my building open.

FIVE

The shower felt as good as I thought it would and I stayed in it until the hot water heater's supply was exhausted and the stream turned cool, then cold. My body was exhausted but my mind was on full alert. Thinking the whole time I was in the shower.

But I hadn't been thinking about Jay Blevins and the race to find him. Instead my mind was occupied with the conversation Cobb and I had had over lunch, when he'd suggested that maybe there was something in Donna's past that had led to the setting of the fire that killed her. That maybe she *had* been the target.

I stepped out of the shower, towelled off, and climbed into sweats and a University of Calgary Dinosaurs hoodie. I poured myself a stout portion of Crown Royal mixed with a lesser portion of Diet Coke, put Del Barber's *Love Songs for the Last 20* and The Tragically Hip's *We Are the Same* on the CD player and sat down to think about what Cobb had said.

What about before she knew you? Something or someone in her past?

I *had* thought and rethought about that possibility in the weeks and months after the fire, trying to make sense of the senseless. And I'd rejected the notion every time.

It simply made sense to me that someone in my line of work — work that involved offending, sometimes attacking people in print that thousands of other people might read — was the target.

Me. It had to be me.

The note had confirmed that, hadn't it? Why would someone send that note *to me* if Donna had been the target? The arsonist would have already accomplished his goal — Donna was dead. That certainty coupled with my absolute belief that no one could possibly have hated Donna enough to want her dead had been the basis for my rejecting the idea that she was the killer's target that night. And I was just as sure now, all these years after her death.

Or was I?

Weirder shit than that — a lot weirder — has happened.

I sipped on my drink, stared at a couple of flecks on the ceiling. *Something or someone in her past.*

A nut job from when she was a teenager, some guy who felt slighted because she wouldn't go to the prom with him or got the scholarship he thought he should have got or …

But would a nut job wait years to exact his revenge? That's why the whole thing seemed so far-fetched, so impossible. Because it *was* impossible.

Weirder shit than that …

I glanced at the clock. 12:42 a.m. I set the drink down and walked to the main closet near the door. In it, below the clothes, footwear, and Christmas decorations I'd need in just a few weeks were some boxes. Including a couple containing Donna's stuff, things that had previously been in the garage and in a storage locker downtown — stuff that neither of us had done anything with in all the time we were married. Most of it I'd never even looked at.

I wanted to look at it now. Between the shower and the drink and the thinking, I was wide awake.

I set the boxes, there were three, in the centre of the room, sat cross-legged on a scatter rug at the end of the bed, and went through Donna's stuff for two and a half hours, feeling like a voyeur, like I was invading her privacy, the only thing that was left of her.

Two and a half hours of fifteen-year-old bank statements, Day-Timers loaded with to-do lists and appointment times, a couple of English essays from what looked like a first-year university lit survey course. I read one, Donna's take on choosing Marlow rather than Kurtz as the hero of *Heart of Darkness*. I read the essay and cried, not for the content but for the creator of the content. I set the second essay aside unread — it was something about Polonius's role in *Hamlet*.

Tax receipts, a phone directory, travel brochures, four letters from me during our courting days ... I didn't read them but I did notice that she had written notes in the margins. "Sweet!!" and "I love that man" were a couple that caught my attention.

I tried not to let the time deteriorate into a nostalgia session and concentrated on finding some tiny hint, some clue that might provide a reason for someone to hate the woman I loved.

Two and a half hours of nothing. I was closing in on comatose. I picked up one more piece of paper. One yellowed piece of three-hole-punched paper like something torn from a school Duo-Tang or notebook. A neatly written note in what I was fairly certain was Donna's handwriting.

Kelly —
The bastard did it again.
D

And under that, what I guessed was the reply.

Pig.
K

It had been stuck between the pages of a battered paperback copy of *To Kill a Mockingbird*. Hundred to one odds it was meaningless — there were a hundred innocuous explanations for the note. And I might have forgotten the whole thing except that it was out of character for the Donna I knew to vent her anger in that way, which wasn't to say she didn't get angry at times, but mostly she dealt with it internally or in some totally civilized and controlled way that didn't involve name calling or writing angry notes.

Still, this was likely high school or even junior high. What kid didn't vent occasionally as part of the growing up/going to school/rebelling against parents and the world phase?

And that was it. Close to three hours of searching had resulted in one hand-written note to someone named Kelly — a note containing six words. Seven if you counted Kelly's one word reply. Not much there to make me change my belief that the arsonist had been targeting me and had messed up.

I left the stuff spread over the bedroom floor and stumbled into bed. Now I *was* tired. Del Barber was singing

"62 Richmond" for the third time. I didn't bother to shut off the stereo. I was asleep before the end of the song.

But not for long. I dreamt. Something about a fire and a fire alarm. At least it started as a fire alarm then morphed into a phone ringing. It took me a while to figure that out. The fog in my brain finally cleared enough that I realized the phone wasn't in my dream. I was actually awake and the reason was that the phone on the end table next to my bed wouldn't shut up.

After maybe the tenth ring, I got it picked up and juggled over to where I was. I rested it more or less against my ear.

"Hello."

Cobb's voice. "Sorry to call at this hour."

"You're hard on rest, my friend."

"Yeah. I called to tell you you're out."

"What? Out what?"

"I won't be picking you up in the morning. You're out of the search for Jay Blevins."

I rubbed my face with my left hand. "You find a better journalist or what?"

"Blevins is dead."

I sat up.

"Jay?"

"Larry. The old man. They got to him before he could turn himself in. Shot in the back of the head but that was after someone did a lot of nasty stuff to him ... something like forty broken bones. The cops couldn't recognize him from his face."

"How did you find out?"

"I was a cop, Adam, I know some people."

"Any idea who?"

"He was found beside a Dumpster a few blocks from his house. Time of death about midnight."

About the time we were getting back to my apartment.

"Shit," I said.

"These are bad bastards, Adam. I can't run the risk of having them come after you."

"Isn't that *my* risk and my decision?"

"No, it isn't. I asked you to help me, you did, and I appreciate it, but things have changed and I'll need to do this without having to ... on my own."

"You were going to say without having to look out for me."

No answer.

"Back to my earlier point, I can decide for myself what risks I'm prepared to take. And besides, you can't fire a volunteer."

"I'm not firing you. Look, I'm sorry, but I need to be on my own and I haven't got time to argue with you about it. Thanks for what you did on this."

I wanted to debate it further but I would have been talking to a dial tone. Cobb had hung up. I set the phone back on its cradle and stared into the dark for a while. Knowing sleep wouldn't be happening any time soon, I got out of bed, pulled on a T-shirt and a pair of jeans, and made a pot of coffee. Finally shut off the stereo. I sat at the table and drank two cups of coffee with milk and more sugar than usual.

I turned on the TV to see if there was anything about Blevins. There wasn't, although there were several reports about the "gangland-style slaying" of two suspected narcotics dealers. No names. Footage of the house on Raleigh, reporters voicing comments that were a collection of generalities, which was probably all they had. I doubted the cops would be all that forthcoming, especially since they likely didn't know a hell of a lot themselves. I wondered how long it would be before they were able to tie Blevins's death to the shooting of the two dealers.

I turned off the TV and started on a third cup of coffee while I leafed through Donna's stuff again. It was a small pile — not much to show for thirty plus years of life. The fire had taken the rest.

But halfway through the third cup of coffee I started to question that supposition. I thought about my own situation — most of the flotsam and jetsam of my past had also been destroyed in the fire. Most, *but not all.*

If I were trying to uncover my own past, where would I look? Parents, best friends, maybe even school. The point was, there *were* places. It all hadn't just disappeared over time. I spent the next half hour making a list of places I might be able to look to reconstruct at least some of Donna's life from before I knew her.

The list wasn't long; the truth is I didn't really know much about Donna (then) Leybrand. I'd lied, I'm not sure why, when I told Cobb that Donna and I had talked about all that kind of thing. In truth we'd almost *never* talked about Donna's life before we knew each other. I never got the impression she was hiding anything or didn't want to talk about the past. We just didn't.

But maybe that wasn't quite accurate either. We'd talked about *my* past. At least the stuff I considered important: the deaths of my parents, Dad when I was twelve, Mom when I was seventeen; my baseball scholarship to Oklahoma

State and a fling with a baseball career that ended at spring training with the Twins when my already too slow fastball got a whole lot slower courtesy of a torn rotator cuff. I had to choose between major surgery that I was told had maybe a fifty-fifty chance of getting me back on the field or getting a job. I decided to find out if my journalism degree was worth the four years it had taken me to get it.

Donna knew all of that, and more, about me. And I knew … not much about her youth. Which isn't to say I knew nothing. I knew she'd gone to university, studied public administration, didn't like it, left school without graduating, and got into retail and worked her way into management. I knew she liked to travel and had done the standard Europe thing and a couple of months in Australia after leaving Carleton.

But as I compiled the list of who I could talk to about Donna's life before I came on the scene, I realized it too was pathetically small.

I knew none of her girlfriends from school (no, that was wrong — there was Kelly, though I knew her only from the note). I did know a couple of people from her college years, a couple more from the job she'd been working at when we met, Dr. Mike McCullers who had been her doctor from when she was a kid, the people who had attended the funeral — their names were listed on the guestbook that was somewhere in the apartment. Donna's mom, Joan Leybrand. Donna's father had passed away three years before the fire and Donna was an only child, no siblings.

Short list.

I decided to start with Joan. We'd always gotten along well. She was far from the stereotypical mother-in-law

— she was more concerned about observing our need for privacy than we were.

I'd call her in the morning. Now that I'd been bumped from the search for Jay Blevins, I had nothing pressing for the next few days. I decided to use some of that time to satisfy my belief, as much as possible, that I'd been right all along. The killer had wanted to get me, had screwed up, and an innocent woman died as a result.

End of story.

SIX

I slept well. Maybe it was the notion that I was active, actually doing something, however trivial, that made me feel good. I decided to start the day with something I hadn't done since Donna died. I went out for breakfast to the place we used to go almost every Sunday of our four-and-a-half years together: Bobby's Omelet on 11th Avenue. I wasn't sure Bobby would still be a part of the place and I was fairly certain the omelets couldn't possibly be as good as I remembered them being seven or eight years before.

Before I left the house I called Joan and told her I'd like to stop by, if it was all right. She said she'd look forward to seeing me. I picked up a *Herald* on the way to Bobby's, parked across the street, and found a table near the back of the restaurant. No familiar faces among the other diners, but the place hadn't changed much. Bobby had tried for homey and succeeded. No two tablecloths were the same but they worked. The walls were adorned with fifties and sixties vintage photographs of Calgary, all of buildings that no longer existed. There were two over my booth. One was of the Capitol Theatre, a wonderful old Famous Players palace that I'd been to a couple of times before they knocked it down. Calgary hasn't always been real big on preserving its heritage buildings.

The other photo was of a church — The First Church of the Nazarene. The cutline below it told of the fire that had destroyed it a decade earlier. What the cutline didn't mention was a murder that had taken place in the church basement in the late fifties or maybe early sixties — a little girl sexually assaulted and murdered. I remembered it because I'd known a family member.

I shivered though Bobby's was anything but cold. It felt like my life was suddenly caught up in some ghoulish theme park of death and murder.

I took the menu from its perch at the wall side of the table and read. It looked pretty much the same as I remembered it — every permutation and combination that involved eggs, bacon, ham, cheese, home fries, and toast. All of it prepared (at least in the old days) by the loving hands of Bobby Panzer, one-time member of the Edsels, Calgary's first really popular teen band, later a morning radio DJ, and for the past twenty years or so, the greatest purveyor of the cheese omelet on the planet.

I was trying to decide between the "Basic" — mushroom, cheese, and ham — and the "Calgary," which was like the Denver that every restaurant served except better. Bobby served it as a torte with herbed cheese and spinach. It had been my favourite back in the day.

"Cullen, been a long time."

I looked up at a smiling face and extended hand. Bobby was thicker by thirty pounds and sported a goatee that stood out on a red face that labelled its owner as either a surfer, which Bobby wasn't, or a drinker, which he was.

I shook the hand, returned the grin, and said, "Too

long. I've missed the place. Thought it was time to stop by, see if you can still remember how to cook."

He slid into the other side of the booth, tapped his temple. "Everything is deteriorating except for right here."

"That's a relief," I told him.

"How've you been?"

"I'm doing okay, Bobby. Doing okay. I guess the fact that I'm here is proof. How about you?"

"Amazing. I'm still fooling the customers, I'm moderately rich, happier than a pig in ten feet of shit, and I got grandkids, three of 'em. That's the best of all. Oldest one's seven — kid plays guitar like he was born with a Fender in his crib. Gonna be the next Edsel."

"Bobby, I heard the *old* Edsels. I hope the kid aims a little higher."

He laughed loudly. "Maybe you're right. Anyway, this grandpa thing is a great gig."

"Yeah."

We were silent for a long minute — old friends savouring a moment. Bobby pointed at the menu. "Made any decisions about breakfast?"

"Better go with the Calgary, I think. Actually do me a favour, make two, the second one to go. The orange juice still freshly squeezed?"

Bobby nodded and grinned.

"I'll take two of those too. But they're both for here."

"Anything else?"

"Yeah. I stayed away way too long."

"I know. And I know why. You don't hear me criticizin'."

"Thanks. That Calgary better be as good as I remember it."

He stood up. "It will be. And don't even think about taking your wallet out of your pocket or I'll make you listen to old Edsels eight tracks the whole time you're eating." He grinned again and was gone.

Forty-five minutes later I was stuffed, happy, and pulling up in front of Joan's sixties bungalow with a take-out Calgary omelet in hand.

Joan greeted me with a smile and a hug, then stepped back to let me in.

"Wonderful to see you, Adam. It always is."

I handed her the takeout container. "Brought you breakfast, or lunch, or brunch. It's an omelet — world class."

"Bobby's?"

"You know it?"

"The best."

"Enjoy."

"I will. Thank you so much, Adam. Come and sit. What can I get you?"

We walked through to the living room, which was tidy and clean without giving the impression that the person living here was a neat freak. Comfortable.

"Nothing for me, Joan. I just drank a lot of juice and a couple of gallons of coffee. Don't need a thing, but you go ahead."

She shook her head, walked quickly to the kitchen to deposit the omelet in the fridge, and was back in seconds. Joan didn't move like an older person. She sat on a couch that had been in the same place for maybe a couple of decades and still looked good.

I sat in a pale blue armchair that sported half-century-old doilies. I looked at Joan, decided to get right into it.

"I … uh … I was wondering if you still had any of Donna's stuff around. You know, her kid stuff, growing up stuff, young woman stuff.… I don't know if you kept any of that kind of thing."

Joan seemed surprised by the request and didn't say anything for probably thirty seconds.

"There wasn't much, not really. You are no doubt aware that Donna wasn't a hoarder. Not as an adult, not as a child. She kept some things, of course, and I still have some of them around, but not a lot. And once she went off to college, there was even less. Some of her favourite texts, a few clothing items, a sampling I suppose, but not much more. Of course, you're welcome to see what there is. I'd just like it back when you're through."

"Absolutely."

"Why are you wanting to see these things, Adam?"

"I guess it's a nostalgia thing," I lied. "I got looking through what's at my place, you know, what survived the fire, and it's next to nothing. I guess I'd just like to feel close to her again. Maybe this'll work. Maybe it won't."

"Are you sure you want to do that?"

A beat.

"Yeah."

There was another hesitation before Joan said, "How far back do you want to go?"

"I'm not sure, really. I guess sometime after her dolls and picture books phase, you know, teenager, young woman stuff as she was becoming the person I knew."

Joan nodded and looked down, adjusting the doily on the arm of her chair.

I said, "I don't want you to do something you're uncomfortable with. I'll be very careful with everything."

Joan looked up, nodded, and smiled. "I know you will, Adam. I guess I haven't stopped being the protective mother. Right, I think we can do this. Although you might regret passing over the dolls phase. We were very big on Barbies around here."

One more thing I hadn't known about the woman I'd been married to.

"Adam, are you sure I can't get you something?"

"Okay." I grinned. "One more coffee can't hurt."

"There's no such thing as too much coffee." Joan laughed on her way to the kitchen.

She wasn't gone long — the coffee must have already been made. "I remember you as a milk and sugar guy, right?"

"Absolutely right." I took the cup she offered and she sat back down with what looked and smelled like herbal tea.

Joan sipped, then set her cup down. "One thought I had — the one thing Donna did keep was her pictures, photo albums. They were like her diaries, she had them all in chronological order with little captions for lots of them. It was really something."

I nodded. "She was the same way with us. I think our wedding pictures were catalogued by the Dewey Decimal System or something close to it."

Both of us laughed, remembering. Joan sipped more tea.

"I'd love to take a look at those albums," I said. "Do you still have them?"

"I do, but it might take some time for me to find them. How about I dig around, and when I find them I give you a call."

"Perfect, but please don't go to a lot of trouble, and if you need any help finding —"

"It won't be any trouble. I'll phone you in the next day or two when I have them located. In the meantime, I have Donna's things — except for the pictures — in a couple of different places in the house. Maybe you can help me with the gathering."

A half hour later, I was on my way back to my apartment with the back seat half full of cardboard boxes and a couple of green garbage bags of Donna's things from before we were married. I felt uneasy. What if I did find something? You snoop around in someone's past long enough, there's a chance you'll find out some things you'd rather not have known. But while that prospect troubled me, I was willing to take the risk if there was something in those old mementos that might offer a clue as to the reason my wife had died the way she did.

I pulled up in front of the apartment but before going in I called Cobb on his cell phone. No answer. I talked to his voice mail. "If you change your mind, I'm ready to jump back into the fray and help any way I can. And I do know there are risks and am willing to accept that. Just give me a yell if you need help."

And, for the second time in as many days, this time after a not badly concocted plate of spaghetti and meatballs, I sat on the living room floor and pored over the earliest strands of Donna's teen and young woman years.

Different background music this time. Bruce Cockburn's *Stealing Fire* CD. Early Cockburn to go with Donna's early life.

Joan was right, there wasn't much. I spent an hour mostly sorting — one pile that I would go through in some detail, the other, items that I didn't think could conceivably give me anything that would be helpful in finding her killer.

And again, I didn't feel I was making headway until I came to her grade eleven yearbook. Northern Horizon Academy.

I'd asked her once why she'd gone to private school. She'd said her parents had wanted her to attend a school that offered excellent academics and a focus on the arts. She'd made sure I understood that it wasn't a Christian school or some offbeat charter school that didn't allow "regular kids" in. I don't remember our talking about her schooling but for that one time.

At first I merely browsed, flipping pages, pausing at a page near the front of the book with its top third missing, the bottom two thirds comprising a roster of teachers — their pictures showing smiles, outdated hairdos, and clothes that would be a big hit in today's retro stores.

I flipped some more, skipping over the section showing the various students activities from the sports teams to the clubs that occupied noon hours and after school time. Several pages were devoted to drama productions, musical performances, a few pieces of writing from the Creative Writing Club.

I leafed through the section of student photos and found Donna's fairly quickly. I moved closer to the lamp, wanting to study the photo — really *see* the woman I would eventually marry. She wasn't one of the school knockouts but she was far from unattractive.

I stared at the photo for a long time, trying to get a feel for what she might have been thinking at the moment the photographer snapped the picture. Got nowhere, scolded myself for getting sidetracked, and set the book aside. Then picked it up again. An idea.

Kelly.

The girl whose name had been on the note.

Kelly — The bastard did it again. D

Pig. K

I started through the yearbook again, looking for Kelly. I started with Donna's homeroom class.

No Kelly. I flipped back to the first page of student pictures and went through the book page by page. There were three Kellys: a ninth grader named Kelly Howe, a grade ten girl named Kelly Blakeley, and a grade eleven student, Kelly McKercher.

Google time. On the way to my computer I switched up the music: this time it was Broken Social Scene's *You Forgot It in People.* I typed in each of the names. Nothing on any of the three girls. Not surprising since it was likely they had married in the decade-plus since they'd been in high school. I trolled Facebook with the same non-results.

Next I tried the various high school social media sites that connected former students with their classmates. I found Northern Horizon Academy and looked for the Kellys. Got lucky with one — Kelly Blakeley, the eleventh grader, now Kelly Kamara, living in Vancouver. I tried Googling every Kamara in Vancouver without much luck. I finally decided to go old school; I phoned the information operator and got the names and numbers of the various Kamaras — five in all.

My first call was to Dio Kamara; the number I called had been disconnected. I got answers at the homes of Ronald R. Kamara and Jaron Kamara, but when I asked for Kelly I was told that I had the wrong number.

I dialled P. Kamara and this time a woman answered.

DAVID A. POULSEN

I asked for Kelly Kamara, got silence, then a slow, "Who's calling please?"

"My name is Adam Cullen. I'm not a telemarketer and I'm not conducting a survey," I said. "I'm the husband of someone Kelly Kamara may have known in high school. Are you Kelly?"

"I don't think I want to —"

I jumped back in before she could hang up. "My wife died a few years ago. I'm trying to find a friend of hers named Kelly. My wife's name was Donna Leybrand. I was hoping, if you were the Kelly Blakeley who attended Northern Horizon Academy in Calgary, that you might have known her."

There was a long pause. I was about to say, "Hello?" when the person on the other end of the line spoke.

"I knew Donna. Well, actually, I knew who she was but we weren't friends. She was a grade ahead of me. I ... I heard she had died. I'm really sorry."

"Thank you, Kelly."

"It was a fire, wasn't it?"

"Yes ... it was a fire."

"I'm sorry," she said again. "I didn't know your wife well but I'm sure she was really nice. She seemed nice, friendly and everything, at least that's what I remember."

"You didn't have any classes with her?"

"No."

"How about mutual friends?"

"No, I don't think so."

"There were two other girls named Kelly at Northern Horizon at the time you and Donna were there. Maybe you knew one or both of them — Kelly McKercher and Kelly Howe."

104

Silence again but I guessed she was thinking. I waited. "I sort of knew Kelly McKercher. She was ahead of me too, but I can't remember if it was one grade or two. She was a cheerleader, one of the really pretty girls at NHA. I remember all the guys were sort of goofy about her."

"You had cheerleaders at Northern Horizon?"

"Yes. Why wouldn't we have?"

"I don't know. I guess when I think of private school I think sort of stuffy, you know — debating club, field trips to poetry readings. I'm sorry, I shouldn't generalize."

"NHA wasn't like that. I mean, we wore uniforms and I guess the academic standards were pretty high, but we had teams — not football, but basketball, volleyball, track, *and* we had cheerleaders."

"I'm sorry," I said again.

"No need to apologize. But didn't Donna tell you about our school?"

"No, she didn't say much about it."

"Oh. Anyway, I heard Kelly McKercher married a golfer — one of those guys who works at a golf course, teaching people and selling equipment, that kind of thing."

"A golf pro?"

"I guess so. I heard they ended up in Phoenix ... at least I'm pretty sure it was Phoenix."

"You don't happen to know their last name."

"Sorry, I don't think I ever heard it, just that she married this gorgeous golf guy and moved to Arizona."

"How about Kelly Howe? Did you know her?"

Another pause while she thought. "Sorry, doesn't ring any bells."

"She was a year behind you — grade nine."

"Kelly Howe," she said slowly. "No, I don't think so."

"Thanks for this, Kelly. I appreciate your time and trouble."

"It was no trouble at all. Good luck with finding the other Kelly. And I'm really ... you know ..."

"I know. Thanks again. Good night, Kelly."

I hung up the phone and stared for a while at the picture of Kelly McKercher. She was pretty much gorgeous all right. I glanced at my watch. 11:25 p.m. The search for the golf pro in Phoenix who had married the Northern Horizon Academy cheerleader would have to wait until morning.

SEVEN

L esson: There are a lot of golf courses in and around Phoenix.

I Googled and copy/pasted phone numbers while I ate breakfast — multi-tasking. Breakfast a la Cullen was a long way from Bobby's: slightly burned toast and choke-cherry jam washed down with store-bought orange juice and two cups of coffee.

By 9:30 I was on the phone making long-distance calls to golf course pro shops. One no answer and three answering machines. I decided not to leave messages, mostly because I couldn't think of a way to say what I wanted without sounding like an idiot. The first four people I actually spoke with sounded like high school students moonlighting at the golf course between classes. The golf pro at all four either hadn't arrived for work yet or was out on the course giving lessons. Two of the kids I talked to were sure the pro's wife was not someone named Kelly, the third told me the pro was fifty-nine years old and the fourth laughed as he told me the pro's name was Sandra, and no, she wasn't married to Kelly.

Call number nine netted me a partial. I actually spoke to the pro there. He was divorced and had been for "thirteen glorious years," but he was pretty sure the pro at the neighbouring Sandstorm Golf and Country club had married a Canadian girl, though he didn't know her name. I called the Sandstorm and was told that the pro, Wes Nolan, had left a few weeks before to take the senior pro job at the Duke, a course in Maricopa, Arizona, about forty-five minutes away.

Next call was to the Duke, where I talked to yet another kid who sounded seventeen, learned the course was named for John Wayne, who had spent a lot of time in the area when he was alive, and that the new pro was off that day.

"Do you happen to know his wife's name?"

"No, sorry."

"Are you sure? Would you know it if you heard it? Kelly maybe?"

"Sorry, I've only seen her once. I didn't get introduced to her. *Damn*, you know what I mean?"

"Hot?"

"Mega."

"Any chance you can give me Wes's cell or home number?"

"Sorry, we're not allowed to give out that kind of stuff."

I thought for a minute, cleared my throat, and decided to resort to good old-fashioned lying.

"What's your name, son?"

"Paul."

"Listen, Paul, this is confidential too but I'm going to have to trust you. The reason we're trying to track down Kelly is that her best friend back in Canada is seriously ill, as in we don't know how long she's got, and her final wish is to see her friend one more time. We need to speak to Kelly ASAP. I'll guarantee you Wes won't find out who gave us the number."

Pause. The kid was thinking. Turned out Paul wasn't a fast thinker. I was beginning to think he'd nodded off or gone to the bathroom when he finally spoke. "This is for real, right?"

I did sombre-voice. "I wish it wasn't, but yes, this is very real."

"And Wes won't find out who gave you the number?"

Aw kid, shut the hell up and give me the number.

"That's a promise."

"Okay." He recited the number. "That's his home number. I'd be in real shit if I gave you his cell number."

"Fair enough. Thanks. I know Kelly's friend won't forget this."

I hung up, dialled the number the kid had given me, and waited.

Three rings, then a female voice. "Hello?"

"Hi. May I speak to Kelly please?"

"Um … who's calling please?"

"I'm calling from Canada. My name is Adam Cullen and I'm looking for a high school friend of my wife. Her name was Donna Leybrand back then. She passed away some years ago and I was hoping to speak to Kelly used-to-be McKercher."

A few seconds of silence, then, "I'm Kelly. It's Kelly Nolan now." A kid screamed in the background. "Maddie, just a minute, Mommy's on the phone.… Thank you, Maddie." Then to me. "I met you at the wedding."

"I'm sorry. I met so many people I didn't know that day."

She laughed. "I can imagine. Donna was totally popular, had a million friends."

"I know. Judging from the caterer's bill, I'm pretty sure all of them were at the wedding."

Another laugh. "Can you hold on just a second?" I heard her set the phone down and speak to Maddie; it sounded like she was picking her up. I visualized the pretty ex-cheerleader getting Maddie arranged on her lap and the phone sorted out so she could talk and keep the kid settled at the same time.

"There, that's better. They always do this when you're on the phone or if someone comes to the door."

"Maddie your first?"

"Uh-huh. She's a year and a half going on thirteen."

"Mind of her own."

"Oh yeah. The terrible two's arrived way early."

"Listen, I don't want to keep you, Kelly. I know you're busy. You're aware, of course, that Donna died in a fire."

There was a pause and a deep breath. When Kelly spoke again, her voice was strained. "I was sick when I heard it. It must have been terrible for you."

I paused. "Yeah, terrible is about how it was."

"I'm so sorry."

"You may also know that the fire was deliberately set."

"I heard some rumours about that but I thought maybe someone just made that up."

"No, nobody made it up. They've never found the person who set the fire. I'm doing some looking into the possibility that there might have been something or someone in Donna's past ... someone who might have had some sick grudge against her. Do you happen to know of anyone like that? An old boyfriend or someone at school who was jealous of her? Anything at all?"

"Okay, Maddie, we'll have juice in a minute." Another pause. "Sorry about that. Donna didn't really have a lot of boyfriends … a couple of crushes but she … in high school she wasn't like some of us, you know — all hormones and attitude. That wasn't Donna."

"She told me she used to think of herself as the ugly duckling," I said.

"She *wasn't* ugly, not even close … just not pretty, at least not then, partly because she didn't spend a lot of time like some of us did trying to make herself *look* pretty."

"Yeah, vanity was never a big part of who Donna was," I agreed.

"But the part about the little duck that becomes a beautiful swan, that part was true."

"I know."

Neither of us said anything for a few seconds. I swallowed a couple of times, took a breath.

"There's no one you can think of, no one at all, who might have had a reason, even an imaginary reason, to dislike Donna?"

She didn't answer right away. "No, I really can't think of anyone like that at all. I'm sorry."

"I came across a note in Donna's high school or maybe college stuff, I'm not sure. It read, 'Kelly, the bastard did it again.' It was signed 'D'. Then it looked like the person — Kelly — answered. Just one word, pig. Then the letter K beneath that as a signature. I thought maybe it was a note she might have written to you and that you answered and sent back to her."

"Just a second. I have to put Maddie down."

I could hear her talking to her daughter, then there was silence for what seemed like a long time.

"Hi, sorry again." A nervous laugh. "I think she should be okay for a few minutes. Toys, a cookie, Dora video — all Mommy's best distraction devices."

"Hey, I'm a big Dora fan myself." Trying to lighten things up.

She laughed, didn't say anything.

"So that note ... 'the bastard did it again.' Ring any bells?"

"No, I don't recall anything like that." The answer came fast, a different feel to her voice.

"Did you two write notes back and forth? I know lots of kids did that."

"Yeah, sometimes. It was way before texting, but I don't remember any of them being important stuff. More silly teenage girl talk, you know?"

"Was there someone at school she didn't like? A guy in your class, or some other class, a teacher, someone outside the school?"

"No, it's like I said. Everyone liked Donna and she liked everyone. I mean, there were jerks in our school just like every school. And I'm sure there were people Donna wasn't totally nuts about, you know? But I ... I wish I could help you. Are you sure whoever set the fire wanted to hurt Donna?"

"No," I admitted. "I'm not sure of that at all. Kelly, would you say Donna was happy at school?"

Hesitation. "I guess so. She was totally smart, got really good grades without having her hand up in class all the time to answer the teacher's questions or ask questions of her own. You know, *those* students."

"Know them well. Pains in the ass."

"Right. Donna was smart without being a pain in the ass."

"You said she was popular, but did she have many *close* friends?"

"I'm not sure what you mean by 'many,' but Donna had close friends for sure."

"Were you one?"

"I guess I was," Kelly said. "Yeah, I think you'd say that."

"But you can't think of what that note might have been about?"

"Sorry, it's been a long time."

"Okay, well thanks, Kelly. Would you do me a favour? Can you take my number and if you think of anything, just give me a call?"

"Sure. Your number is on my caller ID. I'll write it down and if I come up with anything … I just don't think I will, you know?"

"Sure, thanks anyway."

I hung up the phone. Not satisfied. I had a nagging feeling that there was something Kelly hadn't said. It felt like her tone changed — just a little, but it *had* changed — when I brought up the note. Like she did remember it and that it wasn't just chatty teenager talk. But maybe it was me *wanting* something to be there.

I drank another half cup of coffee, then pulled on sweats and a hoodie, went for a walk that became a run … a couple of miles. On my way back, I stopped at the Starbucks on 1st Avenue — part of the new look to Bridgeland since the city had imploded the old General Hospital, a victim of Alberta's cutback mania.

I drank the coffee quickly. Now that I was in action mode I didn't want to sit back and just think about what was going on around me. I wanted to *do* something. I just wasn't sure what.

The walk back to the apartment only intensified my desire to be in motion. I started with a long lukewarm shower, then pulled on jeans and a T-shirt that celebrated spring training baseball. Cactus League. Arizona, home of Kelly Nolan, nee McKercher. For a few seconds I toyed with the idea of booking a flight to Phoenix, finding Kelly, and seeing if a face-to-face would yield more information than what I'd got on the phone.

I abandoned that idea as madness, decided instead to go for a drive. The front seat of the Honda Accord that had succeeded the Volvo looked like the inside of a Dumpster. I gathered and tossed trash in the backyard garbage bin and headed out.

I took 1st Avenue to Edmonton Trail, crossed the Langevin Bridge into downtown, rolled down 4th Avenue through Chinatown, Corb Lund's *Hair in My Eyes Like a Highland Steer* CD playing loud because I needed some cheer-me-up music. Trouble is, it didn't work, not even "The Truck Got Stuck." I guess I just didn't feel like light. I switched to an early Glenn Gould recording of "The Goldberg Variations."

Nothing if not eclectic.

Cruising Chinatown got me thinking about Cobb and our efforts to track Jay Blevins. Maybe that's what made me direct the car back toward some of the places Cobb and I had checked out two days earlier. I swung back east and drove by the Sally Ann; it looked quiet, almost closed, which I knew could not be the case. Next I cruised past the Goodwill store/food bank where I'd talked with Jill Sawley. I tried to get a look inside, but couldn't see much. Finally my sojourn took me to Garry Street and the unfinished building that was home to Zoe Tario.

The place — and the neighbourhood that surrounded it — didn't look any more inviting in the daylight. I drove to the end of the block, made a U-turn, and pulled up across the street from the building. I dropped the volume of "The Goldberg Variations" to barely audible, and locked my doors but let the car run.

I sat and watched in the late afternoon light, waiting for I wasn't sure what, but while I watched, I had a thought that troubled me. Cobb and I had found Zoe without a whole lot of effort. If there were some badass types looking for Jay, how hard would it be for them to get this far? And if they found Zoe and wanted information … I shivered, pulled my collar up, and stared at the building, every once in a while glancing in my rear-view mirror.

I stayed there maybe twenty minutes and decided that nothing much would happen in broad daylight so I did something else I hadn't done since Donna's death.

I hit Peters' Drive-In on 16th Avenue for a burger and a shake — both world class. I read the *Herald* while I ate. The two victims of the shooting on Raleigh had been identified. Freddie "Stick" Schapper and Lucius McGowan, twenty-eight and twenty-five respectively. Both men were known to the Calgary police. Not much more than that. And nothing on the killing of Larry Blevins. I left the paper and went back out to the Accord.

Winter's early darkness had settled around me and I decided to take another pass by Zoe's place. I parked in almost the same place, probably not a good stakeout strategy, but I wasn't thinking stakeout, not really. I wasn't sure what I was thinking.

There was one street light at the south end of the block a couple of hundred metres away and virtually no light at all coming from the building, the result of which left the street in as close to total darkness as I'd ever encountered within the city.

I sat for an hour, not sure exactly what I was watching for and mostly wishing I'd had the foresight to bring along a coffee. I shut the car off a couple of times to save fuel, and both times started it again after about five minutes, opting for warmth and polluting the environment over conserving gasoline and freezing my ass off.

No one had gone into or come out of the building in the time I'd been there. I wasn't sure what I'd do if suddenly a vehicle screamed to a stop in front of the building and three guys leaped out of the car carrying semi-automatic weapons and running for the rear entrance.

I shut off the Honda for the third time and was contemplating that unpleasant scenario as a car did come into view in my rear-view mirror and pulled to a stop just behind me. I had one hand on the ignition key, just in case. Only one person climbed out of the car. It was too dark to see much, but I was pretty sure the person who was now coming alongside my car was a man and wasn't carrying a gun, at least not out in the open. I'm also pretty sure I stopped breathing. I started to turn the key in the ignition.

A tap on the window. I looked out into the darkness as the man bent down and looked back at me, an unhappy look on the familiar face. Motioned for me to roll down the window. I did.

"Nice night for a drive," Cobb said.

"It might be, if I was driving."

"Which leads me to my next question — what are you doing here?"

"Why don't you climb in the other side and we can talk about it without risking frostbite."

He hesitated, then nodded and crossed in front of the Accord. I flipped open the lock on the passenger side and started the car. I was due for a warm-up.

Cobb climbed in and looked across at me. "Frostbite? It's barely below freezing."

"I have thin blood."

"Are you going to be a jerk about this?"

I knew by "this" he meant my being around when he'd told me to get lost.

"Probably."

"To repeat — what are you doing here?"

"I don't honestly know. I just needed to get out of the house, went for a drive, ended up here. Then I got thinking about Zoe and the guys that are looking for Jay. Thought I'd just hang here for a while."

He made a noise that was half grunt, half cough. He looked at the CD player where Gould was wrapping up the eighth variation.

"Classical?" He looked surprised or maybe miffed.

"Yeah."

"You like classical?"

"Among other things, and when I'm in the right mood, yeah."

He made the same noise he'd made a few seconds before, then looked across the street at the darkness of the building, and back at me.

"And you thought you'd 'hang here.'"

"Yeah."

"'For a while.'"

"Yeah."

"Not a bad thought."

Surprised me. "You think she could be in danger?"

He shrugged. "I don't know. These guys are hardasses. They offed the old man, but that might not be enough."

"They could be worried that the kid is pissed off enough to tell the cops whatever he knows about the house on Raleigh."

Cobb nodded. "That's possible. One thing's for sure, if they target Jay, nobody in his circle is home free. That includes Zoe … and you."

"And you."

He nodded again. "This is my line of work."

"You think I didn't run up against some bad guys in my research?"

"I'm sure you did. Encountering violent people when conducting research isn't the same as encountering them when they see you as the enemy."

"I think I can be of some help without doing something stupid. The fact that you're here says you're worried about Zoe. You can't watch her twenty-four-seven and look for Jay at the same time. You need help."

He looked at me. "So what do you do if you're watching this place and a couple of thugs show up, heading for the back door?"

"I was just sitting here having that same thought."

"You call me on my cell, that's what."

"And she's dead before you get here. How does that help anything?"

"So you play John Wayne and go running in there and you're *both* dead before I get here. How does *that* help anything?"

"Fair enough, I call you on your cell ... then what?"

"You wait and you watch and you do what I tell you."

"I'm fine with that."

"Good. Here's your first order. You go get us some coffee, maybe a couple of donuts, no icing on mine."

He didn't wait for me to agree, just got out of my car and walked back to the Jeep. I put the Accord in gear, made a U-turn, and headed back toward lights and civilization. And Tim Hortons.

I was back in less than fifteen minutes. This time I parked behind Cobb and juggled hot coffee cups and old-fashioned plain donuts all the way to the passenger seat of Cobb's Jeep.

I passed him a coffee and one of the donuts. I stared for a minute at the warehouse. "Any action across the street?"

Cobb had just taken a large bite and shook his head to answer. Swallowed, sipped coffee, pointed with his coffee cup.

"The light flicked on, then off in one of the places in there. Maybe ... what was that guy's name?"

"Jackie Morris."

"Yeah, maybe his place. Hard to tell from here. And that's it for ground pounding excitement."

"How do we know she's in there?"

"I took a little walk while you were getting the refreshments. She's there. Alone."

"So she knows we're out here."

He shook his head.

I decided against asking how he'd found out that Zoe was in there by herself without her knowing he was there. We drank coffee in silence for a while. The dash clock read 10:22.

119

"You any closer to finding Jay Blevins?"

Another head shake. "And it might get still tougher. By now he probably knows about the shooting and maybe that his old man was the shooter. If his brains aren't totally addled from the shit he's been putting into his body, he might have figured out that a low profile would be a good idea."

"No profile would be even better."

He nodded.

"Which makes *you* somewhat redundant," I said.

"That thought has occurred to me." Cobb turned his head and looked at me. "I followed up on our conversation with Sharp, the million dollar realtor. The house on Raleigh belongs to a group called the MFs. You know them?"

"I know a little. Catchy name for starters. Bikers. Badass. Shadowy. I was never able to gather enough to actually write about them."

He nodded. "Yeah, it's not like they're on Facebook announcing it to the world every time one of them goes to the john. What is fairly common knowledge is that they're a motorcycle gang that would like to rival the Hells Angels. Drugs, prostitution, loan sharking, history of violence — make that *rumoured* violence. So far nobody's been able to nail them for much more than speeding tickets. Smart guys."

I nodded, took a long drink of my double-double. "I picked up some stuff in my research but a lot of it was rumours. Flamboyant on the surface but pretty low key when it comes to some of their non-motorcycle related activities. The name Blair Scubberd came up a few times. Calls himself Rock. Snappier handle than Blair, I guess.

Not much out there about him either except that he's not a person you want to piss off. I didn't hear the MFs were into the drug industry, I guess that's why I didn't mention them when you asked before."

"Might be a fairly recent development. The place on Raleigh has been a crack house for a while, maybe ten years, but it used to have a different owner-operator. Independent named Jerzinsky."

"Jerzinsky," I repeated. "Never heard of him at all."

"Died a little over three years ago. He was found at the bottom of a ravine on the Calgary to Banff highway. A couple of bullet holes in his head. A year or so later the crack house was up and running again. Under new management."

"Let me guess. No arrests ever made."

"Good guessing."

"Okay, so we fast-forward to the present and the new entrepreneurs are operating a thriving little business out of the house on Raleigh that used to belong to a rival who met with an untimely end."

"Bingo."

"The MFs."

Cobb nodded.

"M and F Holdings."

"Bingo again."

"Mr. and Mrs. Smith, aka Scubberd. Well, at least you know who you're dealing with."

"Sort of. Like you said, this guy Rock is pretty much invisible. The most recent picture I've seen of him is at least five years old. He looks tough, like the name fits. Can't find out much about him other than he's originally from the Maritimes and he's a gym rat. I've been calling gyms to see if I can find somebody who knows him even a little. No luck so far. And his close associates seem to be just as diligent about staying out of the public eye. No names, no faces … so far."

"Except for Schapper and McGowan."

Cobb raised an eyebrow at me.

I shook my head. "It was in the paper."

"Here I am working my ass off and I could have saved myself the trouble and read it in the newspaper."

"We journalists are a bright bunch."

"Paper say anything else?"

"Nothing of note," I answered. "Didn't mention the MFs."

Cobb nodded. "Schapper, the one Zoe called Stick, has been an MF for quite a while, a few years anyway. The other one, McGowan, was a recent recruit."

For a few minutes neither of us said anything.

"So it's back to trying to track down Jay," I said.

"That's all it's ever been. I'm not being paid to butt heads with the MFs. My job is to find and protect Jay Blevins. Period."

"Doesn't matter that your employer is deceased?"

Cobb shook his head. "He paid in advance. But even if he hadn't …"

"You'd keep looking for the kid."

"Right."

"And maybe keep an eye out for a girl named Zoe."

"Which I hope might eventually give us Jay Blevins. And, by the way, watching a warehouse is something I can do by myself. Why don't you take the rest of the night off?"

I nodded. "Sure, but how about I take tomorrow night? Give you a break or an opportunity to pursue other avenues. I've got a whole lot more classical music I can play and I won't do John Wayne."

He looked at me for a minute then smiled and nodded. "Deal. There are a few things I'd like to follow up on and I could use the time … no John Wayne."

I grinned but wasn't in a hurry to leave. "There's something I'd like to talk to you about."

"Sure. Talking during surveillance is good, like classical music."

"Is that what this is? Surveillance?"

"That's what this is."

"I like the word stakeout better. Sounds more detective-ish."

"Detective-ish?"

I shrugged.

"What's on your mind?"

I told him about my looking into Donna's past. Finished up with the conversation with Kelly. When I'd finished he was silent for what felt like several minutes, staring at the building across the street.

"Give me the wording of the note again."

"'Kelly, the bastard did it again. D.'"

"That's all of it?"

"Except for Kelly's answer. One word. 'Pig.' That's it."

"A girl-to-girl note in high school complaining about some guy. It's not much. There can't be more than a few hundred reasons a girl in high school might write those words to a buddy."

"I've already considered that. But the note is uncharacteristic of Donna."

"The Donna *you* knew. This is the teenage, hormonal version, may be a different person."

"Maybe. But there's something else. I'm not sure Kelly was being totally straight with me. I had a feeling she knew what or who the note was referencing but didn't want to share."

"Again, lots of possible reasons for that."

"Maybe. But what about Kelly's response to Donna's note? 'Pig' has a certain connotation. Maybe sexual. A pervert maybe. Or a flasher."

"Or a cop. Or a whole lot of other possibilities, all of them innocuous. Look," Cobb said, "I know I'm the one who got you thinking about this stuff. And I'm not trying to throw cold water on what you've learned so far. There could be something there. I'm just saying it's a long shot."

"You know what's a long shot? That some psycho killed my wife for no reason. Either he was after me or he had some madman's desire to see Donna dead."

Cobb nodded slowly. "Something I've wondered about. If the killer was targeting you, why didn't he try again when he realized he'd failed?"

"Maybe one murder scared him off. Or if I was the target, maybe he figured that having my wife killed was worse for me than dying myself. If that's what he was thinking, he wasn't wrong."

We were silent again. I think Cobb was giving me a minute. I needed it.

Finally he said, "Possibilities for sure. And you're right, a certain kind of twisted bastard may have thought that the pain he caused you was enough revenge … if revenge was the motive. But there's still that other possibility …"

"That Donna *was* the target," I finished the thought.

"Uh-huh."

"I think I'll talk to Kelly Nolan again."

"Can't hurt," Cobb said.

We finished our coffee in silence. I said good night, walked back to the Honda, and was home in twenty-five minutes. Not much traffic at that hour. And the road crews had the main streets pretty much cleared off. I shucked my coat and shoes at the door, pulled a Rickard's Red out of the fridge, and picked up the phone. The tell-tale beeps told me there was a message. It was Joan.

"Hello, Adam … hello, Adam …"

Joan was a with-it senior, but the new technology and things like talking to a machine were troublesome for her.

"I wanted to thank you for the omelet from Bobby's. It was as good as ever. I enjoyed every bite. And I also wanted to tell you that I unearthed those photo albums that we talked about. You can come by any time. Except tomorrow afternoon. I have a doctor appointment and before you get all nervous like people do any time some-one over sixty says they're going to the doctor I'll just tell you it's my regular checkup. Anyway, any time except between one and four tomorrow. Well, uh, bye then."

It was much too late to return the call so I took a long and as-close-to-scalding shower as I could stand, pulled on a pair of checked maroon and yellow lounge pants and a T-shirt, and fell into bed thinking sleep would come in seconds. I was wrong. A half hour later I was out of bed and sitting in the brown leather recliner Donna had bought me on my thirtieth birthday. "Old guys need their creature comforts," she'd written in the card.

I sat for a long time, looking out at the night, sorting thoughts, searching memories. Listening to Blue Rodeo,

Five Days in July. Until sleep finally came. But it wasn't the wake-up-refreshed kind. Too many weird dreams that bordered on nightmares. As with so many of my dreams in recent years, fire was a dominant theme.

The bedside clock — at some point I must have made my way into bed — read 7:14 a.m. I was sweating and had the kind of headache that is usually reserved for the morning after a whisky night.

A shower, shave, and a bowl of Frosted Flakes later, I was feeling almost ready to tackle the day's challenges. Just after eight I returned Joan's call.

"Hope I didn't wake you," I told her.

"You'd have to call earlier than this. You forget I'm an old farm girl."

"Farm girl maybe. Old, not so much."

"You're already in the will so no need for morning BS." She laughed and I was painfully reminded of how much like her daughter Joan was.

"If it's okay maybe I'll pop over and pick up those photo albums this morning … if you're sure you don't mind my having them for a few days."

"Not at all," she said. "There's too much to get through in one sitting. I'll see you when you get here."

I hung up and called Cobb's cell. Didn't get an answer. No surprise. He was probably sleeping after the all-nighter in front of the building on Garry Street. *Surveillance.*

My second call was to Kelly Nolan. I got voicemail. Male voice "Hey. We're either golfing, swimming, taking care of the baby, or making love. Leave a message, and if it's one of the first three, we'll get back to you real soon; if it's that last one, it could be a while." I tried to think of some clever one-liner but couldn't, so I left a message asking Kelly to call me. I wasn't confident she would.

The drive to Joan's was painfully slow — the Glenmore Trail shuffle. It took forty-five minutes to make a twenty-five minute drive.

At the house I rang the bell and heard a voice call out, directing me to the backyard. Joan was sitting on a lawn chair in a winter jacket reading the *Herald* and drinking coffee. Tough lady. The coffee was in a Calgary Flames mug. I'd forgotten that Joan was as big a hockey fan as I'd ever known. She'd been in the Montreal Forum in '89, the night the Flames won their one and only Stanley Cup.

"Coffee, Adam?"

"Thanks. That would be great."

Donna got up and went inside. The photo albums were piled on a table. Piled *high*.

Joan returned with a coffee in hand and held it out to me.

"Thanks." I pointed my chin at the photo albums. "Prolific."

"Mm-hmm. And like I said, actually we both said, mega-organized."

"Mega-organized," I repeated.

Joan nodded. "I looked these over again this morning. There's a photo album for every year of her life from twelve years old on. It's a record of who she was, what she did."

A couple of minutes went by before either of us spoke.

I said, "I miss her."

"I do too, Adam," Joan said, looking up at the grey-blue morning sky.

Neither of us spoke much after that.

EIGHT

On the way back from Joan's house I detoured to the north side of the city. I wanted to drive past Donna's old school. I wasn't sure why.

The building that housed Northern Horizon Academy dated back to just before the First World War. It had originally been a public school, A.C. Rutherford High School, a venerable old brick and sandstone edifice in a solid neighbourhood that was undergoing something of a renaissance — like Bridgeland in that respect. There were lots of in-fills and walk-up style duplexes, new but made to look old, with enough coffee places to keep everyone in the neighbourhood on a permanent caffeine high.

The school had closed its doors in 1971, because of a dwindling student population, but reopened four years later as Northern Horizon Academy.

I parked across the street from the main entrance and watched students going in and out of the massive main double doors that were flanked by tall cedars that looked to have been there for several graduating classes. A hand-painted sign next to the left hand cedar read "Go Marauders, maul those Rams."

I sat for a few more minutes, watching, and listening to Jann Arden performing live with the Vancouver Symphony Orchestra. Finally I climbed out of the car and walked across the street and up the long, wide walkway that led to the front doors. I tried to imagine Donna going in and out of those doors throughout high school and was lost in that thought when I was almost run over by three teenage girls who had crashed through the doors and were running, laughing, and talking — a teenage version of multi-tasking.

They didn't see me until the last minute, managed to avoid me, and were genuinely sorry. Two blondes and a redhead, they looked to be in the upper grades.

I laughed and told them it was my fault. "I wasn't paying attention."

"Are you looking for the office?" One of them asked.

"No, I … well, uh, yeah, I guess so."

"On your left, you can't miss it."

"Thanks."

They moved off but I figured I was committed to at least going inside. A sign just above the handle on the door said, "All visitors MUST report to the office."

I stepped inside and looked to the left. The office door faced in my direction. I started toward it, realized I didn't have a particular reason for being in the school and changed my mind. I turned, glanced up, and saw that the wall between me and the office was adorned with grads' pictures from various years. Four foot by five foot framed collections of headshots — one framed collection for each year. This wall featured recent grads, the years 2001 to 2010.

I was debating whether I should try to find Donna's grad year when the door to the office opened and a woman stepped out carrying a couple of file folders and a thick book in one hand, a coffee cup in the other. She went by me, then stopped. I was facing the pictures on the wall but sensed that she was watching me. With good reason. Schools and the people who work in them have been justifiably spooked by the number of violent incidents that have taken place over the past couple of decades. Strangers, especially those with no good reason for being there, aren't welcome.

"Can I help you?"

I turned to face her. "Uh, not really, I ... my wife attended this school and I guess I just wanted to see what it looked like. She spoke of it often." The last part was a lie but I figured it might help set aside fears that I was in the school for any nefarious purposes.

The person opposite me was my height and conservatively dressed. She wore glasses, utilitarian, not the high fashion kind, and a bun held her brown hair in place. She had a plain-ish face, thin lips, but in a way she was pretty without trying real hard. I guessed secretary or maybe librarian, though she was built solidly and looked fit enough for Phys-Ed.

"She isn't with you?"

"She passed away."

"I'm sorry." She looked like she meant it.

I nodded. "It was some time ago."

"I'm afraid we have quite a strict policy about —"

"I know, reporting to the office. I was just on my way there but then I thought I probably wouldn't stay. No point I guess."

"What was your wife's name? I might remember her. I've been here rather a long time. I'm sure there are students who would say *too* long." A faint smile played at the corners of her mouth.

"You must have come in contact with a lot of students over the years. I'm sure you can't remember all —"

"Try me." The smile got a little bigger.

"Donna Leybrand."

The smile disappeared. "Ah."

"You did know her then."

"I knew her and I remember her. Lovely girl." A pause. "And I read of her death. A fire?"

"Yes."

"I am so very sorry," she said again.

"I appreciate that."

"Would you like to come into my office, Mr...?" She gestured back toward the main office door.

"Adam Cullen."

She held out her hand. I took it. Warm, long, slender fingers, no nail polish, firm grip.

"Delores Bain. I'm the principal here at NHA. I have coffee in my office if you're interested."

Principal. All of my careful stereotyping was merely another botched piece of detective work.

I smiled. "Coffee would be very nice. But you look like you have work to do."

"These?" She raised the folders and book just a little. "These can wait. The longer the better."

She led me into the main office and lifted a hinged drop down door that took us past a counter where two boys were talking earnestly to a short, balding man in a white shirt and tie.

"Just so you know, boys," the principal said without looking at the boys or the man, "even if you convince Mr.

Turley that you shouldn't have to serve those detentions, you'll never convince me."

I heard a groan from one of the boys as I followed her into her office. She closed the door behind me. There was a small coffee maker on a table in one corner. She pointed to a chair, one of two on this side of the desk, and went to the coffee maker.

"It's my one perk for twenty-nine years in the same school," she said over her shoulder. "How do you take it?"

"Just milk or whitener, whatever you've got. One sugar if you have it."

"I have milk, Mr. Cullen, so I guess that makes two perks."

She turned around a few seconds later with her cup refilled and a fresh Marauders mug, which she passed over the desk to me as she eased herself into the chair behind her desk. There were certificates and photos on the wall behind her. The photos were student shots: sports teams, kids posing in front of the school, some receiving awards on a stage. With Delores Bain presenting, smiling, shaking hands.

It looked like she was in all of them. All but one. That one featured a young helmeted driver standing next to what looked like a race car. Stock, like NASCAR. The helmet made it difficult to tell if it was a boy or girl.

If Delores Bain had a family, there was no evidence of it on her desk — no pictures of kids or anyone who didn't look like a student.

I held up my mug. "Here's to NHA," I said.

She nodded and smiled.

We sipped coffee for a few seconds.

"I appreciate this," I said.

She nodded and leaned forward, her elbows on the desk. "Mr. Cullen, I invited you in here so I could tell you what a wonderful student Donna was. You're right, I don't remember them all, I wish I did. But I remember Donna. Anyone who taught her would remember her. She wasn't the most popular or the best athlete or the best … anything, really. But there was something about her. She was someone you looked forward to seeing every day. I'm sure you know better than anyone what I'm talking about."

I nodded. "I guess I do, Ms. Bain."

"Delores, please."

"Delores," I said.

"I was so shocked when I read about the fire. I wouldn't have known it was Donna Leybrand except that the story mentioned she had attended NHA. I did some checking and when I realized it was *our* Donna …" She stopped, looked down at the desk, her eyes moist.

"Ms. … Delores, you must know the fire was deliberately set. The papers were all over that."

She looked up, cleared her throat, working at being composed. A small nod. "That had to be terrible."

"It was. You may have read that I was a suspect for a while."

She looked at me. "I seem to recall something. That too would have been horribly difficult."

I nodded. "Delores, let me ask you something. I've been thinking about the fire a lot lately and there's reason to believe there may have been something in Donna's past that led to this person setting the fire. I know it's a long time ago, but can you recall if there was something, anything, that might suggest there was someone at this school who disliked Donna enough to want to … hurt her?"

Delores Bain didn't answer right away. She looked down at her hands, furrowed her brow, thinking. Then she looked back at me. "I really can't, Mr. Cullen. I wish I could help, I really do. But there's nothing that comes to mind that could have led to something as dreadful as what happened to your wife."

I nodded again, sipped coffee.

"Mr. Cullen —"

"Adam, please. Turnabout's fair play." I managed a half smile.

She returned the smile. "Adam. Are you certain that Donna was the intended target of the attacker, or indeed that anyone was? That it *was* an attack?"

"I received a note one year to the day after the fire. It read 'The Cullens live and love here. I guess not anymore. Ha ha.'" I told her about Donna's hokey little plaque that had been next to the front door.

Delores Bain pushed her coffee cup away as if it were suddenly distasteful. "That's ... beyond belief. But even that, I'm not sure it points necessarily to your wife being the intended victim."

"Actually, I've always believed it was me the arsonist had been trying to get, and I'm not totally convinced that that wasn't the case, even now, but I guess I'm just wanting to satisfy my own desire for the truth, whatever it is."

"That's certainly understandable."

"And like I said, there are a few other things that have come up that have me thinking about it all over again."

She watched me, waiting for me to say more. I thought about mentioning the note to and from Kelly but decided against it. I doubted that the principal of a school would be able to shed much light on the communications between students. I stood up, extended my hand.

"You've been very kind to take the time to talk to me. And I enjoyed the coffee. Thank you very much."

She rose, took my hand, offered a smile that was equal parts sympathy and encouragement. "You are welcome here any time, Adam."

As I turned and walked out of her office I was aware that I could barely remember my high school principal, only that he was tall and seemed too focused, for the most part, on our football team that I seem to recall he once coached. And that was the extent of my memory of him. I was pretty sure that if I had attended Northern Horizon Academy, I'd have remembered my principal.

When I got back to the apartment I wasn't in a real good mood, though I wasn't sure why — maybe the futility of what I was trying to do.

I made myself a bacon sandwich and a fruit smoothie and sat down at the kitchen table with the photo albums. I'd finished the sandwich and the smoothie and was halfway through the second album — grade eight — with nothing in the pictures or the captions to set off any alarm bells when the phone rang.

I picked up on the third ring and barely got hello out before a breathless voice on the other end jumped in.

"Adam, it's Jill Sawley, from the shelter."

"Jill … uh … yeah, hi … thanks for calling." I was caught a bit by surprise with the result that neither my mind nor my mouth were working at full capacity. Again.

"I've just seen Jay Blevins. I tried to talk to him but he got away."

I tried to think. *What would Cobb want to know?*

"Where was this and how long ago?"

"Just a few minutes ago. A couple of blocks from the shelter. I didn't have my cell phone with me so I couldn't call you until I got back here."

"Did you talk to him at all? Get an idea where he was going, where's he's hanging out?"

"I tried. He was across the street and he seemed in a hurry. I called and he stopped but then he waved and kept going. I tried to follow him but I guess I'm not much of a detective. I lost him, or he lost me, in a hurry."

"Was he with anybody?"

"I don't think so. It happened kind of fast. If anything it looked like he sped up when he saw me … like he wanted to get away from me."

"Listen, Jill, I'd like to take a run over there if that's okay. Maybe you could show me where you saw him, what direction he was going … and … stuff." *And stuff.* What the hell did that mean? I was back to sounding like an idiot.

"Of course. I'm working today but there are two of us here so I can get away for a few minutes and take you to where I saw him."

"Great. I'll see you in a half hour or so."

I looked outside to check the weather before I headed for the car, always a good idea in Calgary. I decided, based on my visual assessment, that a down-filled jacket, toque, and gloves were solid choices.

I called Cobb again on the way to the car, got him this time.

"Adam," he said, "I just checked my messages and was about to call you. What's happening?"

"I just heard from Jill Sawley, the woman who works at that shelter in Inglewood. We've got a Jay sighting. Recent, within the last half hour, not far from the shelter. She couldn't catch up with him but got a look at what direction he was headed. I was just on my way there."

"I'll meet you there."

I was there in just over twenty minutes and parked across the street from the shelter. I didn't see Cobb's Jeep and assumed I'd arrived ahead of him. I crossed the street at a trot and stepped through the front door of the shelter.

Jill was talking to a couple of people who were holding bags of groceries and clothing. All three were smiling. She didn't see me right away and I watched her as she shook hands with the man and hugged the woman with him. I guess I'd describe the look on both of their faces as relief and the one on Jill's as joy. *Big* smile.

The couple turned and walked by me on their way to the door. Jill noticed me and waved, the smile still on her face. I crossed to where she was standing.

"Thanks for the call. The urgency level has gone up some since we first talked."

She nodded and her face turned serious. "I heard some reports on the radio. They didn't identify the person who was murdered and I was afraid it might have been Jay. I was so relieved when I saw him. But the person who was killed … his dad?"

I nodded. "Yeah."

We didn't have time for any more conversation. Cobb came through the door, nodded to me, and looked at Jill.

"Hi again. Appreciate the call. Can you show us where you saw him?"

Jill looked around, then called. "Celia." Nothing. "Celia!" she called a second time.

A heavy-set woman whose wardrobe decisions that day had leaned heavily to green came out of the back part of the building. She was adjusting a sweater — forest green, I think they call that shade — that looked like it had fit her several pounds ago.

"The people I told you about are here. I shouldn't be long." Jill pulled on an overcoat and I stepped forward to help her. "Thanks."

Celia shrugged, shook her head.

Jill was still buttoning the coat as we stepped into the street.

When the door had closed, I said, "Doesn't look to me like Celia's a keener."

"Actually, she'd surprise you. She just doesn't like being left alone. I'm not sure if it's the street people or if she's nervous about having to make a decision." She pointed and started across the street. "It was over this way. It'll be faster to walk."

Jill was a fast walker. Cobb and I moved up beside her, one on each side. No one spoke. We rounded a corner onto 9th Avenue, quickly covering one block and part of another. We passed the used bookstore Cobb and I had been in a few days before. Stopped at the corner.

Jill pointed again. "It was here that I saw him. He was over there by that bus stop. A bus was just pulling away but I don't know if Jay had just got off it or was just going by. He was heading that way." She indicated south. "He crossed the street and went through that park. There's a pathway that goes along beside the river and leads down toward the Stampede grounds. A fair number of homeless people haunt this corner … druggies too. Anyway, I called to him just as he was getting to the pathway. As I said, he slowed down when he saw me and waved, not much of a wave really, and then hurried off."

A train was inching its way through the crossing to our left but it wouldn't impact us as the path Jill had indicated went through a tunnel under the train tracks before continuing south.

"Let's take a look," Cobb said.

We crossed the street and hurried through the small park. Several light-coloured concrete sculptures were the park's highlights. Local artists, I guessed. Some of the work was pretty good.

Jill took the lead. "He went right by here going this way. He didn't have all that big a head start," she said over her shoulder, "but there was some traffic and quite a few people on the street. It took me a minute or so to get here even running."

We came to the footpath Jill had indicated. A couple or three meters wide with a yellow painted line down the middle.

Cobb and I moved up alongside her again and we passed through the tunnel. The path snaked past some rough brush on the right leading down to the river. Just beyond the tunnel there was a branch of the path headed back left, parallel to the way we'd come.

Jill stopped. "I got to here and couldn't see him anymore. I looked around but he'd disappeared. I couldn't have been more than a minute behind him, probably less than that. But he was gone."

Cobb stepped ahead, surveyed the path leading away from us. "Anybody else come this way at that same time?"

"You mean like somebody following him?"

"Or someone with him."

Jill shook her head. "No one went down this path between him and me, I'm sure of that. Or even right after me. But Jay was behaving like someone was after him."

"In what way?"

"He looked back a couple of times after he waved to me. But I don't think he was looking at me. He seemed nervous … suspicious maybe."

"So maybe he'd heard about his dad and is scared," I said

Cobb turned back to us. "Could you see what he was wearing?"

Jill looked at the sky, thinking. "He was a ways off so I can't be too detailed, but jeans, a greyish jacket with a hood, a dark toque. And he had a backpack, blue, a couple of shades of blue, I think. That's about it."

"You okay with going a little farther?" Cobb asked.

"Sure." Jill nodded.

We continued south past a car wash on our left. A little farther on, an opening forked off to the left, either a street or an alley; we'd have had to climb up an incline to find out. Cobb seemed to take note of that route, then chose to stay on the path. It continued its way south with a couple of twists along the way then down under a bridge, this one for vehicles. As we came out from under the bridge, we could see Stampede Park ahead and to our right on the other side of the river. Cobb stopped.

"There's a lot of places he could have ducked off and lost you, especially if that's what he was intent on doing."

Jill nodded and all three of us looked around for a few seconds.

Cobb smiled at her, nodded at me. "Jill, thanks again for the help. In fact, thanks to both of you. I'm going to cruise the area for a while, see what I can see. Adam, maybe you can walk Jill back to the shelter."

"Sure."

"I don't need —" Jill began.

"It's okay," I said. "I have to go back that way to get my car anyway."

Cobb said. "If you happen to see Jay again —"

Jill held up a hand. "I know ... call you. I will. I'll keep my cell phone with me from now on, promise."

Cobb nodded. "Thanks." Then he continued down the path away from us.

Jill and I watched him go, then turned and started back the way we had come. We were walking slower than we had when she was showing us the route Jay Blevins had taken. Not talking much at first.

As we emerged from the tunnel a second time, I finally said, "How long have you been volunteering down here?"

"You asked me that before."

"And you didn't answer. Actually, you said something about it being a pickup line as I recall."

She laughed and I did too. "I guess it's been two years, maybe a little more. I had a friend who'd been working with the shelter and she got me into it. Then she moved to Vancouver and I liked volunteering so I just stayed on. I know it sounds corny but when I see people like that couple that were there when you came in today and I know there'll be stuff for their kids to eat at least for the next few days and I see their relief, their gratitude, it's pretty cool."

"I can see that it would be. What about the shelter part? That must be difficult sometimes — people strung out, hypes, people carrying God knows what disease…. I would think there are times —"

"Mostly there are moments when I wonder how much good we're really doing. But every once in a while, not nearly often enough, there's a success story. Someone goes from our shelter right into treatment and comes back maybe three months later and they're still clean. I know three months doesn't sound like much, but to an addict that's a couple of lifetimes. Those are pretty special times."

We walked in silence for a while and were almost back to the shelter.

"What about you and Cobb?" she asked. "You don't seem exactly … uh … the same. How did you two come to be working together?"

"That's a question that's going to need a coffee to answer. If you have time maybe we could —"

"There's a Starbucks up the street."

"Unless that was a pickup line."

"It's okay, mine was too." She smiled.

We were nearing the front door of the shelter. "Are you sure Celia can handle things for another half hour or so? She didn't look confident."

"Confident, no." Jill smiled. "Competent, yes. But we better keep your answer to twenty minutes, just in case."

"Sounds good," I said. And we sped up in unison.

NINE

"What can I get you?" I asked Jill as we walked into the trademark smells and sounds of Starbucks. When I was a kid, I'd lie in bed in the morning and listen to the voices of my mom and dad as they talked in the kitchen and I could smell the coffee they were drinking as they talked. Early on I associated the notion of being a grown up with the act of drinking coffee.

The sounds of that particular Starbucks were two-fold — the first was the high-pitched call of a particularly enthusiastic barista with vivid red hair and a powerful, almost painfully screechy voice. "One venti, non-fat, extra-hot, decaf, Toffee-Nut Latte, no whipped cream, double sprinkles."

She went on a break just after Jill and I came into the place, which saved me the unpleasantness of having to kill her. The second and far more soothing sound was the stereo system playing a compilation CD of Neil Young songs. I'd seen him in concert a couple of times — liked the man, loved the music. Had to be a good omen.

"Maybe I'll have a Caramel Macchiato," Jill answered.

"Great, grab us a table. I'll get the drinks." A couple of minutes later, I handed her the Caramel Macchiato and sat down opposite her with a Verona blend for myself. She smiled her thanks at me.

"I met his dad, you know," I said.

"When you say 'his' could you be more specific?"

I pointed up at the ceiling speakers. "Neil Young. His dad was Scott Young. Sportswriter, wrote kids books, *Scrubs on Skates*. I read it four or five times when I was a kid."

"Neil Young. Now why wouldn't I have known that was who you were talking about?"

"You like him?"

"Neil or his dad?"

"Neil." The speakers were pumping out "Rockin' in the Free World."

"I like him a lot."

"Great," I said. "That means you can stay."

She laughed. I liked her laugh, not just the sound of it, but the way her face and even her shoulders were part of it.

Silence returned. I gave it a few beats, then said, "Well, now about the question you asked earlier. Cobb and me."

She nodded and sipped the Caramel Macchiato.

"My wife died a few years ago. Eight actually. In a fire … a fire that was deliberately set."

She set the drink down, sat up straighter; her face lost its colour. "Oh my God. Adam, I … I didn't know. I'm so sorry. If I'd had any idea —"

I shook my head. "No, it's okay. Really. I hired Cobb to do some investigating and that's how we came to know each other. I hadn't seen him in a long time but he knew I'd done some writing about the drug scene in Calgary and a few other places as well, so when he needed help finding Jay Blevins he thought I might be of some use."

"Did you ever find out who…?"

I shook my head. "Not yet."

She smoothed her hair with one hand and seemed to be studying me. "You're sure that someone …" Her voice trailed off.

"The fire department and cops have people that look into that kind of stuff; they're good at what they do. They're sure it was arson. For a while I was the prime suspect."

"I can't imagine how awful that had to have been."

I nodded. "It was pretty bad." I picked up my coffee cup but set it down without taking a drink. "So was not finding the killer."

Jill looked down at the table for a long minute. "Are they still looking for the arsonist?"

"If they are I don't know about it. I guess it's one of those cold cases now. If some clue happened to drop out of the sky and land on the right person's desk, maybe they'd do more investigating, but otherwise not much is happening."

"You said you hired Cobb?"

"Not right away. One year after the fire I received a note in the mail from the person I believe set the fire. The note was … laughing at me I guess, literally and figuratively. It was a reminder of what happened and the ugliest thing I've ever known. That's when I hired Cobb to try to find the person who murdered my wife. He worked as hard as anyone could possibly work. But we haven't found the killer … yet."

"That's twice you've added 'yet' at the end of a comment about finding the killer."

"That's because someday I'll find him."

Neither of us spoke. Jill held her coffee, I drank some of mine. And I knew that so far my first meeting with her had been pretty much a downer. It was time to change the mood.

As if to help me, "Rockin' in the Free World" came to an end and was replaced by "Harvest Moon," one of the great romantic songs of all time. I said, "So, what about you?"

"What *about* me?"

"Well, you know, who and what is Jill Sawley in twenty-five words or less?"

"Twenty-five words. It takes more than that to tell you about how my being born took fourteen hours and almost killed my mother."

"Fair enough. Dumb idea anyway. How about one thing that's important in your life ... besides the shelter."

"That's much better. And easier. I don't even need the twenty-five words. My daughter, Kyla, she's eight and she's great. Her words, not mine, but I agree with her assessment wholeheartedly."

I smiled and nodded. "A daughter, Kyla. How cool is that."

"Why is it that the words 'how cool is that' felt more like 'that sucks' coming from your mouth? You don't look like one of those guys who can't stand kids."

"I'm not, not at all. And I'm sorry, I didn't mean it to sound like that." I looked down at the contents of my coffee cup for a long minute. "Listen, Jill, I'm not very good at this. Since Donna died you're the first woman I've talked to for more than five minutes who wasn't a relative or someone trying to sell me insurance."

"Well, if it'll make you feel more comfortable I have a terrific special this week on term life. No medical required."

I laughed. "Sign me up. Okay, I need a mulligan here. Let's start over. You ever see *Sleepless in Seattle*?"

Jill nodded and smiled. "A long time ago. Chick flick. *You* saw it?"

"And liked it, even if it was a chick flick. Anyway, you know the part where Tom Hanks is trying to get back into dating again and he's totally clueless?"

"Vaguely. Doesn't he ask one of his friends for advice?"

"Rob Reiner. And that's because the Tom Hanks character has been out of the dating loop forever and doesn't know where to start. Think of me as Tom Hanks. Thing is, I don't know the protocol here. Is this where you tell me your life story, then I tell you mine?"

She shook her head. "Uh-uh. Life stories are first date stuff. This isn't a date so it doesn't qualify. And besides, if I don't get back to the shelter, Celia could stage a mutiny."

She finished the last of her Caramel Macchiato and stood up. I followed her lead.

"Uh, so Kyla, she's eight and she's great — is there a Kyla's dad in the picture?"

"Dad, yes. Husband, no. We split four years ago. He lives in Toronto. Sees Ky three or four times a year. A month in the summer. He's a good father and a good guy but we're oil and water."

I exhaled. I hadn't realized I was holding my breath. "Oh, well … uh … in that case, I was thinking maybe we …"

She swung her purse over her shoulder. Smiled at me, touched my arm. "You have my number. Call me."

And she was out the door. I had planned to walk her back to the shelter but I sat down instead. I was breathing okay but my knees were shaking. "Jesus, I wasn't this bad when I was fifteen."

I hadn't realized I'd said it out loud. A woman, mid fifty-ish, sitting alone at the next table leaned in my direction. "I think the phrase you were searching for goes something like 'maybe we could go out sometime.'"

I looked at her. She was smiling and she looked like somebody you'd like to have for your aunt.

"You could have slipped me a note," I said.

She laughed. "I could have but I would have missed out on some lovely entertainment." She straightened up and picked up the book she'd been reading. I glanced at the title, something I do, or at least try to do, whenever I see someone with a book on the LRT, doctors and dentists waiting rooms, and in coffee places. She was reading *Secret Daughter* by Shilpi Somaya Gowda.

I pulled my parka off the back of the chair. The reading lady looked over at me again.

"A couple of hints," she said. "The daughter's name is Kyla. That's a good thing to remember."

I nodded and said, "Thanks for the tip." I started to stand up again, sat back down. "You said you had a couple of hints. What's the second one?"

"If you're going to reference pop culture you might want to be a little more current."

"*Sleepless in Seattle*? That was bad?"

"Not bad. Just *old*. I recommend cultural references from the current millennium."

"But she'd seen it."

"You were lucky."

I grinned at her and held out my hand. "Adam Cullen." She shook my hand. "Kay Towers."

"Kay, I appreciate the help."

"My pleasure."

"Let me ask you something. You have any nieces or nephews?"

"Five. Plus a couple of grand-nieces. Why do you ask?"

"Just curious, I guess. Kay Towers, you have a great day."

She smiled and said, "I am."

This time I stood up for real. On my way out I put five dollars on the counter and told the barista, "Whatever that nice lady over there is drinking, please take her another one."

And I stepped out into the night to another nice surprise. The wind had swung around to the west and the temperature had come up a few degrees. An Alberta Chinook. I started off in the direction of the Honda humming "Harvest Moon" as I walked.

Neil Young. Good omen.

TEN

I got back to the apartment just after six o'clock. Cobb hadn't said when he expected me to start my watch — *surveillance* — of the warehouse on Garry Street but I figured around nine would be about right.

That left me time to go for a run, warm up a left-over hamburger-noodle casserole, take a hot bath — I'm a shower guy but this felt like a long, slow bath night — and maybe delve into another of Donna's photo albums before hitting the road.

By eight o'clock I was sitting in the living room, Donna's photo albums encircling me.

I found myself studying certain pictures: Donna in the grade nine drama production of *Annie* playing Miss Hannigan with a suitably nasty air about her; Donna as a member of the Lady Marauders, the volleyball team that the caption noted were the Christmas tournament champions that year; Donna with friends at the lake, with her parents at a backyard barbecue; and so on.

I wasn't sure what I was learning. Despite her own claims to the contrary, Donna was not unattractive. In fact, I didn't even see her as plain. Mostly she reminded me of girls I had known who, as the phrase goes, "walked to the beat of their own drummer." Which I think is code for didn't-give-a-shit-about-what-other-people-thought-of-them.

I glanced at my watch. Fifteen minutes until I had to leave. Enough time to get a start at least on the album entitled "Donna Leybrand, 15 Years Old." Donna in her grade eleven year.

But five minutes would have been sufficient to get through that album. While none of the previous albums had used every page, this one's photos took up maybe a quarter of the pages. For the first time, not all of the photos were fastened in place. On some of the pages, pictures lay loose. There were fewer captions too, and those that were there were less detailed than what I'd seen to that point.

It was like Donna had lost interest that year. Teen rebellion? Raging hormones? Or simply attention directed elsewhere, a perfectly normal and common occurrence among fifteen year olds. Changing priorities in a teenager's world.

Whatever it was I didn't have any more time to contemplate. It was time to make my detecting debut. I threw together a couple of tuna bunwiches and a Thermos of coffee, added a giant Dairy Milk chocolate bar and two cans of Red Bull, grabbed my binoculars, and headed out the door.

During the fifteen minute drive to the warehouse on Garry Street I made a phone call. There was a question I needed to have answered.

Lorne Cooney's wife was a high school English teacher. Lorne and I hadn't worked together since the drugs series we'd been putting together when Donna died. But we bumped into each other from time to time, had met for coffee a couple of times, and once for a few beers in the Liquid Lounge at the Westin.

Today, it was Rachelle Cooney I wanted to talk to, to ask just one question. It was she who answered my call. She recognized my voice and said, "Sorry, Adam, Lorne's at a meeting for the Young Conservatives."

"Covering or joining?"

"Are you kidding me? Covering."

"I *was* kidding you, Rachelle. There are so few of us lefties still around in Alberta, I didn't want to think we might be losing another one."

"Nothing to worry about there."

"Actually though, it was you I wanted to talk to anyway. I've got one quick question for you. A school question."

"I'll bet that's one more question than you asked a teacher while you were actually *in* high school."

"I'm deeply offended. And I'll have you know that English was my favourite class."

She laughed. "Yeah, right."

"Well, it would have been if you'd been my teacher."

"Shut up and ask your question before I become ill."

"When do they teach *To Kill a Mockingbird*? I seem to remember it was high school but I don't recall what grade."

"Even though English was your favourite subject."

"Uh … yeah." We both laughed that time.

"Well, fewer schools are teaching it these days, which I think is a shame — it still holds up even after all this time — and it varies. Some schools teach it in grade ten, but I think most still have it as part of the grade eleven curriculum. We do at Crescent Heights."

I'd forgotten that Rachelle had transferred to my former school a couple of years before.

"Okay, that's now … fifteen years ago?"

"I'd say almost all schools would have included it back then."

"Including private schools?"

"Hard to say. Some of the charter private schools do things differently. But most try to follow the Alberta Education curriculum for the most part."

"Thanks. I guess that's about what I thought. How are you enjoying my old alma mater anyway?"

"I love it. Great kids and a really good bunch of teachers and administrators. Hey, it's Alberta, so there are always funding problems, but we soldier on."

"And I imagine my name comes up a lot. The former student who is a wonderful role model for today's students — that sort of thing."

"I've lost track of the times I've heard people talking about you."

"Yeah. Hey, thanks Rachelle, I appreciate this. And say hi to Lorne for me."

"I will."

I powered off the hands-free and thought about what Rachelle had told me and how it fit in with what I knew. Or at least what I thought I knew.

Donna had paid considerably less attention to her photo album in her grade eleven year than she had previously. The note referring to someone as a bastard (and a pig) was in a copy of *To Kill a Mockingbird*, a novel that was studied in grade ten or eleven. And I had a feeling that the person she'd exchanged the note with had been holding back a little in our conversation of a couple of days previous.

Not exactly a mountain of damning evidence. I guessed that any real investigator would have laughed out loud at what I'd pieced together so far.

Anyway it was time to change hats. I'd just turned onto 9th Avenue and was only a couple of blocks from Garry Street. I pointedly turned my thoughts to Jay Blevins and Zoe Tario. And the MFs. Hoping I'd see one or both of the first two. And not so much as a glimpse of the latter.

I'd seen dozens of scenes in dozens of movies and television shows where a cop or detective is watching someone's house. I figured out in the first couple of hours of my first assignment that there was a whole lot of stuff that hadn't received sufficient attention in any of those shows.

The cold, for example. On a November night in Calgary, even during a Chinook, if you were in your car for any length of time, you would want that car to be running and the heater cranked to the hottest setting available. However, when involved in surveillance, running your car means running the risk of being detected while you're detecting.

Luckily I had thrown an extra down-filled jacket, two bulky sweaters, and a blanket into the backseat of the Honda earlier in the day. After a half hour in front of Zoe's building I bundled up. I was uncomfortable but managed to stay this side of hypothermia. It occurred to me that having so many clothes on that I could barely fit behind the Honda's steering wheel and covering my legs with a blanket probably left me lacking something in terms of manliness, which I didn't care about, and mobility, which I did.

Secondly, the movies and TV generally skip right over the part about going to the bathroom. In my case that involved crawling out from under the blanket, unwedging myself from the front seat of the Accord, and, while trying to look casual just in case someone was peeking out from some unseen window somewhere, taking a whiz in the gutter on the passenger side of the car. I tried to be as surreptitious as possible but found it hard to be stealthy when looking — and feeling — like the Pillsbury Doughboy.

The dark helped. Which is the third thing skipped over in all the cop shows. I came to the realization that there is a reason most of the scary scenes in scary movies are shot at night. It's because it's dark and … scarier then. I don't think I'm a coward but I had to admit that the cave-like black of Garry Street — it was cloudy so no moonlight — got to me after a while. While I blessed the darkness during my furtive excursions to the passenger side of the car, I cursed it the rest of the time.

But while I shivered and complained for most of the night, the one thing I did not do was fall asleep. Which meant I was awake at 2:17 a.m. when Zoe came walking up Garry Street in the company of a guy and girl, both of them about her age. They came right by the Honda but none looked inside. I was able to get enough of a look at the guy to be certain he was not Jay Blevins.

Cobb had told me to call if anything interesting happened. I decided the arrival of Zoe and a couple of kids who were either homeless or addicts or both didn't qualify.

Zoe's arrival wasn't the only occurrence. At 4:08 a car turned onto Garry Street from behind where I was parked. It wasn't the first vehicle I'd seen that night. Two others, one from each direction, had gone by my location. The first was just after midnight, the second at 1:46 a.m. While I noted the times in my notebook, neither of those vehicles — the first was a taxi, the second a pickup truck — caught my attention.

This one did. It was moving slowly and without head-lights. It was a dark, menacing object that would pass by the Honda in a matter of seconds, a minute at the most. I slumped down as much as my layers of clothing would allow and eased my head to the left, hoping to get a look at the car and its occupants without whoever was in that car seeing me.

The car slowed still more as it passed me. There were two men in the car, both in the front seat, and as they went by, both were concentrating hard on the warehouse. The man in the passenger seat had his phone out and was talking to someone as they went by.

The car came to a stop three or four car lengths past me. I was afraid they might pull in and hang around for a while but after a couple of minutes it looked like the passenger side guy wrapped up his phone call and they drove off.

As the car disappeared around the corner I started the Accord, waited a five count, and pulled forward. I wasn't planning to actually follow the car, but if I could spot it under streetlights I could at least identify it. I figured that much didn't qualify me for a John Wayne reprimand.

I turned the corner and was almost relieved to see that they were nowhere in sight. I decided to give it one shot. I'd turn onto 9th Avenue and see if they were in range.

I did and they were. There were only two cars moving on 9th Avenue at that moment: my Accord and a sporty silver job heading east about a block and a half ahead of me. I pulled over, grabbed the binoculars, and lined them up.

Audi. Nice car. Expensive car. I put the binoculars away, turned off of 9th Avenue, and took a circuitous route back to the warehouse to make sure they hadn't doubled back and were following me.

When I got back to my post I shut off the Accord and pulled out my cell phone. I dialled Cobb's cell number and was surprised when he answered on the second ring, even more surprised when he sounded wide awake.

"What've you got?"

"How do you know I've got anything?"

"You wouldn't call at 4:30 a.m. unless it was to tell me something. You okay?"

"Yeah, I'm fine. And you're right, I do have a couple of things I thought you should know about."

"Shoot."

"Zoe arrived home with two friends, one male and one female, at 2:17 a.m. They were on foot. They went inside and so far they're the only people who have gone in or out of the building. I didn't recognize either of her friends, but the male wasn't Jay Blevins."

"What else?"

"Just a few minutes ago a car cruised the street, real slow going by the building, lights out, two guys, silver Audi, expensive. The guy in the passenger seat was talking on his cell phone, finished the call, and they drove off.

"Didn't get out of the car."

"Nope."

Cobb was silent … thinking.

"I couldn't get any kind of a look at either of the guys in the car. They only made one pass along the street."

"Did they see you?"

"I don't think so."

"You still at the building?"

"Watching it like a hawk."

"Okay, if those guys come back, dial this number, let it ring once, and hang up. I don't want them to see you talking on a phone."

"Got it."

"It's almost five a.m. Assuming they don't come back, how about I come by about seven, buy you breakfast, maybe we have a chat with Zoe?"

"When you say buy me breakfast, are you thinking of that happening in a restaurant? Because my ass is frozen solid in this car so a donut and coffee in either of our vehicles isn't going to cut it."

That brought a chuckle. "There's a restaurant in the old Kane's Motorcycle place on 9th Avenue. Cool place, real good food. Motorcycle diner motif."

"I know the place."

"Good. I'll meet you there at seven. We'll eat, you can unfreeze your ass, and then we'll pay a visit to Zoe and friends."

"That sounds real good, especially the part about thawing my assets."

"And good work over there. I appreciate it."

"Any time."

"Careful, I might take you up on your offer."

"I meant any time in the summer."

"Right." He hung up the phone.

I bundled up again and started the countdown to seven a.m. … and warmth.

Cobb was already there when I walked into the restaurant. Kane's Harley Diner wasn't fancy but it did what I figured the owners wanted it to do. It featured fifties-ish Formica counters, lots of stainless steel, mirrors, motorcycle stuff everywhere, and big portions of hearty food — a biker's idea of heaven. Except that the clientele extended far beyond the biker community — diners of every stripe.

Cobb was in a booth at the back. I almost didn't recognize him. Peacoat, green toque, unshaven since I'd last seen him.

I slid into the opposite side of the booth. "Is this the can't-beat-'em-join-'em look?"

"Something like that. I've been spending a fair amount of time around here. I figured better to look like a street person than a cop. People talk to street people."

"You been to bed yet?"

He shook his head. "Maybe later today."

"I thought the idea behind me taking on spy duty was to let you get some sleep."

"The idea behind you taking on spy duty was to let me get some things done."

I shrugged. "Fair enough. You getting anything done?"

He didn't get a chance to answer. A tall, skinny, early twenty-something server in a black T-shirt with a Harley-Davidson logo on it, camo pants, and a red bandana wrapped around his head came to the table.

"You guys know what you want to order?"

"Not yet," Cobb told him.

"You wanna start with coffee?"

"Please," I said. "The hotter the better. And if you've got a mug instead of a cup, that would be great."

"That sounds like a plan," Cobb said. "I'll do that too."

When Red Bandana was gone I thought again about asking Cobb what he'd been doing with his free time, but decided it wasn't important.

The server returned back seconds later with two coffees, both in mugs.

Cobb sipped. Tasting it like wine. He nodded approval. "That'll be fine," he said.

Red Bandana started to roll his eyes, looked at Cobb, and changed his mind. Walked off. I grinned at Cobb. "A street person with attitude."

"But lovable when you get to know me."

I warmed my hands on the mug. "You planning on filling me in on what you've learned?"

He shrugged. "Not much really. I've been spending a lot of time down in that area where Jill saw Jay. I figured for him to be going in that direction, he maybe has a place to stay somewhere around there. I've talked to a bunch of the locals and three different people have seen Jay in the last few days, all of them in that same general area, but nobody actually talked to him beyond saying hi. And all of them said the same thing — Jay seemed to be going somewhere, no time to stand around."

"You think he knows the MFs are looking for him?"

Another shrug. "Hard to say. I'm guessing he knows that some bad people aced his old man. Unless he's living under a rock. The underground communication on the street is pretty effective."

"That could explain why he seems to be in a hurry all the time. Maybe he figures he could be next and is scared to stay in one place for very long."

Cobb didn't answer as Red Bandana returned to our table.

"Know what you want yet?"

"Sorry," I said. "We've kind of been talking. We'll get on it right away."

As the server started to turn away, Cobb said, "How long have you worked here?"

The young guy turned back, looked at Cobb, then at me. Tense. "Almost a year."

"You have a bike?"

His body relaxed as he said, "Yeah, a '99 Softtail Standard FXST. Cool machine. I love my Harley." He pointed to the logo on the T-shirt."

"Sounds like a nice machine. So is that part of the deal? You have to have a Harley to work here?" Cobb took a sip of his coffee.

"No, but some of us do."

"What's your name? I like to know my server's name, you know?'

I looked at Cobb. I thought he was laying it on a little thick.

Red Bandana might have been thinking the same thing. He stiffened a little. But he did answer.

"Davy."

"Yeah? I got a nephew named Davy. Not David or Dave. He's Davy."

"Yeah. Well, you just give me a wave when you're ready to order." Davy started to leave again.

"So Davy, you get a lot of people with bikes come in here? You know, it's called the Harley Diner and everything. I figured maybe it's popular with Harley owners."

"Yeah, I guess you could say that. We get some bikers in here. Anyway, I better get back to work. Just yell when you know what you want."

Cobb nodded.

I decided not to ask what the point of the exchange

with Davy was. "Think Jay Blevins has heard about *us* looking for him?"

Cobb shook his head slowly, picked up his spoon, stirred his coffee, though he hadn't put anything in it.

"Scared kid, maybe strung out. Hard to figure what he knows … or what he's thinking."

"Maybe." I wasn't sure I agreed but I wasn't sure I *dis*agreed.

"I keep thinking about what Blevins told me," Cobb said. "About one of the guys in the crack house being on the phone, doing a mock play-by-play of him being in there. Using Blevins's name … and Jay's. Whoever was on the other end of the line on the phone knows about Jay."

"And if it is the MFs and that's what they're thinking …"

"Uh-huh."

"Why doesn't the kid just get the hell out of town for a while?"

Cobb thought about that. "He's a kid. He's not sure what to do other than stay out of sight. And he might be a little shy on travel funds. And if he's using he'll want to be close to where he can get whatever it is he's on."

"Maybe. And Zoe could keep him here too. He might not want to get too far from her."

"Entirely possible," Cobb said.

Neither of us said anything for a while. I drank some coffee. Cobb lifted his mug but didn't drink, studied it instead.

I broke the silence. "What about the Audi cruising the warehouse last night?"

"Yeah, that bothers me. If the MFs know about Zoe, they're likely to try to use her to get to Jay."

"That doesn't sound nice," I said.

"These aren't nice people. Okay, let's order, then we'll talk some more."

Cobb waved an arm and Davy must been looking our way. He came to our table briskly. Businesslike. He had his pad and pencil at the ready.

We ordered. Pancakes for Cobb. Bacon and eggs with OJ for me.

Davy looked up from the order pad. "Anything else?"

"Yeah, one thing," Cobb said. "You mentioned that the biker set comes in here."

"Uh-huh."

"Including gang type bikers?"

Some hesitation as Davy studied Cobb trying to get a read on him. Cobb kept smiling like everybody's favourite uncle.

Davy was shuffling his feet, antsy.

"Yeah, I guess so."

"I'm wondering if any of the guys in the MFs ever stop by. You know who the MFs are." Cobb made it a statement rather than a question.

Davy thought for a few seconds, began backing away, wanting to leave.

Cobb lowered his voice.

"I'm looking for an old school buddy of mine, he's one of the MFs — Blair Scubberd, Rock, the ol' Rockman." Cobb grinned like he was remembering one of the ol' Rockman's most hilarious moments. "You know him?"

Davy shook his head. Licked his lips.

"But the MFs come in here, right? I was told they did and I was also told I might be able to find Rock here, that he stops in himself now and again."

"I better get your order in." He turned away then back to us. "You guys cops?"

Cobb shrugged, which didn't answer the question. "Thing is, I'd really appreciate it if you didn't mention to my pal Rock that I'm looking for him. You know, if he ever happens to drop by. I want it to be a surprise when I finally catch up with him."

Davy turned again and this time kept going.

"You ruined his day," I said.

"Maybe. I've done some more checking on Scubberd. Turns out he was away for a while. Maybe setting up some things in Vancouver. That's the scuttlebutt. I've got a call in to a cop friend of mine out there. See what I can find out. Anyway, our boy Rock has been back in Calgary about a year, and since his return things have been picking up for the MFs, business-wise."

"Drugs?"

Cobb shrugged. "My guess."

"I wonder why the change."

"Starts with M and ends in O-N-E-Y, I'm thinking."

I spent a couple of minutes looking around the place. All shapes, sizes, and ages in terms of customers. Mark of a good place.

Davy arrived with the food.

"That was fast, Davy," Cobb said. "Appreciate it."

Davy set the plates down. "Anything else?"

Cobb looked at me. I shook my head. "We're good, thanks."

For a couple of minutes Cobb and I worked the breakfast in silence. I picked up a piece of bacon, looked across the table at him.

"Let me ask you something."

"Ask away."

"I'm not sure I understand your strategy here. Telling Davy there that you're looking for Scubberd."

Cobb swallowed, dabbed at his mouth with a napkin. "It's a gamble, and if I'm wrong it isn't a big deal, but I see our boy Davy as somebody you tell him not to say something, he'll spill over like Niagara Falls."

"So he tells Scubberd about you and let's assume you don't get shot. What's the best case scenario?"

"We get together, me and the ol' Rockman, and we … talk."

"Okay, let's say Scubberd decides he'd like to chat with you. What exactly do you see as the main topic of conversation?"

"You mean after we discuss the Stampeders' prospects for next season?"

"Yeah, after that."

"I thought maybe I'd ask him if he or his boys snuffed Larry Blevins, and if they did, is that going to be enough to satisfy their thirst for revenge. Or words to that effect."

"Any place in particular you want your personal effects sent?"

"Oh ye of little faith."

We concentrated again on our breakfasts. Mine was excellent, but a night without sleep was beginning to take its toll and I was having to work at eating. Cobb, on the other hand, who had got even less sleep in the last forty-eight hours, was downing his pancakes and ham with gusto.

He came up for air, took a couple of gulps of coffee, and looked over at me. "Anything new come up in your research into Donna's past life?"

"Yeah," I said, "but nothing really definitive." I told him about the photo album from her grade eleven year. "I know it's not much, but combined with the note and my conversation with Kelly, it feels like there might be more out there that I *don't* know."

Cobb looked at me, chewed some more, didn't say anything.

"I stopped by her high school today, met the principal who was also the principal when Donna went there. She was nice but not much help."

Cobb thought for a minute. "You're right. You haven't got a whole lot that could be called definitive. But the album, the note … if it was me, I'd be at least curious. Let me know if there's anything I can do."

"I will. Thanks."

We ate some more, finished the juice and coffee, and Cobb paid for breakfast. No sign of Davy as we headed for the door. Outside the day was looking promising — blue skies, almost no wind, and a temperature that was approaching comfortable.

"Now what?" I asked.

"I'm guessing you're pretty tired, but if you've got anything left in the tank I'd like to have a chat with Zoe. If she's in the line of fire, we need to do something. And we probably need to do it quickly."

"I'm fine," I said. "Let's go."

ELEVEN

We left the Accord and took the Jeep back to the warehouse. No signs of life as we pulled up in front. I had my head on a swivel as I looked for the silver Audi, but there were no signs of it either.

We walked around to the back of the building, stepped carefully through the debris, and once inside made our way up the stairs to the third floor. It was easier to navigate with daylight flooding in through windows and other less formal openings. We walked down the hall to where Zoe was living and Cobb rapped on the door. At first I didn't hear anything inside, but eventually the sounds of someone moving around inside filtered through the door.

A female voice — I guessed it was Zoe's — came from just the other side of the door.

"Who's there?"

"Cobb and Cullen, the two guys who were here looking for Jay Blevins the other night. We'd like to talk to you."

No answer from the voice inside the apartment and no shuffling sounds. Then some whispering, a piece of furniture scraping on the floor, a crash followed by a male voice in a loud stage whisper. "Fuck." More shuffling sounds.

The door opened. Zoe stood looking at us. She was wearing jeans and a grey hoodie. She was in bare feet and sporting a ball cap that said "Beer for My Horses." Her ponytail was pulled through the opening at the back of the cap. She didn't look like she'd just woken up.

Behind her the twosome I'd seen the night before were standing side by side. Both looked worried although the boy's concern appeared to be somewhat distilled by whatever substances he'd taken in over the last hours. I couldn't tell with the girl.

Both were wearing blue jeans with holes in the knees, thighs, and a couple of other locations, and T-shirts. Hers was pink and showed Homer and Marge Simpson proclaiming, "We Are the Best America has to Offer." The boy's T-shirt was the yellow of a cigarette burn on a countertop. No writing. They too were in bare feet, but unlike Zoe they looked as if they'd been sleeping right up until Cobb's knock on the door. Mussed up hair, clothes not quite right.

"Hi," Zoe said.

"Hello, Zoe. Mind if we come in?"

"I've got company." She wasn't being rude, at least I didn't think so, just stating a fact.

"I can see that." Cobb nodded. "But we'd like to talk to you. It's important."

"Is it about Jay? Did you find him?"

Cobb nodded. "Indirectly. It's about Jay, but we haven't found him, not yet."

"Then what…?"

"I think we should do this in there," Cobb said.

The boy inside the room took a step forward, which put him alongside Zoe. "If you don't want them to come in, we don't have to let them in, Zo," he said.

He was maybe as big as me except lighter. He had a soft face and a softer looking body. Actually, he looked like a nice enough kid, maybe even someone I could have a conversation with in a different set of circumstances.

Cobb looked at him. "Son, this would be way over your head even if your head was clear, which it's not, so this isn't the time for you to try to impress your girl there with how tough you are."

The kid swallowed and I could see he was trying to come up with a suitable reply.

"Chill, Owen," Zoe said. "I know these guys."

She pulled the door a little farther open to give us room to move inside. Owen stood his ground for a two count, saving face, then stepped back.

I moved ahead, thinking it might be better for all of us if I was first into the room. I smiled at Owen and the girl. Cobb followed me in. I doubted very much that he was also smiling.

I stopped in about the middle of the room and looked around. Two sleeping bags and a couple of blankets were jumbled on the floor below the window. On the sill a small metal container sat open with five tablets, all different colours, and three of them engraved with words: one said *Kiss*, another *Love*, and the third had *You Me* across the surface.

Ecstasy. I'd seen it before during some of my research into the culture. Cobb was standing next to me but wasn't looking at any of the stuff that had to do with Owen and his girl.

"I think it would be best if we spoke in private," he told Zoe.

"No chance, bud," Owen said.

Cobb turned to look at him. "You got a last name?"

"What?"

"A last name. You got one?"

"Harkness. What's it to ya?"

"Okay, Owen Harkness, you've pissed me off twice and we've only known each other about three minutes. If you talk again when I'm not speaking to you, you'll be eating your meals through a straw for the next couple of weeks. You got that, son?"

"Don't call me son."

A beat. Then Cobb said, "Fair enough."

"Jen," Zoe said. "Why don't you take Owen back in that other room for a couple of minutes?"

"Are you sure, Zo?" Owen said. You had to admire the kid's try.

"I told you I know them. It's okay."

Jen and Owen moved slowly to the other room, Owen looking back as he went in and closed the door behind him.

"You guys want to sit down?" Zoe started moving the sleeping bags out of the way.

"No, thanks. We're fine."

She straightened, looked at me, then at Cobb.

"So you haven't found Jay?"

"No we haven't. A few leads but he's been … elusive. How about you? Have you heard from him?"

"I got a message. He told a person we both know to tell me that he's okay and that he'll see me as soon as he can. I didn't figure there was much there that could help you so that's why I didn't call you."

Cobb shoved his hands in his pockets. "The mutual friend, did he say where he saw Jay?"

"Uh-huh. Outside that pub down close to 12th

Street. He was walking along and Jay came up behind him, called to him. All Jay said was what I told you. Then he disappeared. Went down an alley, walking really fast."

"When was this?"

"Yesterday. Howler came right away and told me about it."

"Howler?" I asked.

"That's what everybody calls him. I don't even know his real name. Kyle maybe, but I'm not sure."

"Okay, Zoe, we appreciate the information, but that's not why we're here. We think you need to take some precautions."

"Precautions?"

"We think the guys who are after Jay might know about this place. If we're right and if they come around looking for him, you could be in danger. Especially if they figure out you and Jay are friends. These people aren't somebody to mess with. They'll get what they want and they won't care who's in the line of fire."

"What makes you think they know about this place?"

"We've been watching the building. For that very reason. But we can't be here or with you all the time. It might be best if you went somewhere else for a while."

"You've been spying on me."

"If we'd wanted to spy on you we'd have followed you. We haven't done that. We were watching your place because we're concerned about your safety."

"I'm not leaving here."

"Listen, Zoe, I get why you want to stay here. But Jay isn't going to be coming by. He told you that himself in that message. And if you do stay here and these guys come around, *Killer* in there," Cobb nodded in the direction of the other room, "isn't going to protect you."

"Do you have a place you could maybe go for a few days?" I asked.

She studied the floor for several seconds, then looked up and nodded slowly. "I guess so. How soon would I need to leave?"

"Right away is best," Cobb said.

"Right away?"

"As in now. We can help you pack up your stuff and give you a ride. Zoe, it's really important that we get you out of here ... now. And that you don't tell anyone where you're going. Not the man down the hall, not your friends, definitely not Batman and Robin." Another glance at the door to the other room.

"You know, calling them names doesn't make you a bigger man." Zoe looked at Cobb.

He looked at her, then nodded. "You're right. Sarcasm's a character flaw of mine. I appreciate that you pointed it out to me." He smiled an apology and I think he meant it. "It's really important that you keep a low profile for a while."

"How long?"

"I don't know."

"And if you find Jay?"

"You'll be the first to know. That's a promise."

Zoe said, "I need a couple of hours to at least set things up with the people I'm going to stay with. I can't just drop in on them."

"Fine," Cobb nodded. "Anything we can do? Give you a lift over there?"

"Uh-uh. I don't want to show up with a strange guy

who's old enough to be my dad and ask if I can move in for a while."

I could see Cobb fighting off a smile. "I understand … I think."

"Just let me go talk to the people I'm going to stay with, then I'll come back here and get my stuff. Meet me here in two hours and I'll be ready to go."

"I've been married for nineteen years, Zoe. My wife's been ready when she said she was going to be maybe twice in all that time."

Zoe laughed at that. "I'll be ready when you get back here."

"See you in two hours." Cobb pulled a twenty out of his pocket, unfolded it, and handed it to Zoe. "Do me a favour and give this to those two. Tell them to get some breakfast. They've got real good pancakes at the Harley Diner."

She looked at the twenty. I could see she was thinking about handing it back to him — one of those *we don't need your charity* moments. But if that's what she was thinking she didn't say it. Instead she pocketed the money, nodded, and smiled at Cobb. "What about me? I just might be hungry too, you know."

Cobb grinned. "No time right now. You need to get moving. We'll take you for something to eat on the way to the other place. Two hours." Zoe was already heading for the other room. We left her place, worked our way along the hall, down the stairs, and back to the Jeep.

Cobb had just hit the automatic unlock button on his key ring when the Beach Boys' "Help Me Rhonda" announced that someone was calling his cell phone. He pulled it from a jacket pocket, said "Hello," then listened. He turned and walked away from me. Private call.

He came walking back a couple of minutes later looking serious.

"Bad news?"

He shook his head. "Listen, Adam, I was ... wondering if you could do me a favour."

"I'll do my best. What's up?"

"That was my wife. I forgot we're supposed to meet with Pete's teachers this morning. He's doing the rebellious thing and not exactly lighting it up in school. I haven't been around much since this thing with Blevins started. This is kind of a command performance and with all the —"

"No need for explanations. What can I do to help?"

"Any chance you could pick up Zoe in a couple of hours? Load up her stuff and get her to her new place?"

"Sure," I said. "No problem. I might just grab a nap for an hour and I'll be fresh as a daisy."

"Are you sure this is okay? It feels like you're doing more than your share here."

"Hey, I majored in moving when I was in college. If it wasn't me it was one of my friends, seemed like every week. I hate to let those hard-earned university skills go to waste."

Cobb smiled and nodded. "Let's go. I'll drop you at your car."

It wasn't the best sleep I'd ever had and it definitely wasn't the longest, but when the two alarm clocks and my cell phone alarm went off, almost in unison, I woke up feeling better than I thought I would. A twenty minute shower-and-shave later, I looked in the mirror. Not what I'd call good-as-new, but an improvement over what I'd looked like pre-nap.

I stopped at a Second Cup on the way back to the warehouse. I picked up four cups of coffee and fixings and pulled up opposite the warehouse with about five minutes to spare. When I hit the third floor without spilling any of the coffee or dropping anything, I was feeling pretty good about myself.

The sense of contentment disappeared about halfway down the hall. I stopped before I got to the door to Zoe's place. There was something wrong. First of all, the door was open. It had been closed all of the times Cobb and I had been there previously.

And it was quiet. Way too quiet. No music coming from the DVD player. No voices. No low hum from the space heaters.

No sound.

I set the coffees down in the hall and eased my way to the door.

I reached for my cell phone and realized I'd left it in the car. Stupid. I looked around for a two-by-four, a piece of metal, anything that I might be able to use for protection once I moved through that door.

There was nothing. I shook myself. "Come on," I said barely aloud, trying to will myself some confidence.

My whispered words seemed to echo off the wall at the end of the hall. I edged forward, closer to the door. Then closer still, trying to stretch my neck forward so I could get a look inside and still somehow keep the rest of my body out in the hall.

As I passed the door's edge I was able to see inside. I could only see the part of the room that was straight ahead. The window looking out at the street below. The sleeping bags were gone, the ecstasy too.

I forced myself to breathe. Once. Twice. Unpleasant smell — I wasn't sure what it was.

I stepped into the room, looking first to the left. Nothing. Messier than before but that was all. I turned.

And saw the blood. Realized that was the smell. I moved forward, careful not to step in it. I knew I had to look behind the door that was blocking my view of that part of the room, the part where the blood seemed to have come from. And except for the night of the fire I have never dreaded more having to look at something I knew I didn't want to see.

But I looked. And instantly felt the bile burning upwards into my throat. I fought the urge to vomit. I looked up at the ceiling and forced myself to take deep breaths, first one, then another. I looked back down at what had been, just a few hours before, a kid named Owen. A boy in his teens, trying to be tough, to stand up to a stranger — and for a friend.

I felt the horror taking over inside me — crushing, hysterical horror — and I knew I was losing control, that I was panicking, even as I told myself *not* to panic, to stay calm, to think, to reason. Not to scream, which was the thing I most wanted to do.

I had to keep breathing. More deep breaths.

I wasn't sure how long I stood there, not moving but for the heaving of my chest. Maybe a minute, maybe two. Finally I looked again at the horror on the floor. It was hard to know where exactly the blood had come from, what parts of him had been stabbed or slashed. Maybe the throat. But lower too — the chest and maybe the stomach.

Owen's unseeing eyes seemed to be fixed on the blood, as they had probably been, watching as the life flowed out of him onto a barren warehouse floor.

I looked slowly at the closed door to the other room. I was shaking, shaking violently, and I couldn't stop. I had to open that door and look in the other room. And I knew that if the killer or killers were in there, opening that door would be the last thing I ever did. Or I could find myself looking at more death — at Owen's girlfriend Jen. Or Zoe. Or both of them.

Yet even as those thoughts overwhelmed me, there was a part of me — of my mind — that seemed to be coming back. I was at least able to think, consider what I had to do. It was that part of my mind that told me not to touch anything.

I raised an elbow and pushed on the door. It slowly drifted open.

The room was empty. No, that was wrong. There were no people, alive or dead, in the room. But it wasn't empty. I'd remembered the first time Cobb and I had been in the place, how Zoe had tried to make the most impossible of spaces into something at least a little orderly.

This room was not orderly now; it was a shambles. Broken pieces of dishes and glass, a mattress that had been cut or torn into small bits of fabric and smashed coils scattered around the floor, a dresser with its drawers strewn around the room, clothing ripped into pieces … that was the room now.

But I didn't see bodies or even blood and for several seconds tried to make sense of what I *was* seeing. None of it felt real.

Cobb. I had to get to Cobb, let him deal with this. He was the detective. He could try to find meaning in all of this — understand it.

I had to get out of the building. I took two steps

backward and turned. I went by Owen's body without looking at him again. I stopped at the door, hesitating, wondering if there was something I should do before I left. I couldn't think of anything. Without touching the handle, I gently closed the door, pathetically, like I was trying not to waken someone who was sleeping.

I shook my head and began to walk, forcing myself not to run. And then I heard it.

A sound. I wasn't sure what. Muffled … a hiccup or sob … something … from over there. To my right. I walked as quietly as I could to where I thought I'd heard the sound. It seemed to have come from the place next door.

The killer or killers? No, whoever had destroyed Owen wouldn't be hiding from a lone, unarmed man. I was counting on that. If I was wrong …

When Cobb and I had come here the first time we hadn't looked in there. There'd been no signs of anyone having been there. Ever. Or at least since this incarnation of the building had come into existence.

Yet I was sure that a sound, almost surely a human sound, had come from behind the door that was hanging from a couple of hinges. I pried it far enough open to allow me to look inside. Still nothing. And no recurrence of the noise, whatever it had been.

I manoeuvred my way inside. It was dark but the darkness wasn't total. I could see well enough to allow me to survey the room. Nothing to indicate it was, or had been inhabited by anything more than whatever crawled the ceilings, walls, and floors of an all but abandoned warehouse.

I turned to go … and heard the sound again, not more than a few steps from where I was standing. It seemed to be coming from the vicinity of where I guessed the kitchen sink would have been located if the building had been completed. Just a space and some pipes were there. And below that several large pieces of cardboard leaning against the wall. No, not against the wall. They were leaning against some framing jutting out from the wall, meaning that there was a space behind the cardboard and below the space for the sink.

A space large enough for …

I pushed the cardboard aside in one motion and found myself looking at two people crouched down. My mind had been working overtime since I'd found Owen, and now it strangely remembered the scene in the movie *A Christmas Carol* where the Ghost of Christmas Present pulls aside his robe and shows Scrooge the two poor and starving orphans.

There *were* two people in the space and they did look like the two people in the movie. But they weren't orphans, at least not *child* orphans. I reached out my hand. Zoe was the first to take it and allow me to pull her out of the space. Then I helped Jen out of there and to her feet as well.

There was blood over the front of the hoodie she was wearing and some on her hands as well.

"Are you hurt?" I kept my voice to barely more than a whisper.

She shook her head and I guessed she had gone to Owen in some kind of effort to help him. It was obvious that it had been Jen who had been doing the sobbing. And now as she realized that she wasn't in immediate danger, the sobs became louder. I put my arm around her shoulder and she leaned against me, shaking.

"Come on," I said. "We need to get out of here."

I steered Jen toward the stairs with Zoe making sure she was right beside me. None of us spoke and Jen seemed to be regaining control. The sobs became intermittent.

We reached the bottom of the stairs and stopped. I raised my finger to my lips.

"Let me make sure we're okay before we go out there."

I poked my head out the door and peered around before stepping completely outside. I couldn't see anything or anyone that raised alarm bells and the only sounds were from distant machinery performing some kind of industrial tasks.

I stepped back inside. "Okay, my car is across the street. It looks clear out there so let's go there together, get in, and get the hell out of here."

"But what about…?" Zoe's eyes flicked upwards in the direction of her rooms.

"We'll deal with that once we know we're safe and away from here."

She nodded and Jen grabbed my arm. She was still shaking. I wanted to say something reassuring but couldn't imagine what might be appropriate in the face of what they had seen in the minutes just passed.

"Let's go," I said and led them out into the daylight.

We hurried to the Accord. Zoe and Jen scrambled into the back seat as I threw myself behind the steering wheel and we roared off. I spent most of the first few blocks looking in the rearview mirror and taking several turns and even a couple of U-turns to thwart any potential tails. But after ten minutes or so, I slowed it down and looked for some place to stop and regroup.

I chose the parking lot of a Starbucks on 11th Avenue, just out of the downtown area. I turned to look at

Jen, who had her head tilted back on the seat, then at Zoe, who was watching me.

"Okay, I need you to tell me what happened. Cobb will want details, but give me the condensed version."

Zoe nodded, spoke slowly. "Well, I went off to talk to the people I'm going to stay with. Owen and Jen headed for the restaurant to have that breakfast and we were going to meet on the way back here. But in the middle of breakfast, Owen remembered that he'd left his ID at my place. He got so worked up about it, Jen told him to run back and get it and come back to the restaurant."

She took a deep breath and looked at Jen, who was crying again, this time silently and with her hand over her face. "When he didn't come back she waited and met me and we went back together. They were going to help me pack up my stuff and be ready for when you got there to pick me up. But when we ... went into ... my ..." she faltered. "You saw ... what we saw."

"Did you see anyone else?

She shook her head. "We freaked. Jen tried to lift Owen but then we heard someone coming so we hid. We thought it might be whoever had ... but it was you."

I nodded and took a twenty out of my wallet. "Okay, go get us three coffees. The biggest they've got."

For some reason I figured coffee was the thing that would most help Jen right at that moment.

"I have to call Cobb and see how he wants us to handle this."

Zoe nodded, looked at Jen, then hurried into the Starbucks.

I pulled my coat off, reached back, and wrapped it around Jen, who was still shaking. I cranked up the heat

DAVID A. POULSEN

in the Accord, pulled out my phone, and called Cobb, hoping like hell he was out of his meeting at the school. He answered on the second ring.

I only got as far as telling him Owen was dead and the girls were with me. He interrupted me. "Where are you?"

When I told him, he barked, "Don't move. Don't talk to anybody. I'll be there in twenty minutes."

It was probably less than that but by the time Cobb got there, Zoe and I had managed to look after a few things. While the girls drank coffee, I had run across the street to a consignment store and bought a couple of changes of clothes and some towels I'd wet down in the store's washroom.

It was contrary to Cobb's instructions but I didn't think he'd object.

Jen was relatively cleaned up, had changed, and was at least somewhat composed when Cobb pulled in behind me. Zoe and I were drinking coffee. Jen hadn't touched hers. Cobb pulled open the passenger door and slid in.

He looked at me, then swung around to look at each of the girls in turn. "Okay, first of all, is everybody okay?"

The girls nodded and I pointed to the pile of bloody clothing on the floor of the back seat. "Jen came in contact with Owen. We got her cleaned up."

Cobb took some time to think about that, finally nodded. "Okay, I need to hear it again. From the beginning."

Zoe, as she had the first time, did the talking. Cobb listened until she got to the part where she and Jen were walking back to the warehouse.

"What time was that?"

"I think it was around two-thirty."

"Where did you two meet?"

"In front of the motorcycle restaurant."

"Then what?" Cobb said.

"We walked back to my … the place," Zoe said. "Jen was worried that we'd miss Owen and I told her he'd probably be stoned or sleeping." She looked hard at Cobb. "Who did that to him?"

"We don't know yet. Okay, you got back to the building, then what?"

"We came in the back way, which is the only way in and out. I guess you know that."

Cobb nodded.

"Then we went up to our floor —"

Cobb held up his hand. "Let's back up a second. Did you notice any vehicles parked on the street?"

The girls looked at each other and shook their heads in unison.

"I … we were like … talking. I don't know if we were paying that much attention to what was on the street, you know?"

"How about across the street or down the street a ways?"

"Uh-uh," Zoe said.

"What about people? Anybody walk by?"

"I didn't see anybody." She looked at Jen, who shook her head again.

"Okay, you went inside. Anything look different? Sounds, smells, anything?"

"I don't think so."

"Jen?"

"I … I didn't notice anything."

"Okay, go on."

"We were talking all the way up the stairs. Everything was all like normal. We got to my place and the door was closed. I pushed it open and Jen called to Owen. We didn't see him at first, but then …" She looked down for a minute then raised her eyes to meet Cobb's. "If those people find Jay before you do —"

"We'll find him," Cobb said. He turned slightly to face Jen. "You came in contact with Owen. Did you move him?"

"No … well, maybe his arm. I wanted him to get up. I thought …" She broke into sobs again and Zoe pulled her closer and wrapped her arms around Jen's shoulders. I thought she'd done well to be as composed as she was for this long.

Cobb waited, his jaw working up and down.

Jen sniffed and sat up straight, making an obvious effort to regain control. A minute or so and she was ready to continue.

"I think I moved his arm," she said again.

"Okay, then what?"

"I wanted to hold him, to kiss his face, because by then I knew he was dead, but … I couldn't. I couldn't even —" The sobs came again and Zoe reached for her a second time.

"Jen," Cobb said, "no one could have done more than you did."

I looked at Cobb. The look on his face as he leaned forward over the seat, as if to be closer to Jen, was equal parts genuine sadness and tightly controlled anger.

"Did either of you go in the other room? The back room?" I asked.

Cobb looked at me, eyebrows raised.

"That room was trashed," I said. "Stuff thrown around, everything kind of torn apart."

Cobb said, "Like the killers had been looking for something."

"We didn't go back there," Zoe replied. "I pulled Jen up to her feet and told her we had to get out of there right away in case the killers were still somewhere in the building or maybe coming back."

"And that's when you heard me coming."

Zoe nodded. "Which is when we hid in the place next door. When we were in there we could hear someone looking around in my place but we didn't know who it was or even how many people it was. And we were afraid if we tried to run they'd get us and …" She looked at me. "We didn't know it was you. Thank God it was."

Cobb turned to me. "Okay, your turn."

I wish I could say I was the ideal, very observant witness. I was not. Truth is I was as shaken as the two girls had been by what I'd seen on the third floor of that warehouse.

I went over it all again, and other than describing in more detail the destruction I'd seen in the back room, I didn't add much to what we knew.

"When you looked back there, did you get the feeling they were searching for something, as opposed to, say, straight vandalism?"

I thought about my answer, trying to recall what I'd seen. I nodded tentatively. "I think so. There wasn't crap written on the walls or anything. It just looked like everything had been either torn apart or thrown around."

Cobb looked at Zoe, who responded without hesitation. "I'm not exactly a neatness freak but that was where

I slept most of the time. It didn't look like what he's describing when I left there this morning."

Cobb didn't say anything for a few minutes. It looked like he was gathering his thoughts. "Okay, here's the deal. No one goes back there unless and until I give the word. The bad guys could come back there any time and we've seen what they can do. Don't think they'll take it easy with you because you're females or because you don't know where Jay is — if that's what this was about.

"We have to let the police know. I'll go there and see if there's anything I can learn, then I'll phone the cops and tell them I just discovered the body. That's probably going to tie me up for a while answering questions."

"Like why were you there in the first place?" I asked.

"Yeah, like that."

"And your answer would be…?"

"I'm still working on that. In the meantime, can you take Zoe to her new place?" He looked at her. "Was the name of the people you're going to stay with or their address, anything that might lead these guys there, anything like that around your place?"

She held up her purse. "In here. That's the only place I have it."

"Good. Then you'll be safe. And Jen, the police are going to identify Owen. In fact, it's probably best if I tell them who he is. That means they may come looking for you. Where have you and Owen been staying?"

"At a shelter up in Renfrew. But we were probably going to be kicked out of there because they have a zero tolerance on drugs and Owen …" Her voice trailed off.

Cobb nodded. "The cops might be able to track

you there, which means you might have to answer some questions."

"Or she could stay with me," Zoe interjected. "The Callaghans are really nice and I know they wouldn't mind. They're basically giving me a room in the basement of their house. They said I could stay as long as I want. And Jen and I could share the room … at least for a while."

"Okay, that should work. Have you still got our cell numbers?"

She nodded. "But that's all I have."

"What do you mean?"

"All my stuff, clothes, everything is back there." She nodded in the direction of the warehouse.

"Sorry, but what I said before still stands. No one goes near that warehouse."

"Which is why God invented Value Village," I said.

Jen was crying softly and Zoe put an arm around her. Jen looked at each of us through tear-filled eyes. "This doesn't seem right. We're all carrying on like nothing happened to Owen. Like he isn't dead. But he is."

Cobb gave her a minute before he said anything. "You're right, Jen. This stinks. But it's not that we want to just forget about what happened to Owen. We don't have any choice. These are very dangerous people and the first thing we have to do is make sure you two are going to be safe.

"As soon as that's looked after, I'm going to do everything I can to make sure the people who did this to Owen pay the price for it. I promise you that."

Jen sniffed and offered a slight nod.

"We better get started," I said. "Mr. Cobb has some things he needs to get on with."

Cobb looked at me. "You okay with this or …" He started to reach for his wallet.

"I'm good. It's been a long time since I've been shopping with a couple of teenage girls. We'll stop by the shelter to get Jen's stuff, then make a Value Village run, and I'll drop the girls at the new place."

"Buy Zoe a cell phone and a pay-as-you-go card. I'll pay for it." I opened my mouth to object but he held up a hand to stop me. "And there's one more thing," Cobb said. "We need to let Owen's family know. The cops will do it too, but I think it might be better coming from someone else."

Jen shook her head. "There is no family. Owen's mom put him in foster care when he was thirteen. He only saw her a couple of times after that and not at all in the last few years. He tried to phone her last Christmas. The phone was disconnected and he had no idea where she ended up."

"What about his father? Any brothers or sisters?"

"Owen never knew his father. Once he told me he didn't think his mother knew him either. If there were brothers or sisters, Owen didn't know them either. I think … he … stopped caring." The tears flowed again though she tried to muffle her sobs. Again Zoe offered her shoulder and stroked Jen's hair as she cried.

"You better go," I told Cobb. "We're okay here."

Cobb looked me. "I appreciate all of this." He looked at each of the girls in turn, though I'm not sure either of them noticed, then he got out of the car and moved off in a hurry.

I spent the next couple of hours helping the girls get sorted and settled.

First, there was a stop at the shelter on Child Avenue in Renfrew, then the shopping trip — Value Village, then London Drugs for a phone and the personal items the girls would need. I learned a few things about them. Or at least about Zoe. Jen had pretty much shut down. Going through the motions. Trying to put on a brave face. It wasn't working and I couldn't blame her.

Zoe was clearly stunned by what had happened to Owen but there was real anger there too. She was in fighting mode. And for her the first part of the fight was to get all her ducks in a row. She seldom took her eyes off Jen for more than a few seconds. It was clear that she had taken on the role of big sister.

Eventually we made our way to the place Zoe had arranged for — the Callaghans'. It was in the Tuxedo area, not all that far north of downtown. It was the all-Canadian family storey-and-a-half, fenced backyard, deck with a barbecue and snow-covered deck chairs, dormant flower beds in the front yard. If there was a place these girls might be safe, I figured this was the place.

If nobody screwed up.

I helped them load their stuff from the Accord up to the house. I didn't go inside. I wasn't sure how much Zoe had told the people who lived there and thought it might complicate things for her to have to explain who I was.

Nobody talked much and Zoe and I did most of the carrying. Jen managed to get a couple of smaller packages up to the house, but beyond that she mostly sat on the steps and stared at the ground.

"You think you'll be okay with Jen?" I asked Zoe as we gathered the last few items from the car.

"We'll be okay." She nodded. Definite.

"I believe you," I said.

"I can get those," Zoe said and took a couple of small bags from me.

"Zoe, what Cobb said about being careful ... he wasn't kidding."

She nodded. "I know."

"Good. You've got my cell number and Cobb's. You call if there's anything at all you think might not be right, okay?"

"Okay."

"For the record, Jay is missing out on an amazing young woman."

She managed a half smile. "I better go."

"Right." I turned to the car.

"Adam?"

I turned back to her.

"It's ... I don't think I've thanked you and Cobb. I just want ..."

I waved my arm. "You just take care of yourselves."

I glanced toward the house. Jen was still sitting on the steps but she had looked up, watching us. I waved but she didn't wave back. I looked back at Zoe. She'd turned and was walking quickly back to the front steps ... and Jen.

I climbed into the Accord, looked in the back seat to make sure the girls hadn't forgotten anything, and drove off. Back to the sanity and sanctity of my apartment.

A half hour later I was there. I dropped my coat and gloves on the hide-a-bed, adjusted the thermostat, and walked to the window that looked out on the street. I stood for a long while, watching the occasional vehicle and a few pedestrians going by in both directions. Thinking about a world I'd written about and seen from the outside.

I was realizing how little I had really understood that world. Until now. And it scared me that kids like Jay Blevins and Zoe and Jen were part of it. And that a kid named Owen had been.

I turned from the window and stepped back into my living room/bedroom. I stopped at the stereo and stared at the stack of albums and discs for a long time. Nothing seemed right for what I was feeling, but I finally settled on Oscar Peterson with Joe Pass, a favourite and for tonight — charms to sooth the savage breast.

I hauled out Donna's photo albums, poured myself an Alberta Premium and Diet Coke, and settled on the couch, determined to make another pass through the last two albums that night. I didn't last twenty minutes before falling asleep. I woke up a couple of hours later three pages into the eleventh grade album and with a serious kink in my neck. I set the albums on the floor and stumbled off to bed, Peterson and Pass gentle in the background.

Bad, bad day.

TWELVE

A peach yoghurt, a bowl of Shreddies, two cups of coffee, and I was ready to start the day. I took Donna's grade eleven photo album, the one that had fewer pages than any of the others and, trying not to spill my too-full coffee mug en route, made my way to the balcony to enjoy one of those spring-in-December Calgary mornings that make winter in this city more than tolerable.

I forced my mind not to think about Jay and Zoe and the MFs and kids with addictions and concentrated on the pages of the album much harder than I had the first time through, first noticing only the obvious, that there was much less content in this book. I'd given the grade twelve album a cursory glance while I ate the Shreddies and it confirmed what I already suspected — that the grade eleven book was an anomaly. Donna's senior year album wasn't as extensive as the earlier ones, but it was far larger than the grade eleven album.

All of them were.

Did that mean anything? Surely there wasn't some prescribed number of photos, some carved-in-stone amount of material needed to make the process valid. Still, why the discrepancy?

As I'd examined the earlier albums, I'd tried to mentally catalogue the photos according to type. It seemed to me there were two categories more or less: Occasions/Activities and Fun Stuff. I'd even made notes and calculations based on my arbitrary classifications.

The first category was made up of pictures associated with Donna being involved with something; there were a few of her playing piano at recitals and receiving awards for her playing. The strange part was that I didn't know Donna played piano. We'd never owned one and she'd never mentioned that she played, even though, judging from the photos, it appeared that the piano had been an important part of her life when she was in school.

There were other occasions too: a provincial volleyball championship (I did hear about that), a couple of academic awards, and one of Donna getting a trophy at the Calgary Music Festival, but not for piano. The carefully handwritten caption informed the reader that she had received a certificate for her recitation of the Alfred Noyes poem, "The Highwayman."

But it wasn't just about awards and achievements. There was a picture of Donna hanging a poster for someone named Trudy Mock who was running for vice president of the students' union; there were a couple of Donna and several classmates building a snow sculpture at the winter carnival. A lot of these pictures showed Donna and others enjoying school and after-school moments. I had to stop a few times, look away from the albums, and sip my coffee.

The "Fun Stuff" group was what you'd expect: people laughing, being silly, mugging for the camera. Mostly pictures of girls, a few with guys. Sometimes Donna was in the pictures with her friends but most of the time she wasn't. It seemed likely that she had taken a lot of those pictures herself.

I calculated that in most of the yearbooks, the breakdown was consistent — about one third focused on occasions and activities with the balance, two thirds, devoted to fun stuff. Until grade eleven.

The change that happened that year wasn't only in the dramatic drop in the number of pictures taken but also in the kinds of pictures. The percentages were altered — drastically. In fact, virtually reversed. What photos of friends there were had a different feel to them. They were more serious and in some cases almost sombre. And something else. No music pictures. None. Had Donna given up playing the piano that year?

Maybe the whole thing was as Cobb had suggested — all hormonal. Donna was going through the mental and physical changes that were part of being a teenager, the angst and rebellion that made for fewer smiles, less laughter … and no music.

The grade twelve album was closer to the pre-grade eleven books in both content and tone. The surprise this time was that music did not seem to reappear in Donna's life. Or at least the pictures of her involvement with music that were part of the earlier albums remained as in absentia from the grade twelve book as they had from the one for grade eleven.

So what did it all mean? Even coupled with the note and my conversation with Kelly McKercher Nolan, maybe nothing. *Probably* nothing.

So why was there this knot in my gut that kept telling there was something out there I was missing?

I fired up my computer and on a whim checked flights to Phoenix. I could leave the next morning. Not a bad price,

I knew where my passport was, and it didn't look like I'd be involved in the search for Jay Blevins, at least not for a while.

I picked up my cell phone, called Cobb. He answered after two rings.

I said, "Why aren't you sleeping?"

"I did that. Fresh as a daisy. How about you?"

"I'm good. The girls seemed okay too when I left them. Any Jay sightings?"

"Nothing. I'm doing the street guy thing, hanging out in the hood, so taking calls on my cell phone isn't great for my cover. What's up?"

"I'll be quick. I just wanted you to talk me out of flying down to Phoenix to talk to Donna's high school pal, Kelly."

"How much is a flight?"

"Under four hundred bucks. Seat sale."

"So you have to ask yourself how much your peace of mind is worth. You go there — maybe you find something. Or you go there and Kelly wasn't holding back and you learn nothing but you hang out in the sun for a couple of days and miss a cold front that's supposed to be coming in. High tomorrow of minus thirteen. If it's me, I'm on the flight. Peace of mind."

"I said you were supposed to talk me out of this."

"Gotta go, some guys are coming this way. I want to talk to them. Enjoy Arizona."

I stared at the phone for a couple of minutes before I went back to my computer, to the Environment Canada site. Cobb hadn't been lying — a system was on its way: north wind, gusts to seventy klicks, temperature dropping.

I Googled the Duke Golf Course and learned that Maricopa is less than an hour south and east of Sky Harbor, the airport in Phoenix. An expensive but not impossible cab ride.

I found Wes Nolan's name on the Contact Us page. No home address — no surprise. I called Arizona information and was asked by an eager-to-please operator if I wanted Mr. Nolan's number or address. I requested both, got them, and, after another Google search, had tracked Wes and Kelly Nolan to 814 West Neely Drive in a subdivision just minutes from the golf course. I'd even written out the directions to their home from the airport.

I bought a WestJet ticket online — leaving the next morning at 10:50 a.m., arriving a little over three hours later.

I had some time to kill. I picked up the phone, stared at it for a long minute, then dialled the number of Let the Sunshine Inn. A voice, very not-Jill-Sawley, answered. Celia maybe. The voice didn't say the whole name of the place.

"Hello, Sunshine Shelter."

"I wonder if I could speak to Jill, if she's in."

"She's with someone right now."

"You think she'll be long?"

"Couldn't say."

"Can I leave a message?"

"I guess so."

I resisted the temptation to say something I'd later regret. "Could you have her call Adam Cullen when she gets a minute?"

Long pause. "She have your number?"

"I think so, but maybe I'll leave it just in case."

"Sure."

She didn't say anything and I wasn't sure if I was supposed to recite the number or wait until she found a pen and paper or what. I gambled, gave her the number.

"Okay," she said.

"Okay, then," I said. "Thanks."

Celia or whoever it was hung up the phone. Maybe she was the screening device for the shelter. If that was her job, she was very good at it.

I cradled the phone, turned on the TV, and watched maybe ten minutes of the news, just enough to remind me that we were all going to die of either the ravages of climate change or a damn good war. All of which was cheerier than watching the media scrum with the prime minister in the halls of the House of Commons as he defended still more cuts to arts funding.

I turned off the TV, thought about putting on some music, but didn't. The phone rang and I picked up. It was Jill.

"Hey, thanks for getting back to me. I wasn't confident you'd get the message. I'm not sure Celia thinks I'm someone who can be trusted."

Jill laughed. "If you heard some of the calls we get here, you'd know why she isn't a little more cordial on the phone. Consider yourself fortunate you didn't get to feel the full force of the Celian wrath."

"My lucky day. Anyway, I thought I'd give you an update on where we're at with finding Jay. Have you got a minute?"

"I've got lots of minutes. I just wrapped up my shift here."

I paused. Was there an invitation there? *So if you want to have dinner ...*

Or was it just a comment and if I did ask her to dinner I'd look like an idiot. I debated the two possibilities long enough that she finally said, "Hello? You still there?"

"Yeah, sorry, still here. I was just thinking that maybe I could give you that update over something to eat, you know, if you didn't have other plans."

"I'd love that. But would it be all right if I went home and showered first? You've been here, you've smelled the place. I could be ready in an hour, well maybe an hour and a quarter."

"That's great. I'll pick you up in seventy-five minutes."

She told me the address; she lived in Glamorgan, in the southwest quadrant of the city. Middle-class neighbourhood, not fancy but nice. I hung up and this time actually put on the music. Emily Spiller. I'd bought the CD a couple of weeks before but it was still in the wrapper. I sat back down and for twenty minutes let the Vancouver singer's voice fill the room. Upbeat. Like my mood had suddenly become.

By the time I pulled up in front of Jill's house, my frame of mind had pendulumed back to just north of anxious, a little this side of terrified. The house was an older bungalow surrounded on both sides by in-fills. It looked sixties vintage, with blue siding, a large living room window facing the street and an uncomplicated but well-tended front yard. A light blue Dodge Caravan sat in a driveway in front of an attached garage to the right of the house.

I sat for a minute, wondering if this was a bad idea, checking the mirror on the off-chance that I'd magically developed Robert Redford looks during the drive to Jill's house. I hadn't but was comforted by the fact that Boris Karloff wasn't looking back at me either.

Finally I stepped out of the Accord and walked up the walk, climbed the three stairs to the front door, pressed the doorbell, heard it chime inside.

Jill came to the door and opened it, smiling. She looked great. Her hair was hanging loose and over the collar of a dark blue turtleneck. Informal but not so casual that our only option was fast food. She pulled the door inward and stepped to one side to allow me to enter.

"Hi."

I stepped in, turned to her, and said, "Hi, you look terrific."

"Thank you. Come in." She closed the door and gestured toward the couch. "Have we got time for a drink before we go or do we have a reservation somewhere?"

"No reservation. I didn't know what you liked so I thought I'd check, then phone."

"Toss your coat on that chair and have a seat. I'll mix us a drink and we can make a serious dining decision."

I dropped my coat on the chair she'd indicated — I liked the casualness of that — and sat on the couch, a pillow-backed brown leather piece that had been around long enough to be soft and deceptively comfortable.

"What can I get you?"

"Have any rye?"

"Crown Royal."

"You said the magic words. A little Diet Coke if you have it. Can I help?"

She shook her head. "I won't be a minute. Just relax."

She went into the kitchen and I could hear her fixing the drinks over Coldplay on the stereo. I looked around. The living room had almost a country feel — hardwood floor, throw rugs that looked a little southwestern, but the pictures on the walls spoke of other things, other places. There was a photo I recognized of Montmartre in Paris, a stylized poster of a museum collection in New York City, and a painting of an island sunset that was stunning.

A desk stood off to one side of the room. It was piled high with what looked like textbooks.

Jill was true to her word. She was back with the drinks before Chris Martin could get through "Square One." She handed me my drink and sat on the couch. I said thanks but she didn't answer. Instead she giggled and put her finger to her lips. Then called, "You can come out now. He's here."

Nothing for ten seconds, maybe fifteen. Then a small head peeked around the door of the first room down the hall.

Kyla.

"Well, come on, you can't just stand there staring. Adam will think you're rude."

The little face and the body that went with it came the rest of the way out of the bedroom and moved down the hall toward us. Kyla's eyes never left my face until she got to the living room. She sat on the arm of the couch on the other side of Jill.

Shy. But not afraid or anti-social.

"I hear you're eight years old," I said.

She nodded and looked disapprovingly at her mother. Like being eight wasn't something you told just anybody.

"Kyla, this is Adam."

"Hi," I said trying not to be over-the-top friendly in that way some adults have of speaking to kids that aren't their own. The same voice they use when talking to someone's pet schnauzer.

"Hi," Kyla said softly. She had Jill's mouth and eyes but, at least so far, seemed more serious than her mother.

I reached into my pocket and pulled out a copy of *The Spoofaloof Rally*, held it out to her. "I brought you something."

She stepped forward, accepted the book, and retreated to beside her mother again.

Jill said softly, "What do you say?"

"Thank you."

"You're welcome, Kyla. I hope you like it. I wrote it about three years ago."

"You wrote a book?" Jill said. "You didn't tell me that."

"It wasn't a *Globe and Mail* bestseller. Besides, I was saving it for tonight's conversation. Now I don't know what we'll talk about."

Jill laughed and she and Kyla flipped the pages of the book. "That is so cool."

I wasn't sure Kyla shared her mother's enthusiasm but after a couple of minutes of looking through the book, she looked up at me.

"The Spoofaloof Rally is a race." She was smiling.

"Uh-huh. But not a car race. And not for people."

"For hippopotamuses."

"Right."

"Hippopotamuses can't go very fast."

"The race takes a long time."

"Is this book funny?"

"I hope so."

"Mommy, can I go read it?"

"PJs and into bed. Anya will be here in a few minutes. You can read for fifteen minutes. Then lights out."

Kyla took off for her room, skidded to a stop at the door, and looked back at me. "Thank you, Adam."

"I hope you like it," I said a second time.

She grinned at me and disappeared into her room, the door slamming behind her.

Jill held her drink up in a salute. "I'd say Adam Cullen, writer of children's books, has a brand new devoted reader."

I clinked glasses with her. "That makes a total of one."

"I somehow doubt that."

"So what'll it be? Chinese? Italian? Or are you a meat and potatoes girl?"

"All of the above. There's a nice Asian place not far from here. Amazing salt and pepper shrimp, not all breaded and deep fried … I mean, unless that's how you like it."

"I prefer amazing to totally breaded and deep fried. Should I call for a reservation?"

She glanced at her watch. "I think we'll be fine."

Ten minutes of small talk before Anya, the babysitter, arrived and we gathered coats and gloves and stepped out into the increasingly frosty night.

"I'd have left it running but I had a sense you wouldn't approve," I said as we walked to the car.

"You sensed right," Jill replied. "There's this thing called climate change."

"I've heard of it."

"Wow, a Honda Accord," Jill said. "I used to have one. I loved that car. Perry got it when we split."

"Best heater on the planet. We'll be toasty in a couple of minutes."

I was right about the heater and she was right about the salt and pepper shrimp. After several wonderful bites, I nodded and said, "This place is a gift from the food gods."

"Told you. So tell me about Jay."

"Right. Well, first of all, we haven't found him. Cobb is masquerading as a street person to see if he can get a lead on him."

"Not great news."

"It gets worse." I told her about Zoe and Jen and the murder of Owen Harkness.

When I'd finished she was silent a long minute … not eating, not talking. For long enough that the waiter came to our table.

"Is the food all right?" he asked Jill.

Jill came back from wherever she'd been and said, "Yes, yes, the food is fine. Very good, thank you."

The waiter moved off and Jill looked at me.

"My God, that boy. That is so awful."

I nodded.

"Did you know Owen? He was a user, I'm guessing regular."

She shook her head. She seemed paler than earlier.

"Sorry to have told you this. But I figured you should know where it's at."

She nodded. "I appreciate that."

"Ever hear of a group called the MFs?"

"The MFs … no, I don't think so. That's the actual name, not the Mother —"

"Nope, the MFs. All about political correctness."

"Who are they?"

"Motorcycle gang. They run the house where Jay's old man shot those two dealers. Apparently big players in Calgary's crime scene … and they play rough."

"As in killing Owen Harkness?"

"We don't know that but it would seem to be a strong possibility."

The talk was desultory after that. Then halfway through dinner Jill set her chopsticks down and looked at me.

"I think it's time."

"For?"

"A confession."

"Is this going to ruin our evening? I mean, assuming our earlier topic of conversation hasn't already done that."

"I hope not."

I couldn't tell if she was serious or not. Confessions can be messy. And if Jill was about to announce that she had poisoned a couple of previous husbands or she hated left-handed men or she was an Edmonton Oilers fan, the tone of the evening would definitely be altered.

"Confess away."

"I Googled you."

"That's it? That's your confession?"

"I hope you're not angry."

"Should I be?"

"Well, it's sort of cyber stalking, isn't it?"

"I'm not sure I see it in quite that light. I am surprised you were able to fit in computer time in your seventy-five minutes."

"That wasn't when I Googled you. It was after we went to Starbucks."

I looked at her. "Why?"

"I … I liked you, I guess, and I wasn't sure if you'd actually call me and I wanted to know more about you."

I laughed.

"What?"

"After you left, the lady sitting next to us gave me some advice on communicating with women. Apparently she thought I was pretty hopeless — especially the *Sleepless in Seattle* reference. I guess she misjudged my animal magnetism."

It was Jill's turn to laugh. "Actually, I'd say she had it about right. You *were* pretty hopeless. But I liked you anyway."

"Thanks, that should give the old confidence a boost. So what did you find out?"

"Not a lot. There were a few stories about the fire, a couple that pointed at you as the probable arsonist. And there were a few mentions of things you'd written for the newspaper. Nothing about a kids' book though."

"Like I said, it wasn't a big hit."

"So you've never Googled yourself?"

I shook my head. "I doubt there's anything there I'd care to read."

We went back to eating. After a few minutes I said, "In lieu of Googling, can I ask you a few things? About you?"

"Sure."

"The shelter is a volunteer position. What do you do for a living?"

"I'm a bookkeeper. I do the books for five different smaller companies. It lets me be at home with Kyla and gives me time for my volunteering at the shelter."

"Sounds like a win-win."

"I'd get better money in the accounting department of an oil company but I like the tradeoff of being on my own."

"Tell me about Kyla. She's eight and she's great, but what else?"

"Grade three. Loves school, especially reading and phys ed. She's read all the Harry Potter books, pretty good for eight. I helped her with the later ones — they're a little tougher. She's also watched the DVDs maybe six times each. I think she has a crush on Harry. She's precocious, only shy when she first meets someone. Next time you see her, you'll be her long-lost pal." Awkward silence. "I mean, if there *is* a next time."

I smiled at her.

"I'm flying down to Phoenix tomorrow morning. I'd like to call you when I get back."

"I'd like that. Phoenix … golf holiday?"

"No, not a holiday." I looked at her for several seconds. Made a decision. I told her about Kelly and my wanting to talk to her in person, that it was part of my ongoing search for whoever set the fire that killed Donna. I wondered how she'd react to hearing that.

She ate a small bite of the shrimp, sipped her wine. "I think if I were you, I'd be doing the same thing. I'd want to do whatever I could to find the bastard." She looked around quickly, afraid she might have been a little too loud.

I smiled again. "It might be a giant waste of time."

"Or it might not be."

"I like your attitude. Dessert?"

"I've been told I have a very positive attitude, *especially* about dessert."

We ordered coffee and shared a baked blueberry cheesecake.

Back in the car later and after the Accord's heater had worked its magic, I put a CD in the player. Arcade Fire.

Jill said, "I love them."

"You know Arcade Fire?"

"Of course. Who doesn't?"

We sat and listened while I drove slowly through residential south Calgary. Between tracks she asked, "So what are you into musically? I mean you like these guys, obviously. So are you a rock fan?"

"I guess I like a lot of different kinds of music. Some day I'll have to show you my collection."

"*This* day would be okay."

I looked over at her. "You mean that? You want to stop at my place? I have to warn you, the record collection is about all I've got. I can't show you my etchings because there aren't any."

"No etchings. I'm devastated." She turned in the seat, looked at me. "Adam, I haven't gone out with anyone in a really long time. I have a babysitter who can stay up past eleven and I'd like to see your music collection. Really."

"We can do that."

I signalled to turn left at the next set of lights.

"Wait," she said. "I've got an idea. Why don't we stop and get my car? That way I can follow you to your place and you won't have to drive me home later."

"Somehow that doesn't feel awfully chivalrous on my part."

"It's okay if I offer. It's right there in the first date manual."

"Yeah, but —"

"I know it sounds odd but some of the things I say will sound odd. Or so I've been told. I just think this is a good idea. For both of us."

Good idea, for both of us. What did that mean? I got to thinking that maybe Jill wasn't comfortable with coming to my house without a mechanism for escape if the need arose. Then why did she suggest my place at all? Okay, so maybe she was thinking he seems like a nice guy but just in case this guy actually started that fire …

I was still embroiled in this interior debate as I pulled up in front of her house for the second time that night.

She leaned across the seat and kissed me on the cheek. "I knew you'd understand."

"Actually I'm not sure I do, but if it's what you want I'm fine with it."

"That's even better than understanding."

I handed her a card with my home address on it. "In case we get separated in traffic."

"I've got my keys with me," she said. "Give me a few seconds to let the van warm up and I'll be ready. Oh, and keep the car running." She was out the door and running toward the Dodge Caravan before I had time to respond.

"Keep the Car Running." Pretty good. A song from the Arcade Fire album *Neon Bible*. This was a woman I could get to like.

I watched her climb into the driver's seat, heard the grudging turning over of the van's motor. It kicked to life after a few seconds. She smiled and waved in her side mirror. I waved back and cranked up the music. Drummed my hands on the steering wheel.

Happy.

THIRTEEN

Forty minutes later we were drinking coffee and Tia Maria at the kitchen table. Well, I was at the kitchen table. Jill was sitting on the floor, barefoot, her coffee on the carpet beside her. She was thumbing through the albums and CDs that took up most of the south wall of the apartment. She hadn't spoken in several minutes.

"This is amazing. Do you have every piece of music ever recorded by a Canadian?"

"No. There's an early Don Messer album I'm missing and maybe a Guy Lombardo or two."

"I'm serious — this is unbelievable." Still thumbing.

"There are some who might think of it as freaky."

"I love it. I want to listen to everything here."

"You better hope your babysitter doesn't have to be home for about six months."

She turned to look at me and grinned. "So what should we play?"

"Your call."

"How about some Bachman-Turner Overdrive and Loreena McKennitt? First we rock, then we chill."

I laughed. "Perfect combination."

"But is it sacrilege that I didn't pick Leonard Cohen

or Bruce Cockburn or April Wine or Joni Mitchell or …
oh my God, I love The Duhks."

"I think you better stay with your first choice. You
can get to some of those others next time … I mean if
there *is* a next time."

She stood up, crossed to where I was sitting, and for
the second time that night, kissed me on the cheek.

She resumed her spot on the floor, just long enough
to put the two CDs in. Then she picked up her coffee and
as Randy Bachman and Fred Turner and the rest of the
band poured out the first track of *Not Fragile*, she went
to the window and looked out at the street. Her body
language seemed to convey that she was deep in thought
and I didn't want to interrupt. But when she stayed there
into the next track I walked across the room and stood
beside her.

After a minute she took my hand, held it. "It's nice
here," she said.

"Yeah, I like it."

"Sometimes I think about some of the people I see
in the shelter, people who must have been okay at some
point in their lives, and I wonder why they would prefer
the lives they live now to stuff like this — just ordinary
life stuff that sometimes is pretty great."

"Maybe they never had a shot at the ordinary life
stuff that sometimes is pretty great."

She nodded. "Maybe. But my God, that's sad."

"And for some I guess the pull of that other crap is so
powerful, they just don't see anything else."

"That's even sadder."

"It is."

"Sorry to bring up downer stuff."

"There's no rules on conversation topics. I checked that first date manual myself."

She smiled and we moved to the couch/hide-a-bed that I congratulated myself on having made up that morning. Folded up, it made the room look a little bigger and more inviting and even conveyed the image that I was domestically organized, which was the case maybe 10 percent of the time.

By the time Loreena McKennitt succeeded BTO, we were on our second coffee and Tia Maria. Jill set hers down on the floor next to the couch and slid closer to me, the warmth of her body flooding over me. I nuzzled hair that smelled like fresh cut flowers as her small body fit comfortably against mine.

We listened to "The Mummers' Dance," and I could tell Jill was caught up in the Celtic pagan feel of the song. Her shoulders swayed gently to the rhythm of the music. When the song ended she turned her face toward me.

I bent to kiss her. Our mouths touched, moved against each other, softly at first, then with more urgency. Her tongue teased my lips and our lips and tongues caressed, the excitement moving through me for the first time in forever.

I moved my hands over her body, felt its heat, felt her moving as she returned my intensity.

I pulled back, looked at her.

"Wow," I said, working at catching my breath.

She nodded. "Yeah." Then, "How fast can you make this become a bed?"

I stroked her cheek with my hand. "Pretty fast."

Neither of us moved. She kissed me lightly on the lips. I looked away.

"But?" she said.

"Jill …"

She sat back a little away from me. "I know. That was way too fast. And that is so not me. I guess I just … look, I'm sorry if —"

"Whoa, whoa. Jill this isn't about too fast or I'm not ready yet or anything in that area code. In fact, there are parts of me that are hating what I'm saying. I like you a lot and I want you *really* a lot. But —"

"Ah."

"But right now there's something else that is eating me up from inside, taking my energy, my thoughts … my … everything."

"Phoenix."

"And whatever happens after that. I guess I'd like to get that done before —"

"Just so you know, there are parts of me that really hate what you are saying too."

I smiled. "Can you understand?"

"No, I probably can't. But I've never had the person I loved most murdered by somebody. What I can do is accept. And I do … with great reluctance." She smiled and I was glad, partly for what I thought the smile meant and partly because it was a great smile.

I nodded, touched my fingers to her lips, her cheek.

"Thanks."

"Adam."

"Yeah."

"The person who killed your wife is very likely still out there … and very likely still dangerous."

I nodded.

"You stay safe, okay?"

"I will. Listen, how about I at least follow you home?"

She shook her head. "Not a chance. I'm fine." She stood up.

I helped her on with her coat and we walked to the door. She opened the door and looked back at me, shaking her head and smiling. "I knew I should have picked the Leonard Cohen."

"Next time," I said.

She turned and was gone.

FOURTEEN

I'm sure the flight to Phoenix was fine.

Truth is I missed most of it as I slept from a few minutes after takeoff to the announcement from the cockpit that we were on final approach to Sky Harbor.

Once off the plane, I carried my bag and computer out to the curb, climbed into a cab, and realized that other than wanting to see Kelly, I hadn't really put a lot of thought into my trip — including where I'd be staying.

I decided to place my fate in the hands of a cab driver. Mine was a bulky guy whose breathing told me it had been a few decades since he'd been in shape. Arizona Diamondbacks ball cap, a T-shirt that may have been a tent in a previous life, and the thickest fingers I'd ever seen.

"I have an appointment at the Duke Golf Course. Can you recommend a hotel close to there?"

He turned around — not an easy task — and looked at me; I guessed he was sizing me up, trying to decide if I was Hilton or Motel 6.

"You a golfer?"

"I hack a little but I'm not here to play golf."

"The Duke. That's Maricopa. Not much for hotels right there. But there's a casino. I've taken some people back to the airport from there. They said the rooms were reasonable during the week and the food was pretty good. You like to gamble?"

"A little. The casino have a pool?"

"I think so. You want me to get on the radio, see if one of the other drivers knows?"

I shook my head. "The casino sounds fine. You know the name? I should call and make sure they have a room."

"Harrah's, same as the one in Vegas."

I called, booked a room for ninety-nine dollars plus tax, and forty minutes later I was in a room, which wasn't bad for ninety-nine dollars plus tax. It looked out on a parking lot populated by tall palm trees and expensive cars. I sipped a bottle of complimentary water and watched gamblers making their way into and out of the casino. Mostly into.

I was antsy, impatient, wanting to see Kelly and get on with what I was here to do.

I'd tried her landline twice in the cab, got voicemail both times, didn't leave a message. Tried it again now, same result. I went down to the casino, had lunch, and dropped forty bucks on a dollar slot. I went for a walk, partly to enjoy the heat, partly to escape the endless racket of the casino.

I spent most of my walking time berating myself for not phoning ahead. What if Kelly had gone somewhere — visiting a relative in Connecticut or to the hospital to have Maddie's little brother or sister or off on vacation to Yellowstone — and I was wasting my time in Arizona. I called Cobb on my cell; he picked up on the second ring.

"You better be phoning from the desert or I'm gonna be some pissed," he growled.

"I just won seventy-five thousand at blackjack and I'm surrounded by scantily clad young ladies, all of whom have expressed an interest in having their way with me."

"Atta boy."

I told Cobb about my concern that Kelly was in some other part of the world and that I wouldn't get to see her.

"You really are one of the all-time great glass half empty guys, you know? This is the busiest time of the year on Arizona golf courses, there's no way her husband could get out of town for more than a day. She was probably at the supermarket when you called. Just chill, maybe spend some of that seventy-five big ones and enjoy all those babes that are dying to have you."

"Got it," I said. "Anything on Jay?"

"Not yet, but I'm using the process of elimination method. I now know a hell of a lot of places where he isn't."

"Yeah," I said.

"And the coroner's report came down. Owen Harkness died from having had his throat cut and twenty-one other stab wounds."

I wanted to say something but there weren't words that fit right then.

"Cops are working it pretty hard," Cobb said. "Don't know how they're doing. It's a tough one."

I found my voice. "And you're okay? I mean you're staying out of the way of whoever killed Owen."

"Yeah, Mom, I'm looking after myself, eating my veggies and everything."

"I'm serious."

There was a pause on the line. "I know you are and I appreciate the concern. Listen, my mother — the *real* one — wouldn't recognize me. So quit worryin'."

"I'll be back in a couple of days," I said. "I'll be ready to help if you need me."

"Right now all you need to do is concentrate on Kelly and your tan."

"Right."

"Right." He hung up and I resumed my walk, spent ten minutes circling the parking lot, and another ten admiring a baby blue '57 T-Bird convertible. Nice car but not nice enough to erase the picture of Owen Harkness that had imprinted itself into my memory.

I found a vacant lawn chair next to the pool, pulled out my cell phone, and dialled Kelly's number again. Three rings.

"Hello?"

"Hi Kelly. It's Adam Cullen calling. How ya doin'?" *My god, I sound like Joey on* Friends. *She'll think I'm hitting on her.*

"Oh … Adam … uh, hi."

"Listen, Kelly, I was hoping I could talk to you. It'll only take a few minutes. There are a couple of things I was wanting to ask you about."

"Uh, yeah, I … guess so."

"Great. How about I pick up some coffee, bring it over, or if you'd rather —"

"Wait, you mean you're here? In Arizona?"

"Oh yeah, I guess I didn't mention that. I'm just down for … a … conference … a newspaper thing in … uh … Mesa and I thought since I was here anyway I could just, you know, stop by or meet you somewhere if that's better."

"No, I just put the baby down. I guess you could stop by for a few minutes. Do you know where I live?"

"Well, only roughly. Maybe just give me the address and I'm sure the cabbie can find it." I'm not sure why I lied to her. Maybe I thought if I seemed overanxious she might just clam up. I also had no idea how far it was from Mesa to Maricopa and hoped I wouldn't have to kill time for too long to make my lie at least somewhat believable.

She recited the address and hung up. I waited what I thought was a decent amount of time, went out to the front of the casino, grabbed a taxi for the ten minute ride to Kelly's house. Small fare. Small tip. Pissed off cab driver.

I walked up the sidewalk to a hacienda-style terracotta house with a parched looking front lawn. Except for the grass, everything about the place told me that the life of a golf pro was pretty good. The house was a nice size and the garage was about the size of the house Donna and I had lived in.

I was reaching for the bell when the door opened. One of the three most beautiful women I had ever seen — the other two work in movies — looked at me and said, "I was waiting for you; the baby." She nodded toward the doorbell.

"Oh ... sorry."

"Come in." A half smile. Not warm and fuzzy but not hostile either. I stepped inside and she closed the door behind me, then gestured toward the living room, which led off to the right. "Please sit down."

I sat in a stuffed chair that was comfortable in the extreme and cast a quick look around the room. Nicely done. Where lots of places have too much furniture, too much *stuff*, this living room was tastefully understated. Not sparse but whoever decorated wasn't afraid of empty space here and there. Southwest décor but again not overdone. Lots of earth colours; moss green and tan were dominant. A couple of desert landscapes that fit the room perfectly. There was nothing inside the home that belied the initial impression I'd gotten from the exterior.

"I made coffee. Would you like some?"

"Thank you. Coffee would be great."

Kelly smiled again, a little bigger this time, nodded, and went off to the kitchen. I glanced around again, noted that the only deviation from the perfectly decorated room was a large framed photograph of a golfer teeing off at what looked like a pretty cool golf course. I guessed it was Wes Nolan in action. Hard to tell, but from where I sat he appeared to be a good-looking guy. Surprise, surprise.

Kelly was back a couple of minutes later with two mugs of coffee on a tray with milk and sugar containers and spoons. As I doctored my coffee, she took hers and sat on a leather chesterfield opposite me. Brown leather with a longhorn skull etched into the cushions. Well, maybe not *etched*.

She held her coffee mug in both hands. "I have to say I'm kind of surprised to see you," she said. "I thought we'd pretty well discussed everything I'd remembered about Donna from school so …"

"I know and I'm sure you're right, but …" I swallowed, looked at the floor, then back up at her. "Kelly, I was wondering, or maybe hoping, that there might have been something you *didn't* say, maybe you didn't want to make me feel bad or say something about Donna that you felt uncomfortable saying. I don't know, I just thought if we met face to face, maybe you'd feel differently."

There was a long silence, broken only by sounds of the baby over one of those child monitors. One soft gurgling sound, then silence, and sleep once again.

I took a sip of the coffee. "I know it's tough remembering and —"

"It's not tough remembering." There was a sudden coldness in her voice that hadn't been there before. Not on the phone. Not today.

"I'm not sure I understand.'

"I didn't tell you because I'm sure there's no connection between what happened to us and Donna's death."

"What happened to you …" I repeated, "as in you and Donna?"

"There were others."

"So the note; you did remember it."

"Not that specific note. But I know what she … what *we* were talking about."

I had to set the coffee mug down. My hand was shaking so hard I was afraid I'd spill on the carpet.

"What was it that happened, Kelly?"

"I told you, it has nothing to do with the fire and … everything. I'm sure of that."

I nodded, waited. This time the silence went on a long time. Kelly was looking in the direction of the monitor's speaker, her eyes filled with tears, one solitary tear trickling down her cheek.

I said, "I'm sorry, Kelly, if it's something painful, I really am, but I need you to tell me."

She didn't answer, the tear falling from her cheek to the carpet, replaced by another. She didn't say anything for what felt like a long time.

"We were … abused."

As much as I thought I was ready to hear whatever Kelly said, as much as those words and others had stamped their sound into my mind so many times in the last few days, when I actually heard the words spoken by someone, I wasn't ready.

This was Donna we were talking about. My Donna. This couldn't be true. This stuff happened to other people. Not to me, not to the woman I had been married to.

The tears came harder now. When she spoke again, her voice was barely more than a whisper.

"There was a teacher at school, our social studies teacher, he was only there for one year. We all liked him as a teacher. He seemed really nice, like he cared about us as students, and as people.

"He had a way of making us all feel special. He was really good-looking, smart, and he let us know we were his equals, his … soulmates. I know how lame that sounds, and you're probably thinking that a girl who was pretty and a cheerleader …"

She stopped again and this time fished a Kleenex out of a pocket, dabbed at eyes and nose.

"I'd just been dumped by a guy, no, not just a guy — the totally coolest guy in the school. Athlete, popular, hot, a complete cliché, and I was nuts about him. We were the 'wonder couple'; oh my God I can't believe I was actually proud of that title back then …" A little half smile through the tears.

"He was the first guy I ever … went to bed with. I was pathetic, thinking we'd get married, kids … Jesus. And then it was, 'yeah, listen Babe, I think we both need to grow, you know? See other people, *fuck* other people.' Those were his words. I thought I was going to die.

"And then along came the new teacher in the school. I think the term they always use is 'vulnerable,' and I guess that was me. He knew what buttons to push, made me think he was in love with me and that I was in love with him. Ridiculous, I know, but I remember thinking *how about that, Joel Carloni, high school superstar. I'm not with some high school kid any more, I'm with a man.*"

A bitter laugh. The tears were gone now, replaced by anger.

"You know something," she looked at me, "you're the first person I've talked to about this since the cops."

"I appreciate it, Kelly. I know this has to be difficult."

"Not as bad as losing your wife in a fire."

I didn't answer.

"I wasn't kidding before," she said. "This guy was a jerk and a predator. But he wasn't a killer. I've thought about it a lot since you phoned me the first time and I know that to be true."

I nodded. Noncommittal. "What happened with this guy and Donna?"

"I don't know the details, and I'm not just saying that to spare you. It was after he'd moved on from me. He'd get tired of us after a couple of months and he'd get rid of one girl and make his move on another. Donna said he never got her into bed with him and I believed her. He did some stuff to her, touched her and stuff, but not … that." Her voice grew still quieter. "Not what he did with me. And the others."

I fought to keep my voice steady. "How many were there?"

She sipped her coffee for the first time, set the mug down, then looked at it. "There were four of us. At least that's how many we knew about. One night Donna told me about what was going on and I told her it had happened to me too. Eventually we figured out that there were two others. Don't ask me how we knew. And the four of us became some kind of sick club. The victims-of-a-teacher club."

She shook her head and stared down at the carpet.

"So you all had him for social?"

Kelly shook her head. "Not Donna. He helped with our school musical that year. He had been a musician, was even in a couple of bands that I'd heard of. He even had the records; I know, I listened to them. Anyway, Donna was really musical, I guess you know all about that …" I didn't answer. "… And it was when she was rehearsing for the musical that he …"

A minute or two passed. Kelly fished another Kleenex out of a different pocket and dabbed again at her eyes. I was able to hold my coffee now and took a couple of sips.

"You said something about the cops."

Kelly nodded. "Donna wanted to go the police right away. The rest of us didn't, begged her not to. We told her that we couldn't live with it being out there. One of the girls said she'd commit suicide if it became known, and I think she meant it. Donna must have thought so too because she let it go.

"And then two years later we heard that he'd been arrested at another school. At first they said all that would happen is he wouldn't be allowed to teach anymore. That's when we went to the police; this time all of us agreed. We wanted to see the bastard in jail. And that's what happened. He went to jail for … I heard six years. I don't know if he served the whole sentence. I didn't want to know anything more; I just wanted to forget it."

"I'm sorry, Kelly."

She shook her head. "No, it's okay, really. And *I'm*

okay … now. I know you had to try to find out everything you could after what happened to Donna."

"Was this in grade eleven?"

"Uh-huh. How did you know?"

"As I was looking at some of Donna's stuff it seemed to me that there were some changes in her that year."

She nodded again. "In all of us. We were depressed. Our grades went down, even Donna's. The counsellor spoke to each of us, she said she'd noticed we seemed less excited about school and life and was there anything bothering us. But, of course, none of us said anything about what was going on."

"You said it happened again two years later. Some of you must have been finished high school."

"We stayed in touch. Funny, isn't it — when you're in school you promise all your friends that you'll stay in touch, be friends forever, all that stuff, and the only ones I stayed in contact with were …" She paused, sipped her coffee, stared off for a long moment.

"Anyway, when Donna heard that he did it again at the other school, she got hold of all of us. I guess she sort of spearheaded the thing."

There were sounds of a baby fussing coming from the monitor.

I stood up. "Listen, Kelly, I don't want to take up any more of your time. I know you're busy."

Kelly stood, smiled. "I'm afraid I haven't been a very good host. Would you like me to warm up your coffee, or get you some fresh? I can go get her and then —"

I held up a hand. "You've been a fine host. I appreciate your seeing me. I know this hasn't been easy. Just one thing more …"

"Yes?"

"What was the teacher's name?"

She hesitated and looked away, the smile gone.

"Kelly, it won't be hard for me to find out. It would just save time if you'd let me know his name."

"What are you going to do?"

I shook my head. I didn't have an answer to that question.

"He didn't set fire to your house, I absolutely know that."

"How do you know that, Kelly?"

"What he did to Donna and to all of us was wrong. It's like that phrase — we were 'robbed of our youth,' or maybe it's 'robbed of our innocence.' Anyway, he did that and I'll never stop hating him for it. But he wasn't someone who could kill anyone … I just know that."

I nodded. "I get what you're saying, but I guess I need to find that out for myself."

"I don't think I can —"

"Kelly, you mentioned that I would know about Donna's love of music. Truth is, I didn't know that. I never heard her play, sing … not ever. As near as I can figure, Donna stopped playing music after that year."

She looked down. "Oh, God." It was a whisper.

"I need to know the man's name."

"What are you going to do?" she asked again.

"I don't know. I … don't know."

I looked at her and she met my gaze, gave the slightest nod.

"Appleton. Richard Appleton."

"Do you know where he is now?"

"I don't. Honestly, I don't. I guess I never wanted to know."

"Thanks, Kelly. You better see to the baby." The noises were getting louder over the monitor.

I started for the door.

"Adam."

I turned back to face her.

"Don't do anything you'll regret … please."

I tried for a reassuring smile.

"Yeah." I stepped out into the Arizona heat feeling as cold as I'd ever been in my life.

FIFTEEN

I'm not sure how long I walked or even where. I was in a pleasant residential area and a lot of the houses had kids playing in yards. On porches.

Families.

Angry thoughts. Anger at Richard Appleton for what he'd done to Donna and at least three other girls. Anger at a school that either didn't pay enough attention to see it happening or saw it and turned a careful, blind eye, concerned more with preserving the reputation of the institution than the safety of its students.

Anger at a school principal who must have eventually been aware of what had happened at her school but had said nothing to me. Although, to be fair to Delores Bain, she may not have known the names of Appleton's victims. The courts are careful about protecting the identities of underage victims and I couldn't say for sure that that protection wouldn't have excluded even the school principal from knowing their names.

Appleton's sentence had been six years. Whether or not he'd served all of it, it wasn't much. Yet that's what the court felt was sufficient punishment for what he'd done to those girls' lives.

It *wasn't* sufficient. Not to me.

My wandering had taken me to a mini-mall and I stepped into a Fry's store to get a coffee and think about what I was going to do next.

I took the coffee to a faux-leather chair not far from the coffee bar and sat beneath a TV where a right-wing politician was telling an interviewer what was wrong with America and how he was the only person on the planet with the will and the intelligence to fix it. Or words to that effect.

I found the remote and turned the sound down and then looked around, I guess as an afterthought. The only person watching was an old black man who couldn't have weighed a hundred pounds. He was sitting at a counter with a newspaper in his hands.

"Sorry," I told him, "if you're wanting to listen —"

He held up both hands and grinned at me. "That's all right, brother, I think he's an asshole too."

I smiled at him and nodded. Took a drink of coffee.

I replayed my conversation with Kelly in my mind. And I thought about what I was going to do next.

Don't do anything you'll regret. That's what she'd said, almost pleading with me. Regret is what you feel when you do something wrong. Was it wrong to want to see the man who had betrayed the trust of teenage girls over a decade before? Was it wrong to want to decide for myself if he was capable of hating one of his victims enough to want to kill her? Or want revenge for her part in putting him behind bars?

I set the half-finished coffee on an end table that stood to the left of the chair, picked up the remote, and stood up. I walked over to the counter where the black man was working on a coffee of his own.

I handed him the remote and gestured at the TV. "He's gone now. It's safe to turn up the volume."

He chuckled and took the remote. "Yeah, I guess it is at that."

I stepped out of the store and saw a cab at the curb, moved forward, and opened the back door on the passenger side. I leaned in. The driver twisted to look at me, raised his eyebrows.

"You have a trip?" I asked him.

He took a few seconds to decide. "No." He shook his head.

He didn't make a move to start the car.

"Does that mean the cab is available?"

A few more seconds before a grudging nod. Apparently the economic woes of the United States hadn't touched this particular cab driver.

I climbed in, gave him the address of the hotel, thinking he'd also be pissed off at the length of the trip and the size of the impending fare.

He said, "Sure," and seemed reasonably content although I noticed he turned off the air conditioning in the car.

Maybe that was his *I'll show the bastard* mechanism. Or maybe it was cool enough already. Maybe.

Back at the hotel I ran up to the room, showered, and changed, then went back down to the lobby. There was a business centre in one corner of the lobby and no one in it. I let myself in with my room key, settled at one of the three Samsung computers, and Googled Richard Appleton.

I found a news story in the archives of the *Calgary Sun*. The story was dated November 22, 1995. An adjacent story reminded me that the date was thirty-two years to the day after the death of John F. Kennedy.

Not a lot of detail but the basics were there, written in the tabloid style of that newspaper.

Creep Teacher Nailed and Jailed

Forty-six-year-old former high school teacher, Richard Appleton, has been sentenced to six-and-one-half years in prison following his conviction on six counts of sexual interference with a minor. The assaults took place over a four-year period at three different schools, two of them high schools and the third a junior high school.

The father of one of the victims who cannot be named under the provisions of the Youth Criminal Justice Act told the *Sun* that he was happy to see justice prevail. "If we get one more predator off our streets even for a while, that's a good thing."

Appleton's lawyer, Christopher P. Hart, told reporters his client would almost certainly appeal the conviction. "We are, of course, disappointed by the jury's verdict. My client is the victim here. It appears jurors were swayed by the testimony of alleged victims who clearly had a vendetta against a teacher with glowing credentials ... this is false accusation of the worst kind.

I stopped reading and went to the next post, a *Calgary Herald* story, same time-frame, same kind of story, different quote from a different parent — a mom this time — and only slightly less inflammatory language.

There was a Wikipedia piece that said even less than the two stories from newspapers.

I stared at the computer for a while, then pulled my cell phone out and called Cobb.

"How's the Arizona sunshine?"

"I need your help on something."

There was a pause on the other end of the line. I guessed that he was surprised by my abruptness.

"You learn something?"

"A little," I said. "I need to find someone, a guy named Richard Appleton. Used to teach school in Calgary. Private school at least part of the time. Went to jail back in '97, or maybe '98. Got six-and-a-half years — don't know how much he served."

"You think this guy torched your place?"

"I don't know, but I need to talk to him."

"What'd he get sent up for?"

"Sexual assault." I paused. "Students."

"I'll call you back." Cobb was gone.

I went back to the computer. There were pages of Richard Appleton references, most of them about an Australian hypnotist-entertainer by that name. I didn't find anything more about *this* Richard Appleton beyond several smaller references to the sexual assault case in other newspapers.

My cell phone rang. I touched the screen, said, "Yeah."

Cobb's voice — all business. "Appleton went to jail

in late 1998. Served most of his time, the last part in a halfway house."

"And now?"

"Looks like he's living in North Vancouver, at least that's the latest I could get on him. Runs a business called School Daze. It's a printing company that produces high-school yearbooks."

"You've got to be fucking kidding. This guy is still going into schools?"

"Unless you can produce and print a yearbook without going into the school, then yeah, that's what's happening."

"Jesus."

"So what now?"

"Like I said, I want to meet him, talk to him."

"Okay, but don't do anything dumb."

Second time I'd heard that particular piece of advice. "Anything new?"

"Not yet. You coming back here?"

"No, I've got business at the coast."

He gave me the address, a couple of phone numbers, and I hung up, dialled the airline. Changed my flight.

The Sylvia Hotel isn't fancy but it's one of my favourite places in the world, mostly because it was one of Donna's favourite places in the world. It's an official heritage building, built in 1912 by a man named Goldstein who named the place after his daughter. It looks out over English Bay. Donna and I had spent hours in the lounge overlooking the ocean and on the beach across from the hotel gazing out at the Pacific Ocean and some of the ships that navigate its thousands of miles.

This stop at the Sylvia was different. I'd arrived mid-morning, checked in, changed, and gone for a run along the beach past the towering magnificence of Stanley Park. After a shower and a lunch of smoked wild salmon chowder and a Keith's IPA in the hotel restaurant, I had moved to the lounge for a rye and Diet Coke. I was flipping through the pages of *Mr. Got to Go*, a children's picture book based on a real story of a stray cat who moved into the Sylvia one day and simply refused to leave. Donna and I had read it together the last time we were at the Sylvia — maybe in this same booth.

Remembering the advice of the wise Kay Towers about the importance of Kyla in any plan I might have to move forward with Jill Sawley, I'd bought this copy at the desk for Kyla.

I put the book down, pulled out my cell phone. The lounge was empty but for one grizzled old guy sipping what looked like a Guinness on the other side of the room. He was wearing a Blue Jays ball cap and a T-shirt that said, "Sailors do it in waves."

Catchy.

I dialled the first number Cobb had given me. A man's voice answered. "School Daze. How can I help you?"

"Hello, this is Rich Maxwell calling. I'm the teacher-advisor for the yearbook committee over here at … uh … Oceanside Junior High. Our student committee met last night and decided they'd like to look at an alternative publisher from the firm we've had in the past. One of the other teachers had heard about you folks and I thought I'd give you a call and chat with you about our book. Perhaps I could come by your office, Mr. —"

"There isn't an office, per se. My wife and I are the company and we work out of our home. When were you thinking you'd like to come around?"

"Well, the kids are chomping at the bit to get going so sooner rather than later would be my preference. I'm tied up in class until 3:15 but I could zip over there right after school — say about four o'clock."

"Well … I … suppose, yes, I think we could make that work."

"Great. Thanks for fitting me in and I do apologize for the short notice. If you could just give me the address and … uh, my colleague mentioned your name, I think, but I can't remember. Sorry."

"It's Richard Appleton." He gave me an address on West 14th Street in North Van and told me that he and his wife lived near the North Vancouver City Library. I glanced down at the address Cobb had given me. It matched.

I told Appleton I'd see him at four and hung up, fairly satisfied with my performance but nervous as I considered what could happen when I got to the house on West 14th Street.

I thought about another drink but decided it wouldn't do for the yearbook advisor at Oceanside Junior High to have liquor on his breath. I ordered a coffee and picked up *Mr. Got to Go* for one more reading.

I eased the rented Impala to the curb and sat looking at the home of Richard Appleton. It was a nice house but not ostentatious. Tans and browns for the siding and trim. Flower beds on both sides of the front steps. A silver Buick LeSabre, early- to mid-2000s vintage and looking brand new, sat in the driveway. A small magnetic sign was visible on the driver's side door. It read, "School Daze, Your One-Stop Yearbook Supplier."

I was nervous but not scared. I'd done interviews with lots of tough guys in my life so it wasn't like I was thinking about the danger of my impending meeting with Richard Appleton. If there was anything to fear it was me, what I might do if I snapped. I'd been storing up hate for the man inside that house since I'd heard about the sexual assaults on his students. If it turned out that he was also the person who had set fire to my house — and killed my wife — all bets were off.

The man who opened the door and smiled at me was not a tough guy, at least he didn't look it. Early fifties, a little overweight, I could see that he'd once been handsome; he wasn't far from that now. My height, brown hair, a long slender nose, wide mouth with straight, very white teeth, solid chin. But it was the eyes that I guessed were a big assist in winning over the hearts of young girls. They were a remarkably deep blue and accented by long, little boy lashes. The eyes knocked at least ten years off his age.

He reached out a hand, and said, "Mr. Maxwell, a pleasure. Please come in."

That was the second thing about Appleton that girls, even women, would have found attractive in the extreme. He had a voice that most radio announcers would have killed for. Sam Elliott without the drawl. It was impressive on the phone, more impressive in person.

He stepped back and I moved inside, found myself looking at a short woman with mousy blond hair, not unattractive but not in the same league as her husband. While they were both in their fifties, he looked to be forty-something and she'd gone the other way — sixty-ish. She seemed friendly but not over-the-moon cordial. Her eyes were guarded. She was looking in my direction but not *at* me. Something — my admittedly biased guess was that it was being married to Richard Appleton — had taken a toll on this woman.

We were in the living room and Appleton gestured toward an arm chair that looked like it had been designed by someone aiming for comfort. I sat and decided the designers had achieved their goal. Appleton sat across from me on one half of a sofa that matched the chair I was in. Mrs. Appleton did not sit.

"This is my wife, Kathleen. She's also my business partner. Can we get you a tea or a coffee, Mr. Maxwell?" Appleton asked.

"Please don't go to any trouble just for me," I said, looking at Mrs. Appleton. She hadn't smiled yet and my feeling was that I could wait a long time before that happened.

"Not at all." It was Appleton who answered. "We were just going to have something ourselves. And we like both, so whichever you prefer …"

"Coffee, then, if that's all right."

Again I looked at Kathleen Appleton, again no visible response. She headed for the kitchen. Appleton watched her go with what looked like regard. But then Appleton had been able to put on enough of a show to captivate several teenage girls, so maybe this too was acting.

He continued to look in the direction she had gone even after she was out of the room. I took that few seconds to look around. If I'm ever given an assignment to write an article on the prototype middle class living room, this wouldn't be a bad place to start. Like the exterior, there was little in the way of pretension. It was pleasant without trying too hard to *feel* pleasant.

The furniture was older but in what the Kijiji ads would call like-new condition. A couple of Robert Bateman prints on the walls. A bookcase along one wall. I couldn't see titles but it looked like a mix of the bestselling thriller writers, some historical romance, and maybe some non-fiction.

What was missing was photographs. There were lots of flat surfaces that often tend to attract framed pictures of kids and newly married couples, but not one photograph adorned one flat surface in the Appleton home.

To Appleton's left was an electric piano and beside it an acoustic guitar—a Martin. I don't know a lot about guitars but I do know that a Martin is a top-of-the-line instrument. *The musician. And unlike Donna, he'd continued to enjoy playing.*

I forced myself to breathe. Appleton turned back to me.

"Oceanside Junior High, you said?"

"That's right." I nodded.

"I was going to check our database to see if we'd included the school in our mail outs but I didn't get off the phone long enough to do that. Maybe you can answer that question for me, Mr. Maxwell."

"I … uh … think so, yes, I'm fairly certain. We let the kids carry the ball as much as we can at Oceanside and it's my first year on the committee so I'm still getting my feet wet, but yes, I'm sure we got your promotional materials."

"Ah, well it's good to know our attempts at promoting are working. And where is Oceanside Junior High?"

"Down White Rock way," I waved an arm in what I hoped was the direction of White Rock.

Mrs. Appleton came into the room carrying two small plates of cookies. She set one on an end table next to me and the other on a matching table near her husband. This time she smiled slightly at me as she turned and started for the kitchen again. "The coffee will just be a couple of minutes," she said as she walked.

"Thank you," I said as she disappeared a second time. "Very nice home, Mr. Appleton."

"We like it. Seems to fit with our lifestyle. We're rather quiet people."

I cleared my throat and looked down at the lone scatter rug that lay on the hardwood floor that looked newer than the rest of the house.

"You should have one of my wife's cookies, Mr. Maxwell. I'm betting you can't stop at just one."

I took one and bit into as good a chocolate chip cookie as I'd ever had.

This wasn't feeling quite right. I was sitting in a comfortable home, having a pleasant conversation with the man who had molested my wife and maybe murdered her. I set the cookie down and nodded to indicate that it was time to get on with discussing the yearbook project.

"There are two or three companies we're looking at and I wondered if I could ask you a couple of things about yours."

He smiled and held out his hands, palms up. "By all means. Ask away."

"How ... uh ... how long has School Daze been in the yearbook business?"

"We're relatively new, just going into our fourth year, but we have been growing every year. Right now there's just the two of us," he nodded in the direction of the kitchen, "but if we get much bigger we'll be looking at taking on a couple of new employees."

"I see," I said. "And how does the process work? Say our student committee decides to go with School Daze, would you be coming into the school to meet with us, that sort of thing?"

"There are a couple of options. Teachers and students tend to be very busy so it's often more convenient for me to stop in, collect the files as they are ready prior to our printing them. Of course, we can also do a lot of this online. It's really up to the school to determine what way they prefer to work."

"Right … That makes sense."

"And now, Mr. Maxwell, I have a couple of questions as well."

I shrugged and tried to smile. "Sure."

"First of all, is Maxwell your real name?"

I sat up straight, stared. "What?"

"You see, I *did* check our database. And there is an Oceanside School but it's on the island, somewhere around Parksville. So you're not who you say you are and perhaps you better tell me what it is you want, Mr. —"

"Cullen. Adam Cullen. But I doubt the name will mean anything to you. It's my wife you'd be familiar with. She was one of your students at Northern Horizon Academy. One of your … victims."

He'd caught me off guard but I was okay now. A thousand interviews, some with people who didn't like me and didn't want to talk with me had prepared me for moments like these.

Appleton stood up and left the room, heading for the kitchen. I heard quiet voices. He came in buttoning

DAVID A. POULSEN

a sweater he had pulled on while he was out of the room. "I find it a bit chilly. I apologize if it's uncomfortable. I turned up the thermostat."

He sat back down and looked at me with a mix of curiosity and apprehension. Curiosity, not malice. Apprehension, not fear.

"There are a number of things I could try to say but I'm not sure any of them would be appropriate, Mr. Cullen. Of course, I knew some of the family members of the young women I was accused of —"

"Accused?" My voice rose and he glanced at the doorway leading to the kitchen. I leaned forward. "If you want me to keep my voice down to protect whatever charade you've got going with your wife, then don't insult my intelligence and don't, for a second, think about denying what you did with those girls."

A few seconds went by before he nodded. "I was merely going to say that this is the first time I have met a husband of any of those young women."

"Well, now you can add that to your list of memorable moments."

I could feel the anger bubbling over and I was close to losing control. I dug my hands into the arms of the chair.

"What do you want from me, Mr. Cullen?"

"I don't know. I want to come over there and hit you in the face. I want you to feel something … something inside that tears you apart the way it tears me apart. I want you to hurt as much as those girls hurt. I want …"

"I paid my debt to society, Mr. Cullen."

"Bull*shit*." My voice was a hiss. "Don't give me that cliché crap. What debt did you pay to those women?" I flung my arm in a half circle. "Things don't look too bad for the Appletons. Comfy little home in a nice middle-class neighbourhood. Bet the neighbours think you're just a nice man who mows his lawn every Saturday morning and sells yearbooks to schools."

"I don't blame you for your venom toward me. You have every right —"

"Shut up. It's better when you don't talk. No, no, I do have one question. How have you managed to operate a business that lets you go into the very places where you preyed on young girls? How did you pull that off?"

"My wife does all the work in the schools. Some of them run police checks so, of course, I can't have any contact with the schools."

"So they know."

"No. The only ones who have suspected that I am the man they read about or heard about don't do business with us. For obvious reasons. Some schools have only asked for the police check for Kathleen. Some don't do much checking."

"Convenient."

"Have you wondered why I let you in my house when I knew you weren't who you said you were? When I suspected you might be someone from … the past?"

"Why was that, Appleton? An opportunity to look into the eyes of one of your peripheral victims, check out the collateral damage?"

"Kathleen and I agreed when I got out of prison that if any of the people I harmed in the past were to come here that we would see them, that even in situations that might be dangerous I would meet my accusers, my … victims and their families and say to their faces how sorry I am for what I did."

"A noble fucking attitude."

"Not noble Mr. Cullen, not noble at all. It is as much for me as for them. I realize that what I did cannot be forgiven but I want to say ... I *need* to say that I am so terribly sorry." His voice caught on the last word and he looked down.

I watched him with as much loathing as I've ever felt for anyone. "You haven't even asked her name."

He looked up at me, eyes moist. He shook his head. "I haven't, I'm sorry ... again. I should have."

"But you already know it, don't you?"

He looked puzzled, shook his head. "There were six girls in all, and I know that that is far too many. Six too many." He paused and rubbed his forehead. "I don't know your wife's name but they ... the young women were not anonymous to me. I knew them. I knew their names. I remember their names. I will know your wife's name when you tell it to me, I promise you."

"And that's supposed to make me feel better?"

"No ... no, I just wanted you to be aware ..." he trailed off, didn't finish the sentence.

Through clenched teeth, I said, "Donna. Leybrand."

There was silence in the room but for a ticking clock in the corner. No sounds from the kitchen. Appleton took a breath, let it out, looked over my shoulder, out the window.

He turned his head just enough to look at me. "Donna was ... a very special person. She was one of my favourite —"

He didn't finish because I was out of the chair and had hold of him, my fist drawn back, wanting to hit him, to smash his face over and over until it was unrecognizable.

"Let him go. Now!" Kathleen Appleton stood in the doorway, a cell phone in her hand. "I will call the police if you don't let him go and get out of this house."

I was close enough to smell Appleton's cologne. *The bastard did it again.* The words crescendoed in my head. Every part of me wanted to ignore his wife's threat and make this man pay. *Donna was a very special person. The bastard did it again.* Words. Terrible words.

I pushed down on his chest and stood up, tears blurring my vision, my chest heaving as I tried to gulp in air.

"It wasn't enough for your pig of a husband to molest young girls …" I looked at Appleton who was pulling himself up straight in the chair. "Does she know about the rest of it? What you did after?"

"I want you to leave." She started hitting buttons on the phone.

"What was it Appleton? Revenge? Donna was the one who spoke out first, got the others to go to the police, to testify in court. Was that your justification for killing her?" My voice had risen to where I wasn't sure the words were making sense and I didn't care.

But they understood the words. Kathleen Appleton stopped punching numbers. Appleton leaned forward. "What did you say?"

"You heard me, you pathetic bastard. You killed my wife." I wanted to yell it but it came out as barely more than a whisper.

"I …" he looked at his wife, then back at me. "I didn't know Donna was dead. I swear I … what happened to her?"

"She died in the fire you set —"

"My God, that's two of those girls … I can't … you have to believe me, I —"

He didn't finish. Kathleen Appleton, her arms above her head, came at me with a scream that was part rage and part wounded animal. I saw the movement out of the corner of my eye and was able to duck but I was off balance and the force of her attack and the fact that it was so unexpected knocked me down. She stood over me, screaming, trying to hit me or kick at me. She was unsuccessful only because Appleton had leaped from his chair and had both arms around her, dragging her back, talking to try to calm her.

Her screams drowned him out. "You make me sick, all of you. You're as bad as those filthy high school sluts with their skirts up to their asses and their tits all over the place wanting men like my husband and then trying to ruin our lives after they got exactly what they wanted, what they begged for."

Her last words were barely understandable as her hate and anger had made her something inhuman, something I'd never seen. She paused to take a breath, to swallow some of the saliva that was bubbling out of her mouth as she screamed at me. But still her arms churned as she tried to get free of her husband in order to get at me.

I got to my feet, stumbled back. I could hear Appleton now, his voice steady as he continued to restrain her, trying to talk her back to sanity.

I knew I had to get out of there. Somehow everything had changed and I had to get away, to try to take away all of what had happened in there. But not yet. What had Appleton said? *There were two of them.* Had he meant two girls dead?

But Kathleen Appleton's fury had not diminished. She was merely resting, gathering strength for another attack. Both Appleton and I knew it. And it came.

"You can all go straight to hell, you Goddamn scum of the earth! Those slut teenage whores and you too! I'm glad she's dead. I can't wait until they're all dead and gone to hell where they belong."

She spat at me but I was too far away and her spittle landed on the carpet at my feet.

Appleton was able to turn his head partly toward me. "Go … now."

"You said —"

"I said go now. Please."

It was a plea. I turned and left the house without looking back. The hate-filled words of Kathleen Appleton followed me out the door.

"Don't come back! You or your sluts. I want you all to die!"

And Appleton's voice. "Kathleen, don't. Kathleen, listen to me."

I drove a few blocks in the Impala and pulled into a parking area for a city park. I was shaking — violently. Part of it was my own anger, the loathing I felt for everything about Richard Appleton. And part of it was knowing I had lost control, that I had done exactly what Cobb and Kelly Nolan had warned me not to do.

But the biggest part of what I was feeling had more to do with Kathleen Appleton than it did with me or what I'd done.

I'd had lots of confrontations with unpleasant interviewees over the years, some of them women. But I'd never encountered the kind of hate, the near insanity that was Kathleen Appleton in those minutes. Maybe some of it was a protective reaction to my going after her husband. But there was something more.

Someone appears to be attacking someone you care about, you do what you have to do to prevent it from happening. This went well beyond that — this was hatred in its pure, uncut form, not just for me but for the young women her husband had victimized.

I leaned my head back on the seat of the car, closed my eyes, and took several deep breaths, trying to get my heart rate back to something near normal and to ease the throbbing inside my skull.

I'm not sure how long I sat, not moving. But eventually I sat up, forced my eyes to focus on the park. I realized the car was still running. I shut it off, pocketed the key, and stepped out into what had become a wet Vancouver day. Not rain exactly but a steady mist-drizzle.

I started forward, into a small neighbourhood park that was populated by trees with very wide trunks and a kids' play area that sat almost in the middle of the trees. As I moved under the protective umbrella of the trees, I felt my body relax. And I tried to think, to make some kind of sense of what had taken place on West 14th Street.

Was I any closer to finding my wife's killer? I wasn't sure. Appleton's reaction to my accusing him of starting the fire seemed to be genuine surprise, maybe even shock. Could he not have known about the fire? Maybe. If he hadn't known Donna's married name, and there was no reason why he should have known it, then he could even have read about the fire and not realized that the person who died there had been one of his victims.

So, maybe. But this was a man whose performances had broken down the defenses of six high school girls.

I stood staring at a long, twisting slide that seemed to be the centrepiece of the old-fashioned playground. It was metal, a throwback. This play area even had monkey bars, my own favourite when I was growing up.

I thought about the simplicity of life as a kid and wondered if Donna had spent as much time in parks like this one as I had. So much I didn't know about her, and never would.

"My wife is not a crazy person."

The voice came from behind me and I spun around to see Richard Appleton, without either coat or hat, standing in the rain looking at me. He was holding a paper bag. My first thought was *gun* and I knew without looking around that Appleton and I were the only people in the park, maybe the only people outdoors for blocks. If it was Appleton's intention to shoot me, I'd made it easy for him.

"I was hoping I might be able to catch you so I set off as soon as I was able to settle Kathleen. I figured it was a longshot, but when I saw the Impala parked on the street …" he gestured over his shoulder, "I'd watched you pull up to the house so I knew what you were driving."

I nodded, not sure what I was supposed to say.

He spoke again. "She is damaged but she is not crazy. As horrible as what those girls must have gone through because of me, Kathleen's suffering has been every bit as awful. I guess believing that the girls were somehow at fault, blaming the victims, is her way of coping with something that is unimaginable to her."

I took a step toward him. "If you're looking for me to sympathize or to forgive you, Appleton, you're wasting your time. You're the worst of scum and I don't give a shit that you caused your wife great pain. I care only about *my* wife and the pain you caused her."

"I'm not looking for sympathy or forgiveness."

"Good, that'll save us both some time."

"You said Donna died. In a fire."

I didn't answer.

"And you believe I may have set that fire."

"Did you?"

Shake of the head, slow at first, then more emphatic. "I did not. I realize you have absolutely no reason to believe me but I did not murder your wife. What possible reason could I have for doing that?"

"I can think of a couple of possibilities. Revenge, for one. Donna was the one who got the others to join her in exposing you. Maybe your wife's not the only one who blames the victims. Or maybe you didn't want to kill her — just teach her a lesson, get back at her for what she did to you. It's interesting that the fire was set *after* you got out of prison. Means, motive, opportunity, Appleton. Check, check, and check."

He shook his head. "I could not seek revenge on someone for doing what was the right thing to do — even if it was to my detriment."

"Words. The basic tools of the seducer, the molester, and maybe, in this case, the killer too."

"You're wrong, Mr. Cullen. I did not set fire to your home. I did not kill your wife."

"And then, of course, there's *your* wife. Seems to me, based on what I saw at your house, that she would be more than capable of exacting revenge on ... let me see if I can get this right ... 'those slut teenage whores.' And I think the other phrase was 'I can't wait until they're all dead.' Sounds like someone who would at the very least celebrate something terrible happening to those girls and at worst could make that something terrible happen."

Appleton, for the first time, became animated — even agitated. "What you saw back there was a woman who has been under enormous stress for a long time. I did that to her and it's one more thing I will never forgive myself for. But Kathleen is not capable of the kind of violence you're talking about."

I watched him for several seconds. "What do you think would have happened if you hadn't held your wife back? She looked to me like a woman who was very much capable of violence in the right set of circumstances."

"She was coming to my defence."

I nodded. I had, after all, come close to smashing Appleton's face to a pulp.

"Maybe that's what it was. The question then is what was she protecting you from … the truth coming out? Seeing her husband go back to jail, this time as an arsonist and a murderer?"

"I swear to you that neither Kathleen nor I murdered your wife." There was a tremor in *his* voice. Emotion maybe — or the actor again.

I wiped rain from my eyes. "The other girl who died … who was she?"

"Her name was Elaine Yu. She was living in Prince Albert, Saskatchewan, at the time and I'm not sure but I think she was killed in a car accident. I never heard the details."

I watched the rain, hard now, running through his drenched hair and down his face.

"Appleton, I want you to know this: I'm going to keep searching and digging if it takes me the rest of my life. If

I find out that you, or your wife, started that fire, I'll be back. And nothing and no one will stop me."

Several seconds passed, then one small, almost invisible nod.

"One last thing," I said. "There were four girls at Northern Horizon and there were two at other schools. Was that all of them?"

The rain fell harder and for several seconds our eyes were locked onto each other, neither of us saying anything. Then as his lips barely moved, words came — barely formed, hard to hear, hard to understand.

But I did hear. I did understand.

"There was one more. She was my stepdaughter — Kathleen's daughter."

I had no words to respond with. I walked past Appleton, out of the park and toward the Impala.

SIXTEEN

I'd been home for almost three hours. I'd finished two rye and Cokes to go with the two I had on the plane. I'd started on a third but it had been sitting on the table in front of me since I'd poured it a half hour or so before. The ice had melted and the Coke had lost its colour and its allure. Great Big Sea had given way to the Downchild Blues Band on the stereo.

My cell phone had rung six or eight times since I'd walked into the apartment and I had yet to answer it. I wasn't sure there was anything anybody had to say that I needed to hear right then.

I now knew what had happened to Donna in her grade eleven year. But I wasn't any closer to knowing who had killed her or why. Maybe the fire had nothing to do with Appleton and his sexual predation on seven young girls. Or maybe it did.

Was it a stretch to think that a man who could do what he'd done to those girls was capable of worse? Likely not. I'd known of cases where convicted criminals threatened revenge on judges, lawyers, witnesses — everyone involved in the case against them. And I had known of a few who tried to carry out those threats with varying degrees of success.

So it was possible that Appleton had killed Donna out of a desire for revenge. And I supposed the same logic could apply to Kathleen Appleton. Despite her husband's protestations, what I had seen in that house was a woman who was dangerous.

And arson wasn't like looking into someone's eyes and shooting or stabbing or bludgeoning and watching them die. You could start a fire and be far away from the scene when your victim's life ended. The kind of murder that might be favoured by a woman?

And how did the fact that one of her husband's victims was her own daughter impact the thing? Wouldn't that have focused any need for revenge on him? Or had Appleton's silver tongue somehow managed to paint himself as the victim even as he seduced his step-daughter?

Was Kathleen Appleton's faith in her husband so great that she could choose him over her daughter? That kind of misguided fanaticism had existed throughout history so it was certainly possible.

And there was the note. The kind of vicious cruelty and hate that would enable someone to send a note like the one I had received one year after Donna's death was evident in the face, the voice, and the actions of Kathleen Appleton when I accused her husband of starting the fire.

Yet, for all of my cop show dialogue — *means, motive, opportunity* — it somehow didn't feel right. I wasn't sure. I wanted to be sure and I wasn't. Richard Appleton was a predator. His wife was a whack job. Hard to argue either point. But coldhearted, coldblooded killers?

I just didn't know.

I picked up the untouched third rye and Coke just as

Donnie Walsh and the rest of Downchild were wrapping up "Cruisin'."

I stood at the window and watched the street lights coming on throughout the streets of Bridgeland.

I set the drink glass back down — still untouched. I didn't feel up to a run but I needed to get outside — walk for a while. Think. I pulled on a down-filled jacket, toque, and mitts, expecting the worst, and took the stairs down to the main floor, stepping out into the dry cold the Canadian prairies are noted for. I shoved my hands into the jacket pockets, turned right when I reached the sidewalk, then left at the bottom of the little hill that led up to my apartment, walking aimlessly and without purpose. I turned again and was opposite the park at 9a Street. There were no kids in the playground there and no one else walking. Too late. Too dark. And too damn cold.

I stepped off the curb and started across the street toward the park.

I heard the car before I saw it, looked up at the roar of an engine that was loud and close…. too close.

The car roared by and I instinctively jumped back, lost my footing, and almost went down. When I'd recovered I turned to … what … yell? Extend a middle finger? Get a licence number to report an idiot driver? I didn't do any of those things. Instead I stared after the car, watching it disappear, tail lights racing into the night.

Dark, maybe blue, hard to say, not a recent model. Big car. *Car*, not the SUV that was the vehicle of choice in this neighbourhood. I saw the back of a head, only one. The car and its lone occupant disappeared around the corner.

A warning? About what? The MFs didn't likely see a need to send a message since I hadn't been a part of the

Blevins thing for a while, and wasn't all that critical to the investigation anyway. Using me to warn Cobb to back off?

Or was it one of the Appletons having beaten me back to Calgary, wanting to scare the crap out of me?

The real answer, of course, was that a bad driver, likely fuelled by a liquid stimulant of some kind, had buzzed me, carelessly but probably unintentionally. Might not have even seen me, noticed me at the last second, was as scared as I was.

The night was even colder than I'd thought. I decided to cut short my walk, stopped in at a Lebanese takeout, bought a takeout sandwich and salad, headed back in the direction of Drury Avenue and my apartment, checking the street periodically for wayward vehicles coming in my direction.

Back in the apartment, I transferred the sandwich and salad to a plate and set it on the counter. I poured myself an orange juice and was pulling Broken Social Scene out of its case when the cell phone rang again. I glared at it, willing it to explode. When it didn't, I picked it up, noting that I had seven messages.

"Hello." I hoped my tone of voice would let the caller know that I preferred shawarma to anything he or she had to tell me.

"It's Cobb. Just checking to see how you're doing."

"I've made a pretty good start on getting drunk but I seem to be losing steam."

"You sound like someone who's losing steam. You okay?"

"Not so much."

"I take it you found the teacher."

"Yeah, I found him. And his wife. Charming couple."

"I'd like to hear about it. Plus I'm hungry. How about I come by in twenty minutes?"

"I'm not in the mood for company."

"Well, get in the mood. I'm on my way."

He hung up. I looked at the phone. "You know, Cobb, you're really starting to piss me off."

I surveyed the room. It wasn't that bad, nothing that twenty minutes of tidying couldn't adequately deal with. I started with wrapping the sandwich and salad in separate cellophane packages and setting both in the refrigerator. I changed my mind on the music and Stan Rogers provided the accompaniment for my cleanup.

The knock on the door came after seventeen minutes and halfway through "Northwest Passage." I hadn't finished the tidying but it wasn't bad — good enough for Cobb on short notice.

I went to the door, pulled it open. Cobb stood, legs apart, grin on his face, like John Wayne arriving in Nome, Alaska, with a prostitute in tow. Except there was no one, prostitute or otherwise, standing next to him.

"Get your coat. I left the car running and we're going for something to eat."

I looked at him for several seconds, decided against arguing. Two minutes later we were heading down the front steps of the apartment.

He hadn't been kidding. The Jeep was running and it was warm inside, a good thing on a night when the thermometer seemed intent on exploring new depths.

"Feel like Chinese?"

"Yeah, sure. Anything."

We'd gone only a few blocks when Cobb's cell phone played the first few bars of Pachelbel's Canon in D. Different ring tone from what I remembered. I hadn't taken Cobb for a classical guy.

"Cobb," he said. And nothing else. He listened for thirty, maybe forty seconds, ended the call, reached again for the gearshift.

"Change of plans. We're still going to eat but Chinese is off the table."

"Jay Blevins?"

"I'll bring you up to speed on that over dinner. This is related … somewhat."

He didn't say anything more, at least not to me. He pulled over to the curb, tapped away on his cell phone for a minute or so. Texting. I resisted the urge to glance over, see if I could spot anything on the screen. Instead I looked out at Lukes Drug Mart, a Bridgeland landmark since sometime in the fifties.

A pause, silence, then more tapping. Cobb set the phone on the dash, put the Jeep in gear, and we were back in motion.

I sat back, let the heat fold itself around me, and continued to look out the side window. There was more snow than when I'd left and the people on the streets looked like figures from a Christmas card. Lots of scarves, bulky coats, and quilted ski jackets, gloves, some mitts. I realized I'd forgotten my own gloves.

Neither Cobb nor I spoke much and I didn't pay a lot of attention to our route until we pulled up in front of Kane's Harley Diner. I could see into the restaurant. Quiet night. People tend to stay at home when it's minus twenty with a wind chill ten degrees south of that.

"Home sweet home," I said.

Cobb said, "Yeah," shut the car off, and got out. I stepped out onto the curb.

Obviously the phone call and the texting had something

to do with our being here. I figured he'd tell me when he was ready. We hurried into the diner, Cobb as eager as I was to get out of the cold. Or maybe he had another reason for wanting to get inside in a hurry.

There was one middle-aged couple in a booth I hadn't been able to see from the street and a guy at the counter reading the paper and drinking coffee. Empty plate on the counter in front of him. Pie maybe.

I looked at Cobb and he pointed to a circular centre table with four chairs that seemed to be the focal point of the restaurant. I followed him to the table. Since the place wasn't busy I figured no one would object to our taking it. Not that Cobb would have altered his plans even if there had been an objection. He wasn't wired that way.

We sat down, waited. Davy came out from the back, spotted us, and came slowly toward us, his body language screaming his lack of enthusiasm. Olympians can run 800 meters in less time than it took for Davy to cover the dozen or so steps that separated us. He arrived at our table and looked at us like he'd never seen either of us before.

"Evening, Davy," I said.

A barely discernible nod as he handed us two menus, then turned to leave.

"You have a special tonight?" Cobb said.

Davy stopped but didn't turn around. "Chili."

Cobb said, "Bring us two specials. And two beers. We won't need glasses."

Davy made the trip back to the kitchen with what could be termed lightning speed — at least in comparison to what I'd seen as he came toward us.

I said, "Davy doesn't seem happy."

Cobb nodded. "Holiday season blahs."

"Must be it."

"I hope you're okay with chili. I seem to remember you telling me once you like it. I didn't want him hanging around our table."

"Chili's fine."

"So tell me about your trip to sun country."

I told him about my meeting with Kelly, the revelation about the abuse, and finally my encounter with the Appletons. I rolled it all out at once, paused only when Davy brought our food and two cans of Coors Light. Cobb watched me, seemed almost to be studying me as I talked, but didn't interrupt or ask me anything until I finished.

And not even then, at least not right away. We ate chili for a while. I piled mine on the toast Davy had brought with the chili; Cobb kept the chili and the toast apart from one another. To each his own.

Halfway through the chili, Cobb stopped eating, wiped his mouth with a serviette, and looked up at me.

"I'm sorry Adam, I really am. All this has to be tough for you."

I nodded. "Yeah."

"You think Appleton is capable of setting the fire?"

I paused before answering. "I've thought about nothing else since that afternoon. And the truth is I don't know. If he was capable of doing what he did to those girls I'd say he was capable of setting the fire. But being *capable* of doing it doesn't mean he *did* it. I just don't know."

"How about the pitbull wife?"

"Same answer. Maybe even more capable if she thought her husband was under threat. She might do anything if she freaked out like she did with me. Thing is he wasn't under threat. This was after the fact. He'd done his time. For all intents and purposes the whole thing was over."

"Except for revenge."

I nodded. "Except for that. And I don't know if either of them could kill with revenge as their motive."

"Either or both."

"What?"

"Just thinking out loud. It's possible that they were acting together on this thing."

I thought about that over a mouthful of chili and toast. "Maybe, maybe not. She didn't strike me as Lady Macbeth. And there's the X factor in all this — he molested her daughter. I haven't got that figured out at all."

"You mean why she's side by side with the son of a bitch when she should be trying to poison his birthday cake."

"Yeah."

He shook his head, which I took to mean it made as much sense to him as it did to me.

We sipped our beer and I told him about the narrow miss with the car.

"You get a look at it?"

"It was dark so it was tough to get a good look. It was a big car, dark colour."

"What do you mean, *big* car?"

"Like those boats people use to drive before we knew about climate change."

"So an *older* big car."

"I'd say so, yeah."

"You saw the Audi at the warehouse. Any chance...?"

I shook my head. "Notta. Not in the same league. I don't know what this car was but it wasn't the Audi."

"And you didn't see the driver?"

"Uh-uh. Back of a head, that's all. I wish I could tell you for sure it was the MFs or that it wasn't, but I can't."

"Maybe we'll just ask them when they get here."

"What?"

"They should be here any time now."

"And you know that because…?"

"I happened to learn that they often come in here on Sunday nights. Not every Sunday, but most of them."

"Just happened to learn," I repeated.

"My man Davy. Picked himself up a two hundred dollar bonus for making a phone call."

"To you."

"To me."

"The phone call you got while we were driving? The texting?"

"The texting was something else. But the phone call, yeah, that was our boy."

"That explains the less than enthusiastic reception we received. He's scared they'll find out and rearrange his body parts."

Cobb nodded.

We ate for a minute. I looked over at him. "I think I liked it better when you were wanting to keep me out of the line of fire."

"Came up a little sudden. I didn't think you'd want me to drop you on a street corner on a frostbite night."

"Good call."

"Besides, there shouldn't be a line of fire. Just a little chat."

"Rock Scubberd going to be one of the diners?"

"That's what Davy tells me. He let it slip during one of my stops here that the MFs phone ahead when they're planning a visit. They like to make sure they're dining alone. I mentioned to Davy that I was aware of a couple of outstanding legal issues he had and that I'd be less inclined to pass that information along to former colleagues, and I'd add a two hundred dollar tip to my next bill if he let me know the next time Scubberd and his group were planning to stop in."

I set my fork down. I'd lost interest in the chili.

"And how will Scubberd take it when he and the MFs aren't the only diners tonight?"

"I told Davy to tell them I got pushy, wouldn't take 'we're closed' for an answer. Basically put it on me."

I glanced around the restaurant, noted that we were the only ones still in the place. "So if Rock and company decide to vent their displeasure, it will be in our direction, not Davy's."

"It was the least I could do for the young man."

"Thoughtful. And why exactly would we want to spend time bonding with the likes of Rock Scubberd?"

"I received another phone call a couple of days ago. From my man Grover."

"Ike Groves."

"The same."

"Informants are a cop's best friend. Or an ex-cop."

Cobb smiled. "Roger that. Apparently my chats have borne fruit. Suddenly Grover can't wait to tell me things. Shared with me that there's a rumour on the street about a drug shipment — big time deal supposed to arrive sometime in the next couple of weeks. Which dovetails nicely with the information I received as to why Scubberd was spending time in Vancouver. Setting up a network for a continuous supply."

"And I'm guessing the shipment is bound for a location owned and operated by the MFs."

"That's the scuttlebutt. Then it gets turned around and is off to Fort McMurray. Popular destination for MF imports. If there's any truth to the rumour, Mr. Scubberd may see the wisdom of chatting with us further."

"And this is the first shipment via the new network?"

Cobb shrugged. "Don't know. Obviously they've been getting stuff from somewhere prior to this. But the Grover tells me this is big."

"And if the Grover's tip is some crack induced hallucination with no connection whatsoever to the reality …"

"Then our night may end unpleasantly."

"Or a setup by a guy who's scared to death of the MFs and wants to get on their good side."

"Even more unpleasantly."

"And you're risking both our necks on the trustworthiness of Ike Groves."

He didn't get to answer. The door of the restaurant opened and the largest man I'd ever seen who wasn't wearing shoulder pads or a sumo diaper entered the restaurant.

What he *was* wearing was a white overcoat that contrasted sharply with the blackness of his skin. He moved a couple of steps farther inside, stepped to one side and two more men, both Caucasian, followed him through the door. They made it unanimous on the overcoats; the three of them likely cost more than my apartment furniture. The second man through the door wore a fedora, the large man and the third guy were bareheaded.

Cobb was sitting with his back to the door, which, when I thought about it later, seemed to fly in the face of the private detective way of doing things. He didn't turn to look or even seem particularly interested. He dabbed at the chili with his toast, took a bite, chased it with beer.

The biggest surprise was yet to come. There was one more person in the group at the door. A woman who, if she had been smiling, would have been striking. She didn't look like someone who was accustomed to smiling. Nevertheless, she was attractive in a pissed-off-at-the-world kind of way. Her clothes — expensive — and demeanor were a long way from biker bitch.

All four came in our direction, then seeing us, stopped, all of them at the same time, like a choreographed dance step. I busied myself with studying the tabletop, whispered, "They're here," at Cobb. "And I think we're going to meet the lovely Mrs. Smith as well."

Cobb stayed focused on the chili. I saw the man with the hat speaking to the big guy. Both were looking at us. The big man nodded and continued on toward us. I whispered "shit."

Cobb looked at me and smiled.

"Good chili," he said.

The big man was now standing beside our table and looking down at us. I was somehow reminded of my favourite TV show from when I was a kid, *The Friendly Giant*. At the beginning of every show "Friendly" looked down on his tiny toy living room and said, "Look up, look way up."

Which is what I was doing now. The key difference, of course, being that the Friendly Giant was … *friendly*.

"The restaurant's closed." The man's voice was Darth Vader-esque but with less charm.

Cobb spoke without looking at the man. "Actually it's not. It closes at nine and here it is," he looked at his watch, "just 8:23. By the way, the chili's very nice."

"The restaurant's closed and you're leaving."

Cobb sat up straight and leaned back against the back of his chair. Managed to look up at the man without it appearing to be a big deal.

"Two things," Cobb's voice had no trace of a tremor. Mine, had I pressed it into service at that moment, would have registered at least 7.5 on the Richter Scale. I looked at Cobb and was aware again that he was not afraid of the guy.

"First," he said, "we're not leaving, and second I'm happy to have Mr. Scubberd join us. I'd extend the invitation to you too but I can see that might be a little problematic, you being the size of a round bale and all."

I'd read several accounts (even written one) about gangland-style slayings in restaurants. We were in a restaurant in which there were no other customers and the only potential witness — Davy — was, as they say, conspicuous by his absence.

And Cobb had just offended someone who looked like gangland-style slayings were his bread and butter.

"Martin." The man in the fedora spoke. I took him to be Scubberd.

The big man must have been Martin because after a few more seconds of looking hard at Cobb, he turned and walked back to the man I presumed to be his boss.

There was a flurry of whispered conversation with the man in the fedora doing most of the talking. The big man said a few things and pointed a couple of times. Mrs. Smith-Scubberd didn't speak but seemed impatient for the conversation to be over. And it was. All four were heading in our direction.

This time the big man passed our table and stopped just beyond it, a little behind me, then turned so that he was facing Cobb. The man in the fedora pulled out the chair to my left and the lady I took to be Mrs. Scubberd sat down. She was even better looking up close but I thought it best not to spend a lot of time looking at her.

Scubberd, if that's who he was, walked to the other side of the table, shucked his overcoat, and sat, putting him on my right, Cobb's left. He had shoulder length, dyed blond hair and a goatee that ran a shade darker than the hair. Starched, pressed, dark brown shirt, open at the neck. Sleeves rolled up one turn.

Muscular. I remembered Cobb saying Scubberd was a gym rat. Whatever workout regime he followed seemed to be working for him.

The third man, maybe five seven and slim even in the overcoat, which he had unfastened except for one button, hovered a few feet behind the woman, close to Martin. He never stopped moving — nervous or high, or maybe both.

"What do you want?" Scubberd demanded.

Cobb pushed the plates to the far side of the table and leaned slightly forward. "My name's Cobb."

"Cop?"

"Private," Cobb said.

Scubberd glanced at me.

Cobb spoke. "He's Cullen. A journalist."

"A private eye and a scribe. You're shittin' me."

Cobb didn't answer, kept his eyes on Scubberd's face.

Scubberd didn't flinch. "I'll say it again. What do you want?"

"I know who *you* are," Cobb said. "I haven't met these gentlemen or this lovely lady."

I tried to glance at Scubberd without appearing to be looking at him. He looked unhappy.

"I'll humour you that much." He nodded toward the big man. "That's Minnis." Another nod, this time at the smaller man. "The Italian's Moretti. And this is my wife. Now I'm asking for the last time, what do you want?"

"I'm looking to make a trade."

"You think you've got something I want."

"Actually I want to trade a favour for a favour."

"And what could you do that would be a favour to me?"

"It's what I *wouldn't* be doing that I think you'd appreciate."

"I'm losing interest fast and I'm also hungry so if you've got something to say you better get it said in the next ten seconds or my associates will see you to the door."

There are people who say tough things just for effect. My guess was that Rock Scubberd wasn't one of those people. I had no doubt at all that he meant exactly what he said.

"I know about the incoming shipment." Cobb said it in the same tone of voice one would use to say *I think I'll have the Thousand Islands*. "I'm guessing that it would be both inconvenient and unprofitable for that information to fall into the wrong hands."

"You gambled and lost, Cowboy. I don't know anything about a shipment because there isn't one. Now fuck off."

"Certainly. I don't want to take up any more of your time. Nice meeting you. I recommend the chili." Cobb slid his chair back and stood up. I wasn't sure what I should do so I did nothing.

Cobb didn't seem to notice my predicament. He was looking at the big guy, Martin Minnis, who had taken one step forward. Neither spoke. Neither moved. Neither flinched.

Scubberd chuckled. "Even if you're as tough as you'd like us to believe, he's not the one you have to worry about. My smaller but equally effective associate favours armaments."

On cue, Moretti undid the last button to let the front of his overcoat fall open, revealing a shoulder holster that housed a serious-looking revolver.

"Impressive," Cobb said.

I wasn't sure how it happened but Moretti was suddenly holding a large, menacing-looking switchblade. He flicked it open as casually as if he'd been opening a glasses case.

"Also impressive," said Cobb. He looked at the knife for a few seconds then turned away from Moretti and back toward Scubberd.

"In fact, that's almost as impressive as *my* associates."

Cobb pointed a thumb in the direction of the door to the kitchen. Two people I'd never seen before came through the door, one carrying what looked to my un-trained eye like a lot of shotgun, the other holding a ma-chine gun–looking piece of equipment that wouldn't have been out of place in a Sylvester Stallone movie. Neither of the two men spoke but took up positions on either side of the kitchen door facing our table, maybe ten meters away from us, their weapons trained on Minnis and Moretti.

The whole scene was surreal. This wasn't New York or Los Angeles or even Montreal — this was Calgary. I'd covered crime in this city long enough to know there was some bad shit that went on. But this was like something from a kids' video game. *My gun's bigger than your gun.*

Neither Cobb nor Scubberd seemed particularly un-nerved by the lineup of well-armed adversaries, who were glaring at each other like North and South Korean soldiers on either side of the demilitarized zone. I, on the other hand, was unnerved enough for everybody.

All of the action was taking place behind Scubberd's wife, who now spoke for the first time. "Rock, I'm sure we can spare these gentlemen a few minutes."

She seemed almost to be enjoying the action around her. I watched her. Her makeup was understated and the open-at-the-throat soft green blouse was classy. Interesting woman. Wouldn't have looked out of place at a fundraiser for the philharmonic orchestra.

Scubberd looked at her, then at Cobb. "Well, now that we all understand one another, maybe you should sit back down and we can finish our conversation."

"I was hoping you might see it that way." Cobb returned to his seat. He turned and nodded to Mrs. Scubberd whose chin tilted down a fraction of a centimetre in response.

Scubberd turned to Minnis. "Tell Davy to get out here with some beer." When Minnis hesitated, Scubberd turned to Cobb, smiling. "I assume your people won't shoot my people for summoning the waiter."

Cobb looked up at Minnis. "You're fine, Slim."

Slim, Cowboy ... Louis L'Amour would have loved this.

Minnis headed for the kitchen, walked between the two guys, who made room for him to pass. The one with the shotgun took two steps farther into the restaurant, turned, and aimed the shotgun at the kitchen door. If Minnis decided to come through there, gun blazing, he wouldn't get far. I was thinking to myself, *these guys are good.* I looked at Cobb. No way to tell what he was thinking.

"Okay, Cowboy, let's get to it," Scubberd said. "You want to talk trade. Now even though there is no shipment,

I appreciate that you came to me with what you thought was good information instead of going to the cops, so let me hear what it is you need and maybe we can work something out."

"Jay Blevins."

Scubberd waited, then said, "Is that supposed to mean something to me?"

"His old man is the guy who took out your boys in the house on Raleigh Avenue. Then you offed his old man. But I have a feeling you and your … associates might feel it's necessary to get the kid as well. Maybe send a message."

"What makes you think I give a fuck about this kid?"

I was surprised that Scubberd didn't deny either the house on Raleigh or the killing of Blevins. Didn't admit anything but didn't deny either.

"Somebody very handy with a knife …" Cobb hesitated but didn't look at Moretti, "carved up one of the kid's friends. And there's been some patrolling at the girlfriend's former residence. Patrolling in an Audi."

Scubberd's eyes flicked a half centimetre in Moretti's direction, then back. I saw it and I guessed Cobb saw it too.

"And you're thinking this person who is all handy with a knife might be one of my people. Along with whoever is doing the patrolling."

"Seems possible," Cobb said. "Bottom line, I don't see that you have any reason to bother with the kid. He was a customer, that's all. He wasn't in on the old man's deal, didn't know anything about it. And you already sent the message when you got the kid's dad. So I'm … requesting … that if your people happen to be on the hunt for this kid, you call them off."

Minnis came through the kitchen door, looked at the shotgun, then walked the rest of the way to the table. Davy was right behind him carrying a tray that held six cans of Coors Light and six glasses. He set the tray on the table between Cobb and Scubberd. Neither made a move toward the beer. Davy picked up the plates from earlier, turned, and hustled back in the direction of the kitchen. Scubberd waited until he was gone.

"What's this Blevins kid to you?"

"Nothing. I've never even met him. Blevins came to me after he wasted the dealers, hired me to keep the kid alive. I'm trying to do that."

"Even though your client is dead."

"Even though."

"An honourable man. Isn't that nice."

Cobb shrugged, said nothing.

"And if I forget about this crack head kid, you'll forget about this *rumour* of some shipment that has no basis in fact anyway."

"That's the deal. I don't hassle you, you don't hassle the kid."

Scubberd leaned back in his chair and rocked a little, looking from side to side as he rocked. His eyes rested longer on his wife than on anyone else. I couldn't see any communication between them. He looked at her. She looked at him.

Scubberd thudded the chair back down to the floor and turned his attention again to Cobb.

"Okay, Cowboy. We can make that work. Now why don't you and the scribe beat it so I can get on with dinner."

I think my breathing became a little more normal. I was waiting for Cobb to move so we could get the hell out of there.

"Not yet," he said.

Oh, shit.

Cobb smiled. Scubberd glared at him. I swallowed.

When Cobb spoke again his voice was flat and cold, devoid of expression, a conveyor of information, nothing more.

"There's one last thing. Recently someone tried to get up close and personal with Mr. Cullen here. Drive-by, a little too close. Maybe a warning, maybe a near miss. Either way — unacceptable."

Scubberd turned and looked at me a long minute, "You see this vehicle?"

I was hoping my voice would work normally. "Older. Eighties maybe, big sedan. It was dark, that's all I could make out."

"None of my people have a ride anything like that. We ride Harleys."

"Except for the Audi," Cobb said.

"That don't sound like no Audi. And since it wasn't a fuckin' motorcycle that almost ran over your ass, it's got shit to do with us." He turned to Cobb. "On top of which I've never seen or even heard of this fuck before tonight."

A loud silence ensued. No one spoke.

Mrs. Smith spoke for the second time. To me this time. "You're a writer. Is that right, Mr. Cullen?"

"I am, yes."

Scubberd snorted. "What kind of shit you write? Letters? Kids porn? Poetry?"

Moretti snickered at his boss's humour. Probably part of the job description.

"Freelance. I write for newspapers when I come across a story that needs telling."

Scubberd poured one of the beers into a glass, reached across the table, and set it in front of his wife. He poured a second into a glass, took a long drink, and wiped his mouth with the sleeve of his coat.

Scubberd looked at me, not unpleasantly. "I hope you're not dumb enough to think that anything you've seen or heard tonight *needs telling*." He drew out the last two words.

When I didn't answer right away, Scubberd emptied his glass, set it down and said, "Because when my guys drive by they don't miss."

"No, I'm not dumb enough to think that."

Scubberd nodded and took another beer but didn't open it.

"Let me summarize. Nobody talks about drug shipments, fictitious or otherwise, nobody kills the kid, and nobody writes anything that ends up in the newspaper That's our *arrangement*, Cowboy. I only use the word *deal* when there's money involved."

Cobb nodded. They didn't shake hands.

Cobb said, "If it's all the same for you, we'll pass on the beer."

"That's good because I wasn't fucking plannin' to offer you any."

Moretti snickered again. Cobb stood up so suddenly that in surprise Moretti took a quick step backward, almost losing his balance. The snicker ended in a growl.

Cobb said, "For a badass killer, you're a clumsy little snake."

Mrs. Scubberd made a noise that sounded like a laugh she was trying to hold in but I couldn't be sure. Moretti's face took on the colour of hail clouds and I knew if it were up to him the deal would be off right now.

Cobb turned to face Scubberd. "Here's how this is going to go. Your associates will sit down at the table. Mr. Cullen and I will walk out the front door. When we're out the door, *my* associates will leave through the kitchen. And we can all enjoy the rest of the evening."

Scubberd nodded once but his lips were pressed together. He was not a man who was used to being told how things were going to play out.

I stood up trying not to look like I was overeager. I'm not sure I pulled it off.

Cobb and I started for the door.

A voice behind us stopped us. "That seems a little harsh, Mr. Cobb," Mrs Scubberd said. I'd have put her voice somewhere between Elizabeth Taylor and Taylor Swift.

We turned back to face them. Mrs. Scubberd was smiling but only a little. "My husband is an honourable man. He's shown good faith. The courteous thing would be for you gentlemen to do the same thing."

Cobb looked at her for what seemed like a minute but was probably five or six seconds. Then he turned slightly and motioned with his head for the two guys with the heavy artillery who were still flanking the door to the kitchen to leave. They did. Cobb turned back to the MFs, nodded once, and we resumed our move toward the door.

I resisted the urge to turn and see if everything behind us was going as Cobb and Mrs. Scubberd seemed to think it would. Cobb opened the door, held it for me, then followed me onto the street. The air outside was oppressively cold but it was the most welcome air I had breathed in a couple of decades.

We walked toward Cobb's Jeep. "Audi across the street."

I looked where he was pointing. "That's the one I saw outside Zoe's building."

"Let's hope we don't see it again anytime soon."

Once we were inside and Cobb had started the Jeep, I turned to him. "Who were those guys?"

He knew which guys I meant. "Ex-cops, one retired, the other on disability."

"And they do this sort of thing?"

"Freelance like you. I called in a couple of favours."

"That's what the texting was about."

"Uh-huh."

"I got the impression Mrs. Scubberd isn't just eye candy."

Cobb nodded. "I'd say she's a player. Maybe not on the same level as her husband but, as you say, a long way from a bad guy's bimbo."

The Jeep's heater had kicked in and I leaned forward to put my hands next to the floor vent. "All we were missing in there was Doc Holliday."

Cobb had been looking straight ahead. Now he turned his head to look at me.

"Something you need to understand, Adam. This isn't some Bruce Willis action movie and that wasn't make believe back there. I had my two guys there because I figured without them there was a pretty good chance that some very messy stuff could happen."

"So why did you want to go face to face with Scubberd at all?"

"Desperation. I haven't been able to find the kid. And if they found him before I did, they'd have snuffed him out like a candle on a birthday cake. When I heard about the shipment of drugs destined for whatever warehouse the MFs use for storing their merchandise, I figured it was worth a shot."

"Scubberd says there is no shipment."

"That was bullshit. He couldn't acknowledge it to me because that would mean that I actually had something on him. This way he pretends he's making nice and sparing the kid out of the goodness of his heart."

"Will he keep his part of the bargain?"

"I don't know. I'm guessing maybe sixty-forty in our favour. Honour among thieves and all that. Mrs. Scubberd assured us that he's an honourable man. We better hope she's right."

"I still think it's risky. You made Scubberd look bad in there. He might be thinking payback."

Cobb looked at me in the semi-darkness of the Jeep. "He might. But I played the only cards I had. What we better hope for now is that the cops don't find out about the drug shipment and stage a raid and blow the whole thing to hell."

"Because if that happens, the Scubberds will think the information came from you and —"

Cobb shook his head. "I don't think so. He knows I wouldn't have gone to him asking for him to leave Jay alone if I was planning to let the cops in on what I know. But he would be worried that there are too many people in the know. And he might decide to start removing those people and anybody he even suspects of having some insider access to what's going on in the MFs world. Then it gets ugly."

"I'm glad I don't have your job," I said.

Cobb pulled out into traffic, driving slowly. "At the very start you told me you were in this for the story you'd be able to write when it was over. You want to write this story, you need to see it all, be part of it. Because if you're not, you could wind up dead in a Dumpster about four hours after your story hits the streets."

"Memo received. Now what?"

"I drop you off at your house. We get a good night's sleep and give Jay another shot in the morning."

I thought about that. "If you just made a deal with the MFs not to waste the kid then what difference does it make if you find him or not? Why bother?"

"I don't like stuff left unfinished."

"Yeah."

We drove in silence for a few more blocks. We came to the lights at 9th Avenue and 19th Street where you turn left if you want to get to the Deerfoot. Cobb didn't turn. Instead he drove on into an older residential neighbourhood for a couple of blocks then turned left, then left again, and one more left to get us back to 9th Avenue. I wasn't paying much attention. A lot had happened and I was still trying to process it. As Cobb turned back onto 9th Avenue heading back toward where we'd just been, I finally broke the silence.

"Cruising, are we? Hoping to see Jay just walking down the street?"

"No."

"Okay ... any ideas? It seems to me this kid is proving to be pretty elusive."

"That's true and I'd like to discuss that with you, but not right now."

That response made as much sense as everything else that had happened so far on this night. And, like most of what had happened so far on this night I didn't like it. "Look, if there's —"

He held up his hand to stop me. "We've got a tail."

"What?"

"Don't look back there but someone is following us."

"Shit. An Audi?"

He shook his head, casting a casual glance now and then at the rearview mirror. "Pickup. This guy's an amateur. Following too close. Easy to spot. He picked us up leaving the restaurant, which means he knew we were there."

"How would anybody know that? *I* didn't even know that."

"He followed us there."

"But if the guy's an amateur how is it you didn't spot him back there before?"

"I was careless."

"Just one guy?"

"Unless someone else is hunkered down in there out of sight. We've got a driver, male it looks like. Dodge half or three-quarter ton, not a dually, I'd say early 2000s vintage."

"So what now?"

"So now we see if we can find out who this person is."

As he finished speaking, Cobb swerved to the right and slid to the curb between a Chevy Nova and a MINI Cooper. As we stopped both of us tried to get a look at the driver of the pickup as it went by. The driver lifted his arm and covered his face as he rolled by so we saw nothing that would help identify whoever was following us.

We waited until the pickup was out of sight down the road. Cobb pulled back out into traffic and drove for a block or so with the lights out, finally turned them back on as we rolled through the traffic lights at 12th Street. The pickup was visible ahead of us but Cobb, unlike the "amateur," stayed well back with two vehicles between us and the Dodge.

I said, "To repeat, what now?"

"Not sure yet. We play it by ear."

Up ahead, the pickup turned right at 8th Street opposite the historic Deane House. Cobb moved into the right lane, slowly eased around the corner. The pickup was nowhere in sight. We drove north one block and turned right again. Cobb and I spotted the truck at the same time; it was pulled into a driveway at a two-storey red brick house on the opposite side of the street. Someone, it might have been the driver, was walking away from the truck and the house. He was walking quickly. Cobb pulled over and we parked alongside a park, neither of us taking our eyes off the guy walking, almost running now.

"Let's go," Cobb said and we both jumped out of the Jeep. "You check the pickup. I got the guy on the street."

We were running now and so was the guy ahead of us. I figured my stop at the pickup was a waste of time — it seemed pretty clear the guy on foot was the same man who'd been at the wheel of the truck.

I did what I was told and ran to where the pickup was parked. I slowed as I got there, and ducked down next to a fence, thinking for just a second about all the things that could go wrong if I just ran up to the driver's side door without thinking.

Unless someone else is hunkered down in there out of sight.

I waited, listening hard, and peered through the darkness at the truck, trying to get a look inside. Not seeing anyone in the truck from my vantage point next to the fence, I slid slowly up alongside until I was even with the back door. Still no one inside that I could see. I yanked the driver's door open and went into a crouch, mostly because that's what I'd seen law enforcement people on TV do. Of course most of those people were pointing guns at whoever was in the vehicle at the time but, as I didn't have that option I hoped the crouch would suffice on its own.

It did but only because there was no one in the truck.

I peered around the interior, saw nothing much of value. A couple of screwdrivers, a flashlight, some empty candy bar wrappers and a coffee travel mug lay spread over the middle and passenger seats. And a box of Trojans, open, a couple gone.

I leaned in, flipped the glove box down, and pulled out a small plastic carrying case that housed the vehicle's registration and insurance. The truck belonged to Roland Nill. I didn't take the time to try to learn more in case Cobb needed my help in the pursuit of Mr. Nill or whoever had been at the wheel of the pickup moments before.

I closed the door of the pickup and started off down the street in the direction Cobb and the guy on foot had taken. I went at a steady, medium-fast jog thinking it could be a long run and that I better conserve some energy for later if I needed it.

I'd gone about two blocks, my head moving from side to side the whole time, hoping to spot either Cobb, his quarry, or both.

I heard them before I saw them. Loud, high-pitched swearing from one voice, Cobb's base growl interrupting it from time to time to state, "Shut the hell up."

They were standing next to an older sandstone building that had been converted to a set of offices. A sign announced that the building housed Jackson MacArthur Enterprises, an accounting firm.

Cobb had hold of someone who was struggling and swearing, neither of which seemed to be having much impact on Cobb, who looked at me as I arrived and said, "Adam, say hello to Jay Blevins."

SEVENTEEN

Jay Blevins's face hadn't been washed in a very long time. That was the first thing I took note of as I looked at the kid we'd been trying to find all this time and who, instead, had found us.

Cobb had a firm grip on the twisting mass that was Jay Blevins but didn't look like he was hurting the kid at all. It also didn't look like keeping him under control, except for his mouth, was much of a job. The kid was as tall as I was, but there was nothing to him.

Jay bore the malnourished, emaciated look I'd seen on the faces and bodies of countless addicts I'd encountered before. Sadly, wasted was the perfect descriptor for what I was seeing.

Owen Harkness all over again.

And like Owen, Jay's mouth was the one part of him that seemed to work just fine.

"Listen, Dipshit, you've got ten seconds to get out of my face, then I call the cops and nail both your asses for assault."

Cobb moved his face to maybe two centimetres from Jay's and said again, slightly modified this time, "Shut the fuck up." Less a directive and more of a threat.

Thankfully it worked. Jay fell silent.

Wrestling with Cobb, if that's what you could call the kid's feeble attempts at resistance, quickly took its toll and he stopped moving except for the heaving of his pathetically small chest. No longer the athlete. Once a football player, now Ichabod Crane.

Cobb released him, straightened the worn jean jacket Jay was wearing, a jacket that was far too light to be even remotely effective in fending off the cold of this night. He wasn't wearing gloves but did have a toque that, like the jean jacket, had seen better, and cleaner, days.

Jay stood up a little straighter, brushed imaginary snow from the shoulder of the jacket, and glared at Cobb, with the occasional unpleasant glance in my direction.

Cobb said, "Okay, Jay, let's start with question number one. Why were you following us?"

Jay shook his head. "Oh no, uh-uh, that's not the question. The question is why have *you* been following *me*?"

Despite the dishevelled, unhealthy look to Jay Blevins, there was something about him that differentiated him from the majority of crackheads, cokeheads, and other addicts I'd encountered over the years. It was the eyes.

This wasn't the wide-eyed, wildly out of control look I had become all too familiar with over the years.

"How long you been clean, Jay?" I asked.

"What's that to you? And who the fuck are you anyway?"

Cobb shook him a little, sort of a show-some-respect shake.

"My name's Cobb. This is Adam Cullen. We've been looking for you. We knew your dad." Cobb said it gently, especially the last part.

I watched Jay contort his face, straighten his shoulders. Trying for tough. "Yeah, well … what's that got to do with me?"

"How about we go someplace a little warmer, maybe get some coffee, and we'll tell you exactly what it has to do with you."

"I don't have to go with you."

"No, you don't. You can stay out here and freeze your ass off. Or we can call the cops — who are also looking for you — or we can go have a cup of coffee and talk a little bit."

A few seconds passed while he thought about it. I hoped he'd make up his mind soon because that "freeze your ass off" thing Cobb had mentioned applied to more than just the kid.

"Where?"

"How about someplace that has some food. Maybe we can get a bite to eat to go with the coffee?"

I said, "There's a place down 9th Avenue a few blocks. Harriet's. Should still be open."

"We talk for a while, then we drop you off wherever you want to go. Fair enough?"

Jay looked at Cobb, assessing the possibility that there was any truth in what he was hearing. I hated to imagine the lies the kid had heard during his time on the street.

Jay shrugged and said, "Okay."

Harriet's wasn't fancy but given the state of our guest, it would do nicely. Better yet, we were the only ones in the place. Cobb parked behind Harriet's next to a Dumpster, which meant the Jeep wouldn't be seen by anyone driving by.

Once inside, Cobb selected a table near the back, again well out of view from the street. This time he sat facing the front door.

Two restaurants in an hour. With interesting people for company in both cases.

To his credit, Jay suggested maybe he should wash. Cobb went with him to the john and stood outside the door to ensure that Jay didn't try to escape out the back. I couldn't imagine why he'd want to take off and miss out on a free meal but I wasn't sure, even if he *was* clean, how lucid the kid's thought processes might be.

He was in the bathroom long enough to have me wondering if he'd decided to vacate via a window, and I could see from his body language that Cobb was having similar thoughts. He looked about ready to kick down the door when it opened and Jay stepped out.

He hadn't been able to effect a miraculous change, but I could see that he'd tried. The hands and face were cleaner and he'd stashed the toque in a pocket and tried to get most of his hair going in roughly the same direction.

I got out of the booth and let Jay slide in first. Cobb sat opposite us. A girl, not much older than Jay, came to the table snapping gum and looking like customers were the worst part of her day.

"What can I get you?" She was looking at Jay with something less than cordiality. In fairness to her, one of the things that the enclosed quarters of the restaurant revealed was that Jay had been less successful eliminating the smell he was emitting than he had been in scraping off some of the surface dirt.

The waitress actually took a step back.

Cobb said, "Jay?"

Jay shrugged. "I don't know."

Cobb looked back at the waitress. "What's your soup, Miss?"

"My name's not Miss."

"What is your name?"

"Virginia."

"My mistake, Virginia." Cobb smiled pleasantly. "What's your soup?"

"Mushroom."

"Great. Bring us three bowls of soup, three coffees, and some sandwiches."

"What kind of sandwiches?"

"Surprise me."

"We've got ham and that's it."

"You just spoiled the surprise, Virginia." Cobb was working at looking pleasant. "Bring us a plate of ham sandwiches as well."

"How many?"

"Surprise me."

She started to answer, changed her mind, and turned away.

"Thank you, Virginia," Cobb said.

She didn't acknowledge his thanks.

"Well, Jay." Cobb smiled. "It's nice to finally meet up with you. We've been looking for you a long time."

"Yeah. And why is that?"

Cobb set his big hands on the table, looked over them at Jay.

"I'm a private detective. Your dad hired me to try to protect you after he killed those two men at the crack house."

Jay's shook his head hard from side to side. "Stupid, stupid, stupid."

"Maybe. But I think he was desperate to do something to get you out of the crack scene and he'd run out of ideas. Besides, he didn't really plan to kill anybody. He went in there to try to scare them off — so they wouldn't sell to you anymore. Things got out of control; he lost it and started shooting."

"What the hell was he thinking?"

"I don't know what he was thinking, but I just told you what he was thinking *about* — that was you."

"And this was supposed to help me how?"

"I've encountered desperate parents before, Jay. They'll do anything to try to get back the kid they used to have. I suspect that was the place your old man was at."

Bubble Gum Girl returned with the soup and the sandwiches. She set the tray down and said, "I'll go get your coffees."

I busied myself distributing the food. I was glad now I hadn't got very far with the chili earlier.

Jay looked at the food as he spoke. "So I don't get where you come in. The old man had already killed those guys. What do I need protecting from?"

Cobb took the bowl of soup I offered and set it down in front of Jay. "Do you have any idea who ran the house you were buying your drugs from, Jay? Who Stick and the other guys were working for?"

"I heard some biker dudes. But I didn't really know. Didn't really care."

Cobb looked at Jay for a long time, like he was trying to figure out how anybody could be that stupid. "Ever hear of the MFs, Jay?"

Jay took a bite of sandwich, chewed for a while, then nodded. "Heard of 'em. Don't know much about them, I guess."

Virginia came back with the coffee. Again I did some
passing and all three of us were busy for a few seconds,
doctoring our coffee. Jay dumped enough sugar into his
to turn it into syrup. He took a drink and looked up at
Cobb.

"What an asshole."

"Who?"

"My old man."

Cobb said, "How about we take a few minutes to eat
some soup? That'll give you time to get some food into
you and it'll give me time to fight off the urge to reach
across the table and choke the shit out of you."

Jay gave Cobb a what's-got-your-ass look but didn't
say anything, which was probably for the best. For the
next few minutes we ate soup and ham sandwiches.

It was real obvious, real fast that it had been a while
since Jay had eaten much. He wolfed down the soup and
two of the sandwiches. Which was a bit of an indicator
that maybe he had been clean, at least long enough to
develop an appetite.

I ate a little soup, drank some of the coffee, watched
Jay take on fuel and looked at Cobb a couple of times. It
was hard to know what he was thinking.

As the pace of the food frenzy slowed, Jay looked over
at me, stared for a long minute.

"You a private detective too?"

I shook my head. "Freelance writer. I've been helping
Cobb try to track you down."

"Guess you both failed, huh?"

"Guess so," I said.

Cobb set his coffee cup down. "Where'd you get the pickup?"

"What?"

"The truck you were driving. Where'd you get it?"

"I borrowed it."

"The owner know you borrowed it?"

"Roland Nill," I said.

"What?"

"Roland Nill, that's who owns the truck."

"Oh … yeah."

Cobb said, "Mr. Nill, he know you borrowed his truck?"

Jay shrugged. "Maybe not."

"So you stole it."

"That's harsh, man," Jay said.

"Yeah, why don't you tell us about it."

"I got the word that a couple of dudes had been asking about me. Two guys driving a black Jeep. I was keeping my eye out for you. I saw you park in front of that biker restaurant. I wasn't sure you were the right guys but I figured I'd hang around, get a look at you at least. Then this guy comes along in the pickup, and he's got this really young chick with him — like a teenager. They park and get out of the truck, head off down the street, probably to a bar or a restaurant. Foreplay." Jay grinned and took a bite out of a third sandwich. "I guess the guy's so horny he leaves the key in the ignition. So I get in and start it just to warm up for a while — I figured I could run for it when the guy came back. Then you came out of the restaurant and I figured what the hey, let's go for a spin and see what happens."

"Which brings us to here and now."

Jay glanced at me. "So you gonna write a book about this? One of those behind-the-scenes real life things?"

"I hadn't planned on it, no."

"Whatever." He looked at Cobb. "My ex-girlfriend, Zoe, I heard she's gone from the place she was living at. You know anything about that?"

Cobb shook his head. "How would it be if I asked the questions?"

"Ex-girlfriend?" I repeated.

"Well ... yeah, we sort of ... broke up."

"When was that, Jay?"

He glared at me, sat up straighter. "What's it to you anyway?"

"It wasn't that long ago, your *ex-girlfriend* was spending her nights in a below freezing dump hoping you might show up. Didn't seem to know anything about how you two had broken up. Maybe you failed to mention that to her."

"What the fuck's it to you?"

I turned, grabbed him by the collar, and jerked him up and toward me. He felt like he weighed maybe ninety pounds. "Listen you little piece of shit —"

Cobb reached across the table, put a big hand on my shoulder. "Easy, Adam. Easy."

He said it in a low, soft voice but it was enough. I pushed Jay Blevins back to where he'd been sitting, my knuckles grazing his chin as I did. Not all that accidentally. Jay busied himself spinning the uneaten crust from one of his sandwiches around on his plate. Sulking.

"Jay," Cobb said, "you know about Owen Harkness?"

He looked up. "What about Owen?"

Cobb looked at him for several seconds. "You don't know?"

"What is this, a little kid game? What *about* Owen?"

"He's dead."

I watched Jay take it in. And for a minute I thought he was going to pass out or throw up. Or both. What he did instead was start to cry. Not loud and not tears streaming down his face but he was crying. And if I was a betting man, I'd have bet it was sincere. It was the first time I felt anything like sympathy for him.

"What … what happened? OD?"

"No, Owen didn't overdose," Cobb said. "Somebody took him out with a knife."

Jay took in air. Looked at Cobb, then me, then the ceiling.

"Shit, who would do that?"

"We think it's the guys that are looking for you."

"The MFs."

"Yeah."

"Goddamn it, man, Owen was all right. He never hurt anybody, you know … he … where did it happen?"

"In Zoe's place."

For the second time he snapped to attention. "Zoe, is she … okay?"

"She's fine."

I said. "Not that you need to give a damn now that you've broken up with her and all."

It was a cheap shot, but I had to get it in. Cobb frowned at me. No anger this time from Jay. He dabbed at his eyes with a napkin, sniffed, and shook his head.

"I thought she should find somebody else. She was trying to get off the shit and I wasn't helping her. I was going to break up with her next time I saw her so she could stay clean and maybe get a life."

I said, "You thought she should stay clean and get a life but you didn't think you should do the same thing."

"It's … it's complicated, man. It's hard, so hard. You don't know. Aw, shit, man … Owen."

Cobb said, "Sorry about your friend, Jay."

Jay looked at him and nodded.

"Yeah."

I said, "Actually, I do know how hard it is, Jay. Not first hand, but I've written about guys who've got the habit — lots of them. They've told me and I've seen it. I do know it's bloody hard."

His head was slumped forward and he nodded again.

"I asked you before. How long have you been clean?"

He shook his head. "Eight days. Eight fucking days. Not much, is it?"

"It's eight days, Jay."

Cobb leaned forward, his arms on the table. "We had a meeting with the MFs, the guy who's the boss. He told us he'd call off his boys … leave you alone."

Jay shrugged. "What does that mean?"

"Good question," Cobb said. "I think there's a chance he's being straight with us, but there's also a chance that he's BS-ing. That's why I think we should play it cool for a while longer."

"Meaning?"

"Meaning we keep you out of sight and safe until we're sure."

Jay didn't say anything. Pushed his plate away to one side. "I need a smoke."

"Sure," Cobb said, "but let's sort this out first, then we'll go outside and you can have a smoke."

"What's to sort out? I think I'd be better off on my

own. They haven't found me so far. Hell, *you* couldn't even find me."

I turned so I could look him in the face full on. "You know, Jay, several people told us you're supposed to be a good guy but so far I haven't found that at all. Your old man dies because he lost it with the assholes that supply your habit, the man sitting across the table from you spent days and nights on the streets trying to keep your ass from getting carved up like sushi, and there's a girl who'd rather get pneumonia than miss out on a chance to see you. And yet with all that, this is still just about you, isn't it?"

"Nice speech, journalist."

I stared at him, wondering what Jill had seen in this kid that I wasn't seeing. Maybe the withdrawal from the crack was messing him up. I wanted to give him the benefit of the doubt. He wasn't making it easy.

Cobb said, "I don't think it would be a good idea for you to be out there on your own, Jay."

"You got a better one?"

Cobb looked at me. My cue.

I said, "You know the place called Let the Sunshine Inn? Just off 9th Avenue?"

Jay nodded. "Jill ... I forget her last name. Good lady."

"How about I make a call, see if I can get you in?"

"I'm kind of *persona non grata* at most of the shelters."

"Why is that?"

"You have to be clean to get into them. And you have to stay clean as long as you're there. I guess I kind of abused the privilege."

"I think Jill would be okay with having you there. Besides ... eight days, remember?"

He smiled a little. "Yeah, I guess."

"What about the truck?" I asked.

Cobb looked at Jay. "The place you left it, that where the guy lives?"

He shrugged. "One in a million chance."

"You leave the key in it?"

"Yeah, didn't figure I'd need the truck anymore."

Cobb thought for a minute. "The owner will call in a stolen vehicle report. Whoever lives in that house will call the police to say there's an abandoned vehicle in his driveway. The cops will connect the dots. I think we'll just let them do that."

"I'll call the shelter," I said.

I slid out of the booth and stepped out into the cold of the night. I kept my shivering under control long enough to tap out the number of the shelter. I waited through six rings, thinking I was about to get the answering machine when I heard a tired, unhappy voice on the other end of the line. Celia.

"Let the Sunshine Inn."

Her tone was better suited to a greeting that went *Let the Fires of Hell Consume You and All Your Kin.* I thought it best not to point that out.

"Hello, is Jill in this evening?"

"No."

I waited for some kind of follow-up and realized that that was the whole answer. I decided not to pursue my request further.

I hung up and called the number Jill had written on the back of the business card. Her home number. This time the answer came just after ring number four. It was Jill's voice, somewhat out of breath.

"Hello?"

"Jill, yeah, hi … uh listen, it's Adam Cullen calling."

"Oh, hi, excuse the breathless thing. I just walked in the door and ran for the phone."

"No problem. A date, was it?"

Someone should do a study on why people say really stupid things during those times when they'd most like to say something profound. Or even adequate.

"Yes, actually."

If I'd had a pen in my hand I would have jabbed it a long way into my thigh but luckily I wasn't carrying anything that would be useful in inflicting self-harm.

"Sorry … I didn't mean … uh … that's great …" I figured if I ever wanted to see this woman again I better get off the small talk in a hurry. "Look, Jill, I'm with Cobb and we've got Jay Blevins with us."

"You found him! Adam, that's great."

"Well, yeah, sort of. The thing is we need a place to put him up and wondered if there was any room at your place — the shelter, I mean, not your house." Nervous laugh. *Where's that Goddamn pen?*

"I can meet you at the shelter in a half hour."

"We'll be there. And thanks for this."

She didn't answer, probably thinking there was no need for both of us to sound like idiots.

When we got to the front door of Let the Sunshine Inn, the lights were on in the main part of the building and the place actually looked welcoming, not an easy task for hundred-year-old bricks and mortar that appeared to have seen only the bare minimum of upkeep and next to no renovations in their tired, decaying history.

Cobb led the way with Jay walking beside him. I hung back just in case the kid decided to run for it.

He didn't. In fact, he seemed almost glad to get to a place where the shower water was hot, the sheets were clean, and the smiles were genuine. Even, by the way, the smile on the face of Celia, who apparently was only unpleasant to detectives and journalists.

Jill hugged Jay and beamed, first at Cobb, then at me. She turned her attention back to Jay.

"It's good to see you."

Jay seemed a little uncomfortable — maybe embarrassed. He mumbled something unintelligible. Jill ushered him to a table where coffee and Oreo cookies were laid out alongside a couple of forms and several pens.

"Just a little paperwork, Jay, it won't take long. Celia will give you a hand if you need it."

Jay nodded and sat at one of the wooden chairs that looked as old as the building. "I've done this stuff before."

Celia poured coffee for Jay and herself, sat across from him, and nudged the cookies a little closer to him. Jay took one, smiled at her, and picked up one of the pens and began to write. Jill directed Cobb and me to a leather couch that was in surprisingly good shape although there were a couple of places where the original dark brown had been worn away to reveal a kind of cigarette stain shade of yellow-brown.

"There's lots of coffee," she told us.

Cobb said, "No, thanks."

I shook my head. It was difficult to have much of a conversation since the topic we most wanted to discuss was sitting a few feet away.

I looked over my shoulder at the two people at the table.

Jay was bent over, working hard at getting the forms filled in, pausing only to take bites of the Oreo. Celia was watching him, her eyes displaying a warmth I hadn't seen. I remembered what Jill had told me about some of the people they had to deal with and I decided to adjust my opinion of Celia.

The front door opened and two people came in: teenagers or early twenties, guy and a girl — neither looked either happy or healthy. Jill stood up, moved to the door to meet them.

The young man spoke first. "We've got no place else, Jill. We just need somewhere to sleep. I swear to God we're not carrying."

"Sorry, Ben. You know the rules. You use while you're here and you're out. You have to go through a program to get back in. Both of you. I can give you some places you can go to register for a program." She stepped back to the desk, opened a drawer, and pulled out a sheaf of brochures, one-pagers, and business cards.

"Come on Jill, for Chrissake," the kid named Ben's voice got louder. "It's winter out there. We could freaking die."

"Sorry, Ben, Jewel … that's something you needed to think about before right now. I'd be happy to pour you a couple of cups of coffee to take with you, but that's the best I can do."

Jay turned to look at the two. "Bro," Ben said.

Jay nodded, turned back to the form he was working on.

"Are you serious?" The edge in Ben's voice was becoming more pronounced. Cobb leaned forward as if to rise but Jill, sensing rather than seeing him move, held her hand out behind her. The message was clear. She didn't want help, at least not yet.

"I am serious, Ben. The steps are detox, program, then here. Get clean and come back, you'll be welcome. Now, would you like that coffee?"

"You can stick your coffee up your ass. If we freeze to death, it's on you." Ben turned and pulled the girl, Jewel, after him. She looked back over her shoulder as she went out the door but I couldn't read what was in her face … or her eyes.

I looked at Jill, who dropped her chin for just a second, then turned back to us. "That's one of the toughest parts of this job," she said.

"Not taking a lot of responsibility for where he's at in his life, is he?" I wanted to say something that would make her feel better. I wasn't sure I'd succeeded.

"There's a lot of that," she said.

Jay looked up. "They aren't going to die," he said simply, much better than me at making her feel better.

"I know," Jill said softly, "I just wish …"

A couple of beats of silence.

"Guess I'm done here," Jay said pushing the forms toward Celia. "I wouldn't mind a shower. Bet none of you'd mind if I had one, huh?" He smiled.

I was finally seeing the Jay Jill had talked about — the kid you could like.

"There's towels and everything you need up there." Celia stood up. "I'll take you."

She started toward the back part of the building, the food bank area, where I'd noticed stairs the last time I'd been here. Jay followed her. He turned back at the doorway into the food bank and looked at Jill.

"Thanks for the room … and the cookies and stuff." His eyes flicked to me, then Cobb. "And, uh … yeah … thanks."

Celia and Jay disappeared and Jill sat back on the couch. She shrugged her shoulders, not for anyone's benefit. She seemed in her own world and neither Cobb nor I spoke.

A couple of minutes passed before she stood up and starting putting coffee things away, needing to be moving.

Cobb stood too. "I'll go start the Jeep. I know how you hate a cold vehicle." He smiled at me and was out the door before I could say anything.

"This table goes over against that wall," Jill said and took hold of one side. I moved to the other side and we lifted it to where she'd indicated.

I watched her as we moved the table.

"Listen, I sounded like an idiot before," I said. "Your dating life is none of my business and I'm sorry if —"

She reached across the table and put her fingers on my lips. "Shh," she whispered. "Come and sit here for one minute." She pointed to the couch and we moved over and sat back down. We were closer together than we'd been before and her leg rested against mine.

She looked at me. "First of all, you're right, it isn't any of your business but I'm going to tell you anyway."

"You don't have —"

"It was a duty date."

"A duty date," I repeated. "I'm not sure I know what that is."

"That's when you owe your girlfriend for helping tile your bathroom floor and she says 'there's this guy I work with and he's seen us together and he'd like to take you out but you don't have to even though I just helped you tile your bathroom' so you say okay. That's a duty date."

"Wow," I said. "I *am* out of the loop. I didn't even know there was such a thing."

"Just be careful who you get to help you with home renovations."

"Thanks, I'll keep that in mind."

"Anyway, it wasn't a great date."

"I wish I could say I'm really sorry to hear that."

"He mostly wanted to talk about how great Stephen Harper is and he smelled like Vicks VapoRub."

"A Conservative with a cold. Not good."

She laughed. "Not good at all. Which brings us to you and me."

"Well, I don't like politics and I don't have a cold but I suck at home renovations."

"Not a bad tradeoff."

"Well, if there's any chance you haven't used up all the time your babysitter has available, maybe we could do something."

"That would sound a lot better if you added the word *soon*."

"How about this weekend? Soon enough?"

"Perfect."

"Saturday night. My place. I cook."

"You can cook?"

I grinned. "Within clearly defined limits. Care to risk it?"

"Absolutely."

"Great." I stood up. "My charioteer probably has the rig toasty by now so I better get going."

"Yeah, I have to get home too."

I walked to the door and she followed me. I turned to face her. "You've seen more of this than I have. A kid like

Jay … you think he has a chance to kick it? Maybe take his life back?"

"Most of them don't. Maybe he'll be one of the ones who does."

"Yeah." I looked toward the upstairs. "Celia's been up there a long time. You think she's showering with the kid?"

"I think she's like your charioteer. Decided we could use a few minutes alone."

"Remind me to stop forming first impressions. I'm lousy at it."

She smiled, stood on her tiptoes, and kissed me lightly on the lips. "Not always."

EIGHTEEN

Neither of us spoke as Cobb circled the block three times.

"Looking for an Audi?" I asked.

"Hell, I missed the kid tailing us to the restaurant earlier tonight and he's not that good. So I figured a little recon might be in order, yeah."

No sign of the Audi or anything else that looked out of the ordinary. Satisfied, Cobb pulled onto 9th Avenue heading east toward my place.

For a couple of minutes I looked out at the restaurants, coffee places, and antique stores that were a part of the new Inglewood.

"So, is that it for you?" I asked after we'd turned north toward the Zoo Bridge.

"Funny, I was just asking myself the same question. I told Larry Blevins I'd try to keep his kid from being killed by the bad guys. But in order to believe that I've done my job, we have to believe Scubberd when he says we have a deal."

"And …"

"And I don't know if I believe that. And if I *don't* believe it then what do I do next? Short of whisking the kid off to something that acts like a witness protection program, I'm running out of ideas. Jay's an addict. His brain and his need for crack or whatever shit is his personal favourite will likely lead him to do stupid things. Dangerous things. Hell, there's no guarantee he'll be at the shelter in the morning."

"Not a lot of wiggle room."

"Not much," he said.

I looked out my side window, watched the Calgary Zoo going by. It was a very different place from the one I'd grown up with. The area we were passing now had once been populated by huge dinosaur sculptures but all of them were gone, moved some years before to a massive prehistoric park that was now one of the zoo's showcases. But just at that moment I missed the way it had been. Wished that everything didn't have to change.

Neither of us said anything for the remainder of the drive. I was caught up in thoughts of my own and I guessed that Cobb was in a similar state.

Cobb pulled up in front of my apartment, slipped the Jeep into neutral, and looked over at me.

"Well," he said.

"Yeah. Listen, this is the second toughest night of my life and I'm pretty much bagged but I can't help but think a celebration drink is in order."

Cobb shook his head. "Not celebration. Not yet. But I could use a drink."

"I happen to know a very capable bartender lives right in this building."

"An offer I can't refuse." He shut off the Jeep and we both stepped out onto the street. I listened to the quiet as Cobb came around the car holding his cell phone.

"I'm just calling home. I want to let Lindsay know I'll be a little while."

He stopped on the curb, punched numbers, and a few seconds later had his wife on the line. I walked up the walk a few meters to give him some space and looked down the street.

I heard Cobb say, "Put her on," and he glanced at me, rolled his eyes, and started toward the building.

It was a dad–little kid conversation that started with "Hi Angel, what are you doing up this late?" It wasn't long and I couldn't hear most of the words but it was a nice contrast to what most of this night had been about.

As we neared the front door of the building, Cobb slowed and turned slightly, I assumed to preserve a little privacy for the final seconds of the call, often the "Daddy loves you" part.

He pocketed the phone, glanced at me, and gave a little nod — ready now for that drink.

As I reached out to the pad to tap in the code that would allow us to enter the building, I said, "Beer your beverage or are a whisky man?"

"He's a fuckin' *dead* man."

The speaker had to have come from around the corner of the building, and moved quickly past a large cedar that had conveniently blocked our view.

Cobb swore softly as first one man, then another materialized in front of us — Moretti, a very large, very menacing knife in hand and grinning, Minnis a step behind him and holding a revolver. I remembered Scubberd's warning that the smaller man, Moretti, was the one to fear because of his skills with a blade. And I remembered the savagery of the attack on Owen Harkness.

I didn't say anything partly because I didn't think there was anything I could say that would alter the situation we were in and partly because my mind was busy weighing all the possibilities. This was one of those moments, like right before a car crash, when everything slows down to a video replay.

It took only seconds to realize that there were no possibilities to weigh. I didn't know if Cobb was carrying a gun or not but it didn't matter. If Cobb tried to go for it he'd be cut down either by Moretti or Minnis or both before he got his hand to his revolver.

Moretti's grin broadened. In that instant I was certain that he had killed Owen Harkness. This was a man who enjoyed killing.

"I guess we're about to find out if the badass killer is a clumsy fuck or not."

I felt Cobb move up alongside me, putting himself closer to Moretti. I looked down at the knife. It looked like it could carve a path through jungle.

Cobb's voice was barely more than a whisper and it was unwavering. "I didn't say clumsy fuck, I said clumsy snake. I hate to be misquoted."

Moretti was done talking. His eyes narrowed and I knew he was about to strike. I figured he'd take Cobb first, that's what I'd have done. I was much less a threat, especially with Minnis's gun pointed at my forehead.

The sound came from our right, from the street. It came fast and Moretti hesitated, though his eyes never left Cobb.

A car pulled to a hard stop at the curb. I turned my head just enough to see the street. Hoping for cops.

It wasn't cops.

DAVID A. POULSEN

An Audi. Mrs. Scubberd was at the wheel. The passenger door opened and Scubberd climbed out, stepping toward the front of the car. He turned, leaned on the hood facing us. He too was holding a revolver, both hands on it, and he pointed it at us.

"Just in case you need us," he said in a voice that was low and blizzard cold.

"Shit," I said.

Moretti took a half step toward Cobb.

It didn't sound like shots, more like two pops, like the sound I remembered my BB gun making when I was a kid. Moretti fell, the knife making more noise as it clattered on the cement than the shots that had killed him.

I looked at the car. Scubberd hadn't moved but he spoke again.

"I warned you once, don't ever think you can go freelance on me." Talking to Moretti like the guy could still hear him.

I looked back at Minnis. He was putting his gun back into the shoulder holster inside his suit jacket. He bent down, picked up Moretti's body like it was a sack of grain, threw it over his shoulder, and bent down again to pick up the knife.

He moved quickly for a big man — down the sidewalk to the Audi. Scubberd was already at the back of the car opening the trunk; Minnis threw Moretti's body in and slammed the trunk lid.

Then he came back up the sidewalk, veered off, and disappeared in the direction he and Moretti had come from. I never found out how they had got to my apartment. But it hadn't been on motorcycles — not on this night.

Scubberd climbed back in the passenger side of the

Audi. The whole thing had happened in less than thirty seconds.

Mrs. Scubberd was looking at us through the open driver's side window. "As I was saying, gentlemen, my husband is an honourable man."

And they drove off.

NINETEEN

The cops questioned us for about an hour each. Separately at first, then for maybe twenty minutes together. Of course, Cobb and I had our story put together in the time between phoning it in and when a small army of homicide detectives and techs arrived.

Cobb had created most of it. We'd arrived at the apartment and were about to enter the building when a man ran up toward the door wanting in. He didn't appear to know the code and asked us to let him in. He was agitated and as I didn't recognize him as a resident and the apartment has a policy about admitting strangers to the building, I told him I couldn't do that. At about that moment a vehicle stopped at the curb opposite the entrance and the man was cut down by a shooter who was in that car. We had dived for cover inside the building. When we looked out again the body of the man who'd been shot was gone. And so was the car.

No, we didn't know the victim. No, we hadn't seen the face of the shooter. No, we didn't get a good look at the car.

One of the detectives seemed skeptical. He seemed to think that as a former cop Cobb should have been able to provide more information. Cobb was apologetic. It was dark, it had happened quickly and our first reaction was to get the hell out of the line of fire.

"So you punched in the code, opened the door, and hid inside the building?"

"Yes."

"Lucky you didn't get shot."

"I guess if they'd wanted to kill us they could have," Cobb said.

"But they didn't want to even though you were witnesses to the whole crime."

"Maybe they thought we didn't really have time to see anything."

"Which would appear to be the case."

"Yes."

"How long were you inside the building?"

"A couple of minutes or so."

"Did you hear the car leaving?"

"Yes."

"And that's when you decided to look outside?"

"Yes."

"You didn't see who removed the body?"

"No."

Of course, all of this was dependent on there being no eyewitnesses, no one in a nearby building who was sitting at the window looking out as it had unfolded. I was worried about that, but Cobb pointed out that there had been almost no noise to draw attention to what was happening. I thought about that and decided he was probably right. There'd been no yelling, no squealing tires, and the silencer on Scubberd's gun meant that Moretti's execution had been less of a disturbance to the neighbourhood than teenagers coming home from a high school dance.

By the time the cops left — after warning us that further questioning at the station was a virtual certainty — neither of us felt like that drink anymore. We agreed to meet for breakfast the next morning. Cobb left and I sat in my apartment for a long time looking at the lights of Drury Avenue and the rest of Bridgeland.

I sat for maybe an hour, not moving. It was all I could do to get undressed before I fell into bed.

But even then sleep didn't come. I tossed, turned, punched the pillow into myriad shapes, read, drank orange juice, then chamomile tea, and read some more. I listened to Valdy, the Barenaked Ladies, and the Saskatoon band The Deep Dark Woods. Finally, desperate, I sorted tax receipts. And fell asleep. Thank God for Revenue Canada.

The next morning I had to go out the back door to leave the apartment. Yellow crime scene tape cordoned off the area around the front entrance.

Cobb and I met at the Diner Deluxe on Edmonton Trail, a terrific retro spot with great food and an upbeat atmosphere. I needed upbeat. It was another of the places I hadn't been to in a long time. It was as busy as I remembered.

Coffee and menus arrived seconds after we sat down. As we fixed our coffee I told Cobb I'd phoned Let the Sunshine Inn. Jill was already there and she said Jay was having breakfast after a night's sleep that "wasn't great but wasn't terrible."

"She said she'll be talking to him after he's eaten, hoping she might get him to commit to a program. I asked her if she thought it would be a good idea if we were to stop by. She said maybe later, that it might be best if she were to try talking to him alone, at least at first."

I drank some coffee. Yawned.

"Not enough sleep?" Cobb smiled.

"Not even close."

"What … an armed standoff in a restaurant, chasing down a druggie, going face to face with two guys armed with a machete and a nine millimetre; follow that up with being interrogated by the cops and you're finding things stressful? What a wuss."

I smiled. "Well, when you put like that I can see I should have slept like a baby."

He nodded. "Actually, kidding aside, we should both be happy. We're alive and that was very much in doubt for a while there last night."

I fought off another yawn. "About last night. One question. How did Scubberd know that Moretti was planning to take us out? What did he call it … free-lancing?"

Cobb nodded. "My guess is Minnis must have let him know, probably called him on his cell phone. Scubberd decided to drop by and … do what he did."

"Honourable man," I repeated the words of the lovely Mrs. Scubberd from the night before. "It's a damn good thing he wasn't a few seconds later."

"He might still have shot Moretti but it wouldn't have done us much good."

"Of course, he might have told Minnis to take care of it if he didn't get there in time."

Cobb shrugged. "I guess that's one of those things that will remain forever a mystery."

"I didn't get the feeling that Scubberd was our biggest

fan. I wonder why he'd sacrifice one of his guys to keep us above ground."

"Two answers," Cobb said between sips of coffee. "The guy he offed wasn't a big sacrifice. The MFs are no different than General Motors or the Royal Bank or the Green Bay Packers. To be effective requires discipline. If people just go off and do their own thing — freelance — the organization breaks down. Scubberd figured it was more important to maintain discipline in the outfit than it was to have that little psycho go rogue and take out a couple of guys who really weren't much more than a minor irritation anyway."

"Rogue?"

"Maybe Moretti thought he was taking care of MF business on his own or maybe he just wanted us dead because I made him look bad at the restaurant. A guy like that doesn't need much of a reason to murder people."

I thought again of Owen Harkness. "Psycho."

"Yeah."

"And reason number two for Scubberd doing what he did?"

"Is this: I guess we found out that the Scubberds keep their word."

"Although technically the agreement was to take Jay off the hit list. There wasn't really anything in there about leaving us upright."

"Now there I disagree. When Mrs. Scubberd asked me to call off the boys in the restaurant, I think what she was really saying was make nice here and we'll take that into consideration sometime."

"And if you'd decided to be a hardass at the diner and kept the guns on the Scubberds and company until we were clear of the place …"

"That's another one of those things that will remain —"

"Forever a mystery. Yeah, I know."

I ordered eggs Benedict with Canadian bacon and Cobb opted for a southwest scramble breakfast burrito.

As we waited for our order, I said, "What's next?"

"We promised Zoe we'd let her know when we found Jay. I'm planning to head over there right after breakfast. Care to join me?"

I nodded. "Yeah, I would care to do that. A lot."

We drank coffee and I people-watched for a couple of minutes.

"Can I ask you something?" I asked.

Cobb sipped more coffee. "Sure."

"Do you think I'm nuts for still wanting to find the son of a bitch who set fire to my house and killed my wife? Because I'm having a hell of a time letting it go. Even in the middle of all of this I … can't let it go. Last night we were a few seconds from being dead and I was thinking I'd never be able to …" My voice wouldn't let me finish the thought.

Cobb's voice was softer than usual. "If somebody hurt one of my family I'd feel exactly the same way."

I waited a few seconds before I said, "Thing is, I don't know what to do."

Cobb nodded.

I ran my fingers along the rim of my coffee cup. "When I found out Appleton had sexually abused those girls … Donna … I was sure there had to be a connection between that and the fire."

"And now?"

I shook my head. "I just don't know. It's killing me that I can't find out who murdered my wife but I don't know what to do next."

"Look, Adam, I'm sorry I haven't been much help to you. I've been kind of tied up with this."

"Hey, no need to —"

He held up a hand. "How about we see Zoe, and I take a couple of days to be a husband and a dad. Then we sit down and look at it all again. Okay?"

"I'm happy to pay you."

"Hell, Adam, you think I'm going to take money? First of all, you've helped me a lot more than you know with this Blevins thing. And you paid me before and didn't get your money's worth. No, that's not right, I gave everything I had like I do on every case. What you *didn't* get was resolution. So how about we see what we can do about that."

"Sure."

"Just promise me that you're not going to go off on your own."

"Damn, I was just starting to enjoy all this John Wayne stuff."

He smiled. "Give me a few days and then we'll see if we can't raise a little hell."

I grinned at him.

"What?"

"My Canadian music collection is having its effect on you."

"Yeah, how's that?"

"'Raise a Little Hell.' Trooper song. Big hit back in the —"

"What, do you think I just fell off the turnip truck? I know who performed 'Raise a Little Hell.'"

He gave me a pretty decent cover of the iconic opening lines, beating out a rhythm on the table top to accompany his singing. Only a few diners turned to look at us.

Zoe was sitting on the front step of the house in Tuxedo wearing a light blue down-filled jacket, sweat pants, and fuzzy pink slippers. The weather guy on the car radio had said it was minus four. Tough kid.

She was drinking something steaming from a Starbucks mug that celebrated Vancouver and reading a beat up paperback. She looked up from it to watch us come up the walk.

I think she was trying to gauge from our faces and the way we were walking if the news was going to be good or bad. She stood up as we got closer. I could see the cover of the book — *Tomorrow, When the War Began.*

"Hi," she said.

"Hi Zoe."

Cobb nodded and smiled.

"Did you find him?"

We stopped a couple of paces from the steps. I figured Cobb should do the talking.

"We did," he said.

"Is he … alive?"

"He's alive."

"And?"

"He's okay."

Zoe tossed the book in the air and leaped at Cobb like he'd just scored the winning goal in overtime, throwing her arms around his neck and screaming. Cobb spun once with her clinging to him and set her down.

She was only slightly less enthusiastic with the hug she

gave me. She left out the scream and I left out the spin. She stepped back and looked at us and the grin faded.

"You guys don't look the way people are supposed to look when something is really good. Is there something about this that *isn't* really good?"

"Like I said, he's fine and it looks like the danger he was in … that's been taken care of."

"Did you kill the bastard that murdered Owen?"

"No. Someone else did."

"And the creeps aren't after Jay anymore?"

"No. Or you either."

"So why don't you look happier? Where is Jay?"

"He's at a shelter."

"Which one?"

"Let the Sunshine Inn."

"I know the place. Let's go."

Cobb looked at me. *Great, I get the bad news.*

"Well, Zoe, it might be a good idea to let him have a couple of days to get himself sorted out … uh …"

"What's to sort out? I want to see him and if you won't take me there, I'll figure out another way."

"The thing is … it's just that Jay … might not want to see you."

"What do you mean?"

"He told us he didn't think you two should be a couple anymore. That he'd just mess you up and keep you from staying clean."

She thought about that. "Is he using?"

I nodded. "Until eight, no, make that nine days ago. He's been clean since then. At least that's what he told us."

"That old joke about how can you tell if an addict's lying?"

I provided the punchline. "His lips are moving. Yeah, I can't say for sure but I would say he's clean. I can't swear to the nine days part. But maybe."

"I want to see him."

I looked at Cobb who gave me a blank face. My call. "Okay. Why don't you go change and we'll wait for you here."

"You want to come in and wait?"

"Thanks, we're good out here," Cobb said.

"I'll be quick." She turned and raced back into the house.

Cobb and I walked back to the Jeep, climbed inside, and turned the heater on high.

"She was sitting outside reading and here we are huddled in our vehicle with the heat cranked. What does that make us?"

"I became a wimp when I turned forty," Cobb said.

I leaned forward and put my hands by the heat outlet.

"I didn't wait that long," I said.

The Let the Sunshine Inn was a happening place. One couple, a woman with a son who looked to be about nine or ten and a family of four, two of them bored teenagers, were in the food bank with Jill moving efficiently between them and the food stocks, filling bags and boxes and chatting idly with the nine-year-old. I heard her call him Tim. Tim looked happier than either of the teenagers, who I guessed were brother and sister. Both looked like they hated life. Maybe they had good reason or maybe they were just being teenagers.

A girl about Zoe's age was sitting at the desk opposite Celia, filling out the same series of forms Jay had the night before. The girl looked like she'd be pretty if she smiled but that wasn't going to happen any time soon. Green appeared to be her colour of choice. Green jacket with a lighter green collar, green sweat pants, green sneakers, and green streaks in her hair. Maybe a Saskatchewan Roughriders fan.

Jay was behind Jill sorting food bank donations as I had done my first time in the place. He was wearing a Montreal Canadiens sweatshirt, clean jeans, and a ball cap that said only *Q*. He looked cleaner and maybe even marginally better than the night before, but his movements were robotic — jerky. This was a guy who was feeling the ill effects of being off the juice.

He was sideways to us, stacking canned goods, and didn't see us at first. Zoe moved closer and was standing opposite him, a table between them, when he turned and saw her. He looked at her, started to smile, thought better of it, looked at his shoes for a few seconds, then back at her.

"Hi." She didn't try to get closer to him, stayed on her side of the table.

"Hi."

"You doing okay?" Zoe sounded nervous, a bit of a tremor in her voice.

"Sure … yeah, okay. How 'bout you?"

The family of four was moving toward the front door, their arms full of provisions. The older of the two teenagers, a boy maybe fifteen, wearing jeans that looked like they'd lost a fight with a cougar, and a jacket with a crest that said, "I'm nucking futs," shook his head as he went by me, letting me know he wasn't happy.

"Yeah, that free food is a bitch, ain't it, kid?" I said.

He scowled and kept on going, shuffling his feet every step. I wasn't envying his parents or his sister the ride home.

The woman with the nine-year-old was getting ready to leave and I stepped forward. "I can give you a hand with those if you like."

She glanced at me, then looked at Jill.

Jill said, "It's fine, Monica. He's a friend of mine."

Monica smiled at me and nodded. I stepped forward and picked up the biggest of the cardboard boxes. Tim took the smaller box and Monica scooped up a large shopping bag in one arm and a king size box of detergent in the other. Cobb held the door for us, earning him a bigger smile than the one I got, which I thought was unfair.

"Have a great week, Monica. Bye, Tim." Jill called.

Monica turned and said, "Thanks again," and Tim yelled "See ya" loud enough to be heard several blocks away.

I followed them out onto the street where the warmest day we'd had in a month was melting some of the snow that was piled up in parking lots, playgrounds, schoolyards, and driveways. Monica led us to a van that looked a lot like the one I had in high school. And my van had been ten years old then.

Rust flecked the fenders and quarter panels like blotchy skin. The van had two side doors that opened out — I remembered that from mine — and Monica looked for a place to put the detergent while she opened the doors.

I bent so she could set it on top of the box I was carrying.

"It's heavy," she said.

"It's okay," I told her and she set the soap atop the box. I winked at Tim and said "Us guys are Supermen" in my best superhero voice.

Jill got the doors open and we set everything inside. Tim high-fived me and said, "See ya, Superman."

"See ya, *Super* Superman," I said.

Monica and I exchanged waves and I stomped off my boots on my way back inside. Celia and the girl in green had completed the paperwork and were headed upstairs. Jill and Cobb were talking in hushed voices and Zoe and Jay hadn't moved. Jay was pushing two cans of SpaghettiOs back and forth on the table and working hard at not looking at Zoe, who gave every indication she was prepared to wait him out.

"It's been crazy here all morning," Jill said. "I need a coffee."

She had decided that whatever was going to happen was going to happen without us. I nodded and Cobb looked as eager as we were to get out of there and give Jay and Zoe some space.

Jill grabbed her coat off one of the nails of the make-shift coat rack and started toward the front door. Cobb got the door again. Jill turned back. "You two want anything?"

Zoe shook her head and Jay mumbled something that I took for a no.

"We'll be back in twenty minutes," Jill said and we headed out onto the street.

We pretty much had the Starbucks to ourselves and it became even less crowded when Cobb told us he needed to get something across the street and could we get him a "tall coffee something or other with room for milk."

He was out the door before we could point out how pathetic his attempts to give us time alone actually were. I shook my head and Jill laughed softly.

"It's a good thing he's a detective because as a poker player he'd go broke in a week."

I ordered the coffee including a "tall something or other with room for milk." That seemed to baffle the barista so I modified the order to a tall Caffé Verona after reading the description as "Rich, soulful, and sweet, this coffee wafts romance."

"I'm not sure about rich, soulful, or sweet," I told Jill, "but I guarantee you Cobb wafts romance."

"Yes, he does." She laughed the laugh I liked.

As the barista worked on our coffees, I turned to look at Jill. "How's your week shaping up for a free evening?"

"The week not so good, but the week*end*, much better. But I have a thought — you know, just in case you can't wait six days to see me." She laughed at what she'd said.

"Actually that's a pretty darn solid supposition."

"I'm glad. Anyway, Kyla has a part in a school play. It runs Wednesday and Thursday and it's called *Bridging the Generation Gap*. It's all hush-hush so I know almost nothing except that Kyla has a fairly significant part."

"The generation gap. Will seeing it make me feel old?"

"I can almost guarantee it."

"When you put it like that how do I say no?"

Cobb returned and I handed him his drink.

We sat for five minutes and drank our coffee, all of us working hard, it seemed to me, to avoid the topic of Jay and Zoe.

"Think twenty minutes is enough?" I asked as we made our way back to the Let the Sunshine Inn at the same brisk pace we had employed earlier.

"Twenty years might not be enough time to get Jay's life back," Jill said. "But twenty minutes might be enough to make a start."

Inside, Jay and Zoe were sitting at the table. Zoe was leaning forward and both seemed to be talking intently.

I looked at Cobb, who answered my look with a shrug. I approached the table; Jill moved alongside me. Jay and Zoe looked up at us.

I spoke to Zoe. "You want us to hang around ... wait for you?"

She looked at Jay. I couldn't see any response but there must have been one. She looked up at Jill.

"We were hoping maybe I could stay here for a couple of days," she said.

Jill didn't answer right away.

"We have only one room for couples and it's taken right now," she said.

"We could stay in the room I was in last night," Jay said. "It's big enough."

I glanced at Cobb. He wasn't showing anything but I felt good that Jay seemed to be thinking of Zoe, however short term and however superficially.

Jill frowned for a moment, then said. "Two nights. I'll bend the rules for *two* nights. Then, unless Lon and Jenna are gone from the couple's room, I'm afraid you'll have to make other arrangements. There are three or four places that have couple's rooms. I'll even make some calls for you. But two nights is it. And that's based on total abstinence from drugs. Use once and you're gone."

She was looking at Jay as she spoke and I watched him take it in. Looked like he received the message, but with addicts — even ones who have been clean for a week or two — it's foolish to take them at their word.

Still, the atmosphere in the place felt positive and I figured I'd let that be my guide. For now.

Cobb said, "We'll stay in touch."

I wasn't sure if the remark was directed at Zoe and Jay or at Jill and it didn't really matter.

I smiled at Jill and mouthed the word *thanks* at her.

Then Cobb and I left.

TWENTY

I chose the Wednesday performance in case I wanted to book tickets to see the show again the next night. It was interesting watching Jill being totally relaxed right up until the moment Kyla first appeared on stage.

At that point Jill grabbed my hand, not out of some romantic sentiment the darkened auditorium engendered, but so she would have something to squeeze, twist, bend, and occasionally pound on as she watched her daughter perform. Fortunately for my hand, Kyla was flawless on stage. Had the kid blown a line, missed an entrance, or tripped over one of the set pieces I would likely have required major reconstructive surgery.

After the show, parents, relatives, and friends gathered backstage to congratulate the performers and exchange relieved smiles with other parents, relatives, and friends.

Eventually I was relatively alone with Jill and Kyla. We were sipping drinks in paper cups. The drinks came from a large drink dispenser and tasted like last year's Kool-Aid. Orange, maybe.

I said, "It would be my honour to take you two out for a post-performance dinner."

"Awesome." Kyla grinned.

"You don't have to do that." Jill looked at me.

"Not a case of *have* to. I'd *love* to take you ladies out on the town. That's what theatre people do," I said.

Kyla nodded sagely. Jill nodded doubtfully.

I looked at Kyla. "So where are we going? I think the evening's brightest star should pick the place."

Jill whispered, "Big mistake."

Kyla beamed at me. "Really?"

"Really."

"Alright, Chuck E. Cheese's, here we come!"

"Big mistake," I heard again.

"Hey." I smiled at Jill. "Might not have been Audrey Hepburn's first choice, but I'm all about … what did you say the name was?"

"Chuck E. Cheese's."

I snapped my fingers. "That's what I'm talking about."

Kyla moved off to tell her cast mates about her good fortune.

Jill shook her head but she was smiling. "I tried to warn you."

"I wonder what the E stands for."

"Eech," she said.

The motto at Chuck E. Cheese's is "Where a Kid Can Be a Kid." Apparently being a kid entails beating the crap out of adults at every game Chuck E. could think of. Kyla had a "mega-blast" and once Jill realized that I was having a pretty good time myself, she relaxed and laughed as hard as Kyla at my pathetic attempts to bowl, toss, shoot, hit, and drive.

The highlight of my night came when I managed to beat Jill at a game that was, as near as I could tell, a cross between a Frisbee toss and slow motion dodge ball. My second-place finish earned me a fist bump from Kyla and a kiss on the cheek from Jill.

On the way out, with Kyla twenty yards ahead of us, Jill hugged me. "You were amazing in there. That was really fun."

"Yeah, it was."

"And if you ever bring me here again I'll break both your legs."

"You're just mad that I beat you at Splat the Brat."

"There is no game in there called Splat the Brat."

"I'm paraphrasing. The point is you're a sore loser, as indicated by your rather nasty threat."

"Okay, a) I'm not a sore loser, b) I beat you at everything but what you're calling Splat the Brat, and c) if you ever take me there again, I'll break both your legs."

I nodded and put my arm around her shoulders. "Do you think Kyla had fun? I mean really?"

"Trust me, she had fun and you have a new fan. Well, actually she was already a fan."

"Cool."

"What eight-year-old girl could possibly resist a man who is a writer *and* a Chuck E. Cheese's guy?"

"Wow, a guy with a fan. What's better than that?"

"How about a guy with two fans?" Jill squeezed my arm and smiled up at me.

"That *is* better."

On the way home Kyla asked me who Audrey Hepner was. I explained that Audrey Hep*burn* was a wonderful Hollywood star and the third most beautiful woman to ever grace the planet, right behind the two women currently in my car. I then launched into what I thought was a thorough and fascinating summary of Ms. Hepburn's life and career but about halfway through my oratory I glanced in the rearview mirror and noted that Kyla was sleeping soundly.

Which meant that when I pulled into the driveway at Jill's house we were able to enjoy a long, slow, warm kiss. Actually two. When I moved in for a third, Jill put a finger to my lips and promised "more where that came from" on Saturday night.

TWENTY-ONE

I was sitting on what passes for the balcony of my apartment, my feet on the railing, as I watched a guy on the balcony of his in-fill across the street. He was cleaning his barbecue.

It was December 14. Maybe he'd misread the calendar.

I was on my second cup of coffee, dressed in navy blue sweat pants, an Oklahoma State hoodie, and sneakers, no socks, no jacket.

Optimist.

Library Voices' *Denim on Denim* was filtering out of my apartment onto the balcony. They were a solid Regina band I'd seen perform a couple of years before. Their sound was helping my mood to improve. That and the smell. Chinook smell. Warm, dry, clean air that southern Albertans get to enjoy from time to time during winter. And might explain the guy working on his barbecue.

I'd made a decision. Cobb had called that morning and we'd set a time for the next day to get together and review everything we knew about Donna's murder. At 9:30 a.m., my apartment — I provide the bagels, he brings the coffee.

It would be good to get going on it again. But in the meantime I was antsy. I wanted to be doing something and I didn't want to be idle for even one more day.

There was only one thing I could think of to do. I wanted to try to find out what had happened to the other girl who had died. Elaine Yu. Appleton had said she'd died in Prince Albert. I'd Googled it and come up with next to nothing other than that Elaine Yu had died in a vehicle mishap of some kind. That seemed awfully general. I wondered if I could find out a little more and take that information to the meeting with Cobb.

And there was only one place my minimal detecting skills could come up with to try to learn more about Elaine and how she had died.

I sipped more coffee. The guy across the road was finished with his barbecue grill and had gone back inside. Probably planning to fire up the lawn mower.

I picked up the newspaper but couldn't really concentrate. Did the headlines and the sports page; the Flames had lost 5–3 to New Jersey.

I followed the lead of the guy across the way and went back inside. I changed into jeans, a bulky knit sweater, added socks to my ensemble, pulled on my down fill, and headed out to pursue the one idea I had.

The students at Northern Horizon Academy were apparently enjoying the spring-like interlude as much as I was. Several were hanging around outside the main entrance, perched on benches or leaning on walls contemplating the weather, sex, and each other. My guess was that few were contemplating chemistry or social studies.

I walked up the walk, ready this time in the event a group of girls tried to mow me down while exiting the main front doors. None did.

I entered the school and turned left, heading for the

office. I stopped, this time intent on finding Donna's photo in the display of her grad year's pictures. I did. It was a picture I hadn't seen before and I had to clear my throat and swallow a couple of times before I completed my walk to the main office.

I stepped into a space I hadn't really paid much attention to the first time I'd been here.

There were three desks in the office but only two of them were occupied. The walls behind the desks displayed pictures, smaller than the collections of student photos in the school's hallways. These were pictures of adults, I guessed the teachers and staff that had served at NHA over the years. Some were black and white.

A hallway led away from the office to a room or rooms I couldn't see. And there were two doors, one on each side of the office. The one on the right, I knew, was the domain of Delores Bain, principal. The other I guessed was the vice-principal's office. Both office doors were closed.

The woman at the desk nearest me looked up from a notebook she was writing in. "Can I help you?"

She was in her forties and attractive. She was wearing a blue jacket over a soft yellow blouse that was open just enough at the neck to activate high school boys' hormones. She smiled as she spoke to me and I smiled back.

"I was hoping I might see Ms. Bain if she's available."

"Is she expecting you?"

"No."

"I'm sorry. She has several appointments this morning and she'll be out of the school at a meeting all afternoon. Can anyone else help you?"

"No. I wonder if you'd give her my name."

"As I was saying —"

"I heard what you said and I'd appreciate it if you'd give Ms. Bain my name and see if she can spare a few minutes."

That had come out much more harshly than I intended and I knew the secretary was only doing her job.

I was thinking about how to soften what I'd said when she stood up and stepped away from her desk. The rest of her looked as good as the part that could be seen over the desk. The smile disappeared.

"What name should I give her?"

"Cullen."

She nodded and crossed to the principal's door.

I scrapped my planned apology — too late anyway. The woman at the second desk had stopped typing and was glaring at me over the top of her computer screen. Her body language made it clear we would never be friends.

The attractive secretary tapped on the principal's door and stepped inside. She closed the door behind her. Maybe thirty seconds passed before the door to Delores Bain's office opened and the secretary came out and headed in the direction of her desk. She didn't look at me. Delores Bain stepped out of her office and offered me a half smile.

"Please come in, Mr. Cullen."

I raised the hinged door that allowed me into the office and crossed between the two secretaries. Principal Bain stepped to one side to let me enter her office, then followed me inside and closed the door.

She stepped around to her side of the desk and sat.

"I'm sorry to stop in without an appointment," I said. "I know how busy you are and I appreciate your taking the time to see me."

She gave me the half smile again but there was no

offer of coffee this time. She nodded at the chair opposite her desk and I sat.

"Faith said you were quite insistent about seeing me," she said.

I nodded. "I guess I was. I wanted to ask you a couple of things."

She sat back in her chair. "By all means."

"I was wondering, first of all, why you weren't more forthcoming with me when I was here the first time."

She stiffened. "I'm afraid I don't understand."

"When I asked you if there was anyone in the school who might have had a reason to want harm to come to Donna, you said you couldn't think of anyone."

"I did, yes."

"Do you not think that a teacher who sexually abused Donna and several other girls in this school and then went to jail for what he did might qualify as a person I should know about?"

She paused. "I see your investigation continues."

"I wonder why you didn't at the very least tell me about what had happened to Donna in her grade eleven year."

"I thought you must already be aware of what happened — that Donna must have told you about it."

"That frankly, Ms. Bain, is lame. Had I known about the abuse surely I would have mentioned it as part of trying to determine if there was something in Donna's school life that might be connected to her death."

Delores Bain thought for a few seconds, sat forward, and placed her arms on the desk.

"Mr. Cullen, I did not see the relevance of that incident to what you were asking me about. You had indicated the fire that killed Donna was deliberately set.

There is absolutely no chance that Richard Appleton set fire to your home."

"That's what everybody, including Appleton himself, says. I'm curious what makes you so sure that a man who could prey on teenage girls would draw the line at arson — or murder."

"It is my business to know people, Mr. Cullen. I know that Richard Appleton did not set fire to your house."

"Did you hire him?"

"Pardon?"

"Did you hire Richard Appleton to teach at this school?"

"I was part of the hiring process, yes, along with my superintendent and someone from HR."

"Apparently your *knowing people* didn't preclude hiring a sexual predator."

She took a breath, let it out slowly. "I didn't go into this the first time you were here because it has no bearing on what happened to your wife, and frankly I didn't want to add more pain to what you had already suffered. If I erred in keeping that information from you, I assure you that it was done for the right reasons. Nevertheless, I apologize."

I wanted to tell her I considered her apology a crock but decided there was little to be gained from a full-blown confrontation.

"There's something you can do that might be of help," I told her.

"Of course … if I'm able."

"Another of Appleton's victims, Elaine Yu, died a few years ago in Prince Albert, Saskatchewan. I'm sure you are aware of the incident."

She nodded and looked down at her desk, then up at me. "I did hear that Elaine died. It was a few years ago — a traffic accident of some kind, I believe. I found out some weeks after it happened so was unfortunately unable to attend the funeral. And frankly, that's all I know about it."

"Do you know what kind of traffic accident?"

She shook her head. "I never heard any of the details. I suppose I didn't really want to. When I learned that Elaine had been killed I sent a note to her family expressing my sadness. I didn't hear back from the family and hadn't expected to. It had to have been terrible for them with her so young."

I nodded.

"Are you asking this because you think there's a connection between the two girls' deaths?"

I shrugged. "I don't honestly know. I just thought I should check it out."

"Of course."

I wasn't sure what else I could ask her.

Her features softened and her voice, when she spoke, was gentler. "It would seem that you have been quite diligent in your investigation."

"I've talked to some people," I said. "But I'm not sure I'm any farther ahead than when I started."

"Adam … I don't want this to end badly. I really am sorry I wasn't more forthcoming in our first meeting. And I hope you will accept that my reasons for not telling you about Richard Appleton were genuine, if flawed. I do wish you well in your pursuit of the person who set fire to your home."

"And killed my wife," I said softly.

"And killed your wife," she repeated.

I stood up.

"Thanks again for your time. I'll let you get on with your day."

She stood, smiled, and offered her hand. I shook it, then turned and walked out of her office. In the outer office I thought about saying something by way of apology to the two secretaries, but changed my mind.

As I left the school it seemed to me that the temperature outside was sinking again. Like my mood.

TWENTY-TWO

I stopped for groceries and wine in preparation for cooking dinner for Jill the next night. Then I drove the rest of the way home and cleaned house and drank a slow rye and Diet Coke as Gordon Lightfoot, then the Rankin Family provided pleasant background sounds.

I called Jill on her cell and left a message telling her to come any time after six and not to bring anything. The house looked decent and the Rankins were wrapping up *Endless Seasons*, my favourite of their albums.

I built a second rye and Diet Coke and sat down in the leather recliner to think. The meeting with Delores Bain had been unsettling.

I hadn't enjoyed pushing her. But she had kept information from me the first time we'd met — information that, despite her assurances that Appleton the predator could never be Appleton the killer, might have been important to me.

Thing was I knew nothing more than I'd known before I paid my second visit to Northern Horizon Academy. I sat and drank my whisky and thought hard. And no matter how I dissected and analyzed it all, I kept coming back to Richard Appleton.

What I didn't have was anything that looked remotely

like evidence. The man had preyed on young girls from a position of trust. What could be slimier? And he had gone to jail because of the testimony of those girls. And now two of those girls were dead, one the result of a deliberately set fire, and the other....

Revenge is a powerful motivator. And if it turned out that there was anything at all suspicious in the death of Elaine Yu, then that would be significant. But would it point any more clearly to who killed Donna?

That was a question I couldn't answer. I hoped that Cobb, a few days of R and R under his belt, might have more answers — even *one* more answer — than I had.

And that was the last thought I had before falling asleep in the recliner.

When Cobb arrived just after nine the next morning I was no longer in the chair. I had woken at around three a.m. and shifted to my bed for the last few hours of sleep, sleep that was punctuated with a dream about a car race in which I was driving the Accord. It was a sort of NASCAR, sort of Formula One race and I was frustrated that no matter how hard I tried I couldn't seem to make any headway in the race. As stupid as that sounds, dreams never seem stupid when you're having them and I woke around seven a.m. in a bad mood and nursing a headache.

By the time Cobb arrived I'd gone for a run, had a shower, downed three extra strength Tylenol, and four glasses of water. Half the recommended daily intake. I was ready.

Cobb set two Starbucks take-out coffee containers on the counter and took up residence in the recliner. He had dressed winter casual. Jean jacket over a Route 66 sweat-shirt, faded jeans, sneakers not laced up.

The bagels had been staying warm in the oven. I had cream cheese and jam set out on a TV tray that was older than I was.

I pulled the bagels out of the oven.

"Whole wheat or plain?"

"Whole wheat? There's a whole wheat bagel?"

"Sure, they got lots of flavours now."

"But whole wheat?"

I shrugged.

Cobb shook his head. "There are rabbis all over North America in shock right now."

"I take it you'll want the plain."

"Good call," Cobb said.

I sat on one of my kitchen chairs opposite him. I'd poured my coffee into a New York Yankees mug Donna had given me for a birthday present. Cobb left his coffee on the counter for the moment, working instead on a bot-tled water he had brought along.

Probably just getting started on his recommended daily intake.

For a while we ate bagels and talked about the Flames.

Then I told him about my encounter with Delores Bain. He furrowed his brow but didn't say much.

"It feels like it's so close," I said. "That the answer to who killed Donna is just out of my reach and if I could just put a couple of things together it would all be right there."

Cobb nodded. "It's like that in my business a lot of the time. Sometimes it all comes clear and sometimes it doesn't."

"So what's next?"

He leaned forward, rested his elbows on his knees, and looked at me. "I called a few people in Prince Albert, some local cops and an RCMP guy I know. The accident that killed Elaine Yu may not have been all that accidental."

I set my coffee mug down.

"More."

"Elaine Yu was a home care nurse. Travelled around to people's homes administering their meds, doing minor tests, changing dressings, bandages, and the like. She had come to Canada with her family from a little village just outside Beijing. She was twelve, went into grade seven. Never looked back. Bright, hard-working, I heard a lot of the same things about her that you've told me about Donna.

"The RCMP cop I talked to, First Nations guy named James Moostoos, he worked on the case. He told me Elaine was returning to Prince Albert after a home visitation. Sometime between nine and nine-thirty at night, she went off the road at probably close to the speed limit. Dry road, good visibility, no alcohol involved."

I leaned forward, watched Cobb.

"Moostoos told me their investigators' best guess was that her car, which was a 2002 Toyota Camry, was forced off the road on a highway south of Prince Albert. Near a place called St. Louis. The car rolled into the ditch and she was killed instantly. No witnesses."

"Then how do they know she was forced off the road?"

"Damage to the driver's side of the car was inconsistent with a rollover, consistent with a vehicle being smashed from the side. Paint on the Camry that was from another vehicle. Could have been from an earlier fender-bender but there was no report of an accident involving the Camry prior to that night. The investigating cops wrote it up as a suspected road rage incident."

"Road rage," I repeated.

Cobb nodded. "It happens. Idiot gets pissed off, pulls up alongside the person he's pissed off at, bumps the vehicle, maybe not wanting to put it right off the road but making a point."

"And if it *does* go off the road …"

"Too damn bad."

"Except maybe this wasn't road rage."

Cobb shrugged. "Maybe not."

He spread cream cheese over the last of his bagel and popped it into his mouth.

"When did it happen?" I asked.

Cobb pulled a notebook out of his jean jacket pocket and flipped it open. "October 18, 2005."

"Less than six months after Donna was killed."

"Yeah. And just over a year after Appleton was released from prison. And one other interesting tidbit Moostoos was able to tell me … one year to the day after the crash, the family received a note in the mail that read, 'Too bad your daughter didn't spend more time taking driver's ed.'"

"Jesus. Didn't that tell them something?"

"They already figured the thing was deliberate. Checked with all the body shops for unreported repairs. Nothing. Back to road rage. The note was consistent with someone with anger management issues."

I stared at the floor for a long while. "So where does this take us?"

"It takes *me* on a flight to Saskatoon in the morning, then a rental car journey to Prince Albert, and maybe St.

Louis. It's pronounced St. *Louie*, by the way. Maybe I can learn something from the incident reports. Or maybe not."

"I could come with you."

Cobb drank some water and shook his head. "Not really a two man gig. Besides, I owe you one … maybe more than one."

"You don't owe me. Something I just thought of. What about the other girls. There were six victims, not counting Appleton's step-daughter. What about…?"

Cobb nodded. "I thought about the same thing. Did a little checking during my time off. All are alive and well, although one girl, a Casey Kingsbury — lives in Nanaimo now — had her dog run over, got a new dog, and it was run over just a few weeks after the first. Both times the dogs had somehow got out of a fenced yard. Might be nothing or …" He shrugged.

"Weird," I said. "But the girls themselves, they're all okay?"

"Uh-huh. Anyway, I plan to be in and out of Saskatchewan in a hurry. I'll stop by Monday, Tuesday at the latest, and let you know what I found out."

He stood up, took his coffee from the counter, and sat back down.

I watched him swirl the cup around, then take a long sip.

"You think there's a connection between Donna's death and what happened to Elaine Yu?"

His eyes narrowed. "Too early to say 100 percent, but I've never been a big believer in coincidence. And the notes both one year to the day after each of them was killed screams same killer."

"Okay, so let's say we can connect the two deaths, what then?"

"I don't know. Maybe we have to take another look at the Appletons, Mr. *and* Mrs."

"You think a woman is capable of doing the things that this person did?"

"Adam, there are women, clearly not as many as men, but they're out there, who are capable of unimaginable horrors. I'm not saying Mrs. Appleton is one of them, but I'm saying we can't rule it out."

"I was thinking of the physical act of forcing someone's vehicle off the road; that feels more like a man."

Cobb shrugged. "Ever hear of Danica Patrick? Okay, I'm being flippant, but the truth is there are actually very few physical acts that you can rule out the possibility of a woman doing, other than those that require the strength, that men, because we're bigger, might have."

I was having trouble with that. "And yet, most all of the mass killings have involved male shooters."

Cobb nodded. "True. Along with the vast majority of violent crime. And I'm probably like you — this feels like a male perp. I'm just saying we can't ignore the possibility that either of the Appletons, or both of them working together, are responsible for both deaths."

I nodded. "Maybe."

He took another sip of coffee. "The part that bothers me is the same thing that's bothered me all along: any harm either of the two girls could do Appleton had already been done, which means they were no longer a threat."

"Yeah."

"Which makes revenge the only possible reason for Appleton or even the charming Mrs. Appleton to kill those two women." He leaned forward as if to stand up, then changed his mind and leaned back again. "Begs the question — could either of them kill out of revenge?"

I didn't answer right away. "Based on my conversation with them, I honestly don't know. Appleton seemed genuine in the things he said to me. If my wife hadn't been the victim and if I was assessing the guy for someone else, I probably would say he doesn't seem capable of setting fire to someone's house knowing that someone might die as a result."

"And you may be right." Cobb tapped an index finger against the side of his coffee container. "Except that he was able to deceive so many people the first time around. Can we be sure he isn't doing it again?"

I nodded. "And there's Mrs. Appleton, who we know is capable of violence, but to what extent?"

Cobb didn't move. He was staring at a point on the wall just above and to the right of my left ear. Not saying anything. Barely breathing. Intense.

After a minute or so, he stood up.

"Okay, so I go to Prince Albert and I talk to some people and maybe I learn something."

I stood up and reached out my hand.

"I appreciate what you're doing."

He shook my hand. "I want to find the person who did this, Adam."

I nodded as he turned for the door. "So do I," I said.

And he was gone.

I looked down at my plate. I hadn't eaten much bagel. I'd lost my appetite.

TWENTY-THREE

I was nursing a glass of red wine, surrounded by veg-etables, condiments, and salad-making implements. I'd planned the menu carefully. A mussels starter I had gleaned long ago from a Peter Gzowski column in *Cana-dian Living*, then my own variation on a popular green salad that employs green leaf lettuce, red onion, cucum-ber, tomato, chopped yellow pepper, cashews, and a bal-samic vinegar dressing. And finally a fettuccine carbonara that I had made once before and had actually worked. Why mess with a proven winner?

I had chicken parts I'd bought the day before sim-mering in water on the stove, creating a stock for the mus-sels. With the chicken, onion, salt, and pepper bubbling away, the apartment smelled pretty good.

I'm far from a gourmet and even farther from being a chef, but I like to cook and was kind of enjoying trying to come up with something that would dazzle Jill. She was bringing the dessert and no amount of wheedling from me could get her to drop even a hint as to what it might be.

I'm painfully slow in the kitchen, which was why I was working on the salad and the stock for the mussels at three o'clock, a full three hours before Jill's ETA.

Michael Bublé was belting out "Heartache Tonight" (yes, *that* "Heartache Tonight") with my help when I heard a rap on the door.

I set the cucumber down, turned down the flame under the stock, and wiped my hands on a nearby towel, headed for the door. I figured with my luck the caller would be a religious proselytizer, an insurance salesman, or a member of the Wildrose Party.

The person at my door was none of those.

I hadn't seen Lorne Cooney in a few months. It was good to see him now. He was wearing a dark blue sweat suit, a tan and blue toque, and light, what looked like cotton gloves. He was grinning at me, which came as no surprise since Lorne Cooney grinned more than anyone I had ever known. Just a happy Jamaican.

I grinned back at him, then threw an arm around him.

"It's been way, way too long," I said.

"Truer words," he said and returned the hug.

I stepped back and pointed the way in.

He stepped in a couple of steps, and I closed the door behind him. He stopped and looked around.

"Joint ain't changed much."

"Hard to be creative in seven hundred square feet."

"Especially when three hundred of 'em is taken up with the music collection. I see that ain't changed either. Why don't you get rid of all that Canadian shit and lay in some reggae?"

I laughed. "Find a spot in there and I'll get us a beer."

"Talked me into it."

He talked as he headed for the recliner and I pulled two bottles of Rickard's Red from the fridge, putting my red wine on hold for now.

"I wasn't going to stop, man, but I was running by here and the door downstairs was open, I figured what the hell."

I handed him a beer and crossed to the hide-a-bed and sat. "I'm glad you did. I should've called you a long time ago but —"

"Shit, man, don't say that. You think I don't get what's been going on for you?"

"Thanks, Lorne."

He took a pull of the beer and looked at me. "How you doin'?"

"I think it's getting better, I really believe it is, but there are times …"

He nodded and we drank beer without saying anything for a while.

The grin came back to his face. "Hey, guess who I had lunch with the other day?"

"Simon Cowell."

"He called, but I told him I was busy. We talked Caribbean music and he said he'd call again sometime."

"Right. Who?"

"Janice."

"Janice Mayotte?"

"The same. Except she's Janice Flynn now and got a belly on her that says there's gonna be another Flynn sometime soon."

"Hey, that's great. I heard she'd moved to Toronto."

Lorne nodded. "Married an architect and the next thing you know his firm sends him to Calgary to work out of the office here. Anyway, once she's done having this baby she figures we ought to get together and maybe do something cree-ay-tive, revive our little trio, maybe take the journalistic world by storm."

343

I finished my beer and set the bottle down on the floor. "Another one?"

"I can't man. I got to finish my run. I'm trainin' for a half marathon, only five weeks away." He looked at his beer. "I've already sinned."

"Have to keep your strength up," I said. "Anyway, the idea of working with Janice again sounds cool. You, on the other hand, I'm not so sure about."

The grin. "You forget, I'm the brains of the outfit."

"You're right, I did forget that. Did you two ever finish that series on the drug scene in Calgary, the one we were working on when …" I stopped as the bad memory hit me.

Lorne shook his head. "We kind of lost the desire with you out of the deal. Maybe that's something we should talk about when the three of us get together."

I nodded. "Let's do that. I might have a few new insights that could be useful."

Lorne stood up, looked around. "I see you got some stuff goin' on and I better be getting back to my run."

I thought about explaining what the cooking prep was all about but figured it might be a longer story than either of us needed just then.

We walked to the door, I opened it, and we shook hands. "I'll call you, Lorne. I mean that."

One final grin. "I know you do, man. And if you don't, I'll come around, maybe flatten your tires."

He started bouncing on his toes. Getting back into running mode.

"Gotta run. Literally."

"Don't sprain an ankle out there."

"An athlete like me?" He laughed and headed off down the hall toward the stairs.

I picked up the beer bottles, put them away and re-turned to my salad. Three minutes later there was another knock at the door. I was laughing as I opened it, working on a one-liner to lay on the returning Jamaican, who had no doubt forgotten something. Or maybe decided to blow off the training for one day and have that other beer.

I pulled the door open.

And was wrong again.

Delores Bain looked very different out of school. She was wearing a long, black leather coat trimmed with silver-grey fur and high, laced leather boots that looked both chic and expensive. She was also sporting a hat that could best be described as funky — a black twenties throwback thing that looked much better on her than I would have thought. She was holding her gloves in one hand and smiling at me.

"Well … uh … hello," I said. I'm pretty sure the sur-prise I was feeling was reflected in my voice.

"I won't stay long," she said as if to set my fears on that score at ease. "I've been thinking hard about all this, and I'm not sure, but I may have something that could be useful to you."

I stepped back from the door. "Please come in. I was just working on some dinner things for later. Can I take your coat?"

She stepped in, I closed the door and she shrugged out of the coat, handing it, the gloves, and the hat to me. My closet is the size of a kitchen pantry and is full of that part of my wardrobe that needs to hang. There was no room in there for Ms. Bain's winter outerwear, so I set her things on the recliner, meaning that she and I would both have to sit on the hide-a-bed.

"Can I get you a drink or a glass of wine? Coffee?"

She smiled again. "Coffee would be good."

She may have noticed the half full coffee perk on the stove and been trying to be nice or maybe she just liked coffee. I gestured at the hide-a-bed and made my way for the kitchen. I poured two cups of coffee and set them in the microwave. Coffee, beer, and wine in the space of twenty minutes. Eclectic.

While the coffee was heating I turned to her. "I'm sorry I don't have any cookies or much to go with the coffee."

"That's quite all right. I wasn't kidding when I said I wouldn't be long. I can see you're getting ready for company."

I couldn't think of a response so I smiled. The microwave beeped and I turned back to it and fetched the two mugs.

"How do you like your coffee?" I asked her.

"A little milk if you have it."

I fixed her coffee, added milk and sugar to mine, and made my way back into the living room area. I set her coffee in front of her, turned down the stereo, and sat down next to her.

"You said you had something that might help."

She nodded and sipped the coffee.

"You mean help with who set the fire?"

Her shoulders moved slightly. "I don't know … maybe. I … do you think I could trouble you for just a little more milk? It's a bit … strong."

"Sorry, it's been sitting there a while."

She handed me her cup. I took it, stood up, and headed for the fridge.

When I came back she appeared to be studying what

was going on in my kitchen. I couldn't blame her; the place was smelling better all the time.

I sat back down and looked at her. She seemed to be waiting for … what … the right moment … the right words? I sipped coffee and waited.

"First of all, I apologize again for the other day. I'm afraid I wasn't at my best, which doesn't excuse my treating you with less courtesy than you deserved."

"No apology necessary."

"You're very kind but there is and I do."

She was struggling with getting into whatever it was that had brought her here and I didn't want to rush her. Neither of us spoke for maybe a full minute. She took in air, breathed it out through her nose.

"I'm … I'm not sure it means anything at all," she said. "There was a teacher at the school; he died last year. Mr. Levinson, Gerard Levinson. He'd taught at NHA for almost twenty years and was, I suppose you could say obsessive in terms of his pride in the school."

She paused, drank some coffee, so I did too.

"I know I'm probably imagining things, but I recall something he said once. He seemed as angry at the students who had spoken out against Mr. Appleton as he was at Appleton himself. Like they'd brought shame to the school by going to the police. Like they should have kept silent even after what Richard did. I remember thinking it was an odd reaction."

"What was it he said?"

"I want to try to get it exactly," she said and stared at the ceiling, searched her memory.

"He said, 'It would serve those girls right if more shit happened to them.' I remember it was oddly vulgar of him to put it that way. He seemed … very frustrated."

"Do you think this guy, Levinson, was capable of hurting people?"

"I suppose I've never thought about it before, but since we talked the other day I've found myself wondering if Gerard might've been so angry at seeing the reputation of a school he cared about so much being damaged, that he might have … done some things."

I thought about what she was saying. Was it possible that someone could be as obsessive as the guy she was describing? Obsessive enough to kill people?

"Top up on the coffee?"

"I'm fine." She smiled.

"What did you say the guy's name was?"

"Mr. Levinson. Gerard Levinson."

"Right," I said. "Gerald …" I stopped. That was wrong. She hadn't said Gerald. I looked at her and tried to think.

Come on, you've had one beer and less than a full glass of wine. Focus, for Christ's sake.

But that was the problem. I wanted to take in what she was saying. This could be the breakthrough I'd been waiting for. Someone who could hate enough to kill two girls. But it didn't feel right. *I* didn't feel right.

I looked at her and tried to form a question.

"How … old …" I couldn't think of how the question was supposed to end.

She was watching me.

"Are you all right, Adam?"

"Yeah … I … no …"

"Adam?"

"I just … Gerard, that's it, isn't it … you said Gerard, not … that other name."

"Yes, Adam, that's what I said."

She was smiling now and I knew. But what did I know? There was something wrong. Something wrong with me. She'd done ... what? I was so tired, so dizzy, so ...

It was right there. *Right there.* I knew what she'd done and I knew it was too late for me to do anything about it. The coffee. She'd put ... something ... in the coffee. I tried to get up. But my legs wouldn't help me. If I could just sleep for a minute or two, just a few minutes, but no, I can't sleep now, not now or —

I tried again to stand up. And almost made it.

The woman ... I couldn't think of her name either but she was right there, looking at me. The smile ... that damn smile was bigger now. Her face was closer to me. And she was speaking to me. But it wasn't making sense.

"You are a Goddamn fool. Did you really think I'd stand by and let you destroy what I've spent my life building and creating? Northern Horizon Academy is a wonderful place of learning. And it's a wonderful place of learning because of *me*."

Why is she...? Sleep, just for a minute ...

"You aren't going to ruin my life's work. Those pathetic women tried to do that and they paid the price for their interfering. Not all of them. Not yet. But they will. They all will. Just like your wife and that other little bitch. They got what they deserved."

What's she holding ... a needle ... hypodermic ... what is she...?

"All of them will pay. But there's no hurry for them. You, on the other hand, made yourself more of a priority, didn't you, Adam?

I tried to focus, felt my head, no, my whole body wanting to lean forward and just ...

"How does it feel to know you are dying? I'm sure someone as stupid as you are thinks you'll be joining your wife in some blissful state of eternal joy. Well, good for you, you pathetic bastard. Good for you. You just hang on to that. While you die."

I forced my body to a half turn and looked back at the stove. It was so far away.

I have to turn the burner off … the mussel stock will burn. I have to … move … have to.

That was the last thought I had as a black curtain settled over me. *So … heavy.*

And all was darkness.

TWENTY-FOUR

I opened my eyes. She was still there. Still smiling. Looking down at me and smiling. But ...

No, it wasn't *her*. It was Jill ... looking down at me.

"If you didn't want to have dinner with me you could have just said so."

I blinked at her.

"Oh, and by the way, you owe your life to a lemon pie," she said.

I tried to shake my head but I don't think it moved. What it did was ache. Badly.

"Lemon.... Where am I?"

"Foothills Hospital. You've been out for ..." she looked at her watch, "almost thirty hours."

"Out ... thirty hours ... lemon pie ... what ... what's going on?"

"We were hoping you might be able to tell us."

Different voice. Other side of the bed. I turned my head. Not a good idea. It hurt like the worst hangover in the history of alcoholic beverages. I forced my eyes to focus on the speaker.

Cobb was wearing a Cleveland Browns ball cap. I thought I must be okay if Cobb's hat could register with me. If I could just get my head to stop hurting and if someone would be kind enough to remove whatever it was that was in my mouth that was making it taste like compost, I'd be a hell of a lot better.

"Why aren't you in Saskatchewan?"

"I've been and I'm back."

That was just one more thing that made no sense. I'd get back to that later. I turned my head very slowly back to Jill.

"You want to explain the lemon pie thing? No, on second thought, start with the thirty hours part."

"You've been unconscious, out, zombie-like for thirty hours, give or take."

"Jesus," I said.

"And technically it wasn't the lemon pie, it was the whipped cream that saved you. I came to your apartment early because I wanted to get it in the fridge before it went all scoodgy —"

"Scoodgy," I repeated.

"Nobody likes scoodgy whipped cream," Cobb said.

Jill smiled. "The ambulance guys said another half hour and you'd have been dead. But maybe they were just being dramatic. To make me feel good."

"Dead," I repeated.

"Drug overdose. When you didn't come to the door I knew there was something wrong. I tried it and it was unlocked. Lucky. I guess it's a good thing we were having dinner."

No one said anything for a minute. I was trying to sort it all out … to remember.

"You a user, Adam?"

"What?"

Cobb set the paper down, leaned forward.

"You've been through some bad shit, pal," he said. "I get that, but you damn near died. You would have if anyone but Jill had been the one to find you. And if the paramedics had been more than five minutes away. She knew to keep you breathing. She knew to —"

"Stop." I tried to hold my hand up. It wanted to fall back down but I made it stay there. "What are you talking about?"

"I'm talking about heroin," Cobb said.

"No."

"You OD'd on heroin, Adam."

I tried to shake my head.

"You're wrong. I didn't take anything. I mean, I didn't … myself."

They were looking at me. I couldn't tell if they believed me. I tried to get the words sorted out … the words I needed to explain … to make them understand …

"She had a syringe," I said, the memory of Delores Bain coming slowly into focus.

I felt rather than saw Cobb lean closer still. "Who Adam? Who had a syringe?"

"Delores Bain. The principal at Donna's school. She's the one. She set the fire, she killed the other girl, and she wanted to kill me."

"You know this?"

"She told me … all of it."

"Can you take us through it?"

"Yeah, I think so. It's a little fuzzy but I think I can remember a lot of it. Is there anything to drink?"

"They brought some juice a while ago," Jill said. "You want to try it? They said it might be hard to keep anything down for a while."

"I need to drink something."

Jill passed me the juice and helped me sit up. I gulped down half a glass or so of the best orange juice I'd ever tasted.

I lay back on the pillow and thought for a minute. I needed to get this right.

"She came to the apartment a little after three, I guess. Just after Lorne Cooney, a guy I've worked with, just after he left. In fact, I thought it was Lorne coming back for something but it wasn't. It was her."

I looked at Jill. It was important to me that she understood.

"Keep going, Adam," she said.

"She told me she'd remembered one of the teachers, a guy who died a year ago, I think she said … some guy who was so obsessive about the school's reputation that she thought maybe it was possible that he could hurt people to protect the school from further scandal."

I took another drink of the juice. I was feeling slightly better, like after you come out of anesthetic and things start to make sense again.

"But it was bogus. It was all bogus … an act. And I was already wonky … losing consciousness. She drugged me. Must have put something in my coffee. Then injected me with…"

I turned my head toward Cobb.

"It was her. *She* was the one who hated the people she thought had hurt the school. Once she knew I was too far gone to do anything, she told me … told me she'd killed Donna, and the other girl, Elaine Yu, and that she's going to kill the others. But she wanted to get me first … saw me as a more immediate threat.

"I realized she'd done something and could feel myself getting woozy and I tried to get up and do something but I couldn't."

"Probably one of the date rape drugs or something like it," Cobb said.

"Whatever it was I was as helpless as a baby. Pretty sick feeling."

"That *and* the heroin," Cobb said. "You are a lucky S.O.B."

I was starting to feel almost human. I sat up on my own and smiled at Jill.

"Enter the lady with the lemon pie."

"And whipping cream," she said.

"That she didn't want all scoodgy." Cobb grinned. She laughed. "Uh-huh."

"You … you said thirty hours. I've been out that long?"

She nodded her head. "Pretty close."

"And you've been here the whole time?"

"Not quite. I went home for a few hours. I wanted to be there when Kyla got home from her friend's house. I slept a little, then came back."

"Wow," I said. Which didn't come close to covering what I was feeling. But it was all I could come up with, given the state of my brain cells.

A doctor who looked barely old enough to be out of high school came into the room. He was tall, fit looking, and smiling. He stopped at the foot of the bed and looked at me.

"Well, you're looking a whole lot better. Feeling better too, I bet."

"Maybe not ready to run a half marathon, but I think I'm going to live. If I don't starve to death."

He came around to the side of the bed and bent down to get a better look at me. "If you're hungry, that's a good sign."

"I'm hungry."

"Mr. Cullen, you took a massive overdose of drugs tonight and almost ended your life. Clearly there's a problem that needs to be addressed and …"

I might have laughed if I could have been certain it wouldn't hurt. I settled for shaking my head.

"Thanks for the concern, Doc, but it turns out that someone drugged me and shot the stuff into me. I'm not a user."

He looked up at Cobb. "Is that true?"

Cobb nodded. "Yeah, it is. And I checked his arm when I first got here. No tracks. He's telling the truth."

The doctor frowned and looked back at me.

"I guess that's good and bad. Good that you're not an addict, bad that someone tried to do you harm. We need to report this to the police."

Cobb spoke. "I'm a private detective, Doctor. This happened as the result of an investigation we're involved with at present. The police will need to be brought into this but we can handle making that happen. For now, it's not something that you need to worry further about."

"The law in Canada requires physicians to report any admittance of harm by one person to another. I have no choice."

Cobb nodded. "I understand, Doctor, but we'll be reporting the incident to Deputy Police Chief Capuano. I've worked with him — and for him — and I've already texted him to say we'll be in as soon as Mr. Cullen is able."

The doctor didn't answer right away. "You're sure this man isn't in immediate danger?"

Cobb said, "The person who did this is, we think, unstable. And clearly diabolical. But the danger is manageable."

"Who will manage it?"

"I will," Cobb said.

The doctor turned back to me. "I'd like to keep you in overnight just to make sure everything is as it should be. You've taken a double hit and it might be best —"

"Thanks, Doctor, but I'm feeling a whole lot better and I'd like to get out of here as soon as possible."

He looked at Jill. "I'll be honest, it's nuts in here tonight and we could use the bed, but I'm a little reluctant …"

"We'll watch him like a hawk, Doctor. I've had experience with overdose situations."

"As your actions tonight clearly showed." He turned back to me. "In that case, how about you just take it easy for a little while longer. We'll check your vitals in a while and if everything's good I think we can get you out of here. But if you start feeling worse —"

"I'll get my butt back here in a hurry. Promise."

An hour and a half later Cobb, Jill, and I stepped through the hospital's main entrance and into the cool evening air. Air, like the orange juice earlier, had never tasted so good. I took a couple of deep breaths.

"What time is it anyway?"

Cobb glanced at his watch. "A little after nine-thirty."

"You still hungry?" Jill asked as she took hold of my hand.

I looked at her.

"Okay, dumb question." She looked over at Cobb. "I think we better get him some food."

Cobb grinned at me. "What's your preference? I'm buying."

"I'd like to say steak and lobster but I don't think I'm up to a dining experience tonight. Maybe something pleasantly plebeian."

"I have the answer." Cobb was still grinning.

We were sitting on three plastic moulded chairs around one of the Formica-covered fibreglass tables that are a design feature at Tim Hortons restaurants from sea to shining sea. Pleasantly plebeian.

I had finished off a toasted BLT, two old fashioned plain donuts, and was nicely into my second large double-double before serious conversation resumed. Since the two of them seemed to be waiting for me to give some kind of cue, I set my cup down, wiped my mouth with my napkin, and looked first at Jill, then at Cobb.

"So, what happens next?"

Cobb shifted around on his chair. "I've been thinking about that. I'm worried that a good lawyer could get her off."

"Are you nuts?" I was a little louder than I meant to be. I leaned forward, set my elbows on the table. "I'm an eyewitness *and* the intended victim. And she confessed the whole thing to me. Okay, maybe confessed isn't the right word, bragged is closer to what she did, but the point is she told me all of it."

Cobb nodded. "I get that and I know it sounds crazy, but think about it. You didn't actually see her put anything in your coffee, or stick the needle in your arm, and all we've got is your recollection of her telling you she was the killer while you were in a reduced state of consciousness."

I stared down at my coffee.

"I could see her walking away from this," Cobb said again.

"That stinks." Jill's voice wasn't as loud as mine had been but she clearly felt the same way about Cobb's revelation as I did.

I leaned back in my chair. "Which I suppose brings us back to my earlier question — what happens next?"

"I'm thinking it might be time for me to get back on the surveillance regimen."

"You can't watch her twenty-four hours a day," I said.

Cobb regarded his coffee cup. "I can't. But I have a couple of colleagues I can call on for help."

"What's she likely to do next?"

Cobb flicked his thumb against his chin several times. Thinking.

"I'm not sure. We're okay until she learns that you survived her attack. Which, of course, she will, eventually. The big unknown is what will she do then? This is someone who is psychopathic, sociopathic, and clearly capable of great violence. Factor in that she's also very intelligent and unpredictable and what we've got is the potential for some bad shit."

Jill and I mulled that over for a while. I drank more of my double-double while Jill stared out the window.

"And she'll realize that since no one has shown up to arrest her that you haven't given her up to the cops yet. She'll also know that you're out there and that you know she's the one. If I'm her I'm thinking I can't just let this guy that I tried to kill wander around out there until he does decide to go to the police."

"She'll want to silence me. Permanently."

Cobb nodded. "That's my guess."

I nodded. "But for right now, I'm okay. She thinks I'm dead."

Cobb nodded.

"For now," he said.

I tried to think of something to say to lighten the mood a little but couldn't come up with anything. I looked at Jill. She was pale and worry had drawn her eyes into narrow slits. I reached over and covered one of her hands with one of mine.

"Hey," I said. "Mother hen. Take it easy. I'll be okay, I promise."

She jerked her head up to look at me. "Oh, crap," she said so suddenly I actually jumped and spilled a little of the coffee on my jacket.

"What?"

"That reminds me — I forgot to tell you when we were at the hospital. Your mom called three times wondering how you were. One of the nurses told me that while you were still unconscious. You better call her and let her know you're okay."

I set my coffee cup down and took a deep breath, let it out slowly.

"That's going to be a little tough," I said. "My mother passed away in October of 2006."

TWENTY-FIVE

There was silence around the table for several seconds. All of us knew what this meant but it was Cobb who put it in words.

"Looks like Ms. Bain already knows you survived her attack."

"But how?"

Cobb shrugged. "Maybe she hung around, watched your place for a while. Saw the ambulance take you away. Maybe followed it to the hospital. I'm guessing, but it has to be something like that."

I felt like I did after a horror flick — the kind where you come home after the movie and check under the bed and in the closets. I actually looked around the Tim Hortons at each of the people sitting at tables. There were six. None of them were Delores Bain. Two more people, a man and woman, were at the counter ordering. Neither of them were Delores Bain either. I stared out the windows at the parking lot and the residential streets beyond. Was she out there?

Cobb had his cell phone in his hand and was punching numbers. He held the phone to his ear, listened, then spoke.

"Lalonde, c'est moi, Cobb." That's about all I got of the conversation as Cobb spoke French for the next couple of minutes — one more surprise from a man I thought I was starting to know.

When he clicked off, he set the phone down and spoke to Jill and me. "I'm setting up a couple of guys to keep an eye on each of you for a couple of days until we get a plan of action in place and see what our school principal lady has in mind."

He pulled his notebook out of his pocket and said, "I'll need your address, Jill."

"Whoa, wait a second." Jill put a hand up. "Do I have any say in this? Who says I want anybody keeping an eye on me?"

Cobb closed the notebook and nodded. "Sorry, I should have talked to you first, but this lady is dangerous and I can't protect both of you at the same time. You won't see this guy; you won't know he's there unless something happens and you need him."

Jill was silent but she didn't look happy.

"And you have your daughter to think about," Cobb added.

"Do you think Kyla could be in any danger?"

Cobb took his time answering her. "Truth is, I don't know, Jill. The last thing I want to do is over-dramatize. But we've seen what Delores Bain is capable of. I really think we should take every precaution, at least for the present, until we can get a little better read on this."

Jill's features softened and she managed a smile. "I get that you're just being cautious and I appreciate your concern. I guess I was just a little concerned about my privacy."

Cobb returned the smile. "My bad, I should have talked to you before I called Lalonde. I'm sorry."

Jill waved off his apology. "Not necessary."

"What about the cops?" I asked. "Should we be involving them in this?"

"It's an option." Cobb nodded. "Problem is, we haven't got anything that could be called hard evidence. And even if the police agree to watch Jill's place, I'm fairly certain it will be in the short term only."

"And your guy ... guys?"

"As long as it takes until we get enough on this woman to put her away. That'll be my job."

Jill shivered. It wasn't cold in the restaurant. "I'm sorry. I must sound totally unappreciative of what you're doing."

Cobb smiled. "You said the very things I would have said if I'd been in your position."

Jill managed a small smile. "Thanks, Mike." She gave him the address.

Cobb wrote it down. "Lalonde can start right away. I'll call him and give the address." He turned to me. "I'll be putting a guy on you as well. Same deal. These guys are good at what they do. Discreet and effective."

I was less reluctant than Jill, mostly because I'd seen Delores Bain in action. "You know my address."

"I do."

"And what about you?"

"I'll be watching Delores Bain."

"You'll need help."

"I can get help." I opened my mouth but he cut me off. "I know what you're thinking and the answer is no. I don't think it's a good idea to have the potential victim performing surveillance on the suspect."

"Unorthodox, I agree, but potentially effective." I was trying for levity but the gallows humour wasn't working. Neither Cobb nor Jill laughed or even smiled.

I kept shifting my eyes back to the big windows, trying to decide if any of the cars in the parking lot looked like the kind Delores Bain might drive.

Cobb called Lalonde a second time and gave him Jill's address. When he ended the call — again all of it but for Jill's address in French — he turned to Jill. "He'll be there by the time we get you home. Don't look for him, you won't see him. And I think it would be a good idea for you to take Kyla to and from school for the next few days."

"Maybe I'll keep her home. I can phone the school and get what she needs to do."

"Even better." Cobb's next call was to somebody named Merle Jankowsky. This call was in English. Jankowsky would be watching me, or at least he'd be watching my apartment.

After that call Cobb set the phone down, sipped his coffee.

"I didn't know you spoke French," I said.

"I took three years of French at university before I switched to criminology. Spent two summers in Quebec with French-Canadian families."

"International man of mystery," I said.

"I think I'd like to be getting home," Jill said. "Kyla's with a babysitter and if this woman is as sick as you think …"

"You're right. We should make a move."

Walking out to Cobb's Jeep, I scanned the parking lot once more. I'm pretty sure Cobb was doing the same thing but he was less obvious about it.

I wasn't even sure what I was looking for since I didn't know what kind of vehicle Delores Bain drove. But I was beginning to think that it was more and more likely that she had been at the wheel of whatever it was that almost picked me off the sidewalk a few days earlier.

"Both he and Jankowsky have some people they work with. As good as they are. Jill and Kyla will be watched round the clock."

The snow was falling harder now and Cobb turned the windshield wipers on to a faster speed. Visibility was becoming a little difficult.

"When we get to your place I'll come in for a second just to …" He didn't finish the thought.

He angled right onto Memorial Drive heading east toward my part of town. I wanted to talk. *Needed* to talk. Nerves maybe. I needed to talk about something that didn't involve people trying to kill people.

"I have to tell you, the French thing, that blew me away."

Cobb glanced at me. "Really? Why?"

"I don't know. I mean I think it's great. It just surprised me. I guess I didn't see you as a bilingual kind of guy."

"We all have our surprises."

"I guess so."

"Now take you, for example," he said. "I didn't figure you to have the most complete collection of Canadian music on the planet."

I peered out into the snow that was getting still heavier, hoping Cobb could see the road okay. I could barely make out the huge poplars that dotted the boulevard on the south side of Memorial Drive, trees that had been planted after the First World War in memory of men and women who gave their lives. I'd always thought the trees were one of the coolest things about Calgary.

I looked back at Cobb. "First of all," I said, "I doubt it's the most complete."

"Maybe, maybe not. But it is pretty damn impressive.

How long you been at it?" It was like he sensed my need for conversation — normal, everyday, mundane conversation.

I shrugged. "I guess I've always bought a lot of records but after the fire I needed something to think about that wasn't Donna or the fire or what my life could have been if there'd never been a fire."

"Any particular reason that the something you decided to think about was Canadian music?"

I shrugged. "Not sure. I mean, I'm not some nut-bar nationalist. My all-time favourite song is Barbra Streisand singing "Memory." You know, the song from *Cats*."

Cobb nodded.

"And if I could only go to one concert for the rest of my life, it would be Bruce Springsteen. My favourite singer of all-time is Frank Sinatra, my favourite group is the Beach Boys, and watching Mark Knopfler play the guitar is like watching Derek Jeter play shortstop. But one day, for no particularly good reason, I decided that I wanted to listen to the Rankins and Sarah McLachlan and Lightfoot and Cohen and Cockburn and Bachman and a whole bunch more amazing artists I'd never heard of but found out about on CBC. So I did. It became the focus I needed, an escape maybe. But the thing is, I really like this stuff."

"Wow, sounds like a speech somebody ought to give to some parliamentary committee on funding for the arts."

"Probably already been done. Probably didn't help."

"So you've got music by other people," he said.

"Sure, tons of it, but most of it's boxed up and in a storage locker in the basement of the building."

Cobb nodded something that looked like approval. "That's a cool story."

I shrugged. "Maybe."

The snow had let up some and we could see a little better. We were approaching the intersection at 10th Street Northwest and the light was green so Cobb picked up speed a little to make the light. As we cruised through the intersection, a dark blue one-ton dually pulled alongside us in the inside lane and I happened to glance over.

"Cobb!"

I was too late. Delores Bain, at the wheel of the pickup, jerked the steering wheel hard to the left and slammed into my side of the Jeep. Cobb wasn't ready for it and we were propelled to our left, into the westbound lane and directly into the path of an oncoming City of Calgary sanding truck.

It was one of those moments when everything slows down and your mind speeds up. I remember thinking the truck was probably a five-ton but seemed like a monster semi-trailer. I remember thinking too that there was no way it could miss us.

But it did.

Or at least we missed it. Cobb, instead of trying to get us back to our side of the road, spun the wheel left and crossed in front of the truck, trying for the far lane on the other side of it. If there'd been a vehicle in that lane we'd still have been hit head-on, but afterward I figured Cobb was gambling that whatever was in that lane had to be better than the sanding truck.

I'm guessing the truck driver must have done some nifty driving too, though probably about all he could do was hit the brakes. We hurtled by the truck and into the inside lane of westbound traffic.

If there's a God for journalists and detectives he or she was smiling down on us at that moment. There was no one in the inside lane, at least not for a few hundred meters, which gave Cobb time to get the Jeep stabilized and heading straight — even though straight was still on the wrong side of the road.

But not for long.

Cobb cranked the wheel back as we came out of the intersection and slammed the accelerator to the floor. We spun some, although the road was better in the intersection than almost anywhere else, and we rocketed back to our side of the road, this time narrowly missing a furniture van. *That* driver gave us the finger as we roared in front of him.

"You okay?" he yelled.

"Yeah," I yelled back at him.

"Was it her?"

"It was her."

"Hang on," he shouted again, I figured more from adrenalin than the need to make himself heard over the noise.

We were several car lengths behind her but she must have seen what had happened in her rearview mirror. She sped up and began changing lanes and swerving around and between cars to try to lose us.

As good as Cobb was at driving at high speed in close quarters — and I found out that he was very good — Delores Bain was proving to be *as* good. I had a flashback to a picture on the wall of her office. The photo of someone standing helmeted next to a race car, face difficult to see in the helmet. I had assumed a former student. Maybe I was wrong.

We gained ground slowly. Both vehicles careened through the snow-covered streets with a couple of near misses for each of us and one that wasn't a miss at all as Cobb swerved around a cab only to come face to face with a Dodge Caravan that had pulled onto Memorial from 4a Street directly in front of us.

Cobb braked and threw the steering wheel to the right this time, sending us into a sideways slide toward the van, then at the last second, with a hard crash seeming inevitable, he released the brake, hit the gas, and spun the wheel hard back left. The Jeep brushed the van but we avoided the worst of what had the makings of a bad wreck. It was Cobb's side of the Jeep that made contact with the right rear of the van, but again he was able to keep us on the road and for the moment at least we were once more travelling in a straight line.

I looked back and the van seemed okay.

I don't know how long the chase lasted. It seemed, I'm sure, much longer than it actually was. At Edmonton Trail, Cobb ran a light that had just turned red. Had anyone been entering the intersection even a second or two early, we'd have hit them at high speed.

"Let her go!" I screamed. "Either she's going to kill someone or we will."

Cobb didn't answer but seemed to bear down even harder. I focused again on the road. At least for the section immediately ahead of us, there didn't appear to be anyone but us and the truck ahead of us with the woman who had killed my wife at the wheel.

And though I knew that, I also knew that the police abandon high speed chases when they pose a danger to the public. This chase was clearly a danger to the public.

"Let her go, Cobb," I said again. "I'll call the cops. Let them handle this." I reached for my cell phone.

Cobb eased off on the gas pedal and we slowed. I looked up to watch the taillights of the pickup disappear from view.

Except that they *didn't* disappear from view. I calculated that Delores Bain was maybe a kilometre ahead of us. But the distance between us wasn't increasing, even as Cobb slowed. It was just seconds until I realized why.

The pickup was slowing too, at the turnoff to the zoo. She started to the right, then spun into a U-turn.

And suddenly was coming back down Memorial Drive, now racing back to the west.

Straight at us.

There could be only one reason for her to do what she was doing. She clearly intended to hit us head-on — to kill herself and us. The hunters were once again the hunted.

"Jesus Christ," I said in not much more than a whisper.

Cobb did the one thing I hadn't thought possible. He floored the Jeep and propelled us ahead, at greater and greater speed straight at the oncoming pickup, two vehicles racing headlong at one another. If this was chicken I hoped Cobb was prepared to lose the game.

"Cobb," I said and looked over at him expecting to see someone who had lost his mind.

Instead what I saw was concentration and all-consuming anger but not someone who was, even temporarily, out of his mind. And there was something else — control. Whatever was happening, it was clear that Cobb was acting, not out of desperation, but in a calculating and unnervingly calm way.

Or was I delusional? Desperate and hoping, praying that the crash that was only seconds away could somehow not happen.

"Hang on!" Cobb yelled for the second time.

I was already doing that with every ounce of strength I possessed. Cobb ripped the steering wheel hard right and we careened off the pavement of Memorial Drive and onto the boulevard that ran along the south side of the road. We were travelling fast when we hit the curb, flew up, then back down with a crunch that brought my jaws together in a jarring flash of pain.

The Memorial Drive trees were now an obstacle course with Cobb trying to somehow slalom us between them. A massive poplar loomed up in front of us, but it looked like we might get by it. *But what then?* Beyond that a steel street light pole, just as deadly.

I looked left past Cobb and my stomach lurched as I saw the headlights of the pickup coming at us, blinding in their intensity.

Like a mirror image the truck and its deadly driver were careening toward us on the boulevard at the perfect angle, in fact, aimed at a spot just a little ahead of us. And somewhere inside me there was a tiny appreciation for this woman who even now had been able to realize that she'd have to lead us by just a bit to guarantee the impact that was now inevitable.

That impact came.

The massive pickup hit the light pole with a force that I thought would snap it off like a dead tree branch and allow the truck to continue its missile-like mission into the driver's side of the Jeep.

The light pole buckled and its light exploded like the detonation of an aerial firework. The noise of the crash was a sound I'll never forget — the scream of metal on metal with a jarring of the senses and obliteration of the night in a way that could surely only be duplicated by the weapons of war. If there was another scream — the human kind — it was lost in the noise that for those few seconds was everywhere.

Cobb was able to finally get the Jeep stopped. He wheeled it around, without speaking, and took us back to the scene at the light pole. Our lights illuminated the horror that was the end of the chase. The front of the truck was unrecognizable, the rest of it a twisted, terrible distortion of what it had been.

It was over.

The silence was as intense and eerie, and somehow as frightening as the noise that had preceded it.

And eeriest of all, one shard of metal, I couldn't tell if it was from the truck or the light standard, pointed in the air, a single arm extended skyward like a cobra stretching ever higher to the sound of the charmer's notes.

Delores Bain was pronounced dead at 11:57 p.m., three minutes before December 14.

TWENTY-SIX

"Why didn't she just shoot us? When she came up alongside us, it would have been easy." I ran my finger around the lip of a faded blue porcelain coffee mug.

Cobb and I were sitting in an all-night pizza place in Forest Lawn.

We'd ordered a pizza, but between the two of us we'd eaten half a slice. Appetites dulled from being frontline players in a bizarre special effects clip.

A twenty-something waitress with big, dark eyes and what sounded like a level four cold came by every few minutes to fill our coffee cups and eye the pizza as if to determine what was wrong with it.

"It's not the pizza," I finally told her. "It's been a tough night and we don't have much of an appetite."

The waitress smiled, apparently reassured that neither she nor the cook had screwed up, and filled our cups one more time.

When she'd gone Cobb nodded. "I thought about that too. A few reasons, I think. First of all, it isn't as easy to shoot a moving target, in this case two moving targets, as they make it look in the movies. Especially when the shooter is trying to drive and shoot at the same time. Second, until that moment she still had a chance of getting

375

DAVID A. POULSEN

away with it. Two guys get bumped into a fatal head-on with a sanding truck, the driver of the bumping vehicle is distraught, blames road conditions, and even though there are some connections to other questionable events, there isn't much for evidence. Had she been successful with getting us out of the way, she stood a good chance of getting away with all of it."

"Yeah, I guess so," I said.

"And third, not everybody's a shooter. She'd succeeded once before with the sideswipe thing — why abandon a winning strategy? She'd been waiting for the right moment and the gravel truck was the right moment."

I told him about the picture on the wall of her office at the school. "Maybe she drove race cars or demolition derby cars back in her youth."

"That would explain some things. Using vehicles as weapons. The killing of Elaine Yu. How well she handled that truck on a slick road. Guess it doesn't much matter now."

I wondered if I looked as tired as he did. Guessed that I did. I drank some of the coffee, trying to make sense of all that had happened.

After the wreck on Memorial Drive Cobb and I had been grilled yet again by the cops — first from the traffic side, then by two homicide detectives named Weller and Twistleman. The nature of the crash that killed Delores Bain had taken it out of the realm of a traffic investigation.

I'd got the impression Weller didn't like Cobb or me very much. Or maybe it was the good cop–bad cop routine and Weller was the bad cop. If that's what it was, he was good at it.

He was pencil-thin with dark, dull hair that lay against his skull like a bandana. Weller had eyes the same colour as his hair. And about as friendly.

I wouldn't have called Twistleman *good* so much as just *less bad*. He was the size and approximate shape of a cube van and red-faced in a brown wrinkled suit and shoes that hadn't seen polish in a long time. If I'd been the casting director I'd have put him in the role of bad cop.

Cobb and I had talked about it while we'd waited for the ambulance and cops to arrive at Memorial Drive. We agreed we'd be as truthful and forthcoming as possible but that the word "follow" might be preferable to "chase" or "pursue" when we described our efforts to stay close to Delores Bain.

Weller was a little smaller than me, and though his tan dress pants and corduroy jacket probably looked fine on Dustin Hoffman in *The Graduate*, the ensemble didn't say *retro* so much as *out of style*. Weller was also a hardass, like the cops in the old movies who hated all private detectives and lived to make gumshoes' lives miserable.

But maybe I'm not being fair to Detective Weller. I have to admit that from the moment I first heard his name, I had a visual of Pickwick's man, Samuel Weller, firmly Photoshopped into my mind. Probably didn't help foster a relationship based on respect.

Weller made it clear that he'd like to nail Cobb's "vigilante ass" for reckless driving and leaving the scene of an accident. He'd flipped open his notebook to inform us that "Doris Pahk had called in a complaint to the effect that a Jeep Cherokee had, while driving erratically, struck her vehicle, a 2005 Dodge Caravan, and fled the scene at about 9:50 p.m. the previous evening."

Cobb stayed silent and so did I.

"Is that about what happened?" Weller flipped the notebook shut. He seemed to enjoy the act of flipping — maybe for dramatic effect.

"A vehicle like the one you described pulled out in front of me as I was trying to recover from being struck from the side by the pickup driven by the deceased woman as I've already described," Cobb said. "But, to be honest, things were happening rather quickly and I may have missed the secondary contact after the violence of the first one and my desire to follow the person who had struck us."

It was quite the oration from a man who wasn't known for long speeches. Weller turned to me. "What about you? You being a newspaper man and all and trained to observe what's going on around you — were you aware of contact between *Mr.* (he emphasized the mister) Cobb's vehicle and the Dodge Caravan?"

"No, sir."

"But you saw the van."

"Yes I did."

"But you don't know if your vehicle hit Ms. Pahk's."

"As Mr. Cobb mentioned, things were a little chaotic just as that moment."

"So you *don't* know if your vehicle hit Ms. Pahk's," he said again.

"No, sir."

Another cop had come into the room. I didn't pay much attention to him at first. After a few minutes he spoke to Weller.

"Is the central issue here a traffic violation, Detective?" We learned later the newcomer's name was Hannigan.

He was senior to Twistleman and Weller and a harder ass than either of them.

"Sir?" Weller said.

"We have what appears to be a deliberate attempt to cause bodily harm with a vehicle, arguably attempted homicide; we have the person who is alleged to be the perpetrator of the attempted homicide now deceased as the result of a violent collision, perhaps of her own doing, and you appear to be focusing on a possible traffic infraction."

I'm betting cops hate to be humiliated in front of guys they are trying to impress with their toughness, and since they can't really take out their frustrations on the superior doing the humiliating, I'm pretty sure Weller filed away Cobb's name and mine on his I'll-get-these-bastards-one-day list.

There was more, but after Hannigan's comments it was pretty smooth sailing. We were finally cleared to leave with the warning that follow-up questioning might take place.

"There's a lot about this I don't understand," I said.

"Me too." Cobb poured milk into his coffee.

"She had to have been following us."

Cobb nodded slowly. "Maybe I'm getting too old for this. That's two tails I haven't made in the last few days."

"There was a blizzard out there. How could you have seen her?"

"She saw us." He drank some coffee. "Thing is, I did see the truck and I ruled out a one-ton dually. Shouldn't have."

"That last part — trying to ram us head-on — that was pretty much suicide."

"The only person who could tell us what was going on inside her head at that moment is dead, but maybe she thought her luck had run out and she had nothing to lose. Or maybe her hate was so great that she was willing to do whatever it took to kill you."

"Suicide," I said again.

Cobb nodded. "Whatever it took."

"It doesn't make sense. How could the reputation of her school be enough to make her want to kill people?"

"People kill for a lot of reasons that don't make sense. Nutso sports fans have tried to kill players on opposing teams. Mothers have tried to murder girls that were going to beat out their daughters for spots on the cheerleading team. There are a whole lot of crazy people out there who've never seen the inside of a psychologist's or psychiatrist's office."

"Yeah," I said, but it still wasn't clear to me, none of it.

Cobb looked at me. "If she was obsessed with her school and it was all she had in her life and she saw first Donna, then you, as a threat, then clearly this was a woman sick enough go to any extreme to punish — or eliminate — that threat."

"And for that ... obsession, Donna died."

"Yes."

I stared at my coffee cup for a long time. Finally I looked up at Cobb.

"You were pretty damn good out there yourself, you know."

Cobb sipped his coffee, looked at me, and smiled.

"Maybe. But we were lucky too. If that light pole wasn't there ..."

"Yeah."

"What was your plan when she turned and came at us? You couldn't have calculated that she'd hit the light pole."

"You're right, but I knew we had no chance at all as long as we stayed on the road. I figured if I got off Memorial and onto that boulevard at the last possible second maybe she'd miss us."

"And if she'd missed us *and* the lamppost? What then?"

Cobb shrugged. "Maybe the river. I can't say I'd thought that far ahead."

"I need sleep," I said. "What do you say we get out of here?"

"Why don't you take the pizza home," Cobb said. "Shame to waste it."

I shook my head. "You've got kids. You take it."

Cobb nodded. I waved at our waitress and gestured that we needed a box for the pizza. While we waited, Cobb chuckled.

I looked at him. "Are you overtired or delirious?"

"I was just thinking," he said. "We're like those duos in the detective novels. Maybe we'll have to team up again in the future. I can sometimes use a good researcher."

"Hey," I said. "I've read some of those books. I know what happened to Sam Spade's partner. He was dead by chapter two."

"Yeah, that was unfortunate." Cobb chuckled again. "But maybe I'm a better detective than Sam Spade."

"Yeah, but maybe I'm not as good a partner as Sam's was."

"I'd say you were pretty damn good."

"Thanks."

The waitress came with a box and we packaged up the pizza. Cobb threw twenty dollars on the table and we headed out into the starless night to where Cobb's Jeep sat beneath a street light, a wounded warrior, both sides showing the evidence of what had happened earlier that night.

To be honest, whether Cobb was serious or not about our ever working together again, I was thinking I'd be perfectly happy if my detective days were over.

TWENTY-SEVEN

The dinner preparations were proceeding well.

I'd altered the menu a little. I decided that *carbonara* must be an Italian word that meant *some-really-bad-shit-is-going-to-happen-to-you* so I switched up the pasta course to a pesto primavera over spaghetti. I stayed with the mussel appetizer and a similar green salad to the first time around.

I'd cleaned the apartment to within an inch of its life, bought flowers for the table, and set them between two bottles of Amarone. I wore a light orange sweater I had bought in Vancouver a year before, over designer jeans and new sneakers and wondered, like Tom Hanks's character in *Sleepless in Seattle*, if I was trying too hard.

This time there were no visitors during my preparations and I was relaxed when Jill arrived — promptly at six, apparently not worried this time about the whipped cream going scoodgy.

We sat on the couch with glasses of wine. Shania Twain was soft in the background. It felt comfortable. Jill was wearing a brown, bulky knit sweater and Cruel Girl jeans. She tucked her legs up under her and with her bare feet and ponytail she looked casual and in a word, good.

"How are things at the inn? Is it okay if I call it the inn? The actual name's a little long."

"Only those who have actually sorted food bank items and stocked shelves get to call it the inn, so you're … uh … in." She smiled the smile that I was getting to like more all the time. "And things are good," she said. "I saw Jay and Zoe yesterday."

"How're they doing?"

Small shrug. "Both clean as far as I could tell. Jay's hanging in there with the program for the moment, saying all the right things but … it's hard to know for sure."

"What do you think are their chances?"

"Reality? Maybe seventy-thirty against, at least for Jay. I'd say Zoe's going to make it okay unless he goes back to the stuff and takes her with him."

"Seventy-thirty," I said. "Not great odds."

She shook her head. "What happens with a lot of these kids, adult users too, is they start out trying real hard and maybe even do okay for a while until there's a bump in the road. Something happens; they lose a job or they get dumped by the boyfriend or girlfriend or somebody they're close to dies, and they're so fragile that they just fall back to the old ways. So we'll see what happens with Jay when some of the garbage life throws at us comes his way. With Zoe there, he'll have a better chance than if she wasn't. But the whole thing's a crap shoot; unfortunately when someone does break the cycle and actually takes their life back, it comes as a pretty big surprise. Sad that it has to be that way."

We sipped wine and sat for a couple of minutes without talking.

"How are you doing?" Jill asked me.

I set my wine glass down and looked at her.

"It's getting better, I think. Having the answers is helping even if some of the answers are painful."

"Like what?"

"Are you sure you want to talk about this stuff?"

She nodded.

"Okay," I said. "I went to talk to Donna's mother. I guess I was upset … not angry really, but upset that she had known about the abuse but hadn't told me. She said Donna had made her promise that she would never tell anyone — *anyone* — what had happened."

"And you think she should have broken that promise with you?"

"I guess after Donna was killed I thought … I don't know what I thought."

"Tough position for a mom to be in."

"Yeah."

Jill reached over and put her hand on mine.

"Adam," she said softly. "If it had been me, I would have honoured my daughter's wishes."

I nodded. "Yeah."

We sipped our wine then, each of us lost in thoughts of our own.

"Okay, enough melancholy talk," I said and stood up and headed for the stereo. "Time for some mussels and dinner music." As Shania was wrapping up "Rock This Country" I hit the eject button and said over my shoulder, "k.d. lang, okay?"

"k.d. lang is wonderful."

As the music began, I took Jill's hand, and led her to the table. I topped up our wine glasses and set the mussels on before I sat down.

"A toast," she said.

I raised my glass. "What should we toast?"

"Well, 'to us' is such a cliché," she said.

"Absolutely." I nodded.

"To us." She smiled.

"To us."

During dinner we talked about Kyla (she loved *The Spoofaloof Rally*), what the Flames should do in the off-season, horses (Jill knows a lot — I know only how to bet on thoroughbreds), and we talked again about Delores Bain.

"There's still so much I don't understand," she said.

"Me too."

"The part that's hardest to figure is that she hated the victims. If you want to kill someone, why not kill the guy who brought all the pain to the school?"

"Maybe she thought he paid his debt to society for the shame he'd brought on the place. And the girls hadn't."

"That's crazy."

I nodded and took a sip of wine. "It is crazy. I don't know what defines insanity, but I think to be so obsessed with your school's reputation that you'd kill ... that has to be getting awfully close."

Neither of us spoke for a few minutes.

I said, "I guess there's one thing I wish I knew the answer to."

Jill looked at me. Waiting.

"The note. Why the note?"

I watched her think about it for a while, then shake her head. "Part of the hate, I guess. It wasn't enough to destroy the girls, she had to cause as much pain as she could to the people they were closest to."

"Maybe," I said. "Maybe that's it."

We sat, sipped our wine, and felt the warmth of each other. And slowly, some of what had been my life for the past few years ebbed away. Not all of it. But some.

"Okay." Jill stood up. "I say we clean up."

"No need," I said, "I can do it in the morning."

"Uh-uh. Come on, it'll only take us a few minutes."

She was right and after the dishes were in the dishwasher and everything was put away but the second bottle of Amarone, she headed for the stereo.

"Okay if I pick the next music?"

"Absolutely."

She sat cross-legged on the floor next to one of the speakers and studied the CDs and albums that covered, some would say *littered*, the floor along the wall next to the front window. Apparently Jill attached considerable importance to the music selection because she spent quite a long time at it. I sat on the couch, drank wine, and watched her. I liked watching her.

She put two CDs into the stereo unit, stood up, and returned to the couch.

"Well?"

She pressed her index finger to her lips. "Shh, it's a surprise."

I didn't have to wait long. The Deep Dark Woods's "The Place I Left Behind" slipped through the speakers and into the room. Jill had started the album on the title track.

"You know those guys?" I asked. It surprised me a little. The Saskatoon band had a pretty solid following but weren't really a household name. At least not yet.

"Know those guys, love those guys." Jill grinned as Ryan Boldt's gentle vocals insisted on our undivided attention. Jill joined me on the couch, sitting closer this time and we let the music take us.

"That's such a great CD. I keep saying I have to get it but I just haven't done it so far."

"And now there's no need. You can come here and listen to it any time you want."

We listened for a long while before either of us spoke. It was "The Ballad of Frank Dupree," a song about a murder that got us talking again.

"You want to know something strange?" I asked. "Everything that Delores Bain did — even killing Donna, the note, all of it — I'm not glad she's dead."

Jill didn't answer right away. But she moved so that her body was against me.

"I like you better for that," she said.

I reached around her and pulled her still closer and we sat like that through the rest of the CD.

"And now part two of the surprise recordings," I said.

"Uh-huh."

I listened as the CD player made the change and Leonard Cohen's *The Future* filled the room. I tilted my head down and brushed my lips against her cheek.

"You remembered," I said.

"I did."

She stood up, crossed the room, and turned out the light.

I set my glass down and stood up. Darkness filled the room, broken only slightly by the lights of Drury Avenue and the rest of the city outside my window. I could see only Jill's shadow. She was moving toward me, slowly, soundlessly, and as she came closer I could smell the gentle apple scent of her hair, feel again her warmth as she moved against me.

"If you were to kiss me ..." she said softly.

I put my arms around her and held her, neither of us moving for a long time. I thought of other times, other places, and other people.

And I knew that at *this* time, in *this* place, she was the person I wanted to be with.

And I kissed her.

ACKNOWLEDGEMENTS

Thanks are due to the following for their invaluable help: Mike O'Connor, long respected, now retired member of the Calgary Police Service; Dr. Adam Vyse, dedicated and gifted physician in High River, Alberta; my editor, Jennifer McKnight, for her perceptive and always thoughtful comments and suggestions; my agent, Arnold Gosewich, for believing in me; Sylvia McConnell, for opening the door and guiding me through it; my wife, Barb, for her spot-on insights and never-ending support; and the Saskatoon Public Library, where I served as Writer in Residence while much of this book was written.

While I have been fortunate to have twenty-three previous books published, this one is special because it is the book I have always wanted to write and frankly never thought I could. I owe so much to the mystery writers I have admired and read with such delight — from Sir Arthur Conan Doyle and Earl Stanley Gardner, whom I first encountered, to Christie, Dixon, Stout, Hammett, Chandler, Buchan, James, Parker, Hillerman, Kellerman, Connelly, Rankin, Robinson, and Bowen. I am indebted to all of them.

 DUNDURN

VISIT US AT

Dundurn.com
@dundurnpress
Facebook.com/dundurnpress
Pinterest.com/dundurnpress

CPSIA information can be obtained
at www.ICGtesting.com
Printed in the USA
LVOW10s0500170117
521177LV00001B/1/P